John looked over at his brother Samuel and nodded in Calling Crow's direction. "Tell him we'll be taking the black with us."

"No," said Calling Crow.

John glared at him. Calling Crow turned and spoke to Samuel, who then looked up at John. "He says that the black man has already told him he wants to stay."

"Who cares what he wants?"

Calling Crow spoke rapidly to Samuel in Spanish, and he relayed the Coosa chief's words. "Calling Crow says that black people have not come here in ships and sold guns to his enemies, and that he holds no bad feelings toward black people."

John grew visibly angry. "But he's worth quite a few pounds, brother. We could . . ."

"No!" Calling Crow looked up, his face resolute . . .

Calling Crow Nation
The epic conclusion to Paul Clayton's brilliant historical trilogy

Berkley Books by Paul Clayton

CALLING CROW
FLIGHT OF THE CROW
CALLING CROW NATION

CALLING CROW NATION

PAUL CLAYTON

BERKLEY BOOKS, NEW YORK

CALLING CROW NATION

A Berkley Book / published by arrangement with
the author

PRINTING HISTORY
Berkley edition / January 1997

All rights reserved.
Copyright © 1997 by Paul Clayton.
This book may not be reproduced in whole or in part,
by mimeograph or any other means, without permission.
For information address: The Berkley Publishing Group,
200 Madison Avenue, New York, New York 10016.

The Putnam Berkley World Wide Web site address is
http://www.berkley.com/berkley

ISBN: 0-425-15604-4

BERKLEY®
Berkley Books are published by The Berkley Publishing Group,
200 Madison Avenue, New York, New York 10016.
BERKLEY and the "B" design
are trademarks belonging to Berkley Publishing Corporation.

PRINTED IN THE UNITED STATES OF AMERICA

10 9 8 7 6 5 4 3 2 1

These writings relate divers' actions taking place in the late sixteenth century in the area of the Caribbean Sea and along the east coast of that land that the mapmakers call Terra Florida.

The port town of Isabela, on the north coast of Hispaniola in the West Indies, 1572

Chapter *I*

Samuel Newman, merchant, stood on the quay and looked worriedly down the red dirt road that led away to the town. Where in hades was that bloody fat Spaniard? he wondered. Nearby, ropes as thick as a man's arm tied his three-masted, lateen-rigged caravel tightly to the pilings of the quay. More than sixty years old, the ship's rigging was frayed and its triangular, age-browned sheets worn and full of patches.

Thirty-five years old, Samuel wore a padded blue doublet, black breeches and brown boots. He wore a mustache and beard like most Englishmen his age, and his were trimmed close. Unlike most Englishmen, however, his teeth were still white, perhaps because of his dislike for sugar and sweets. His thick, curly brown hair hung down over his collar.

Again he looked down the road. Where was their buyer?

A sudden surge in the calm sea leaned the ship over noisily. Named the *Contempt,* it had been seized from the Spaniards in the channel by English privateers. It was then quickly sailed into Bristol. The Spanish crew, after being stripped of their belongings, were rudely run off and told to make their way home any way they could—begging passage on one of the many freight-carrying ships calling in Bristol, perhaps, or swimming. The hold of the ship was then emptied and the goods sold. Finally the ship itself was sold to Samuel Newman.

Samuel glanced down the road and then turned to William. In addition to being a smith, the old Englishman was also their pilot, having learned about the coasts of the New Lands from a Portuguese named Mendes. "How seaworthy is the *Contempt* now, William? She's leaking an awful lot."

William, his silky white hair and beard contrasting with the rugged brown of his leather jerkin, turned an iron rod in a small, charcoal-fired forge that sat upon a stack of quay stones. A ship's boy of fourteen or fifteen worked the bellows beside him. William glanced surreptitiously to both sides. "She'll get us home, all right, m'lord," he said finally, "but we'll have to have her careened when we get there. The teredo worms are finding her old beams a tasty meal."

Samuel nodded. "Yes," he said absently, "when we get back." Over the steady hiss of the bellows, an angry shouting erupted. Samuel and William turned to watch some crewmen wrestle one of the heavy bales of cloth into position on the other side of the quay. As tall as a man, the bales now stood in orderly rows, thirty-eight in all, linen cloth from Munster and dyed woolens from London. Only two more remained in the hold of the ship. But where was their damn buyer?

Fenwick, a short, thick-necked, red-faced tailor, came up beside the small iron forge. Smiling at the boy, he put his finger in his mouth and removed a gob of spit. He deftly pressed it against the side of the forge, where it popped and hissed, eliciting a smile from the boy.

Samuel turned away and looked up to the half deck of the *Contempt*. The rest of the crew busily sewed canvas, spliced ropes and readied the hold and deck to receive its new cargo. Periodically they, too, looked down the road upon which the buyer should have arrived at sunup.

"Where do you suppose he is?" said Fenwick to Samuel.

"I left my crystal ball on the ship, Fenwick," said Samuel impatiently. "I cannot give you an answer."

Fenwick smiled sadly but said nothing in return.

The men remained silent. Not far away Samuel's brother John argued loudly with the only Spaniard member of the trading expedition, Señor Gredilla. John was thinner than Samuel, but stood a full head taller. He wore a red-banded felt hat, and beneath it, his hawklike nose gave him a predatory look. Gredilla, a thin, compact, leathery-skinned man from San Lucar, backed away involuntarily. Although Samuel and John had put up all the money for the venture, they had made the Spaniard Gredilla a full partner because his name and nationality made the venture possible. It had been the coin with which they had purchased their license from the Casa de Contracion. They had even temporarily put ownership of the *Contempt* in Gredilla's name. All this was necessitated by the fact that Spain limited trade with her New World colonies to Spanish merchants operating out of Seville. But Spanish merchants alone could not supply the growing demand of her colonies for finished goods, and so more than two thirds of the goods arriving in the New World came from merchants in London, Flanders, Paris and Venice. Off-loaded in Seville, they made the trip across the Sea of Columbus on Spanish ships.

Under Samuel Newman's direction, they had carefully navigated the shifting winds and jagged shoals of commerce, and yesterday their efforts had seemed ready to bear fruit. The quay had swarmed with local merchants and landowners, and the bidding for their cloth had been intense. Señor Fernandez, a wealthy merchant from the town, had made the best offer and they had struck a deal. Did his absence mean he was now backing out of the contract?

Señor Gredilla came over as if to escape from John, but the thin Englishman followed him. John looked at Samuel. "I told you at the beginning of this that they were not to be trusted!" He looked angrily at Gredilla. "I cannot stand the smell of them!"

Gredilla flinched visibly and turned away. They stood in angry silence. "Ah," Gredilla exclaimed suddenly as he looked toward the town. He tapped young Samuel Newman on the back. Samuel turned and fixed his sharp brown eyes on the smaller man. "Señor?"

Gredilla indicated the road leading back to the town.

At last, thought Samuel, as he recognized Fernandez's black two-horse carriage leading a caravan of twelve flatbed wagons.

Samuel's smile constricted into a frown as the wagons drew closer—they were all empty! The old Spaniard was to bring his payment of hides and sugar today. What had changed?

"He comes," said Gredilla, stating the obvious in broken English, "but he brings nothing in his wagons."

"Then he will take nothing away," said Samuel. Samuel looked up at the ship. She was small, a hundred feet in length. A half dozen men were wrestling a bale of cloth toward the rail. He called up to them. "Leave it for now. I'll tell you when to bring it down."

Samuel's brother John started over. John, five years older than Samuel, pushed Fenwick and Gredilla out of the way. He watched the approaching wagons for a few moments then turned suspiciously to Gredilla. "What is Fernandez up to, anyway?"

Gredilla blanched at the look. "Señor, how would I know?"

Samuel shook his head. There wasn't an Englishman alive who hated Spaniards more than his brother. He almost regretted having brought him along on this venture. But, soon they should be finished here. Then everything would slowly return to normal.

Although a head shorter than his older brother, Samuel was broader in the chest and stronger. He had a quiet, confident, commanding nature and none of the men ever doubted who was in charge when both brothers were present. He started walking toward the upright bales. "Let us go see."

Samuel walked to where the street met the quay. John, Gredilla and Fenwick followed him. Up on the half deck of the ship, the men had stopped their work and crowded around the rails to watch. Others were coming up from the hold.

Fernandez's wagon came to a stop. Holding tightly to the side of the wagon, he carefully lowered his great belly down the steps to the road. A tall, emaciated Indian jumped from the rear of the wagon and ran around to Fernandez, opening a parasol to shade the rotund grandee from the sun.

Samuel nodded a greeting to Fernandez as John, Gredilla and Fenwick came up behind them.

"*Buenos dias, señor,*" said Samuel pleasantly. Samuel had learned a conversational Spanish while a boy at the knee of a Spanish Jew, a refugee of the Inquisition.

The Spaniard nodded. "*Buenos dias, señors.*" Despite the circle of shade his attendant's parasol provided, Fernandez perspired profusely. He glanced worriedly behind him at the road that led to the town, then turned round. Recognizing Gredilla from the day before, he spoke rapidly in Spanish. Fernandez then turned and waved commandingly at his men. They jumped down from the flat wagons and started toward the bales of cloth.

"What did he say?" said Samuel to Gredilla. "He speaks too fast for me to follow."

"He has told his men to start loading the bales," said Gredilla.

"What?" said John angrily, his hand going to his sword.

"Calm yourself," said Samuel.

John frowned, but seemed to relax some. Samuel turned and shouted over at the approaching men. "*¡Espere!*" The men stopped and stood where they were as they waited for Fernandez to countermand the Englishman's order.

Gredilla spoke rapidly in Spanish to Fernandez.

"Ask him where our hides and sugar are," said Samuel.

Gredilla's brow furrowed into a dozen lines as he translated Samuel's words for the old Spaniard.

Fernandez looked at Samuel furtively before replying. He spoke slower, and Samuel understood the old Spaniard's words.

"Late, eh?" said Samuel to Gredilla. "Should we believe him?"

Gredilla nodded. "The wagons may even be loaded by now. He said they will be here soon."

Fernandez turned away and shouted to a mestizo wearing a wide-brimmed hat, "Miguel," he said, pointing. The man walked toward the bales.

"Where in blazes is he going?" said John. He started over and Samuel took his arm, stopping him.

"Wait," Samuel called up to the men on the ship. "Collins, Butler, bring the others." He turned back to Gredilla. "Tell him nothing will be loaded until we have our hides and sugar."

Gredilla blinked nervously. "But, señor, he has already explained. The men were late in rising. They will be here at any moment."

"Tell him!" demanded John angrily.

Gredilla looked at Samuel.

"We will wait for the hides and sugar," said Samuel calmly. "Tell him."

Gredilla relayed the Englishman's words and Señor Fernandez replied rapidly and angrily in Spanish.

"What was that?" said John suspiciously

Samuel smiled at Fenwick. "Maybe we don't want to know."

Gredilla looked chagrined. "He did not add anything else, señors. He simply repeated what he has already said."

No one spoke as the men stood about waiting for orders. Samuel watched his brother carefully. John's hand was again on the hilt of his sword, his face reddening. Samuel knew he should not have brought him along, that he was a liability, but he had felt sorry for him. John's fortunes had fallen of late and he needed money badly. Samuel felt guilty too. When they were boys, their father had favored Samuel over his older brother, apprenticing Samuel to a kindly wool broker, while turning John over to the strict charge of Mathew of Rose Lane, a fishmonger. Samuel had worked hard and learned much, and now had a thriving wool business. John, on the other hand, had thought the work beneath him. There were many beatings and John had left Mathew when he was of age and done a tour of soldiering in the Irish campaign in Munster. It had been a very brutal, bloody experience and John had never been the same since. Each brother had inherited one of their father's houses at his death. John lived the life of an idle lord, although he really couldn't afford it. From time to time he was forced to work for his brother in order to pay his debts. This was one of those times.

But, Samuel comforted himself. They were almost finished with their business here. He felt confident he could control the situation now. "John, give me your sword."

"What?" John laughed.

Samuel faced him. "Give it to me. I'll not have you threatening these people and ruining the business."

John looked at him wryly. He pulled his sword and handed it to Samuel. Samuel tucked it into his belt.

The tropical sun burned down and for a while the only

sound was the gentle slapping of the waves against the stones of the quay.

Señor Fernandez walked over to a stone block sitting by the road and sat tiredly upon it. Señor Gredilla walked over and stood beside him. They talked softly in Spanish, occasionally looking over at the Englishmen.

"They get along rather well," said Fenwick.

Samuel frowned. "Yes, and the friendship of the old señor will be all Gredilla brings back if Fernandez does not bring his hides and sugar."

"Enough of this," said John angrily. He walked over to the two men and rudely pushed Gredilla aside. He glared down at Señor Fernandez.

Samuel walked quickly over to them, Fenwick following. "Calm yourself, John," said Samuel. "We will give him a little more time. We've waited this long already."

John's face was fierce with anger as he turned to his brother. "Why? I have invested heavily in this venture too. I only want to question him, brother. He is up to something."

As John stood over Señor Fernandez, the Spaniard cast his big, moist eyes plaintively toward Samuel and then looked down at his feet. John continued to stare down at him and then turned angrily to Gredilla. "Tell him that if his bloody hides don't get here soon I will take him over there and throw him into the sea."

Samuel moved closer.

Gredilla looked at him. "Señor," he said, "surely you don't want me to say such a thing?"

Samuel would not let John hurt the old man, but there was no harm in putting a scare into him. Samuel nodded to Gredilla. "Say it."

Gredilla translated.

Fernandez looked down at his boots as he answered.

Gredilla looked ashen as he translated. "He said he is very sorry, señors. He said that he wanted to do business with us, but that the Hidalgo of the town has instructed him to confiscate your goods and put them in his warehouse."

"What?" said Samuel incredulously.

"I told you we couldn't trust any of them," said John.

Samuel held up his hand. He looked at Gredilla. "The ship is in your name," he said, striving for calm, "we have our license, everything is legal. What has changed?"

"The corsair who is called Drake," said Gredilla somberly.

"Francis Drake?" said Samuel.

Gredilla nodded. "He has been ravaging the ships and towns along the Main. Everyone knows it now. Señor Fernandez says that word has come that any English who dock in these ports will be detained and their cargo impounded until there is a hearing."

John pushed closer. "Like hell they will!"

"Here come more wagons," said Fenwick.

Samuel turned with the others to look. A distant smudge of dust hung in the air. He squinted his eyes in the bright light but could not see the wagons yet. "Ask him what he thinks the outcome of the hearing will be," said Samuel.

Gredilla put the question to Fernandez and listened to his reply. "He says he thinks it will come out in your favor. He knows several lawyers in the town who he is sure we can bribe to ensure that."

Samuel looked down at the Spanish grandee in disdain and then turned back to look at the approaching wagons. Shading his eyes with his hand, he saw that the approaching column of dust was thrown skyward not by wagons but by a column of Spanish cavalry. He could now make out the distinctive Spaniard comb helmets glinting in the sun. He turned angrily to Fernandez.

"Soldiers! What is the meaning of this?"

At the sight of the approaching column of soldiers, Fernandez's nervousness changed into fear. He got to his feet and began speaking rapidly.

"What is he saying?" said Samuel to Gredilla.

"He said that he is very sorry for you, that it is not his fault, that the Hidalgo ordered this."

Samuel was about to reply when John suddenly pushed past him. "Bloody papist!" he screamed. "There will be no hearing!"

Samuel grabbed for his brother, but John's dagger was already out and glinting in the sun. It flashed down and into the fat Spaniard's chest. Fernandez's eyes closed as he grabbed John's doublet reflexively and held on to him. Fernandez's eyes issued tears through their tightly clenched lids as much blood soaked through his white silk shirtfront.

John pulled his dagger out and pushed Fernandez away. He fell to the ground and his Indian men looked about, unsure of what to do.

Samuel turned to his brother. "For the love of God, man, have you lost your mind?"

John's face was a mask of rage and he appeared not to have heard his brother.

Samuel turned to Fenwick. "Get his knife."

Fenwick approached and John turned to him wildly. Fenwick backed off, looking at Samuel.

"John," shouted Samuel, "you have killed him! Now we shall all hang!"

John seemed to come out of his fog. He sheathed his dagger. "He betrayed us!" he shouted, his voice thick with anger.

Samuel turned away in anger and disgust. He watched the approaching column of soldiers. They would arrive in another few minutes. A wagon brought up the rear. Samuel frowned as he made out the long, black cylinder of a gun taking up the length of the wagon. They would have to flee, he decided; John's bloody rashness had seen to that. Immediately, all Samuel's sailor's senses came to life, measuring the slight breeze coming off the land, which moved the hairs of his beard; it was weak, tepid. Samuel scanned the harbor, judging the maneuvering room he would need in which to turn the *Contempt;* there didn't appear to be enough. They would move like a slug, a perfect target for the Spanish on this sunbright perfect day.

Samuel watched William the Smith hurriedly throwing his tools into a leather sack beside his forge. What was he doing? he thought. They were not going anywhere. They would hang in this balmy, mosquito-infested place. In a black mood, Samuel watched the heated air ripple off the small forge. The distortion tickled his eyes, then his brains, and an idea came to him that might save them. If it didn't, he reasoned, it was better to die a quick death fighting, perhaps a musket ball between the eyes, than slowly swinging and strangling with a Spanish rope around one's neck.

Samuel shouted to his men. "Back to the ship! Cast off the ropes! Quickly now."

Fenwick looked at Samuel as if he were crazy. "Samuel, have you lost your mind? They have a gun! They'll blow us to matchwood."

"Yes. If they can see us."

Fenwick sputtered and looked around to see if any of the others had heard Samuel's crazy utterances. "See us? For the love of God! They are not blind!"

Samuel shoved him. "Shut up! Get on the ship . . . unless you want to hang." Samuel grabbed Fenwick's hat off his head and ran back toward William's forge. The old man had already gone back to the ship. Using Fenwick's hat to insulate his hands from the red-hot iron, Samuel picked up the forge and ran to the bales. He lifted the forge high, dumping some of the coals onto a bale; he then ran to the next and did the same thing.

John ran over to him. "Our goods," he said in a shocked voice, "you're burning our goods." John attempted to scrape the coals away with his dagger.

Samuel ignored him and hurried on to the next bale. Soon ten of the bails were smoldering and emitting smoke from their tops like the chimneys of miniature cottages.

Samuel gave John his sword and started back to the ship. "Come on," he called to John, Fenwick and Gredilla, who were still standing around. Fenwick and Gredilla followed him grudgingly as John tried futilely to stop the spreading fires.

Fenwick stopped and looked back. "Half of everything I own was invested in those bales," he said sadly. "I'll be wiped out."

Gredilla nodded. "My commission . . . up in flames!"

Samuel ignored them and called over to his brother, his voice sharp with anger. "Give up, John. That is all our monies burning up! All because of your rashness!"

John looked at him angrily then turned to look back at the

approaching soldiers. "I will stay and fight. I'll not run away."

Samuel stopped and Fenwick and Gredilla waited for him.

Samuel called to his brother. "Come to your senses, John. Our only chance is to take to the water. Otherwise we will all hang."

John said nothing as he watched the soldiers. They rode at an unhurried pace, not yet having noticed the head-high tendrils of smoke that were now moving toward the *Contempt*.

Samuel shook his head angrily. "As pigheaded as you are, I'll be damned if I'll let you hang!" He turned to Fenwick and Gredilla. "Help me with him."

Samuel threw his arms around John, pinning John's arms to his chest, while Gredilla and Fenwick each grabbed a leg. John struggled furiously as they carried him back to the ship.

John's hat fell off as they dropped him roughly onto some coiled ropes. For a moment he seemed dumbfounded, as if coming out of a faint. Then he retrieved his hat.

"Get the ropes aft!" Samuel shouted at him. John frowned painfully and ran to the rear of the ship.

Samuel went to the bow, where another set of ropes tethered the *Contempt* tightly to the quay. Gredilla stood passively, watching the soldiers' advance. Fenwick stood next to him, looking down at his boots and rubbing his hands together nervously. "I'm going to hang!" He looked at Samuel. "Why did I come here? I'm just a tailor!"

Samuel began pulling the ropes away. "You're a greedy little tailor and you thought there was a lot of money to be made, that's why you came here. Now, both of you help me get these ropes off or, so help me, God, you will hang!"

Fenwick and Gredilla knelt and frantically pulled at the ropes. The ropes fell away and they could then hear the clatter of the horse's hooves on the paving stones. The bales were putting out a thick smoke now, but no flames were visible.

Samuel looked aft. John and the teenaged seaman Peter Butler struggled with the ropes there, but they still held. Another man who had been helping them had panicked and was now clambering aboard. The weak, smoky wind had moved the ship only a few inches from the pilings.

Samuel looked back at the column of soldiers. They were at the end of the quay now, putting the ship well within the range of the Spanish muskets. Fernandez's Indians watched the drama complacently, seeming not to care about the outcome.

Samuel turned round to the ship. Fifteen or so of the twenty-man crew were hauling on the ropes, raising sail. Fenwick started climbing quickly up to the rail. Gredilla stood still, watching the approaching soldiers worriedly.

"Señor Gredilla," shouted Samuel, "go help John with the ropes."

Gredilla nodded, but didn't move. He looked over at John and took off running toward the soldiers. "The English are escaping!" he shouted at them. "Hurry!"

Samuel ran back to John. He pulled his sword and began hacking at the remaining ropes. A partly severed rope snapped like a whipcrack and the ship immediately lurched outward from the quay. Samuel and John leapt for the ropes and began climbing. John tumbled over the rail. Samuel clung to the ropes, looking back. Peter Butler stood unmoving, looking at him openmouthed.

"Jump," shouted Samuel as the ship slowly moved away, "save yourself!" He clung tightly to the ropes, holding out his hand.

Peter Butler's eyes were wide with fear and indecision.

"Come on, boy," shouted Samuel.

The ship slid out of reach, Butler remaining frozen, unable even to lift his hand.

As the weak, smoky wind pushed the ship away, Samuel watched a dozen soldiers run up to the quay. Two of them grabbed Butler, throwing him to the ground, while the others quickly set their muskets into their shooting stands. The soldiers in the gun wagon wheeled it around, almost turning it over.

Samuel climbed over the rail and ducked down on the deck as the first volley from the muskets slammed splinteringly into the ship. He got to his feet. There would be a few minutes before the Spanish reloaded their muskets. Flames now sprouted from half of the smoking bales and the smoke was growing thicker, partially obscuring the ship. Samuel crouched down and a moment later another volley from the muskets cracked into the *Contempt* as it drove sluggishly forward toward the breakwater. Before they got there, Samuel would turn her and attempt to head her out to sea. Until then they would be broadside and vulnerable to the Spaniards. Samuel got to his feet. His men seemed okay. He looked to port, searching through the thickening smoke for the Spanish cannon. He prayed the smoke would continue to thicken; he prayed that the gunners were hungover and bleary eyed from drinking too much wine the night before, and he prayed for a miracle. How else could the Spaniards miss at this range?

Samuel hurried forward to check the depths. His men were busy readying the saker, a bronze, muzzle-loaded cannon of eight feet in length that fired three-inch-caliber shot. Mounted in the stern, it would be useless until he brought the ship about. Samuel shouted back to them, "Get that damn gun loaded. Quickly!"

"Almost ready," came a shout. Samuel peered down at the bottom through the clear water. Without the cargo they were not drawing much water and had plenty of draft.

Somewhere above Samuel a musket ball punched a hole through the sheets with a slap. He looked back at the quay through the patches of thick smoke. Gredilla was gesticulating wildly to a mounted soldier as the bales burned wildly. Black smoke obscured the quay now, and Samuel saw several Spanish soldiers attempting to wrestle one of the bales over to the edge of the quay and dump it in the sea. Other soldiers carefully aimed their long muskets at the ship. Then, through the tendrils of black smoke, Samuel finally saw what he feared most—a large flash of orange fire from the Spanish gun. He prayed that their aim was poor. It wasn't. A crash came from aft and a cloud of dust and debris blew seaward. One of his men screamed. He lay on the deck, his hands covering his eyes as blood ran between his fingers. His mates ran to him and carried him below. Samuel saw that the shot had stove a hole in the superstructure of the stern. It wouldn't sink them; he'd have William begin the repairs when next they anchored.

Samuel signaled the helmsman and turned the *Contempt*.

Then his men fired the saker. Samuel watched in appreciation as the shot struck one of the burning bales, knocking it over like a ten pin. The Spanish musketeers broke ranks in a panic and ran for the protection of a low wall not far from the quay. The *Contempt* moved faster now, showing only the slim silhouette of her stern. Samuel saw the Spanish gun flash fire again. He waited a few moments and breathed in relief as a geyser of seawater erupted off their starboard. The water rained down on him and his men and a cheer went up. They would be well out of range before the Spaniards could reload. Samuel could hardly see the soldiers moving about on the quay now as a stronger wind spirited them out to sea. Thanking God, he went back to look at the damage.

Chapter 2

Twelve hundred miles north, above the Florida peninsula, the forest was unnaturally quiet—and full of activity. The four-leggeds and winged-ones remained stone-still as they waited and watched the two groups of men moving stealthily closer to each other through the ferns and bushes. In one of the groups, Calling Crow, chief of the Coosa people, looked over at his son, Swordbrought. Swordbrought was only sixteen summers upon the earth, but his face showed no trace of fear, just a stern resolve. Calling Crow felt a quick twinge of pride, then nodded over at Red Feather, his most trusted brave. Red Feather gave the signal and the ten other braves immediately knelt, disappearing from sight.

Calling Crow remained standing as he listened for sounds of the others. He and his men had been hunting two days south of their village when they ran into the signs on the trail. These were Coosa hunting lands and this affront could not be overlooked. Otherwise there would be more incursions.

Calling Crow was taller than most of his men. His skin was the color of a leaf in autumn and his nose proud and full, its prominence offset by deep brown eyes that were thoughtful and wise. In the late middle of his earth journey, he was still very strong physically, without a trace of fat on him. He wore a breechclout of woven brown/black bark fibers and a sash of the same material. Bands of decorative, black tattoos encircled his neck, arms, chest and legs. Around his neck he wore a necklace of iridescent black crow feathers and a carved wooden cross, a relic of the time when the Spanish moved in his world. Given to him by a woman that he had loved, it was powerful medicine and had once stopped an arrow.

Calling Crow heard a sound. He whistled like a robin and Red Feather and the others immediately knew what he wanted. They got to their feet, moving into position as they prepared to ambush the approaching Timucua invaders.

Like many other tribes of the southeast, the Timucua were a Muskogee-speaking people. They fought wars against, and held alliances with, the tribes to the north, west and south of them, but a balance of power had long been achieved and borders remained fixed. This changed with the arrival of the Spanish along the Floridas in the middle of the sixteenth century. The Timucua received the brunt of the invasion. Their numbers quickly decimated by disease and superior technology, some Timucua village leaders submitted to the invaders, reluctantly embracing the cross and servitude in the plantations; others fought back and were driven off; still others made a pact, allying themselves with the powerful invaders, thus ensuring their own survival. This group fell in the last category.

When all his men were well hidden behind the bushes and ferns, Calling Crow signaled them again. Eyes narrowed with determination and righteous indignation, they drew back their arrows and waited. Soon the gentle rustle of the invaders' footsteps could be heard and a file of grim-faced, topknotted Timucua braves appeared coming down the trail. The man in the lead held his bow at the ready as his eyes rapidly swept the trees and bushes for signs. The brave behind him carried one of the long, iron muskets the Spanish called harquebuses tightly to his chest.

Calling Crow let the enemy braves advance until he was able to determine their numbers. He squeezed the medicine pouch hanging from his belt and said a quick, silent prayer to guide the arrows of his warriors. Then he gave the signal to attack, a turkey call. His men stood suddenly and released their arrows. The lead Timucua brave fell to his knees, staring down in angry disbelief at the arrow that pierced his chest. By the time he had fallen forward, the other Timucua, having sustained only minor wounds, had dropped out of sight.

There was very little sound as Calling Crow and his men moved stealthily about, seeking advantage. They rose quickly here and there, their arrows flitting through the hot, still air like angry insects. As Calling Crow peered through the thick foliage, he thought it strange that the Timucua were fighting so poorly. Most of their arrows were hastily and wildly shot, and it almost seemed as if they didn't want to hurt Calling Crow and his men. The harquebus boomed suddenly and deafeningly, distracting Calling Crow's thoughts.

Calling Crow and some of his men had seen or heard the Spanish harquebus on at least one occasion, and so its awful voice did not frighten them. The puff of smoke from the fired gun oozed through the bushes, giving away the location of the shooter. Immediately, several arrows cut through the leaves and he collapsed with a crash of branches. The remaining men continued their maneuvering and shooting.

The fear that the harquebus could inflict on Indians who had no experience of it was not the sole reason the Timucua brave had been carrying it. The explosive report of the gun traveled far under the canopy of forest, farther than would the shouts and cries of fighting men. Upon hearing it, another, much larger group of Timucua who had been lying in wait all night got to their feet. They began a well-practiced flanking movement, quietly closing in on Calling Crow and his men.

"Red Feather," Calling Crow called to his most loyal supporter, "how many have we killed?"

Red Feather stood motionless next to a tree across the trail, disdainfully exposing himself to the enemy. "Just the lead brave and the thunderstick shooter." Red Feather was no longer the young, tentative boy who had first welcomed Calling Crow into the Coosa tribe. Now he was a man with high, stern cheekbones, brave eyes, and a wide mouth with which he spoke wisely and confidently. Because of Red Feather's loyalty and bravery, Calling Crow had made him his *tastanagi,* his right-hand man in all things concerning war and the security of the people.

The voice of the fierce young brave named Crying Wolf cut through the stillness. "These cowards hardly raise their heads."

"They're not cowards," said Calling Crow in warning. "Something is not right."

"What is it?" It was Swordbrought, from somewhere behind Calling Crow.

Calling Crow turned quickly and looked into the fearless eyes of his young son. Before he could answer, an angry scream cut through the sounds of their battle. He and his men turned as thirty or so Timucua braves rushed out at them from between the trees. Many of the Timucua carried what looked to Calling Crow like bundles of coarse cord.

"Red Feather, Swordbrought," shouted Calling Crow, suspecting the worst, "you and the others, break and run!"

Then the Timucua were upon them, heaving their cord bundles. Calling Crow rose and drew back his bow as a cord bundle blossomed in midair into a large, coarse net. The net fell about him, deflecting his arrow. He dropped his bow as he struggled with the entangling cords of the net. A moment later several Timucua smashed into him, knocking him to the ground. Blows struck him and he heard a strangely accented voice cautioning the Timucua braves not to hurt the captives too badly. Calling Crow's arms were bound behind him and he was yanked to a sitting position. He looked about and saw that two of his men, Half Knife and the young brave, Crying Wolf, had been captured. Half Knife was lying prostrate, his wrists bound behind him, but Crying Wolf was still fighting with the two braves who were attempting to tie him up. Calling Crow saw that his son Swordbrought, Red Feather and the others had evidently escaped.

A stocky, bearded white man stood calmly next to a tall Timucua brave with a small arrow decoratively braided into his topknot. Both men watched the struggle to subdue Crying Wolf. The top of the bearded man's cheeks were pocked with the holes of smallpox. Calling Crow assumed him to be a Spaniard. The arrow in the Timucua man's topknot indicated rank; he was the chief of these braves.

"He's a slippery one, Mantua," the bearded one said in Spanish, confirming Calling Crow's hunch.

The one called Mantua was slender and muscled, with a broad, rocky face. His eyes seemed incapable of mirth and were as sharp as arrow points. The Spaniard turned back to watch the struggle on the ground. "*Rapido,*" he said impatiently. "We must be gone before the ones that escaped return with more braves from their village."

Still, the two men could not get their cords around Crying Wolf's wrists and legs. The Spaniard pointed and Mantua walked over and hit Crying Wolf on the head with his axe. The blow stopped Crying Wolf's struggling, but to Calling Crow's ears, it hadn't sounded hard struck enough to have killed him.

Mantua looked down at Calling Crow. Curiosity moved his leathery face as he noticed Calling Crow's cross and iron axe. He knelt and took the cross and axe, tucking them under his sash. Ripping one of the feathers from Calling Crow's necklace, Mantua inspected it briefly. He scoffed and threw it on the ground. "How far away is your village?" he demanded.

Calling Crow said nothing and Mantua kicked him angrily, knocking him over. Calling Crow rolled backward and up into a sitting position as Mantua looked at Half Knife. Deciding that he too would refuse to talk, he walked back to the front of the group and addressed the bearded one.

"Señor Avila, they are all bound securely now. We are ready."

The Spaniard who was called Avila glared over at Calling Crow and nodded. "*¡Vamonos!*"

Two of the Timucua carried Crying Wolf as they began walking at a fast clip down the trail. Soon they began running. The trail broadened and passed through a thick forest and they ran along it for the better part of the day. When the sun had moved lower over the trees, they came upon a smaller party of Timucua braves guarding about thirty captives. There were men and women in the group, many of them old, and they were not of Calling Crow's village. The Timucua stopped for a rest. Calling Crow heard the cry of a hawk and thought of his son, Swordbrought. The hawk was Swordbrought's spirit guide. Calling Crow looked up and saw the hawk swiftly disappearing to the west. The Timucua ordered some in this new group of captives to carry Crying Wolf and they hurried

on. The trail turned to skirt a great swamp, and at this point
the older captives began panting loudly. The braves in the
lead slowed to a walk. Suddenly a disembodied voice floated
out from the hot air of the swamp. "Stop!" it commanded.

The column halted obediently. The voice had quieted the
swamp's cicadas, but now their drone started up again. As
they waited, Crying Wolf regained consciousness. He looked
at Calling Crow dumbly, wondering where he was. The mysterious voice hailed them again and Calling Crow recognized
it as Red Feather's voice.

"Calling Crow," he called, "we will get you back!"

Mantua's flinty hard eyes frowned. Avila came and stood
beside him. They slowly searched the scattered bald cypresses
in the distance. A woodpecker's rapping echoed over the hot,
still water. Avila and Mantua consulted quietly. Mantua
waved over some of his men.

Another voice called out from the swamp. It was Swordbrought. "Father, I will free you!"

Calling Crow was overwhelmed at the sound of his son's
voice and could not keep himself from shouting out. "Go
away or they will catch you too!"

"Never!" Swordbrought's voice rasped with anger and determination and it seemed to come from everywhere at once.
The captives looked around as if there were an invisible spirit
hovering about nearby. "I will never abandon you, Father."

Calling Crow watched nervously as Avila and Mantua gestured and talked quietly with the braves. Four of the braves
crept off, heading stealthily in the general direction of the
highest bald cypress. Avila gave the signal to move on and
Mantua and his men struck the captives, ordering them to
their feet. The column began running again.

Toward the end of the day, when it grew too dark to move,
the column stopped. Avila formed a large perimeter camp
with the braves and put Calling Crow and the other captives
in the center. Mantua then gave each captive a handful of
parched corn to eat and posted guards. Then a Timucua brave
walked about, roughly pushing Calling Crow and the others
down on the ground and ordering them to sleep. Calling
Crow's head was full of thoughts of escape and his body was

taut with energy, but his arms were bound too tightly and he could see no way out. His only hope was that Red Feather had dispatched a fast runner back to the village for help. But, he wondered, would they be able to reach them in time? He thought of his wife, Green Bird Woman, and his daughter, Bright Eyes. Bright Eyes, a grown woman now, would be crying at the news of his capture, her face wet and miserable. But Green Bird Woman's still-pretty, middle-aged face would be stern and dark with anger. He could almost hear her shouting angrily at the men who returned to report their capture. She was a good woman.

Just before the light of day faded completely, some of the heaviness in Calling Crow's heart lifted. The four men that had been dispatched to catch Red Feather and Swordbrought returned empty-handed. Still, Calling Crow could not sleep. He quietly called to Half Knife and Crying Wolf, urging them to rest. They would all need their strength if a rescue party were to reach them in time.

The Timucua woke Calling Crow, Half Knife, Crying Wolf and the other captives at dawn with kicks and blows, and forced them to their feet. They set off immediately and began trotting down the trail. After a while they came to a seemingly deserted Timucua village. As they ran past the timber palisade, Calling Crow wondered why Mantua and his men seemed unconcerned at the absence of people there. The column quickly left the village behind and continued to run south along the wide trail.

The trail entered a forest of tall pines. After they had penetrated its stillness deeply, Swordbrought's voice suddenly called out to them. Calling Crow's heart twisted in anger and sorrow. Here they were, deep in Timucua territory, and still his brave, foolish son would not obey his wishes and save himself!

Avila held up his hand and the column halted. Mantua and his top braves looked about as they conferred quietly with Avila. Again Mantua dispatched four braves to try and capture the brazen intruder, and again Calling Crow felt despair deep inside. It was bad enough that he had allowed himself, Half Knife and Crying Wolf to be captured, but if his only son also ended up a Spanish slave, it would be too much for him to bear.

The column hurried on and toward full day the Timucua braves returned alone. Again Calling Crow's mood brightened. Perhaps Swordbrought had finally come to his senses and started back. Hope started to build in Calling Crow that perhaps a group of his men were now hurrying after them. They would have to move very fast, however, for the Timucua had kept up a steady, grueling pace. The older captives were in great pain and even Calling Crow was tiring of it. Finally, later in the day, the column slowed to a walk.

The column left the trail and came out onto the banks of a small river. They followed this out to the beach and the sea. Calling Crow saw a scattering of thatched huts and a great mass of people on the sand. Out on the sea, a large, solitary ship rested at anchor and a small boat moved slowly across the pale blue water toward it. Most of the people on the beach were captives. Twenty or so Spanish soldiers busily unloaded two small Spanish boats. The sight sickened Calling Crow and he felt his pain and fatigue double. They would soon be on the ship and then his men could not help them. The captives slowed to a bone-weary walk through the hot, thick sand. The Timucua braves yelled at them to hurry, but did not strike them, knowing perhaps that they could no longer move any faster. They approached another large group of captives. Avila halted the column and spoke with a soldier.

Calling Crow looked at the great mass of captured people. They sat on the hot sand in a large circle. Their arms were, like Calling Crow's, bound tightly behind them and they were tied one to another like animals. Crowded into mixed groups of men, women and children, they stared sadly at their feet as they waited. Between the different groups, topknotted Timucua braves walked about freely. Spanish soldiers in their distinctive baggy breeches and comb helmets carried pikes and crossbows as they paced and watched carefully. Spanish boxes and bundles rose in orderly stacks and piles. Several Spanish women tended two large black-iron cook pots.

The Timucua braves pushed Calling Crow, Half Knife and Crying Wolf toward one of the large groups and ordered them to sit. One of the men captives looked over at Calling Crow as Mantua and his men walked off.

"What people are you?" said the man to Calling Crow.

"We are the Coosa people," said Calling Crow.

The man's eyes narrowed suspiciously and he seemed to move away a bit. Calling Crow looked at the man's topknot. "What people are you?" he said.

"Timucua."

Crying Wolf spat at hearing this.

Calling Crow frowned as he looked at the Timucua man. "It was your people that captured and brought us here."

The man said nothing.

"Why are you and these other people bound?" said Calling Crow, "while others of your people walk about free?"

The man grew visibly angry. "Mantua has betrayed us to the Spanish, Avila. Mantua and our chief had a disagreement. Using that as a pretext, Mantua, with the help of Avila, came and made us prisoners. Mantua has sold us to Avila for shooting sticks and the powder and ball that go into them! They say that they will take us out to the ship in the morning."

The man looked away, shaking with impotent rage. "One day Mantua will pay for his treachery. I will find a way to kill him. I swear it!"

Calling Crow looked at the many soldiers and braves walking about, some of them peering over at the captives suspiciously, and he doubted that this man would ever have his revenge. He said nothing.

Calling Crow heard voices speaking in Spanish. He strained to listen as, a few feet away, Mantua argued with Avila the slaver.

It was official government policy of the Audiencia of Santo Domingo not to trade harquebuses to the *Indios*. Pedro Avila, however, was not a government official. He was a businessman, dealing in slaves and pearls, and lately the demand for slaves had been growing. Although blacks were being brought in to the islands in growing numbers, there was still money to be made in Indian captives. The rogue cacique, Mantua, had been his tool in exploiting this demand. Mantua provided

Avila with the manpower and information for the operation, and for a bargain: fifty captives per harquebus. Now he was trying to increase his price.

"No," said Avila, "the price stands. But here is something extra." Avila pulled a bone-handled knife from his belt. "This is a gift for you."

Mantua brought the knife close, inspecting the filigree carved into the handle. "*Gracias, señor,*" he said thickly in Muskogee-accented Spanish. He pointed in Calling Crow's direction. "Where these people came from, there are at least three more villages. My scouts have told me this."

Avila looked over at the new captives and shook his head. "That may be, but I want you to concentrate in the south for the next eight to ten months. The season of storms approaches and I don't want to venture too far north. I will tell you when to go north again."

"*Sí.*" Mantua tucked the knife under his belt.

Avila walked off and Mantua knelt beside the box on the ground. He lifted the harquebus from it and inspected it carefully. Bringing it to his cheek, he sighted along the octagonal black-iron barrel, aiming it squarely at the big captive who had worn the cross. The man glared back fearlessly and Mantua thought that he must not know what the shooting stick could do to a man. Ha! For him it no longer mattered. But someday his people up north would know. Mantua's flinty eyes narrowed in contempt. He, Mantua, would show them.

As the sun began to set, the Timucua braves left the area, going back into the forest. When the light was gone, the Spanish lit torches and moved about. They ordered the captured people to sleep, but of course, they could not. Hidden by the dark, more and more of the women and children gave vent to their despair and cried disconsolately at their plight. Calling Crow was moved by their deep sorrow and wanted to tell them something to raise their spirits, but could not. Having once been a Spanish slave, he knew that they were in for much worse than their tormented minds could ever imagine.

The night passed slowly and daybreak brought not hope, but more sadness, for the people knew that it would be the last day they would spend in their lands. Soon they would be put aboard the Spanish ship.

When the light was bright enough, the soldiers and the Timucua braves began shouting and moving the people down onto the beach. Many dugout canoes had been brought up onto the beach at first light and the people were loaded into these and paddled out to the ship. The loading took all day and Calling Crow, Half Knife and Crying Wolf were with one of the last groups to leave. As Calling Crow was paddled out to the ship, he remembered the recurring vision he had had. In it, he was on a boat going away from his people. Always in the vision it had seemed to him as if he were making the journey of his own volition, but now, sadly, it appeared that that was not to be the case.

The canoe carrying Calling Crow and the others reached the other canoes that were all jammed together around the ship as they waited to unload their captives. The loading went very slow and Calling Crow looked back at the shore. In front of the fort many soldiers worked busily at unloading boats of supplies from the ships, and Timucua braves walked about freely. Calling Crow's eyes moved north along the shore. For a long stretch the forest grew right down to the water's edge, obscuring the white sand beach. Then Calling Crow's eyes came to a little patch of white beach where the land curved in, as if a giant sea creature had taken a bite out of the trees on the land. As his eyes rested on this place, a figure came out of the green forest and stood on the sand, looking out at the ship and the canoes. Calling Crow had the distinct feeling that the figure was looking directly at him. He could not make out any facial features on the tiny figure but he knew from the man's weight and height and from the way he stood that it was his son, Swordbrought. Although Swordbrought was too far away to actually see Calling Crow, he continued to look directly at him for a few more moments and then he disappeared back into the emerald green of the forest. A painful sadness welled up inside Calling Crow as he realized that this would be the last he would see of Swordbrought.

The canoes crowded so tightly together that Calling Crow and the other captives were able to step from one of the rock-

ing vessels to another as they made their way to the ship,
where they were roughly hauled up. The belly of the ship was
filled with tied-up people. It echoed with their screams and
shouts, like the hell the Spanish believed waited for those who
failed to worship the Great Spirit in the Spanish fashion. Calling Crow, Half Knife, Crying Wolf and the others from their
boat were made to sit up on the open deck. Then their cords
were tied securely to iron rings set in the wooden deck planks.

The sun set behind the trees. Iron clanged on iron and
booted feet thumped on oaken beams as Spanish soldiers
shouted orders. Calling Crow wanted to question the soldiers
in Spanish about where they were going, but his knowledge
of their language would expose him as a runaway slave and
he might be taken away from his men, down into the belly
of the ship. As the sky turned from orange to violet, more
and more of the captives lost their courage and began la-
menting their fate. With the approach of night, the sea swells
picked up and the boat rocked more pronouncedly, making
many people sick. Later, when the moon and stars came out,
a boat bumped dully into the hull of the ship. Calling Crow
and the others watched the ropes move as someone climbed
up. A soldier's helmeted head appeared, then another. Two
soldiers struggled as they pulled and pushed something
aboard. A wooden thud sounded as what looked like a large
bundle of cloth or grain fell onto the deck. The two soldiers
climbed over the rail. They bent at the waist, grabbing at the
bundle at their feet. Then they yanked Swordbrought roughly
to his feet.

Calling Crow's pain and anguish knew no bounds now. He
watched helplessly as the soldiers roughly dragged his son's
unconscious form across the ship and tied him to some other
people. Swordbrought's head hung limply on his chest when
they finished. The soldiers climbed back over the side and
disappeared.

For what seemed like a long, long time, Calling Crow
stared sadly at his son's still form. Then Swordbrought awoke
and brought his head up to look around him. Despite the poor
light, Calling Crow could see that his face was badly bruised
from a beating. Swordbrought was studying the faces of the

people tied near Calling Crow when he recognized Half Knife and Crying Wolf. Next his eyes met Calling Crow's. Calling Crow's look cautioned him to say nothing. As they stared at each other, a woman's anguished cry floated up from the belowdecks. "Our days are completed," she wailed between her sobs. "These Spanish value us less than their animals; our lives are over!"

The other captives looked down at their feet in shame, not wanting to meet one another's eyes.

Chapter 3

The rosy light of early evening flooded horizontally into the airy palm-thatched hut, illuminating the orderly array of intricately woven baskets, the pretty, patterned weavings on the walls, and the reed mats that were there to walk upon. Green Bird Woman stood against the west window opening. She wore a garland of beads and shells about her forehead. Despite having moved into the middle period of her life, Green Bird Woman was still very attractive. Her well-proportioned body and her smooth face exuded health and strength. Her eyes were proud and confident, but they had a sad tint to them, for they had seen much tragedy. She looked out at the palisade wall and the forest beyond. A single, iridescent-green feather was woven into her long, scalloped hair. The feather, and five others like it tucked away in a basket, were all that remained of Dancer, the big wonderful parrot she had once owned. It was Dancer that had caused her to be named Green Bird Woman, and he had filled many of her houses with his color and voice. He had even outlived her first husband.

A cool breeze moved through the hut, bringing with it the promise of a nice cool night. It was the first corn harvest. Two more corn plantings and harvests would follow before the rains of winter arrived. Tonight the people danced at the square ground in celebration. Green Bird Woman was going to watch the festivities.

A woman half Green Bird Woman's age entered the hut and smiled over at her. Bright Eyes's pretty face vaguely resembled her mother's, with full lips and soft, doe-brown eyes. Although now as tall as her mother, her figure was not as full.

Green Bird Woman smiled sadly at the sight of this fine

young woman. Green Bird Woman's own daughter had died seven years earlier of the black vomit. Green Bird Woman had adopted this girl from among a group of Santee captives. She had been almost the same age as Bright Eyes and bore a resemblance. Green Bird Woman had, of course, given her new daughter the name of the daughter she replaced. Strangely, like Green Bird Woman, Bright Eyes, too, had lost her first husband, and these losses had formed a very strong bond between them.

"Mother," called Bright Eyes chidingly, "Calling Crow has not yet returned, and the corn cares not whether you wear your feather."

Green Bird Woman turned to her daughter and laughed. "The corn knows," she said, "and the people expect me to dress well. They would worry if I did not." Green Bird Woman sighed appreciatively as she looked at Bright Eyes. She needed little to accentuate her beauty. Every unattached man in the village had his eyes on her.

The two women went out into the early evening. They walked the hard-packed dirt street that bisected the palisade-enclosed village, past the corn and bean fields that filled one side. They arrived at the square ground as young men began lighting torches tied to tall poles. Green Bird Woman and Bright Eyes had gone over to talk to some women who were cooking at a pot when they heard a commotion. Several men were running toward the square ground. Green Bird Woman saw the fierce-faced top brave called Swift Arrow and the big hulking top brave called Little Bear. Both men had gone with Calling Crow and the others; her heart sank.

Swift Arrow came right up to Green Bird Woman when he saw her. He leaned forward, putting his hands on his knees as he fought for breath. He turned to Little Bear. The big man's wide, placid face showed nothing of the pain he must have felt. "Go find Two Clouds and bring him here."

Swift Arrow coughed and turned to Green Bird Woman as Little Bear lumbered away. "We were attacked, ambushed," he said quickly.

People pushed in closer to hear his words.

Small birds darted about in the dark sky overhead as if

they sensed the tension in the people below. Green Bird Woman shouted at Swift Arrow. "What happened to Calling Crow and Swordbrought?"

Swift Arrow coughed again. "They are alive, I think, but prisoners. There were too many for us to fight." Swift Arrow looked around at the gathering crowd and went on. "Calling Crow told us to flee, to come here and get help."

Green Bird Woman looked around wildly. "My husband . . . my boy," she said to no one in particular, "we must go get them." Spotting two boys with lances, she called to them, "You two! Come with me. We will leave right away."

The two boys did not move; instead, they looked at Swift Arrow in confusion.

Green Bird Woman addressed the bigger of the two boys. "What are you called?"

"I am Flat Head."

"Come here."

The boy approached and Green Bird Woman took his lance from him. "I will go get them myself," she said, looking around at the gathering darkness with worry.

"Mother," said Bright Eyes anxiously, "wait."

Green Bird Woman did not hear her. Then a deep voice called Green Bird Woman's name and she turned. It was Two Clouds. He was flanked by Little Bear and another young brave.

"Green Bird Woman," Two Clouds said gently, "you must not rush off. The warriors are being assembled and Sees Far must prepare them for battle before they leave. At first light they will go and pick up the track." He walked over and stood by her. "Now, please come back to the *chokafa* with me and we will talk."

Green Bird Woman's eyes were glossy with unshed tears as she shook her head. "No," she said dreamily, "I will go get them myself." She turned away from the stately figure of old Two Clouds.

Bright Eyes hovered close to her mother as Two Clouds motioned to the braves. Little Bear gently took Flat Head's lance from Green Bird Woman's hand and gave it back to him. Then he and another brave each took one of Green Bird

Woman's arms. "Come," said Little Bear, "we will take you to your house."

The crowd had left, embarrassed and grieved at the sight of Green Bird Woman's pain. Only the two boys remained, nervously watching as the braves led the woman away. Bright Eyes cried softly as she followed along behind. Out of the growing darkness, a skinny old man hurried up behind Bright Eyes. It was Bent Ears, a friend of Green Bird Woman's late uncle. He took Bright Eyes's hand consolingly. "I heard," he said.

Bright Eyes squeezed his hand in reply.

Bright Eyes kept the fire in her mother's house burning brightly. She dipped a gourd cup into a pot of soup and extended it to her mother. Green Bird Woman shook her head and looked into the fire.

"They will find them," said Bright Eyes. "Our young men are the best trackers. You will see."

Green Bird Woman looked at her and tried to smile. "You are right, Bright Eyes. I was so worried about your father and brother . . . I wasn't thinking clearly."

Bright Eyes patted her hand. "It is all right, Mother."

Outside, the night passed slowly as the two women stared into the fire. Neither spoke and finally Bright Eyes tried to rest, laying her head down upon her upraised knees. Periodically the slapping footfalls of a runner passed outside. Sometimes the distant singing of the warriors as they prepared themselves seemed to swell as a breeze carried it into the hut. Green Bird Woman listened to these things blankly as she stroked her daughter's head lovingly.

Bright Eyes awoke suddenly and looked up.

Green Bird Woman smiled sadly at her. "You know," she said, "when they said that Calling Crow and Swordbrought had been captured, I found myself thinking about how it felt to hold Swordbrought when he was a new, wriggly little thing."

Bright Eyes smiled at this description of the beginnings of the brave young man her brother had become.

Green Bird Woman's eyes lit up at the infectious smile of

Bright Eyes. ''You had to hold him tightly or he would jump out of your arms. Calling Crow said he would probably run before he crawled.''

Bright Eyes laughed bravely. She struggled for something to say and fell silent. Green Bird Woman patted Bright Eyes's hand and knelt to push a stout stick into the fire. Outside, the distant drumming grew with hopeful intensity. Green Bird Woman sat back down and lay her head upon her knees.

Chapter 4

Almost directly east of the Spanish slave ship, the dark bulk of the *Contempt* sailed slowly north in a steady wind. Below, out of the weather, Samuel Newman stood in a pool of flickering lamplight before John, Fenwick and two dozen others. Heads down, they concluded their prayer for their captured mate, Peter Butler: "May the Lord God deliver him from the bloody Spaniard!" Samuel intoned solemnly.

"Amen," the others mumbled.

Samuel looked round at the men. "We will have to land somewhere and secure victuals and fresh water for the return crossing."

"When?" Fenwick said.

"Tomorrow, the day after, as soon as we spot a good anchorage."

"Victuals and water, yes," said John loudly, "but I'm not for going home yet."

"Very well," said Samuel, "after we get our water and victuals, we will leave you ashore."

Several men laughed.

John's face grew dark. "No, brother, you will not get rid of me so easily."

"Ho ho," said a man on the outer perimeter of the gathering, enjoying the brothers' argument.

"Then what is it you are proposing, John?" said Samuel tiredly.

John's voice resonated with simmering anger. "After we victual, we should lay low until we spy a Spanish prize. Then we will take it, refilling our purses and repaying them for their bloody treachery."

"Yeah," said a man tentatively, with several others mumbling their agreement.

Samuel looked round at them. "What about the rest of you? I thought you had had enough of the bloody heat and mosquitos. Do you really want to go off privateering?"

The majority of the men had become emboldened and grumbled affirmatively.

"We've all lost money back there, sir," said Fenwick, "and we'd like to get it back."

"With interest!" said a man, fired by the thought. More of the men now grumbled affirmatively.

"Very well," said Samuel. "We'll give it two months and no longer. If we spot a ship in that time, we'll go after her. If we don't, we'll go home. Old Tom lost an eye and Peter Butler's as good as a dead man. I'll not risk any more of the lads. Agreed?"

"Aye," the men said heartily, and the meeting broke up.

Samuel made his way forward. He touched the lookout on the shoulder and the man walked off. Samuel leaned out on the bowsprit, the large spar projecting forward from the prow. He stared into the darkness, watching and listening for the phosphorescence and thunder of surf that would indicate shoals. Samuel's soul ached from the events of the last long day, the treachery of the Spanish, Gredilla's cowardly departure, the destruction of their goods and especially the loss of the Butler lad. He would probably be burned at the stake as a heretic in some colonial town square, or worse, chained to an oar in one of the Spaniards' hellish Mediterranean galleys. Now the men wanted to go privateering! Samuel's anger flared hot over his mercurial brother's actions and interference. All their misfortune was partly his fault and he still insisted on meddling. Samuel thought back to the bloody death of the grandee, Fernandez, on the quay. If not for that, they could possibly have won their case; the Spanish courts were as riddled with corruption as a cheese. They could have bribed someone and still turned a profit for the venture. But John's hot head had closed that door.

Samuel forced his mind to change its tack. He could not

change John, and it was his own fault for having brought him
along. Well, it would be the last time. Now he must think
only about what was needed to get them all home safely. They
would put in somewhere and stay for two months. With luck
and God's grace they'd all get home safely. Then he could
again relax around his hotheaded brother. But from now on,
he'd bear watching.

Just aft of the mainmast, down below on the gundeck, Patrick, the Irish ship's boy, was working the ship's pump handle
back and forth. The sound, a dull, rhythmic thudding, provided accompaniment to a ballad he sang about an unfaithful
maiden and a vengeful knight. His voice was plaintive and
not unpleasant and Samuel gave himself up to the mournful
tune, feeling it a salve for his bruised soul.

Chapter 5

In the night, a steady stream of debris floated along in the black tidal current, moving past the anchored Spanish slave ship—seaweed uprooted by a recent storm, the husks of fruits, branches fallen from trees. The ship would sail for Santo Domingo in the morning. The debris bobbed in the water as it moved south, past the ship and out to sea. Red Feather clung to one of the things, a small log, as it moved in the flow toward the ship. The swells rose and fell gently and powerfully as the swift current bore him along. In the dim starlight, Red Feather saw something that made his heart pound in his chest. The jumbled line the debris formed now turned, curving outward to sea, away from the ship. He began pulling the water with one arm as he held on with the other, attempting to change the course of his drift, but the log stubbornly followed the other things on their path out to sea. He abandoned the log and began swimming toward the ship. The current was much stronger than he had thought and after a while he seemed not to have gotten any closer. He clenched his jaw grimly and forced himself to swim harder. Calling Crow was on this ship, the man whose courage and vision had led the village through many dangers in the past, the man who was loved and respected by all. Calling Crow was a man that he, Red Feather, loved like a father; he would drown before he would let the white people take Calling Crow away. *Aieyah!* Red Feather put all his strength into his swimming. If he could not free Calling Crow, then he would join him in captivity.

Red Feather's breath was coming fast when he noticed that the ship had grown slightly in size. He was closer! He said a prayer of thanks to his spirit guide and swam on as hard as he could; he would make it! Finally, in his exhaustion, his fist banged carelessly into the timbers of the ship with a dull thud, but the little noise it made went unnoticed by the soldiers on guard above. Red Feather jammed his hands into the gaps in the timbers and clung tightly as he rested. Later, he became another shadow on the black sea as he moved along the bulk of the ship. Coming upon some ropes, he quietly began climbing up.

He stepped over the rail and looked around. People slept everywhere. The light was almost nonexistent, but before too long he found who he was looking for. Red Feather stood over Calling Crow's sleeping form.

Calling Crow slept shallowly. He sensed a presence and looked up into Red Feather's eyes. Calling Crow's face conveyed his appreciation to his *tastanagi*. Only Red Feather could have done this thing. Calling Crow indicated, with a nod of his head, someone among the people tied up to the rail on the other side of the deck. Red Feather silently crossed the wooden expanse. Finding Swordbrought, he quietly cut him free. They came back and Red Feather knelt before Calling Crow, Little Bear and Crying Wolf. Red Feather was sawing at the thick cords wrapped around Calling Crow's wrists when they heard a sound.

Swordbrought knelt and pulled the knife Red Feather had given him, ready to fight. They looked about and waited. Booted feet thudded heavily somewhere on the wooden deck. Not caring how much noise they made, the Spanish clumped closer along the side of the ship. In another few moments they would be close enough to see what was happening.

The disembodied footsteps left the rail and started over toward Calling Crow and his men. Calling Crow called out commandingly in Spanish, "*¡Rapido!* Señor Avila wants to see you in his cabin."

The men immediately turned and hurried back the way they had come. Swordbrought and Red Feather looked at Calling Crow in awe as the captives stirred around them. "Quickly," said Calling Crow, "cut Little Bear and Crying Wolf loose."

The Timucua brave next to Calling Crow watched Swordbrought and Red Feather cutting the others loose.

When Calling Crow was on his feet, he turned to Crying Wolf and indicated the Timucua brave. "Cut his cords loose and give him your knife so he can cut his people loose."

Crying Wolf's face was a mix of anger and incredulity. "But they are Timucua," he said, "the same people who captured you!"

Calling Crow's voice had an edge of angry impatience to it. "Haven't you learned anything the whole time you have known me? They are not Timucua! They are Spanish slaves. Cut him loose!"

Crying Wolf's face was stiff with shame as he knelt and cut the Timucua man's bonds. He gave the Timucua his knife and the man quickly cut the man next to him free of the ropes.

Calling Crow said to the two Timucua. "Cut the ropes from your people as quickly as you can. The soldiers will return soon."

Silently, Calling Crow and his men went over the rail and climbed down the side of the ship. They eased their bodies into the sea without making a splash.

The water enveloped Calling Crow like cool freedom. He swam quickly, powerfully pulling the black water past him without a sound. Saying nothing, he and the others swam toward that part of the beach north of the Spanish fort where the forest grew down to the sea. Halfway there they could hear the splashes of the other Timucua as they jumped into the sea. Calling Crow trod water momentarily to listen, then swam on to join the ghostly white combers racing toward the sand. Soon they were running heavy legged through the strong, foaming surf. They entered the forest and heard the shouts of the soldiers and then the boom of a gun as the alarm went out.

They pushed through the forest and found the big trail. All night they ran along in the dark. When daylight began to push down through the thick canopy, they stopped and listened to hear if they were being followed. Hearing nothing, they ran on.

It was the second day of their search for Calling Crow, and Swift Arrow, Little Bear and the other four Coosa braves had easily followed the track the raiding party had left. Now the pine forest came to an end at a grassy plain bordering a great swamp of water lilies and bald-cypress islands. Swift Arrow strode down to the water's edge in a tall thicket of bushes. Little Bear and the other braves knelt on the sandy bank to inspect some prints. Swift Arrow pushed noisily into the thicket toward the water. He thought he could see something where a creek ran out to the sea. Little Bear came up beside him and together they pushed through the thicket till they could go no farther and stood in water up to their waists. At this point the thicket was cage-like, with wrist-thick branches rising from the water to reach and twist overhead.

"I saw it swimming this way . . . Here."

Swift Arrow and Little Bear froze. The strangely accented, Muskogee voice had come from just the other side of the thicket. Clear and distinct, and no more than a stone's throw away, it had reached their ears with no warning, no footfalls, no splashing through the water. Swift Arrow and Little Bear remained motionless. Through a myriad of holes in the thicket they watched a dugout canoe glide slowly to a stop, the muscles in the paddler's thick legs tensing visibly as he shifted the oar to brake. Swift Arrow and Little Bear and the others saw that the men in the canoe were Timucua. One of them held a long paddle, the other a lance. The Timucua with the lance peered into the water.

A splash came from near the dugout. "I've got him!" said a triumphant voice. Swift Arrow and the others saw a flash of silver as the Timucua hoisted the gar he had impaled on his lance up out of the water and into the dugout. Another canoe glided into view. "The ship is leaving," said a man. "Yes," said another, "they say there were so many slaves on it that they had to stack them two deep." The others laughed.

Swift Arrow looked through the holes in the thicket and saw the ship. Small in the distance, it headed straight out to sea, taking his beloved chief with it.

"Come," said one of the Timucua voices, "we'll cook this big fellow over a nice fire. Can we get through here?"

The Timucua began beating the thicket with his oar as he

probed the thickness of it. Swift Arrow turned and motioned
to Little Bear to begin backing away.

Little Bear pointed to a ripple of movement on the surface
of the water behind him. A large water moccasin was swimming toward him. It wrapped itself around his broad back to
rest, preventing him from moving.

Swift Arrow insistently waved him back. Little Bear grimaced and backed up. Immediately the serpent came to life and
bit Little Bear on the back before swimming quickly away.
Little Bear exhaled audibly, but did not cry out. Sweat beaded
on his wide, dark face as he pushed slowly and silently
through the water to the bank. After running for a while, the
Coosa braves were forced to stop. Although Little Bear had
been bitten many times before, he was reeling from the poi-
sons in this snake's bite and needed to rest. Swift Arrow and
the others took up position, watching the approaches, as the
big brave lay down on the ground. After sleeping for half a
day, Little Bear woke and they ran on.

Chapter 6

The *Contempt* lay anchored in a small bay into which a muddy river emptied. The sun climbed into a nearly cloudless sky, burning off the hazy mist that hung low over the shoreline. Samuel Newman, John Newman and Fenwick the Tailor sat in the skiff tied to the ship. Two men began climbing down the ropes from the ship. One, a big, ruddy-faced, blue-eyed Flemish tanner in his forties named Breuger, who had emigrated to England to escape persecution from the Catholics five years earlier, carried a loaded crossbow over his shoulder.

Fenwick called up to him. "Be careful, my friend, don't fall. That crossbow might go off."

"It's okay, Fen, for even if it should shoot a bolt into you, I have several more in reserve."

"Ho ho," laughed Fenwick.

Samuel smiled at their banter. He knew they were nervous about going ashore, but go they must. They would have to procure victuals and water somewhere, enough for their stay here and enough to get them back home. Samuel looked back at John, who appeared not to hear the other men as he stared intently at the misty forested shore. Samuel's smile faded. John's black moods would be his own undoing, but he must make sure they didn't threaten the rest of the men and the venture.

Breuger hunched over low as he walked carefully through the middle of the skiff, keeping his weight in the center. He took a seat next to Samuel. Three other men climbed down. The first, a strapping lad of nineteen years from the Bristol countryside named Thomas, put his weight on the skiff, pushing it lower in the waves. He carried an old, German matchlock musket. Thomas went carefully to the prow of the skiff and lay the musket there. He came back and sat at one of the oars. The second man, a quiet, emaciated, pock-faced chandler named Miles, sat in the stern. Then young Patrick Fitzgerald from Munster climbed down. Keeping his eyes to himself, he sat at the other oar. Samuel nodded and they pushed off.

They began pulling for the shore. The two young men put their backs into the task and the boat soon traversed the bay. By the time Samuel directed them to start up the river, the mist had burned off. They rowed quietly beneath great dark bald cypress trees, leaving a large V-shaped wake in the black water. John rested his hand on the hilt of his sword as he watched the shores. The birds make a racket and the men saw many turtles sunning themselves on rocks and logs. Samuel pointed out a large tree on the bank to Patrick and Tom and they headed for that. A few moments later Patrick and Tom shipped the oars and they drifted toward the bank. The skiff grounded gently on the muddy bottom.

"Fenwick," said Samuel, handing him a coiled-up length of rope with which to tie up the skiff, "you shall have the honor of being the first ashore on Florida. Over you go."

Fenwick looked anxiously down into the black water.

"He's worried about the alligators," said John drily.

"It's all right, Fenwick," said Breuger, "they will only bite you if you step on them."

"Are you sure?" said Fenwick.

"Of course," said Breuger.

Fenwick smiled as he held out the rope. "Then you go."

"Hurry, man," grumbled John.

Fenwick jumped into the water, muttering quietly to himself. "After two weeks of no meat and nothing but dried peas and biscuits, the alligators better worry about me!"

The others laughed as Fenwick pushed through the water and climbed onto the bank. He began pulling the skiff in hand over hand. When it would come no farther, the other men began climbing out.

"Secure it well to the tree," said Samuel. "The tide has

gone out and she sits low. We don't want to lose her when the tide returns and have to swim home.''

Wordlessly they pushed through the thick bushes and ferns, listening to the sounds of wildlife all around them. Used to the ever-reaching vistas of the long-ago deforested fields and towns of England, they marveled at the wild lushness of the forest. Here there was no horizon; there was no road. They heard birds overhead, but saw none flying about for there seemed to be no sky.

Young Tom was the first to speak. "I've heard stories about the inhabitants of these lands," he said softly to Miles, who was walking in front of him. "They say that there are wild men in these forests who live up in the trees."

Miles turned round to him briefly and nodded. "I have heard the stories too. Tailed men, they say!"

"There are some who believe that we all had tails at one time," said Breuger from behind them. "But most of us lost them over the centuries."

"Yes," said John, "all but the Irish."

Patrick's cheeks grew red at the taunt, but he said nothing, continuing to walk.

Fenwick winked at him, then turned back to Samuel. "Tailed men?" he said, but Samuel was staring intently into the dense growth and did not hear him.

"Supposedly," said Breuger, "the natives of these lands are tailed. But worse than that, they are said to be cannibals of the worst kind, fond of burning their captives alive and then eating their blackened flesh."

Fenwick again turned worriedly to Samuel. "Is it true, Samuel?"

"What?" said Samuel, "that they are cannibals?"

"No, that they are tailed."

Samuel peered at the thick foliage. "When I see a live *homo caudatus,* all bound up, or a dead one for that matter, then I'll believe it. But I'll not settle for children's stories of such."

"A homo what?" said Fenwick.

"*Homo caudatus,*" said John. "That is the Latin word for tailed men."

The forest thickened and the men lapsed into silence as they were forced to hack and push at the vines and bushes. With their heads as wet as if someone had doused them with buckets, they finally pushed out onto a trail. It was not a hip-high animal trail through the thickets, but a well-traveled, dirt-smoothed trail, almost wide enough to allow a carriage to pass, definitely wide enough to allow three men to walk side by side.

"I wonder where this goes," said Fenwick nervously as he picked his nose.

"To a village, no doubt," said Samuel.

John and the other three men were looking down the trail in the opposite direction. John came up to Samuel.

John wiped his brow with the back of his hand. "It sounds like every bloody animal God ever created is about and making noise, but you never see one to put an arrow into it."

Samuel nodded tiredly. "Perhaps we should follow the trail and see if there's a village. We could trade with them for food."

"Oh," said John, "how, I pray you? We don't speak their language, we don't even know if they have the capacity of language. Do you think it will be like trading with the bloody French or the Irish? Hah! If we find a village, our best bet is to take what we need." John lay his hand on Tom's musket. "Keep your match lit, boy. We'll put the bloody fear of God into them with that and get what we need."

Samuel found his temper rising. "No," he said emphatically. "The Spaniards trade successfully with the natives. If we find any, we will trade for what we need." He glared in warning at the other men and then at young Tom. "Do you understand?"

Tom nodded.

John laughed as he looked at his brother. "Samuel has read too many of those French books about the natives of the New Lands." John turned to the others. "It is written in these books that the New Found Lands are a paradise where the rivers flow with wine. The birds in the trees and sky are already roasted to a golden brown and sing like angels before they fly into one's mouth." John turned back to Samuel.

"Brother, do you think the natives will victual us with these birds and wine for our return voyage?"

"Stop your rot," said Samuel angrily. "It was your doing that got us into this mess."

"By my soul," said John hotly, "I thought a fat, old grandee named Fernandez had some hand in it."

Samuel shook his head angrily as the other men waited for the two brothers to settle their argument. "Enough, enough already," he said, "let's go."

John smiled as he pointed first one way on the trail and then the other. "This way or that way?"

Samuel started down the trail toward the north and Fenwick fell into step behind him. Wordlessly, Breuger, Miles, Tom and Patrick followed, and then John. They had not gone far when a curious sound came from the trees off to their right.

"What was that?" said Fenwick.

"I don't know," said Tom.

"Some kind of local bird, I think," said Samuel.

"Well," said Tom, hefting the musket up, "if it shows itself, it's going in the cook pot tonight."

They walked on and heard the same call from the thick foliage on the other side of the trail.

"There's another one," said Breuger worriedly.

"Pay it no mind," said Samuel, "keep moving."

As the men walked along, the sound came again and again, as if there were now many of the creatures and they were following them. The Englishmen walked faster, their breathing heavier, and the creatures seemed to become more bold, coming closer. Breuger took off running down the trail. "Wait," Samuel called. The others ran after Breuger, and Samuel followed them. The sound grew much louder and the men fell into a panic, running wildly. A horrible scream rang out and they stopped, looking about at the inscrutable green foliage. A large feathered form raced across a small clearing.

Tom raised the musket to fire and an arrow pierced his chest. He opened his mouth to scream but no sound came out. Then a swarm of arrows found him and he fell like a stone. Samuel and the others looked around frantically. A chorus of horrid screams erupted and the bushes seemed to come alive with natives. Feathered and hideously painted, they rushed at the surprised Englishmen as they pulled their swords.

Samuel faced the attackers but turned at the last minute when he sensed movement behind him. A strong arm closed around his neck and he was thrown to the ground and clubbed in the head. The blow stunned him. He was aware of the sounds of the others' struggle, but could do nothing to help them. Then someone was pulling him to his feet. Samuel felt a small degree of relief when he saw that John and the others were unhurt. Like him, they, too, were bound up tightly with leather straps of some kind.

"John," said Samuel, "are you all right?"

"Yes," said John, looking around sullenly at their attackers.

Samuel estimated there were more than fifty native men, all of them painted red and black and decorated with feathers, stones and the like, all of it designed to give them a menacing, wild-animal look. They were tall and stout of frame, and wore their hair pulled up into a knot that stuck up from the middle of their heads for about the length of a finger.

Samuel glanced back at the others. Fenwick's mouth hung open in fear and he looked about wildly. Breuger was on his feet and evidently unhurt, but his face was bruised badly and he appeared to be in shock. Miles and Patrick sat on the trail, their hands bound behind them.

One of the natives began shouting and they pushed Samuel and the others back in the direction from which they had just come. They passed Tom's body where the natives had left it lying on the trail, stripped of his sword, boots and clothing. The natives had retrieved their arrows and Tom's pale white body was a mass of bloody holes.

"Christ in Heaven!" Fenwick said fearfully, "he looks like a bloody pincushion."

They were led along the trail for most of the day, until they came to what appeared to be a large timbered fort. They passed through the entrance and walked down a main street of packed dirt. Samuel stared at the groups of small huts, corralled off with crude fences, that lined both sides of the street. There were no people anywhere to watch their entrance and he thought this strange. When they came to a square of sorts, one of the native men called a halt.

As Samuel looked about, he heard a commotion behind and a large, muscled man who was evidently the leader came up to him. Inspecting him briefly, the man issued orders. His men then pushed Samuel and the others rudely toward some poles set in the ground. The poles formed a circle the diameter of which approximated the height of a man. The poles were spaced such that people tethered to them would not be able to see one another. A native shoved Samuel back so hard his head cracked into a stout pole. As his hands were being tightly bound, he fell again into unconsciousness.

Samuel came out of a fog and heard voices. The air was cool. He opened his eyes. He was in the center of the village, his arms tied painfully behind him. The sun had set and the light was dying. A breeze washed across the open square of the village, chilling him. He looked about but could see none of the natives anywhere. Behind him he heard Fenwick and Breuger talking, but he could not turn his head around enough to see them.

"Where are their women?" Fenwick was saying, "and their children?"

"Perhaps there are none," said Breuger, "perhaps they are a species like the Amazons, with only one sex."

Samuel called to them. "Are you all right back there?"

Breuger's voice came. "We're alive."

"But for how long?" said Fenwick plaintively.

"Shut your trap," snapped John.

"Is Miles alive?" said Samuel.

"I'm all right, sir," came the man's reply.

"Patrick?"

"He's still unconscious," said Miles.

Samuel wondered where the natives had gone. He wished he hadn't blacked out. "Where are they?" he asked the others.

John answered. "There is a big hut back here which you cannot see. They all went in there, to rest up, we think."

"Have they been out since then?"

"No," said John.

"They know we're not going anywhere," said Fenwick.

The air continued to cool and the men fell silent, each with his own thoughts.

Someone cried out as if in great pain.

"What was that?" said Samuel.

"It's Patrick," said Miles, "he's coming round."

"Is he all right?"

"I think so."

"They're coming out now," said Fenwick, "a dozen or more of them."

Samuel was vexed at not being able to see what was happening. "What are they doing, Fenwick?" he said. "Keep me informed."

"I don't know," replied Fenwick sadly, "bringing up wood."

Samuel could hear the sound of branches being broken. He heard the occasional shouts and laughter of the natives.

"About fifty paces from here they have stacked quite a large pile of wood," said Fenwick.

"What are they doing now?" said Samuel.

"Nothing. Just standing around."

"Christ in heaven!" said Breuger.

No one said anything and Samuel called out anxiously. "What is it?"

"Someone is bringing a torch."

It was dark now. No one said anything. After a while Samuel could hear the crackling of the fire. He knew it must be large because even from the distance, he could soon feel its warmth on the back of his neck. Were they really going to throw them into the fire? he wondered. The thought was too much to bear and he pushed it out of his head. He watched the flickering light that now fell on the ground, and allowed his mind to take him back to a lawn party at his estate. Torches cast their quivering glow upon his grassy lawn. His five-year-old son ran with some other boys, shouting as they played the catching game Last-in-Hell. A small, warm hand clasped his finger tightly. It was his two-and-a-half-year-old daughter, Catherine, the joy of his life. Her happy eyes beseeching him, she pulled him out onto the lawn for a dance. Her fat cheeks shone like red apples above the round white-lace collar of her black velvet dress. He spun her around and her delight issued forth in a tomboyish belly laugh. His wife, Frances, heard and looked over from where she sat with the others. She smiled at him. Then she turned round to smile and talk with the guests as the servants made the rounds with cakes and drinks.

Chapter 7

Calling Crow and his men arrived at the deserted Timucua village he had passed the day before. The sweet smell of hickory smoke was in the air. Calling Crow knew now, of course, what had happened to the people of this village, but he still wanted a look inside. He ordered his men to halt. Moving well away from the high timber palisade, they found a place to rest where a thick wall of trees and vines would obscure them from the eyes and ears of anyone in the village. Calling Crow sent Red Feather over the wall to scout.

Calling Crow, Swordbrought and the others waited watchfully, quietly talking of the escape of the night before. Although Calling Crow had taught Swordbrought Spanish, he could not speak the language with the same facility as his father. Now, together with the other braves, Swordbrought marveled at Calling Crow's use of the Spanish soldiers' own language to fool them. They laughed at the thought of the men's plight at having to explain their actions to their chief later.

Red Feather returned quickly, his eyes shining with excitement. "Mantua and his men are camped in there," he said quietly to Calling Crow.

Calling Crow frowned thoughtfully in the growing dimness. He wanted to recapture his cross and iron axe. He also wanted to teach this Mantua a lesson. Perhaps this was his chance.

"He has five Spanish prisoners," added Red Feather.

Calling Crow frowned and momentarily put away his thoughts of revenge. "That is strange," he said, "why would Mantua capture and hold any Spanish? It would jeopardize his relations with Avila the slaver."

Red Feather frowned. "I don't know. But inside he has five of them tied up."

"I will go see," said Calling Crow, getting to his feet.

Swordbrought quickly got up. "I will go with you."

Crying Wolf pointed to Swordbrought as he said jokingly, "Notice how now he will not let his father out of his sight."

Swordbrought gave no indication that the other brave's words had bothered him, but Calling Crow knew his son well enough to know they had. Crying Wolf should not have said this. After all, Calling Crow himself had ordered Swordbrought and the other men to flee. But that was the way it was between these two. Although Crying Wolf was three turnings of the sky older than Swordbrought, and of a different mother, the two of them competed and fought like brothers.

Calling Crow and Swordbrought quickly climbed up and over the back wall of the village. The darkness was almost total now, for there was a new moon and only starlight to see by. They moved as quietly as owls, fleeting shadows winding their way between the small huts. Calling Crow saw the light of the big fire up at the square ground. He and Swordbrought crept past the huts, staying out of the light as much as possible. Having nothing to fear in their own territory, most of the Timucua braves had congregated in one group. But, Calling Crow knew, there would be a few men moving about and he must watch out for them. Calling Crow drew closer to the large group of braves. Mantua was nowhere in sight. Perhaps he was sleeping. Calling Crow saw the white men tied up behind the fire. They could be French, he thought, but long ago he himself had seen the French fort destroyed and all their people either killed or run off by the Spanish. That memory brought up much sadness for him, for it was at that time that his first woman, Swordbrought's natural mother, Juana, had been killed. Would the French be foolish enough to settle again in what the Spanish arrogantly claimed as their lands? He didn't think so. So who were these white people?

Calling Crow and Swordbrought peered through the entryway of a hut, listening to the shouts and laughter of the Timucua braves. But, try as he could, Calling Crow could not make out their words. Perhaps he should just retrieve his cross and axe and leave the white men to their fate.

Harsh laughter came from the Timucua braves. Calling Crow remembered the conversation he had overheard between Mantua and the slaver, Avila. Mantua and his men would concentrate in the south in their search for slaves. But eventually, in eight or nine moons, they would come north to Coosa Town—with shooting sticks! What then? Calling Crow had been thinking about this for some time. There was only one way his people could protect themselves; they, too, must have shooting sticks. But how?

Calling Crow looked back over at the white men. Could they be the answer? Would they get them the shooting sticks they needed to defend the village? *Aieyah,* they must! That was why his footsteps had been guided here. Ho! It must be so!

Calling Crow turned to Swordbrought. Stealing the white men away from the Timucua would be dangerous, but his men would thrill to the challenge. Calling Crow signaled to Swordbrought that they would go back to talk to the other braves.

Later, Calling Crow faced his men. "There are too many Timucua warriors so there must be no fighting. There will be plenty of fighting some time in the future.

Red Feather, take Crying Wolf with you and go to the back of the village. Lure the Timucua braves your way."

Calling Crow looked at Crying Wolf sternly. "There must be no fighting, do you understand?"

Crying Wolf nodded slightly.

Calling Crow turned again to his faithful *tastanagi,* Red Feather. "Remember, don't be seen. Swordbrought, Little Bear and I will go in the front to get the white men. Go now."

Red Feather turned and led his men away.

Samuel could feel the heat of the fire lessening in intensity. It grew quieter and he called round to the others. "What are they doing?"

"They are going off toward the back of their houses," said Fenwick. "One of them has evidently found something back there and now they are all going to see what it is.''

Samuel stared into the blackness. All his strength had gone and he sagged from the ropes. He was vaguely aware of Breuger's and John's voices when a dark shape appeared before him. It was a tall man, a native. He wore his hair long and did not look like the others that had captured them. His neck, chest and arms were decoratively banded with black marks and he wore a necklace of black feathers. Out of the corner of Samuel's eye, he saw two others moving about. One was marked like the first man; the other was an unmarked young man in his mid-teens. The unmarked youth moved as confidently and stealthily as the two men.

The tall man put his hand over Samuel's mouth momentarily, indicating that he should be silent. ''Are you Spanish?'' he asked quietly in that language.

Startled, Samuel shook his head.

''Are you French?''

Samuel again shook his head. ''*Ingles*,'' he said. Samuel saw that the man seemed confused by his response.

The native man's eyes bore into Samuel's. ''Do you have a ship?'' he said.

Samuel nodded.

The man pulled a knife from a sash he wore around his waist. Samuel's strength was gone and he felt strangely detached. He noted that it was a knife much like his own, made of steel. He thought the man might use it on him and he found the prospect better than the fire. Instead, the man cut Samuel's hands free. While Samuel was gratefully rubbing his wrists, the man disappeared.

Samuel walked around to the other side of the poles and saw John, Fenwick, Breuger, Patrick and Miles standing in a group, while across from them the three natives held a whispered conference. When they finished, the younger one, a boy really, indicated by signs that they should come with him.

As Samuel followed him, he noticed the man who had released them walking off alone toward where the natives that had captured them had gone. Samuel and the others walked behind the boy, coming to the village entrance. John whispered to Samuel. ''He speaks Spanish.''

"Who?" said Samuel.

"The boy."

Samuel nodded. "So does the big one. Rather well too."

John frowned. "Imagine!"

The older of the two natives turned round to them and motioned them to silence. Using signs, he indicated they should crouch down and wait. He then crept stealthily forward to reconnoiter the area.

Calling Crow spotted two somber-faced Timucua braves standing guard outside a hut and he knew Mantua would be inside. Calling Crow went around the back and found an opening big enough for him. He climbed in. Giving his eyes a moment to adjust, he located Mantua's long form stretched out on a sleeping shelf across the hut.

Calling Crow pulled his Spanish iron knife and crept silently across the hut. He stood over the sleeping man, looking down at him. Calling Crow's cross and iron axe lay on the shelf. Calling Crow looped the cross around his neck and slipped the axe under his sash. Removing a black crow's feather from the necklace about his neck, Calling Crow lay it gently on the man's sweaty, rising and falling chest. This Mantua, this chief who sells his own people into slavery, would never forget this night.

One of the braves outside said something and Calling Crow crouched down, making himself smaller. The man stuck his head in and scrutinized the blackness. Satisfied, he turned again to talk quietly with his companion. Calling Crow went quickly back to the opening and left.

Samuel and his men waited in the darkness outside the palisade until the older, tall native leader arrived. Samuel noted the cross now hanging upon his chest. The native led them away from the walls of the village until they came upon the wide trail. They then began running. After a while Samuel and the others were breathing heavily and falling behind. The tall native man called a halt and they rested, Samuel and the others in one group, the native men in another.

Samuel watched the natives as he caught his breath. They

did not sit, but rather squatted down, their buttocks almost touching earth. They said nothing as they stared out into the blackness. Samuel got to his feet.

"Where are you going?" said John between rasping breaths.

"To talk to the big one. He is evidently in charge." Samuel walked up to the native men and squatted down in their fashion. In Spanish he said, "Thank you for helping us."

The native man seemed surprised at Samuel's words. "It was the will of the Great Spirit," he said.

"The Great Spirit?" said Samuel.

The man indicated the night sky and the trees. He touched the ground beneath their feet. "He who rules over all."

Samuel nodded and touched his own chest, indicating the man's cross. "What is that?" he said in Spanish.

"Spanish medicine," said the man, "very powerful. It stopped an arrow once, saving my life."

Samuel tried not to frown. The Spanish had already infected him with their cross worship. What else had they taught him? he wondered.

"There are many Timucua," said the native man, "very bad men. They were going to trade you to the Spanish for shooting sticks."

"But . . . the fire," said Samuel.

"That was for a celebratory dance."

"I see," said Samuel. "Why did you help us?"

"Because you will help us."

"How?"

"We will speak of that later."

Samuel nodded. "Very well." He pointed in the direction he thought the sea was. "We must get back to our ship. Our people will think we are dead and leave us."

"We will take you," said the man. "And then you will take us onto your ship and take us to our village."

"How will you find the ship?"

The man stared off into the distance. "We will follow the tracks you and your men made."

"In the dark?"

"Yes."

Samuel paused a moment to catch his breath. "What is your name, sir?"

"I am called Calling Crow."

Samuel nodded. "I am called Samuel." He went back to his men, who had been watching the exchange anxiously.

"What'd he say?" said Fenwick.

"His name is Calling Crow," said Samuel, "and he will take us back to our ship before morning."

"In the dark?" said Breuger.

"That is what he said," said Samuel.

None of the men said anything for a few moments.

"Did you see his cross?" said John. "Imagine, savages with crosses!"

"The Spanish gave it to him," said Samuel, "along with their religion, no doubt."

"Did you see their markings?" said Fenwick in awe.

"Yes," said Breuger.

"Like the ancient Picts," said Samuel.

"The Picts?" said Fenwick.

"A wild white tribe of England and Ireland, long gone. They, too, went about naked and marked themselves up like that. They were also known for taking the severed heads of their vanquished enemies home with them."

Fenwick scratched his head exploratively. "You think these fellows are Picts?" he said worriedly.

"No," said Samuel.

"What rubbish," said John angrily, "wild white tribes. What else did the big savage say to you just now?"

"He said," said Samuel patiently, "that those natives, Timucua, he called them, were going to sell us to the Spanish."

"What?" scoffed John. "They were going to eat us! What in blazes do you think the fire was for?"

"A dance. He says they were going to dance around the fire."

"A bloody dance!" John's voice rose in volume and the one called Calling Crow looked over disapprovingly. "And you believe him, I suppose," said John in a softer tone.

"Why shouldn't I?" said Samuel. "He set us free, did he not?"

"Yeah," said John, "but why? What does he want? I don't trust him."

"Me neither," said Fenwick.

"Nor I," said Breuger.

Patrick and Miles said nothing, staring into the surrounding blackness.

"Well," said Samuel, "we have no choice."

The natives got to their feet in the darkness, silhouetted against the faint starlight. The one called Calling Crow waved at Samuel. As Samuel and his men stood, the natives took off running quietly. After a while, when Samuel and the others began to fall behind, Calling Crow slowed the pace. They left the broad trail just as the sun was coming up. Samuel and his men were staggering as they pushed through the bushes. Finally they came out to the tied-up skiff.

Fenwick, Breuger, Miles and Patrick immediately collapsed onto the mud of the bank. Samuel and John held on to a tree trunk, breathing heavily. Calling Crow got into the skiff and sat. His men followed his example.

"What the hell's he think he's doing?" said John.

Samuel waved his brother's comment away and went over to Calling Crow. "Wait!" he said, "we must rest." Samuel pointed to the six casks sitting in the front of the skiff. "*¡Agua!* We would like to fill those up with fresh river water and perhaps attempt to catch some game animals."

"*¡Vamonos!*" said Calling Crow. "There is no time."

"What'd he say?" said Fenwick.

"He said that we must go now." Samuel frowned and turned back to Calling Crow. "How far do you reckon it is to your village?"

"Not far," said Calling Crow. "A day, maybe two, in your ship. Go now." He turned away and would say no more.

Samuel turned resignedly to his men. "Let's go." He climbed into the skiff and took his seat.

Fenwick, Miles, Breuger and Patrick followed behind him. John watched them sullenly from the bank. Samuel nodded to Breuger and Patrick, who were sitting at the oarlocks, and they shipped the oars.

"Since when do we follow his orders?" said John sullenly from the bank.

"We don't," said Samuel tiredly. "We follow mine. Now, get in."

With a grunt, John stepped into the skiff and they glided smoothly out into the black water of the river. The diffuse light of early dawn painted the thick foliage along the banks a dull green. Breuger and Patrick pulled steadily at the oars. They had not gone far when something plopped noisily into the river a few feet behind them.

Fenwick nervously looked over the side into the black water. "What was that, a fish jumping?"

Breuger smiled as he leaned back into a stroke of his oar. "Perhaps it was an alligator, Fen."

Patrick smiled nervously.

Fenwick did not laugh as he moved slightly toward the center of the skiff. Calling Crow and his men sat rock-still, saying nothing. Movement along the bank caught Samuel's eye. One of the topknotted Indians was running parallel with the river, just inside the bushes. He came to an opening and quickly shot one of his arrows at them. It struck the side of the skiff, shattering loudly.

"What in hades was that?" said John.

"The ones that captured us," said Samuel, pointing. "The Timucua."

John and the others turned to see several dozen Indians pushing through the thick foliage to get down to the muddy bank.

"God in heaven!" said Fenwick.

The natives quickly shot their arrows and the men ducked. Two of the arrows struck the skiff harmlessly and the rest landed in the water.

"Pull hard, damn it," said Samuel.

As Breuger and Patrick leaned into the oars, they craned their heads awkwardly, following the flight of the arrows. Samuel, John, Fenwick and Miles watched the natives worriedly while Calling Crow and his men sat in the middle of the skiff, staring fixedly forward, their faces showing no emotion. The river widened as it neared the ocean and Breuger and Patrick moved the skiff into the center of the stream, just out of range of the arrows. The nearest of them fell a dozen feet away.

"We'll be all right now," said Breuger. "Their bloody arrows can't reach us anymore."

Fenwick stood up. "Yeah," he said, "but *that* can!"

Breuger craned his head around to see. Fenwick pointed to a sandy spit of land that jutted out ahead just before the ripple where the river pushed into the sea. Four Timucua waited there for them to pass. One had the musket they had taken from Tom set up in a shooting stand made from the fork of a tree.

Breuger was red-faced from exertion. "Christ in heaven," he said. He stopped rowing and looked at Samuel and John. "Do you think they know how to use it?"

John scoffed. "Savages? I bloody well doubt it."

"Pull hard now," said Samuel angrily. "Calling Crow said they use muskets quite effectively. They were going to trade us to the Spaniards for muskets."

Fenwick pointed to the waiting braves. Two of them were wading into the water. "They're swimming out," he said worriedly, "pull hard."

The skiff moved in a straight line down the middle of the river as the two braves swam purposefully closer.

"Fenwick, Miles," shouted Samuel, "get forward!"

Fenwick watched the progress of the two braves in the water as he stood and moved forward. Calling Crow and his men continued to sit sedately and mutely on the floor of the skiff, as if the struggle no longer had anything to do with them.

When the first of the swimmers drew close, Fenwick pulled his sword. Holding onto the gunnel, he leaned outward and swung. The man dived under the water and disappeared. Something thumped the bottom of the skiff and it lurched sideways, its forward progress slowed. On the spit of land ahead, the Timucua brave patiently sighted down the long barrel of the musket as he followed their progress. With a loud splash, a Timucua brave surfaced at the rear of the skiff, grabbing the transom and attempting to pull himself in. Samuel slashed at him with his sword and the man jumped back into the water, but not soon enough. A smear of thick blood adhered to the gunnel. The man's bloodied head surfaced not far away and he began swimming feebly for the banks. The skiff suddenly wrenched sideways.

"Miles!" shouted Samuel, "get him!"

A brave had found solid footing on the mud of the stream and now held onto the bow eye, trying to pull the skiff to shore. Breuger and Patrick pulled hard at the oars as Miles leaned over the bow. Cursing, he brought his sword down and the brave let go. With the pull of the oars, the skiff lurched seaward again.

"He's going to take his shot now," shouted Fenwick.

"Christ in heaven," said Breuger.

"Everybody get down," said Samuel.

They ducked their heads down as the musket erupted like thunder. The wood at the side of the skiff shattered and Breuger and Patrick quickly sat up to have a look.

Samuel shouted at them. "Keep rowing, damn it."

Just forward of Samuel, a hole as big as a man's hand had been opened in the side of the skiff only inches above the water line. With every swell, a quart or more of water slopped into the skiff. The musket ball had smashed one of the casks to splinters, spending its velocity before it could do any further damage. Samuel judged the distance to the ship and felt sick. Like most Englishmen, neither he nor his men could swim, and if the skiff took too much water . . . He pushed the thought away; it was too gruesome to contemplate. He quickly knelt and took off his doublet, rolling it into a ball. He jammed it into the hole, but as soon as it got wet it collapsed and came out.

Fenwick came back to look at the hole. "Lord above," he said, "we'll drown like rats!"

"Shut up and bail," said Samuel, "and get me a bloody bailing bucket."

Samuel got to his feet to take the bucket from Fenwick while Breuger and Patrick continued to pull for the ship.

As he scooped up bucketsful of water, Samuel cursed. It was a losing proposition. He looked for something to fill the hole with. He noticed that one of Calling Crow's men was hurt; his arm ran with blood. It didn't matter, he thought, they were all going to drown anyway.

Fenwick knelt to look at the man's arm. "Wood splinters," he said. "He'll be all right."

Breuger and Patrick continued to row steadily but the skiff moved sluggishly as it filled with water. "We're sinking!" said Fenwick plaintively.

"Shut up and keep bailing," said Samuel. Despair threatened to overwhelm Samuel and then he noticed that they had left the choppy waters where the river met the sea and the skiff was riding smoother in the long ocean swells. Very little seawater now came in the hole. Soon the water level had dropped and they were within hailing distance of the *Contempt*. The young native who was called Swordbrought touched Samuel on the shoulder. "*¡Mire!*", he said, pointing back to the shore. A hundred or so Timucua braves crowded on the beach, watching them expectantly.

"Christ in heaven," said Fenwick, "look at all of them."

"Give 'em something to remember us by, Fen," said Miles.

Fenwick smiled and turned. He pulled his breeches down, exposing the pale white moon of his buttocks. The Indians on the beach grew visibly angry, some of them waving their lances, others shaking their fists in the air. Calling Crow and his men remained seated and said nothing. A while later they bumped into the ship and began climbing the ropes.

The people of Coosa Town knew by the looks on the returning braves' faces that they had not brought back their chief. The strong, brave men looked downward, their faces grim as they ran through the village toward the meeting house, the *chokafa*. The big brave, Little Bear, brought up the rear and seemed barely able to keep his feet. Reaching the large building, they filed inside and sat facing the sacred fire. Soon the Council members entered and took their seats solemnly. Several honored women entered, led by Green Bird Woman and Bright Eyes. They sat to the side, between the Council and the returned braves.

Two Clouds stood. "Coosa warriors, what do you have to tell us?"

Swift Arrow got to his feet. The other warriors looked downward at the mats. "I am sorry, but they are gone."

A deep moan escaped the people.

Two Clouds's voice boomed out. "Tell us what happened."

Swift Arrow looked around at the people and recounted the story of their search. "When we found the place where they had taken them," he concluded, "there were still many Timucua warriors in the area. It appears that they are going to set up a camp there. We looked everywhere for our chief and could find no evidence of him, his son, or the others . . ."

"No!" shouted Green Bird Woman. "It cannot be." Bright Eyes embraced her mother and she began crying.

Swift Arrow went on, "We searched a place where many captives had been held and then some Timucua approached. We hid and overheard them talking about the raid. They said that all the captives had already been taken away on the white man's floating house."

"Maybe they were lying," said a man in the back. "You should have stayed and searched longer."

"Our great chief is dead," an old woman shouted mournfully. Several other women began wailing. "We must pick someone else to lead us!" called out an old man fearfully.

Green Bird Woman stood. "Stop," she cried and the commotion died down. "Calling Crow is not dead! He will come back to us."

For a few moments, the people tried to hold the hopeful words of Green Bird Woman close to them, to believe in them and draw courage from them. Then Swift Arrow turned slowly to her and said sadly, "It is true. We saw the floating house going away with our own eyes."

The people's fear began to build again, manifesting in a sad buzzing of voices. Green Bird Woman bravely wiped away her tears and remained standing. Bright Eyes embraced her sadly.

Two Clouds held up his arms. "This is a blue day for us; we have suffered a great loss. Now we must make preparations for war. The Timucua took our chief and his young son, and several of our best braves, and took them away on the white man's floating house. For that we will take thirty of their best men. Let the preparations for war begin!''

The *Contempt* sailed smoothly through calm seas, pushed by the trades. Samuel, John and Fenwick stood in front of the cowl built over the helmsman's cutaway. On the deck below them, Miles manned the whipstaff, only his head visible as he steered the ship according to Samuel's commands. Fifty feet away, Calling Crow and the other Indians stood in a group on the foredeck, watching the green-shrouded coast slip by. Samuel had offered them quarters out of the weather, below in the great cabin, the name given to the long, dark, unventilated deck that ran the length of the ship. Calling Crow had seemed to approve of the idea, but his men were loathe to go below and so they had spent all their time under the weather. Fortunately, the weather had been good—cool and balmy at night, warm with steady breezes by day.

Samuel's fascination with the Newlanders was growing by the day, but they kept themselves aloof and Samuel thought it better not to approach them. They were so solemn and quiet, as if possessed of great secrets. And they seemed to be aware of the Divinity. How did they come to this knowledge? And their markings . . . He thought of Fen's wanting to know if they were Picts. The idea had seemed amusing, but now he wondered about it. Could there possibly be some connection between these men and the ancient wild people of England? Samuel was intrigued by this question and others. He wondered about their relations with the Timucua people. He especially wanted to talk to their leader, Calling Crow, about the crudely shaped iron club or axe in his belt. Did he get it from the Spanish?

Calling Crow left his men and walked back toward the mainmast. He went over to one of the two remaining bales, which was lying on its side, and knelt to inspect it.

"I'm going to talk to him," Samuel said to the other men.

"I am going with you," said John.

"Why is that, brother?"

John frowned. "We don't know this fellow."

Samuel shook his head. "Control yourself this time, man. I'll not have any more outbursts on my ship!" John held his tongue, Samuel knew, at great effort to himself. They walked over to Calling Crow.

Calling Crow looked up at them and said in Spanish, "How many shirts would this woolen cloth make?"

"Over a hundred," said Samuel.

Calling Crow continued to examine the cloth.

Samuel knew the Indian wanted the cloth. "Perhaps you would like to trade for it," he said.

Calling Crow looked up. "Perhaps." He went back to inspecting the cloth.

"He must have spent a long time as a Spanish slave," said John. "He speaks their bloody language well. What is he saying?"

"He is interested in the cloth."

Calling Crow addressed himself to Samuel. "Why have you come to these lands?"

Samuel found the man's eyes penetrating, as if he were trying to get inside his head and know his thoughts. "We came to trade with the Spanish," he said,

"I thought the English and Spanish were enemies."

"Yes, yet there is still trade between our two nations. But I will no longer be a part of it."

Calling Crow continued to study the two men. Finally he said, "I would like to trade with you."

Samuel nodded. "We have another bale of woolens in the belowdecks."

Calling Crow shook his head and looked at Samuel piercingly. "Wool is very good, but I want shooting sticks."

"Muskets?" said Samuel in surprise. He thought back to the Timucuas and the idea repulsed him. He shook his head. "No, I'll not trade any muskets, or swords. As I have said, we have another bale of woolens in the belowdecks. I will trade that.''

Calling Crow paused for a few moments to look back down at the cloth. "Very well. After all the worry I have caused my people, I would like to bring home some presents for them.''

Samuel nodded. "What would you give for the two bales?''

"What do you want?'' asked Calling Crow.

"Enough food and water for our journey home.''

"How long a journey?''

"It will take us forty to fifty days.''

"Come to my village,'' said Calling Crow. "For the two bales of cloth I will see that you get enough food for your men for the return journey. Then we will talk more about shooting sticks.''

"Well?'' said John impatiently. "What is he saying?''

"He wants to trade for muskets. I already told him we would not. Now he wants us to come to his village. He will victual us for the voyage home in return for the two bales of cloth.''

John cast a quick look at Calling Crow and then looked back at Samuel. "Have you lost your senses, brother? Victual us? He will bloody victual *on* us if we go back with him!''

"I will trade with him, John.''

John's face contorted in amazement. "Brother, making deals with the likes of him is like trying to make friends with a wild boar or an alligator.''

"You are welcome to your opinions, John.'' Samuel looked over at Calling Crow and went on. "This fine fellow has been a godsend. We must have victuals and fresh water, and he does seem to put great stock in honor. Therefore, we will trade with him.''

Calling Crow watched the exchange between the two brothers and then continued to inspect the cloth.

John spat over the rail. "I don't want any more savage hospitality and I think you'll have a hard time getting any of the others to go ashore with this lot too.''

"Some will go.''

"And the others and I will not rescue them if they get into trouble." John walked off angrily.

"Your brother does not like us," said Calling Crow in Spanish.

Samuel frowned. "No, it is not that," he lied. "He is still angry and suspicious over what happened with the Timucuas. He will calm soon."

"You love him very much," said Calling Crow.

"He is my brother." Samuel's face grew tense. "Calling Crow, I would like you to pray with me now."

"Why?" Calling Crow continued to inspect the cloth.

"I would like to ask for God's blessing on our friendship."

Calling Crow's eyes narrowed as he looked up. "I will pray when I return to my village."

"But you don't know how. I will teach you."

Calling Crow got to his feet and his face became hard. "Is your god like the Spanish god?"

Samuel shook his head. "There is only one God."

"Then he is the same god?"

Samuel nodded. "Of course."

"Then I already know how to pray to him. I have done so before in the Spanish churches."

One of Calling Crow's men called over to him and he turned to listen.

"I want to teach your people of God and his ways," said Samuel, trying to hold the man's attention.

Calling Crow's men continued shouting to him.

"We are nearing our lands," said Calling Crow. "Come, I will show you."

The *Contempt* hove to and anchored in the muddy waters a small river spewed into the sea. Seabirds wheeled inquisitively in a sunny blue sky as the skiff was lowered. Miles and Breuger climbed down with their muskets, setting them carefully in the skiff before taking up the oars. Samuel, John and Fenwick, and Calling Crow, his son Swordbrought and the other Indian men took their seats and the skiff slowly moved toward the shore. When they were halfway there, they spied some boys upon the sand. They quickly disappeared and a few minutes later a dozen or so people appeared to watch their approach. Samuel grew concerned at the number of young men among them. Armed with bows and greatly agitated, their numbers grew by the minute.

"Calling Crow," said Samuel, "your people seem angry. What is the matter?"

The tall Indian seemed unperturbed. "There is no need to worry."

John picked up one of the muskets, rapping his ring metallically against the barrel to get Calling Crow's attention. "Tell him," he said to Samuel, "that if there is any trickery, I shall open him up with this!"

Miles and Breuger turned and cast worried looks at the growing group on the shore.

Samuel's voice was steady. "You keep yourself calm and steady, brother. If you can do that, then we shall be fine."

"Fine?" said John angrily. "Look at them! You are putting us at great risk. We should turn the boat around now before it's too late."

Samuel said nothing.

By the time they stepped ashore, the crowd had grown to more than a hundred noisy Newlanders. They crowded around the men from the skiff as they walked up the beach.

John glared at them angrily and called to Samuel, "Tell the big one to move them back."

Breuger, Miles and Fenwick stayed close together, their hands on the pommels of their swords.

"Calm yourself, John," said Samuel. Samuel turned and had to shout into Calling Crow's ear to make himself heard. "What is the matter with your people?" he said in Spanish.

Calling Crow spoke without turning. "Some of them think it was you that took us away on your ship. They think that I am your hostage. I have told them that I am not, but there are still a few who think that I am in danger. Don't worry, I will calm them."

One of the young warriors separated from the crowd and spoke excitedly to Calling Crow.

Calling Crow raised his arms and the people quieted. Samuel noted the respect they accorded him. They evidently held him in great regard. Calling Crow spoke to his people in their tongue for a few minutes, calming them. He turned to Samuel and the people began talking among themselves again, the noise level rising. "We will go to our meeting house now," said Calling Crow. "You will stay the night there and tomorrow there will be a feast in your honor. Come."

Calling Crow walked off, flanked by his lieutenant and his son. Samuel and his men followed close behind. The crowd of people closed in around them, staring excitedly at the Englishmen and their strange clothing.

They followed a path that paralleled the river until they came to a small palisaded village. Samuel estimated there were about fifty houses. Calling Crow led Samuel and his men to a large building constructed atop a mound of packed earth. He spoke briefly to his lieutenant and then entered. Calling Crow indicated some woven mats in the center of the building, toward the front. "Samuel, sit. You will be fed."

Calling Crow turned to go and Samuel called out to him. "When will you return?"

"In the morning. Make sure your men remain in here tonight."

Calling Crow turned and spoke to his men. They quickly filed out of the building, leaving the stunned Englishmen alone.

Outside, Calling Crow turned and faced Red Feather. "Stay here tonight. See that the Englishmen do not wander around and do not allow anyone to get too close to them. There may still be a few in the village who mistakenly assume they had something to do with our capture."

"As you say," said Red Feather.

Calling Crow walked off.

People called out to Calling Crow warmly as he walked slowly through the village streets in the gathering dimness. With a rolled-up length of the English woolen cloth tucked under his arm, he entered Green Bird Woman's gate. Calling Crow ducked his head slightly as he entered her hut. Green Bird Woman knelt as she painted one of her pots. She turned and smiled at him, getting to her feet. She wore a doeskin gown with a pattern of geometric stick figures marching in squares and rectangles, all of them made up of colored stones. It was the prettiest gown Green Bird Woman owned and Calling Crow was touched that she had put it on for him. In her wavy black hair she wore one of her prized green feathers from the great parrot she once owned.

Green Bird Woman came to Calling Crow and put her arms around him. Tears ran down her face and she wiped them away. "I worried so," she said. "It is a good thing for the Timucua people that you escaped."

Calling Crow laughed. He took the bundle of woolen cloth from under his arm and gave it to her. "What do you think?"

Green Bird Woman brought the new cloth up to her face to examine it closer. She rubbed it between her thumb and forefinger. "It is a fine weave, much tighter than what we do with the bark. But it could use some decoration. Is it from the strange white people?"

Calling Crow nodded.

"Our daughter, Bright Eyes, said she thinks the leader of these people is attractive. Imagine."

"He is called Samuel."

Green Bird Woman shook her head. "Bright Eyes had better not let Red Feather hear such talk. He is so fond of her."

Calling Crow said nothing.

Green Bird Woman frowned in mock disgust. "All that hair on the Englishman's face!" She laughed. "She'll come to her senses soon. How can she find that attractive?"

Calling Crow pulled her close. "Enough of such talk. Let us lie down together. I want to show you how much I have missed you."

Green Bird Woman pulled away from him and went over to the hut's entryway. She untied the thong that held the skin covering off to the side; the skin flapped into place, closing off the hut from the outside. Green Bird Woman giggled girlishly in the dimness as she pulled her gown over her head.

Samuel, John and the others sat upon the mats in the center of the large, airy hut, their weapons within arm's reach. At one end of the structure, a small fire burned in a stone-lined pit. Periodically old native holy men came in to attend to it and Samuel decided that it served the same purpose as a devotional candle in a church. Aside from the holy men, and the women that had brought them food, they had been alone here since Calling Crow left. As night drew near, people, children mostly, occasionally looked in at them from the entryways, but did not venture inside.

John threw a twig into the fire. "We ought to go back to the ship in the morning, brother. We are too vulnerable here like this."

Fenwick, Breuger and Miles looked over at Samuel to see what he would say.

Samuel said nothing, hoping his brother would drop the subject. He knew the others were afraid, none of them able to sleep, but he judged their situation to be safe.

A commotion came from outside. Several young men bearing torches came into the building to peer over at them in curiosity.

John moved slowly toward the musket on the mat.

"Do nothing," said Samuel.

John glowered at him angrily, but then the men went back outside. Muffled conversations in the strange native language wafted into the building for a few moments and the men went away. Samuel thought they would be safe. After all, the native king, Calling Crow, wanted muskets, lots of them. What would he gain by murdering them here for only two muskets? Still, Samuel wished Calling Crow had stayed here with them.

"Where did the king and his lieutenant go?" said Fenwick, voicing everyone's concern.

No one answered him.

Samuel was visited by a dark thought. He truly believed Calling Crow to be an honorable fellow, but perhaps some treachery had befallen him. Had another, rival lord in the village usurped his power in his absence? Perhaps John was right.

Samuel looked over at the entryway. There was still three or four hours of night left. They would never be able to get back to the ship in the dark. They must wait for the morning's light.

Samuel was about to speak to the others when a boy in a great state of agitation ran into the hut and looked over at them.

"What does he want?" said Fenwick.

"Just a look, that is all," said Samuel.

They heard voices outside. The sound grew; people were coming. Several young men with bows walked boldly through the entryway. Samuel and the others scrambled to their knees, grabbing their muskets and swords

About a dozen young men with bows stared at the Englishmen with a mixture of astonishment and wariness. One of them, a muscled, wild-looking man with an animal pelt draped over his privates, grew agitated and shouted at them angrily and incomprehensibly.

"What in bloody hell?" said John as he, along with the others, quickly and nervously clipped into the serpentine mechanisms the glowing match cords that would enable their weapons to fire.

John brought the musket up and pointed it at the men.

"No," called Samuel, "wait."

The bowmen saw the move as threatening and hung back, but the wild one grew more belligerent. Nocking an arrow into his bow, he advanced on John in an exaggerated stalking walk. John moved slowly forward, aiming the heavy musket at the young man's chest.

Samuel put himself between the two. "John, go back."

A commotion ensued at the entryway and Calling Crow's lieutenant and son pushed through the mob. The son yelled at the bowmen and they grew silent. They all seemed in awe of the young man, except for the wild bowman, who continued to stare menacingly at John.

Calling Crow's son angrily addressed the wild bowman. From the dark looks on the faces of the others, Samuel could tell it was a grave threat of some kind.

The bowman's manner became less threatening, but he would not lower his bow.

"John," called Samuel, "get back here!"

"Not until he puts that bloody bow down."

Samuel hoped the son could reason with his bowman, for he knew his brother was beyond reason now.

Calling Crow's lieutenant watched the bowman's angry display, then, evidently having seen enough, pushed through the others and accosted the man. The bowman appeared to be taken aback. Then, with one quick movement, Calling Crow's lieutenant took the bow out of the other's hands and broke it loudly over his knee. The bowman's face collapsed in shame and he rushed from the building.

Calling Crow's son came over to Samuel. "How are you and your men?" he said in Spanish.

"*Muy bien, gracias,*" said Samuel.

Calling Crow's son pointed to the mats. "*Sientese, por favor,*" he said.

Samuel turned to his men. "He wants us to sit." Samuel sat and his men followed his example reluctantly.

The lieutenant and the son sat across from Samuel. Using Spanish and some signs, the son told Samuel that these men had just returned from a hunt and thought that Samuel and his men were part of the group that had kidnaped Calling Crow. They would not bother the Englishmen anymore, and why didn't they sleep? Samuel told him that they would and the son and the lieutenant withdrew. Despite the assurances of the two Indians, however, and the great weariness of Samuel and his men, none of them slept. Instead they spent the night warily watching the entryways to the great hall and saying nothing.

In the morning, young men brought in many more reed mats and lay them down. Three young women brought the Englishmen gourd cups full of a wonderfully hot and refreshing native tea. Afterward, Calling Crow entered, followed by his court, composed mainly of old holy men. One of them, was ancient looking, and carried in on a young man's back. Samuel thought by his dress and feathered decorations that he was the wizard or conjurer for these people. About twenty young women came into the airy hut. With turtle-shell rattles tied to their feet, they did a kind of stomping dance around the Englishmen and the sound was rhythmic and compelling.

Next, women brought in wooden platters of roast fish and

fowl, corn, beans, fruits, roasted walnuts and divers roots, all
excellent of taste, and conch shells and gourd cups full of
wonderful native teas made of ginger, sassafras and cinna-
mon.

The feasting took several hours and after they had finished,
Samuel and his men gave Calling Crow, the king, some
knives and iron axes, which he said he would give to his most
loyal warriors. More dancing followed and Fenwick, Miles
and Breuger smiled broadly at the goings-on. Even John
seemed to relax. Samuel forgot about his capture by the Timucua and his worries of only a few hours earlier. Here were
a people he had read about in a book, people who hearkened
back to the golden age of antiquity. Yes, they had their share
of hot heads, but overall, they were a loving and kind people.
He was certain he could use his relationship with them to
further the cause of commerce and Christianity.

Chapter 9

Samuel looked around the small town as he walked along one of the hard-packed dirt streets with Calling Crow at his side. He thought of the complaints of his brother and the others about this place—that the Indians had no fine things, no theaters or taverns, no markets or docks, no chessboards, spring clocks or featherbeds. But, Samuel knew, they had no need of them. They had all the food they needed, a comfortable climate, and they seemed genuinely happy and content. The air was filled with the evidence of this: the occasional smell of roasting meat or boiling vegetables; from inside the huts, the sound of laughing children and the occasional cry of a healthy babe; conversations spoken too softly to be deciphered, floating on the hot air. In the compounds on either side, people worked at their daily tasks, stretching skins for drying, making pots, preparing and storing food.

Calling Crow stopped and pointed south. "We lived south of here, about a day's march, but the game began to move on and so we did too." He pointed to the west. "We have burnt many fields over there . . . It brings the deer in to eat the young shoots. And the fishing is very good here. You will enjoy your stay with us." They walked on.

Calling Crow paused in front of a newly built hut, the palmetto thatch roof was still green, the dirt floor freshly swept. A pile of firewood was stacked beside the gate. Calling Crow pointed to the entryway. "This will be yours while you are here."

Samuel nodded his thanks. He was continually amazed at the generosity of these people. In the streets of his own country there were now many footloose people begging and stealing. The parishes were overburdened taking care of them. But these people did not have that problem. The bounty of their fields and hunts was great and it was shared with the old and the sick. While Calling Crow's people lacked the knowledge of Christian teachings, in the area of giving they were model Christians. Samuel saw that perhaps the answer to his own country's problems lay here. If he could establish commerce here, then they could perhaps get financial backing for a colony. England needed a colony in the new world and, given the helpful nature of these people, this was an ideal place.

"Samuel," said Calling Crow, "my people and I were wondering why you stay here and your men stay on your ship."

Samuel's eyes narrowed thoughtfully. Not too long ago the others had rowed back to the ship. "They want to be ready if a ship is spotted," he said, "a Spanish ship they can raid. I pray there will be no ships for I want to conclude our business and go home. Also, while I am here I wish to spend my time with your people in order to learn your language and ways."

A messenger ran up to Calling Crow. They spoke briefly and Calling Crow turned to Samuel. Calling Crow had a hint of a smile on his face. "The people are going to play ball now," he said. "Would you like to join us?"

Samuel was intrigued. "Yes, I would like that."

It was early afternoon and the air had not yet heated up fully. A good breeze came off the sea as Calling Crow and Samuel walked to the field in front of the *chokafa*. It was in this large, rectangular field that all the ball games and many of the ceremonies were held. A crowd of people had already gathered for the game. After Calling Crow and Samuel arrived, more people came quickly. Samuel was surprised at how many women were in the crowd. Calling Crow waited until the crowd had swelled to over a hundred people, at least half the village.

Calling Crow pointed to poles set at opposite ends of the field as he explained to Samuel. "We must get the ball to over there; they will try to get it down there."

To Samuel's surprise, all the women were moving to one side of the center line, the men to the other. Someone gave

Calling Crow a stuffed skin ball about the size of a melon.

"Surely we are not going to play against the women?" asked Samuel in amazement.

"We are," said Calling Crow, "and a good game it will be." Calling Crow tossed the ball skyward. Shouting erupted as both sides ran to catch it. Then, like a great wave slamming into a rocky cliff, a mob of women crashed into Samuel and the other men. A matronly woman with braided hair caught the ball. Whooping shrilly, she and her sisters ran for their goal while Samuel and the men laughingly chased after her. Halfway down the field a young man darted into the women's midst to tear the ball out of the woman's hands, and the mob reversed direction. Samuel, not being able to run as fast as the men because of his boots, ran at the edge of the men, where the most fleet-footed of the women were now pressing them. The men slowed a bit and soon they ran as one happy, shouting pack, every single sweaty face intent on trying to locate the ball. The crowd stopped and many people attempted to push into the center. Samuel found himself pressed up hard against a comely maiden. It was the same girl who had smiled and laughed at him earlier that day when she passed with some others. He realized that she had deliberately put herself here in front of him and a great passion rose in him at the feel of her soft warmth. She seemed to know his mind and smiled at him. With an explosion of laughter, the mob broke up in confusion and the girl disappeared. Another round, middle-aged woman now had possession of the ball, a phalanx of women and girls surrounding her protectively. Samuel laughed as he and the pack of men ran after them. Someone behind Samuel tripped him and he tumbled on the grassy field. Calling Crow's lieutenant, his *tastanagi,* Red Feather, ran on.

Samuel quickly pulled off his boots, wondering angrily if Red Feather had intentionally tripped him. Then Samuel was on his feet and running swiftly. He soon caught up with the men. Putting on a burst of speed, he positioned himself behind Red Feather. He was about to trip him when the crowd suddenly changed direction. Ahead, Samuel saw the pretty woman running with her sisters and forgot about Red Feather.

The woman tossed him a look over her shoulder. Samuel smiled and ran as one with the others, not thinking about the ball game or Red Feather. His thoughts were only of the pretty woman running ahead, her laughing eyes, her tan shoulders and slender legs, the swell of her buttocks under the soft, white doeskin gown.

The beautiful blue sky stretched away forever, with only a few small white clouds moving slowly across it to the west. Five native boys followed Samuel, John and Breuger as they walked the dirt street toward the large prayer house that the natives called the *chokafa*. Samuel looked up at the slowly moving clouds, wondering briefly about what lay to the west. Calling Crow and his son who was intriguingly-called "Swordbrought," had told him stories of the Mountain People who lived there. There were, however, several other, more interesting stories going around. John and Breuger swore that one day they had seen a black man among a crowd of native people at the far edge of the village. They hurried there, but the man had quietly slipped away before they could find him. And Fenwick had been told by some of the village boys of a white man that lived in the town somewhere. When the boys took him to the man's house, there was no one there. Samuel had asked Calling Crow about these things and had been told that Calling Crow would explain it all to them today at their *chokafa*.

As Samuel and the other two Englishmen approached the now-familiar *chokafa* sitting on its mound of earth, the boys who had been following them fell back. Samuel and the others headed for the entrance flanked by columns with red and green serpents coiled around them. Samuel paused inside the dim interior, John and Breuger at his side, as their eyes adjusted. Samuel found the cool air inside the big structure refreshing. A bright column of down-pouring light, as wide across as a standing man, illuminated the interior of the *chokafa*. Calling Crow sat beneath it with Swordbrought and two other men. Samuel saw with amazement that one was indeed black, and that the other appeared to be a white man.

"I told you," said John quietly.

They walked over and Calling Crow motioned for them to sit. The Spaniard had no beard, evidently being in the habit of plucking his hairs out in the fashion of the natives. He was bare-chested, dressed only in a breechclout, as was the black.

Samuel, John and Breuger stared at the two men.

"*Buenos dias,*" said the Spaniard. "*Yo soy Gregorio.*"

"*Buenos dias,*" said Samuel. "*Yo soy Samuel.*" John and Breuger nodded a greeting, as did the black man.

"How did you come to be here?" Samuel asked the Spaniard in his own language.

The man frowned. "There was a war between us and the French settlement. We attacked; they attacked . . . There may have been others who escaped, but only Wilfredo and I came here." He nodded in the black man's direction.

"How long has he been here?" Breuger asked Samuel.

Samuel put the question to the Spaniard in his own language. "Almost sixteen years," Samuel translated for Breuger and John.

"Well," said John, "tell him that his ordeal is over. We will take him back with us. No white man should have to live like this."

Samuel looked at the Spaniard. "We will take you with us."

The Spaniard shook his head. "No," he said. "I will stay here."

"He wants to stay," Samuel said to his brother and Breuger.

John scoffed. "He must have been running around with this lot in the sun too long; it has damaged his brains." John turned to Breuger. "I've seen and heard enough." He got to his feet and Breuger followed suit. Samuel remained seated, as did Calling Crow and the others. John pointed at the black man and said to his brother. "Tell Calling Crow we'll be taking the black with us."

Samuel translated John's words into Spanish.

Calling Crow replied and Samuel translated. "He says that the black man has told him he wants to stay."

"What?" said John angrily. "It matters not what he wants."

Calling Crow spoke rapidly to Samuel in Spanish and he relayed the Coosa chief's words to John. "Calling Crow says that black people have not come here in ships and sold guns to his enemies. He said he holds no bad feelings toward black people."

John frowned in frustration. "But he's worth quite a few pounds, brother. We could—"

"No!" Calling Crow looked up, his face resolute.

John turned and walked off, followed by Breuger. After they had gone, Gregorio and Wilfredo got to their feet. As they prepared to leave, Calling Crow questioned them thoroughly. Both men's faces were without emotion as they answered. They then walked away.

Samuel faced Calling Crow and Swordbrought. On the periphery of the large, round structure, other braves and elders talked softly as they conducted their business, staying well away from the three men in the center.

Two young women entered the *chokafa* and approached. Samuel recognized one as the pretty girl from the ball game. Both women kept their eyes demurely downcast as they placed calabashes of water before the men. The pretty woman from the ball game raised her eyes briefly and smiled at Samuel. Having finished with the calabashes, the women quietly walked away.

"My daughter is intrigued by you, Samuel," said Calling Crow. "How do you find her?"

Samuel looked at Calling Crow, surprised to learn that the woman was his daughter, for she did not seem to bear any resemblance to him. "She is very beautiful," he said.

"What is her name?"

"She is called Bright Eyes."

Samuel thought the name a good one as he remembered the woman's beautiful, playful eyes. He felt a stirring as he remembered the feel of her body. Then he thought of his own wife and a pang of guilt stabbed through him. He had been away too long and his lust was growing, attempting to lead him astray.

Calling Crow unwrapped a doeskin-covered bundle. He extracted a long, carved, brightly painted tube with a thumb-sized bowl at one end. A fringe of white and gray turkey feathers hung from it. Samuel realized it was a pipe for smoking the herb, tobacco.

Calling Crow held the pipe up, either to inspect it or to pray to it, Samuel wasn't sure which. Calling Crow then took some tobacco from a pouch. His mouth moving into the faintest suggestion of a smile, he sprinkled some on the earth and packed the pipe. Taking a half-consumed stick from the small fire nearby, he held it to the pipe and puffed until a blue column of smoke rose skyward. Calling Crow drew smoke into his lungs and paused. He then blew it in four different directions and handed the pipe to Samuel.

Samuel drew on the pipe. He coughed harshly, then felt a pleasant dizziness. He expelled the smoke as Calling Crow had done.

"Do you like it?" said Calling Crow.

Samuel nodded. "I have heard they smoke it in rolled-up sticks in Spain." He passed the pipe to Swordbrought, who sucked at its smoke slowly.

Calling Crow reached over and touched the green shirt Samuel wore, which was cinched at the waist with a belt. "My wife is charmed by the bright color of your shirt. She wants it. I will give you tobacco for it."

Samuel shook his head. "I have a bolt of cloth like this on the ship. I will trade it for my weight in the roots and herbs with which your women make their teas."

Calling Crow nodded. "Bright Eyes will take you into the forest and show you those roots and herbs."

Samuel found his heart beat quicker at the prospect of spending time with Bright Eyes. He took another pull on the pipe and passed it to Swordbrought. The young man tapped the embers out, then wrapped the soft white doeskin around the pipe with such reverence that Samuel thought it must be part of the ceremony. He waited till Swordbrought finished before speaking.

"Calling Crow, the Spanish are behind these Timucua that

are threatening you. How can you be sure that Gregorio and Wilfredo will not betray you?"

"It is true that they once lived with the Spanish," said Calling Crow, "but now they speak our language and have become one with us. I have given our word that we will not harm them and they have given their word that they will be loyal."

"Perhaps you put too much stock in their word."

Calling Crow grew angry, but his voice remained calm. "The word of our people is sacred. When our people give their word, they will never go back on it, even if it should mean their own deaths."

Samuel nodded. He thought of his own men. Could their word be relied upon such as that? He doubted it. Samuel had to admit to himself that Calling Crow's men seemed to have great loyalty to him, a loyalty such as Englishmen had for their kings in days long past.

Chapter I I

The target, a square of soft white doeskin, hung from a tree branch about a hundred yards across a harvested cornfield of dried and brittle, knee-high stalks. Samuel, John, Miles and Breuger, along with Calling Crow, Swordbrought, and the young brave called Crying Wolf, stood together as the summer sun shone down brightly upon them.

Samuel set the heavy musket into its shooting stand. The English had agreed to trade the two bales of cloth to the Coosa chief for enough food to get them home. Calling Crow had again attempted to get Samuel to trade for muskets, but Samuel would not. He had, however, agreed to demonstrate the use of the musket for Calling Crow.

Samuel took the match cord from where it hung around his belt and blew on it until it glowed. He then clipped it into the serpentine firing mechanism of the musket. Wetting his finger to test the wind, he nodded to Calling Crow.

Calling Crow took Samuel's place behind the musket. Swordbrought and Crying Wolf moved closer to watch. Although Calling Crow had seen muskets on many occasions, and, sadly, knew personally of the damage they could do, he had never fired one.

"Remember," said Samuel, "you sight along the barrel just as you would along the shaft of an arrow."

As Calling Crow sighted down the long barrel, Fenwick approached, leading a column of five Coosa bearers carrying baskets of corn.

Swordbrought held up his hand for them to stop. Fenwick and the bearers waited quietly for Calling Crow to take his shot. Calling Crow said a quick prayer to his spirit guide and fired. His prayer was answered as a moment later the doeskin fluttered as if an invisible hand had smacked it.

"Good shooting, m'lord," said Fenwick jovially as he came up to them. "Good shooting!"

Calling Crow said nothing.

Samuel took the musket and primed it for the next shot.

"He is an excellent shot," said Fenwick.

John and the others ignored him.

Samuel nodded and placed the ball and wadding into the muzzle. "Fen," he said, "how are you progressing with the loading?"

"Very good, m'lord. We've got more than half of it aboard now."

"Carry on then."

Fenwick walked on. Samuel rammed the ball home as Calling Crow and the other two Indians stood silently.

Miles said to John, "Well, soon we shall sail."

"The bloody sooner the better," said John. "If I eat any more corn I'll puke."

Breuger and Miles scoffed mirthfully.

"More awaits you on the ship," said Samuel calmly.

Breuger and Miles laughed aloud as Samuel turned to Calling Crow. "Who shoots next?"

Calling Crow pointed to Crying Wolf. Like his own son, Swordbrought, Crying Wolf was very brave and showed much promise. For those reasons Calling Crow had taken an interest in training him. Crying Wolf competed fiercely with Swordbrought, as if they were brothers. Calling Crow thought that good for both of them.

Samuel lay the musket in the shooting stand and Crying Wolf took hold of it. Laying his cheek against the thing as he had seen Calling Crow do, he pulled the trigger. The musket bucked and boomed and the men eyed the doeskin across the field. It did not move.

John and Breuger laughed, Miles smiling nervously. Samuel said nothing.

"What is the matter?" said Crying Wolf. "Why did the skin not move?

"I don't know," said Calling Crow. He suspected that Crying Wolf's prayer had been unfocused. What good was medicine without a strong prayer? He asked Samuel what was the matter.

"There is nothing the matter," said Samuel. "Tell him it is his fault, that his aim was off." Samuel began reloading the musket for Swordbrought's turn as Calling Crow translated Samuel's words for Crying Wolf.

Calling Crow was displeased with Crying Wolf's reaction. The young brave grew tight-lipped and sullen, saying nothing.

Samuel nodded to Swordbrought. Swordbrought took hold of the musket, butting his cheek up against the stock. He fired and a moment later the doeskin jumped backward and fluttered to the ground.

"Good shooting," said Samuel.

"He's got his father's eye," said Breuger.

"Bloody luck, is all," said John.

Crying Wolf tried to grab the musket from Swordbrought. "It is a trick," he said. He glared at Samuel and the Englishmen suspiciously. "You used your medicine to make the skin move for Calling Crow. Then you made it move for Swordbrought, but not for Crying Wolf. Why?"

Not sure what Crying Wolf had said, Samuel said nothing.

Crying Wolf looked angrily from Calling Crow to Swordbrought, then stormed off.

"What did he say?" demanded John.

Calling Crow ignored Samuel's brother. A runner was approaching. Calling Crow listened calmly as the sweating man reported in a state of great excitement. When the man finished, Calling Crow gave him instructions and the man ran off in the direction he had come from.

Calling Crow's face showed no emotion, but Samuel had spent enough time with him to sense that the report had been troubling. "What is it?" he said.

"A trading party has reported that many Timucua raided a large Alibamu village ten days' journey to the south and west of us. They took many villagers prisoner."

"That is too far away to concern you," said Samuel.

"Perhaps for now," said Calling Crow, "but the Timucua will come eventually. They will launch small, probing attacks first." Calling Crow pointed to the musket cradled in Swordbrought's arms. "If we had many shooting sticks like that, they would leave us alone."

Samuel said nothing.

Calling Crow went on. "Samuel, you English hate the Spanish very much. Why don't you help us?"

Samuel shook his head. "I am sorry. Soon we must go. There is nothing we can do for you." He took the musket from Swordbrought.

Calling Crow could see that the Englishman would not easily change his mind. They would be here for another five or six days. Perhaps Calling Crow could enlist the help of the medicine man, Sees Far. His medicine might cause the Englishman to change his mind. Calling Crow said, "I go now. I will talk to you later."

John, Miles and Breuger, who had been watching and listening to the exchange with interest, watched the natives walk off.

"What was he saying?" said John.

Samuel turned to him. "He still wants to trade for some muskets."

"Surely you're not going to trade the savages muskets," said John.

"No. I have told him no."

Samuel waited in the shade of his hut as the heat of day grew. Today Bright Eyes was to take him into the forest and show him the trees from which they took their bark for teas. Samuel thought of her amazing, Eve-like beauty—her big, soft eyes, her hair, jet-black and scalloped, some flowing down her back, more of it hanging down over her breasts, for she often wore nothing above the waist, as was the custom of the women here. She had come to symbolize this wild, beautiful land to him.

He noticed her at the gate. She was bare-breasted, wearing only a skirt that hung clear down to her ankles. Made from long tendrils of the moss that hung from the trees in the area, it allowed her legs to move out of it, revealing their pleasant brown color to him. She carried a basket upon her back and a staff of sorts in her hand. Samuel joined her on the dirt street and a crowd of boys followed them as they walked to the gates of the village.

Bright Eyes's beauty made Samuel light in the head as they walked in the forest. He glanced surreptitiously at her breasts; such a display would have caused riots in his own country. Bright Eyes saw him and smiled innocently, totally without shame. His face flushed crimson and he stared straight ahead, not daring a second look. The forest grew thicker, the light dim. They walked for some time, saying nothing. Bright Eyes stopped after a while and left the trail. Samuel followed her as she pushed through the underbrush, coming out into a small clearing. A waist-high pile of tree branches sat on the ground, bound up with still-green vines.

She pointed to them. ''They are drying,'' she said, using a

combination of signs and Spanish and Muskogee words. "I will show you where there is more."

They walked on, Bright Eyes occasionally turning to speak. Once she stopped and, composing her face very seriously, asked him something. Samuel was not sure, but he thought she was wondering why he had not brought his wife with him. He tried to convey to her that it was too dangerous, but he did not think his words were sufficient to make her understand. They walked on.

They came to a small structure off to the side of the trail. Made of willow poles lashed together, it had a thatched roof and open sides. Many bundles of roots and branches were piled atop one another inside. The afternoon light was dappled by the overhanging leaves; the ground was warm beneath their feet. Bright Eyes pointed to some trees at the edge of the clearing and they walked over. Much freshly turned earth remained strewn about, evidence of their root harvesting.

Bright Eyes knelt at one of the digging sites and Samuel sat beside her. A slight, warm breeze moved through the trees, bringing the scent of wild flowers and sassafras. Bright Eyes pulled up a section of root and held it to a shaft of sunlight to show him. He leaned close. The root's tiny hairs caught the light, glowing like gold as the musky loam of the earth tickled his nose. She smiled at him. Unable to stop himself, he looked down at her breasts. He very badly wanted to hold his face to them, to have her suckle him.

She knew his desire and leaned closer to him. He could not stop himself from taking her bare shoulders in his hands, from pulling her close. He kissed her sweetly on the lips. Shame and guilt suddenly overwhelmed him and he drew back.

She looked at him in confusion, touching her lips exploratively. "What you do?" she said.

"I kissed you, m'lady."

Again she brought her fingers to her lips. She smiled sweetly and lay back suggestively.

His compunction caused him to look away. His face was burning. Not knowing God's laws, she could be forgiven for having no shame, no sense of wrong about this, but he knew it was a sin. He got to his knees. "I should not be here with you," he said guiltily. "I am sorry."

She looked at him in confusion and turned away. He got to his feet and leaned against a tree.

"What do you want?" she said.

"I don't know," he said. "I don't know."

She repeated her question, a tinge of hurt now in her voice.

Calling Crow walked quickly through the palisade entrance and toward the forest. He had not been able to locate Red Feather and had only just realized where he would be. Red Feather's agitation over Bright Eyes's interest in Samuel was growing. Calling Crow had noticed this, but had hoped that his *tastanagi* would put the peoples' problem before his own. And Calling Crow had hoped that the reluctance of the Englishman to trade them shooting sticks could be overcome. Was not the medicine man Sees Far praying for that very result? And had not Calling Crow's spirit guide led him to the Englishmen for this reason? Ho! It must be so! But Red Feather's jealousy could undo all this.

When the cool shade of the forest enveloped him, Calling Crow began running. The joy this activity normally released in him was quieted by his growing concern. All around, the winged ones and the four-leggeds went about their business, gathering food for the winter, feeding their young, stalking one another, eating one another, unconcerned with the Coosa chief's hurried gait, knowing that he was after other game and that they were safe.

Calling Crow came to a bend in the trail and slowed. He saw where someone had pushed through the foliage, and he followed their trail, entering a small clearing. Red Feather was thirty paces away, peering intently through the leaves at the trail. Clutched tightly in his hand was his war club, set with bear's teeth and adorned with red paint and white feathers.

Calling Crow walked up behind him and Red Feather whirled about suddenly.

"What animal is it that you stalk with your club, Red Feather?"

Red Feather's face was dark as a stormy sky. "An animal

of great cunning and deceit that walks upon two legs, an animal that will kill all of the people if we don't kill him first."

Calling Crow's face showed a tinge of sadness. "Go back to the village, Red Feather."

Red Feather did not move.

Calling Crow's voice remained soft. "I came to your village when you were but a boy, still afraid of the shadows in the forest. I taught you courage and the noble ways of the warrior. Do you remember these things?"

Red Feather's shoulders slumped and he could no longer look at Calling Crow. "Samuel will destroy the people, and he will destroy you, Calling Crow. He must be killed."

"You say you are concerned for the people and for me, Red Feather, but your concern is really for yourself. Go home and I will try to forget what I saw here today."

Red Feather struggled for words as he looked at Calling Crow. Both men heard a twig snap and Samuel pushed noisily through the bushes.

The Englishman looked at them in surprise. "I thought I heard voices."

Red Feather shouted at Samuel loudly in Muskogee. Samuel moved backward, his hand on the hilt of his sword. "What is he saying?"

"He says," said Calling Crow, "that you will kill us all."

"Has he gone mad?" said Samuel.

As Calling Crow was about to reply, a terrified scream cut through the still summer air. It was Bright Eyes. All three men pushed through the bushes and out onto the trail. Samuel was the first to reach her. She knelt in a clearing, blood running down her neck and arm. Samuel knelt beside her and she embraced him, crying. Red Feather looked away angrily. Samuel inspected her wound closely. A cut ran along the line of her jaw, causing much blood to run out, but it was not a fatal wound. Samuel stanched the flow of blood with the palm of his hand.

Calling Crow and Red Feather went out onto the trail. Red Feather knelt to inspect the earth. "The one who did this is alone," he said to Calling Crow. "I will run him down."

"No," said Calling Crow. He put his hand on the younger man's arm, stopping him. "They will be waiting down the trail. We will punish them later."

Samuel helped Bright Eyes to her feet, continuing to press his hand against her cheek to stanch the flow of blood.

Red Feather's face darkened with anger. He glared threateningly at Samuel and went to Bright Eyes. "Who did this to you?" he demanded.

Bright Eyes would not look at Red Feather. "The one with the arrow in his hair." She looked at her father. "He said to tell you that he will be back before the second corn harvest."

Samuel started to lead Bright Eyes away.

Red Feather blocked his path. "You left her unprotected!"

Samuel addressed Calling Crow, ignoring Red Feather. "I did not think it would be dangerous this close to the village."

Calling Crow's face was dark. "Now that the Timucua have shooting sticks, it is becoming more dangerous for all my people. They will stop coming here only when we, too, have shooting sticks."

Samuel frowned. "I will leave one of our muskets with you and your village. We can discuss trading for more later."

"Yes," said Calling Crow, "that is good. Take Bright Eyes to her mother. We will talk more of this trade when I return."

Samuel and Bright Eyes said nothing as they walked quickly back to the village. When they were within sight of the palisade, Samuel said, "Red Feather cares greatly for you. How long has he wanted you?"

Bright Eyes looked down. "Since my husband died."

Samuel said nothing.

"And what about you?" said Bright Eyes, "how long have you wanted me?"

"Since I first saw you . . ."

"And now?" said Bright Eyes.

Samuel said nothing. He thought of the turn things had taken. Red Feather was becoming unstable, threatening to damage his relationship with Calling Crow. And he had hinted at trading more muskets to Calling Crow and his people. And then there was his wife and daughter back home . . .

Despite his strong attraction to Bright Eyes, getting involved with her was wrong for many reasons.

"I think I should stay away from you," he said finally. "I'm afraid I bring you only bad luck."

Bright Eyes said nothing as they entered the village palisade.

"*You're* not serious, brother," said John.

They were standing in the square ground of the village. The morning dew was still on the grass, the sun not yet having risen over the distant trees. John, Breuger and Miles had just come up from the river and Samuel had told them of his intention to leave a musket with Calling Crow, and to discuss trading for more.

"I *am* serious, John," said Samuel. "They are threatened now by this other tribe the Spanish are arming. Just the other day Calling Crow's daughter was attacked by one of them."

"Arming them could be dangerous for any ship calling here," said Breuger calmly.

Samuel scoffed. "There will not be any ships calling here. And I shall give them only enough powder and shot as they require for hunting their game, and defending their village from attackers. And when they need more shot, they'll have to trade with us for it."

"What has he to trade for muskets?" scoffed John. "More corn?"

"There is much in the way of merchantable commodities here," said Samuel, "if you have eyes to see it."

John scoffed.

Samuel pointed to the tall trees around them. "Our choicest forests in England have long ago fallen to the farmer's axe. Look at all this lumber for shipping, for masts!"

John looked at Miles. "So now we're to take the forests home with us, are we?"

Miles chuckled.

Samuel turned to Breuger. "I'm sure you have noticed their excellent deerskin garments, as I have. Their deerskins are of a high quality. We would do very well with them in the London markets.''

Breuger nodded. ''I agree.''

John scoffed disparagingly. ''You agree? The savages would never be able to get us enough to make the venture worthwhile!''

''Just yesterday,'' said Samuel, ''I watched five braves bring in seven deer, big creatures too.''

''Here they come,'' said John.

Samuel and the others watched Calling Crow and Swordbrought approach.

''How many muskets would you require?'' Samuel asked Calling Crow in Spanish.

''*Veinte.*''

Samuel nodded.

''Twenty?'' said John. ''Brother, surely you are not going to trade twenty muskets to them?''

Samuel ignored him. ''We want deerskins in trade,'' he said. ''How many would you be able to get?''

Calling Crow looked over at his son momentarily then back at Samuel. ''Let us go to the *chokafa* to talk about it.'' Calling Crow spoke in his own tongue with Swordbrought and they started toward the *chokafa*.

Samuel and the others followed Calling Crow and Swordbrought through the darkened entryway of the meeting house. The air was comfortable inside, scented with wood smoke. Calling Crow directed the Englishmen to sit on some mats and sent Swordbrought to summon the other braves and wise men who would discuss the trade. Calling Crow then walked to the entrance to speak with another of his men.

Samuel turned to Breuger. ''How much do you think we could get for one of their skins on the market?''

Breuger's blue eyes shone in his reddened face as he figured enthusiastically. ''For one of the bigger ones, at least ten pounds.''

Samuel nodded. ''That is what I would calculate.''

From the entryway, Calling Crow watched them quietly as he spoke with one of his men.

''Get eight skins for each musket,'' said John.

"Eight?" said Samuel. "They would be forever collecting them. Five skins will give us a fat profit."

Swordbrought arrived with four other braves, one of them carrying the ancient-looking lame wizard on his back. After they had seated themselves across from the Englishmen, Calling Crow came over and sat.

"Where will you get the shooting sticks?" Calling Crow asked Samuel.

"Through the London market," said Samuel. "There are many traders in London and I am sure I can get them."

"We will give you two skins for each of your muskets," said Calling Crow.

"Six skins for each musket," said Samuel.

Calling Crow turned and talked quietly with his men. The lame wizard spoke softly and Samuel looked at him closely. He was blind, his eyes clouded over with a purplish scarring.

"It would take too long to kill that many deer," said Calling Crow after a while. "We will give you four skins."

"That is not enough," said Samuel. "You have helped us much, and so we will take five skins for each musket."

Calling Crow looked at him calmly for a moment. "We will give you half of the skins to take to England, and half when you return."

Samuel shook his head.

"Half the skins," said Calling Crow, "will enable us to be away soon. Your men are anxious to go home and I must return by summer."

Samuel grudgingly agreed with the native's logic. "Very well," he said.

"There is more," said Calling Crow.

"What?"

"They don't believe you will return with the muskets. Two of us will go with you to England and two of your men must stay here."

"Agreed," said Samuel.

Calling Crow turned and discussed the business further with his men. Samuel could see that some of them were becoming agitated. "What is the matter?" he said.

Calling Crow turned to him. "It is not good to kill that

many deer. But, our holy man says that in this case it will be all right if he makes a special offering to placate the deer people."

Calling Crow turned back to his men and continued the discussion. Finally he turned to Samuel. "I will convene a council. If the others agree, we will begin hunting the deer tomorrow!"

"Very good," said Samuel.

"What did he say?" said John.

"He agrees to the trade, but he must get the approval of his councillors. He wants to send two of his men back with us and he wants us to leave two of our men here in order to guarantee they will get their muskets"

John looked at Breuger and Miles. "We will leave these two behind."

Breuger said nothing; Miles laughed nervously.

Calling Crow and his men began talking again. Samuel noted their growing excitement as they discussed the venture.

"Calling Crow," said Samuel, "is there a problem with the offer?"

Calling Crow turned to him. "Some of them are still afraid and do not want to send men and skins back with you. I will convince them, but it will take time. Leave us for now and we will discuss this further among ourselves."

Samuel nodded and turned to the others. "Let's leave them. They want to talk it over some more."

The Englishmen went out into the bright afternoon light. They crossed the dirt street from the big meeting hut and stood in the shade of a smaller hut. Several women walked past carrying skin bundles and baskets of nuts and fruits. They looked over at the Englishmen and smiled. Bright Eyes was among them. Under her mother's ministrations, her wound had healed with hardly a scar. When they had gone farther down the street, Bright Eyes turned to look directly at Samuel. She put such longing into her eyes that he felt a great stirring. He watched as she and the others disappeared from view. He continued to wait with his men. Finally someone exited the meeting hut.

"Well," said John, "here comes the king's son. They have

talked with their ministers of state and the Papal emissary. A decision is at hand."

Swordbrought walked up and spoke to Samuel in Spanish. "Well?" said John.

"They want to speak with me alone." Samuel walked back to the *chokafa* with Swordbrought.

John, Breuger and Miles walked toward the palisade entrance. Exiting the village, they headed in the direction of the river. Two small boys and a dog followed them curiously for a while before losing interest and wandering off.

Breuger looked over at John. "I think we will make a great deal of money on this deal, John. After we purchase the muskets, we can make a profit of forty percent on each one."

John looked at him as if he were crazy. "What do you mean, 'purchase the muskets'? There is no need to purchase anything. We will simply take the skins back and sell them and that is the end of this whole business."

Breuger looked worriedly over at the meeting house. "But Samuel would never agree to that."

John waved away his words.

Miles frowned. "And what about the men the king will send back with us? And the men we will leave behind?"

"I can talk Samuel into leaving the two Irish lads behind," said John, "and the savages'll be easily gotten rid of on the ship." He paused and the other men stopped. "But remember, when it is time to do it, Samuel is not to be hurt. I will deal with the Bristol savage myself."

Breuger and Miles smiled at the name someone had jokingly given to Samuel for spending so much of his time with the natives.

John looked around disapprovingly at the village. "He sees a great deal of money to be made here. Hah! Aside from the skins, there is nothing here."

"I don't know about this," said Breuger, "even with the savages gone, your brother will be wanting to come back here with the muskets. You know how determined he is to establish commerce between these people and our own."

John shook his head in annoyance. "Damn it, man, I tell you we will not be back. With the savages gone, I can talk

Samuel out of this foolishness.'' John looked around. ''Now, when the time is right, we will simply toss the savages into the sea and that will be the end of it.''

Breuger laughed and Miles nervously stroked the stubble on his jaw.

Chapter 14

Two months passed. The people of the village had become used to the sight of the strangely dressed, hairy Englishmen and they no longer drew large crowds. The Council still debated the idea of sending men and skins off with the English, but more and more, people were coming around to Calling Crow's side. Despite the demonstrated treachery of the white people—everyone still talked of the time the Spanish had taken the old chief, Atina, hostage for food—Calling Crow's wisdom and loyalty had always proved true and his forceful speeches in council were winning him more and more support. He argued that not all white people were the same, that these men were different from the Spanish. Indeed, they were enemies of the Spanish. Furthermore, Calling Crow argued, he had seen all of this in his vision anyway and therefore he must act upon it. The forty skins now curing in the drying sheds were testimony to what everyone knew would be the outcome of the debate. In fact, the only thing that was still unsettled was which braves would go back with the English.

On one particularly hot day, four men sat in a circle on a pallet of skins and reed mats in the sweat house. Bright sunlight from the entryway illuminated the hut. Calling Crow, Red Feather and Swordbrought wore only breechclouts, and the forth, Samuel Newman, wore breeches and hose and a linen shirt which clung wetly to his skin.

Calling Crow talked softly to Red Feather about the progress they were making in accumulating the skins while Swordbrought sat silently. Two young men carried the ancient, blind medicine man, Sees Far, in and lowered him to the mat. Sees Far deftly packed tobacco into his pipe. No one knew exactly how old Sees Far was, but the second oldest man in the village, Long Arms, swore that when he was only a tiny sprig of a boy carried about on his mother's hip, Sees Far was already an old, old man.

Sees Far's heavy-lidded eyes quivered as he stared up at the skin-covered ceiling of the hut and listened to the men talk rapidly in Muskogee.

"Is Samuel here?" asked Sees Far.

"Yes," said Swordbrought; Calling Crow and Red Feather did not hear the old man ask his question.

Sees Far frowned. "These English . . . they smell like the Spanish."

Swordbrought frowned in puzzlement; he had never smelled the Spanish. They had left these parts by the time he was born.

Red Feather's voice rose suddenly. "No, Calling Crow, I fear for you!" Red Feather angrily glared over at Samuel. "I will go instead, and perhaps Little Bear. But not you. It is too dangerous."

"I saw it in my vision," said Calling Crow calmly, "therefore I will go."

"I will argue against it in the Council," said Red Feather.

Sees Far reached out his small withered hand and placed it on Red Feather's arm. "No, Red Feather. If Calling Crow saw his going in a vision, then he must go. I will make him medicine to help bring him back and I will pray for him while he is over there. Then, hopefully, he will complete his days in these lands, instead of the lands of the English men."

Red Feather's face was fierce with determination. "Very well, Grandfather." 'Grandfather' was an honorific term used for all old men. "But," Red Feather continued, "we should send at least ten braves with him to protect him."

"Ten braves or three," said Calling Crow, "over there it would make no difference if the English betray us."

Red Feather looked over at Samuel suspiciously. "Then why go?"

Calling Crow rebuked him sternly. "Red Feather, were your eyes closed back at the Spanish fort? Did you not see the shooting sticks being traded to the Timucua?" Calling Crow's tone softened. "The Timucua will be probing our defenses. We need all the braves here so they are not tempted to launch an attack.''

Red Feather was at a loss for words and fell silent. Again he glared over at Samuel. ''Why must the English man be here?'' he said.

Calling Crow and Swordbrought looked over at Samuel, who sat with his head bowed. His hands were folded in front of him and his eyes closed.

''He asked for this sweat bath,'' said Calling Crow. ''He wants to know everything about us.''

Swordbrought frowned. ''Why are his hands like that?''

''That is the way the English pray,'' said Calling Crow.

''*Aieyah!*'' said Red Feather. ''He looks like a squirrel chewing on an acorn.''

Swordbrought laughed softly.

Calling Crow frowned at Swordbrought and Red Feather. His look told them that the Englishman's efforts to understand their ways were to be regarded as sincere, and that he was not to be scoffed at.

''It is time,'' said Sees Far. ''We will begin the ceremony. Perhaps the English man will have a vision.''

Swordbrought smiled broadly at this and even Calling Crow allowed himself a small, barely discernible smile at Sees Far's comment. Visions were not easily come by. A man had to pray long and hard over years, begging for a vision. Some men spent their whole lives seeking a vision and were never blessed with one.

They began by smoking the pipe. When they finished, the attendants brought in the first of the large hot rocks, cradling them in the antlers of a deer. ''Hello, old friends,'' said Sees Far as the attendants lay the rocks in the pit, ''straight from the house of the sun.'' One of the men went out and one remained inside to pour water. The man outside flipped the skin covering of the sweat house down, plunging the interior into darkness. The rocks glowed in the center.

Sees Far shook his turtle-shell rattle as the attendant poured a calabash of water over the rocks. Steam quickly engulfed the men and they gave themselves up to Sees Far's chanted prayers. ''Oh, Great Mystery,'' the old man's brittle voice

cried out, "we humbly pray you will honor us with a vision."
Time seemed to stand still as the heat built in the house and
Sees Far sang the prayers. The seekers prayed silently as the
attendant tended the rocks and poured water. Once someone
cried out in the mist like a child crying for its mother, and
then the hot silence again wrapped itself around them.

Later, upon receiving word from Sees Far, the attendants
took the rocks away and the air began to clear. No one said
anything for a while. Red Feather stood without a word and
exited the sweat house. After a while Swordbrought spoke to
Samuel.

"My father will be going to England with you, along with
one other brave."

"Why doesn't he send one of his men in his place?" said
Samuel. "That is what Red Feather and others want."

"A long time ago he had a vision of himself going on this
voyage, that is why."

Calling Crow called over to Samuel. "Samuel, did you
have a vision?"

Samuel shook his head. "I was thinking of my son who
died of fever. I could see his face and hear his voice. I don't
know why God took him from us, or what I did to be pun-
ished so. I still pray to know why."

Calling Crow's eyes conveyed his sympathy. "I, too, have
suffered such a loss. But why one dies as a babe and another
lives to be a very old man, no one can know these things.
They are simply part of the Great Mystery."

"No, he was not a babe. He was five years old and strong,
then he took sick with a fever. He shouldn't have died."

Calling Crow and the others were silent.

Samuel stared at his feet. He admired these dusty-colored
men who seemed so content with their simple lives. He had
even thought he might get some solace from their sweat bath.
Logically, he knew that the effect could be no more than the
heated blood putting pressure on the brain. After all, an ig-
norant plowman sweat buckets during the course of his day
and that certainly didn't make him holy, or even less crude.
Still, because of Calling Crow's childlike belief, he had been

willing to try it. But all he had gotten for his efforts were painful memories.

Samuel got to his feet and left the sweat house. As he walked down the hard-packed, earthen street, his head felt empty, devoid of all thought. A warm wind had come up while they were in the sweat house and now swept across the land. Samuel stopped to stare at a large, ancient poplar tree across the fields. It was the biggest tree in the area and its long branches moved in the wind like waving arms, its leaves and flowers whipping about like a head of hair tossed wildly in a dance. The sight cheered Samuel, blowing away the last vestiges of his sadness like so many dried-up leaves. He saw the tree as alive, as alive as a friendly dog, as a bird, as alive as he, and the realization thrilled him. He was suddenly aware of Calling Crow standing beside him.

"It's alive," said Samuel in amazement, "alive!"

"Yes," said Calling Crow, "do you love it?"

Samuel turned back to watch the tree. "Love it? I don't know . . . But the sight of it dancing so fills me with joy."

"If you love it, it will ease your heart," said Calling Crow, "such is the power of the Great Mystery."

Several little boys ran up to Samuel and Calling Crow. Their eyes were wide and playful as they looked at the Englishman. Samuel thought he heard someone call his name in the distance and turned away briefly. When he turned back, Calling Crow was walking away toward the *chokafa*. The boys spoke to Samuel rapidly in Muskogee, one of them tugging at his sword. He growled playfully at the boy and he and his fellows laughed as they backed away.

Samuel smelled something sweetly familiar in the air . . . What? He felt strangely compelled to walk in the direction of the river. Pollen filled the air as Samuel walked the village streets toward the palisade. He left the palisade entrance and walked down the path to the river. When he reached the river path, he thought he heard someone behind him. He walked away from the direction in which the skiff would be. Someone had been along here; he was sure of it. It was very hot and the air was awash with the fecund smells of the river and flowering trees. A noise came from ahead, but Samuel saw nothing. Intrigued, he walked faster—still nothing. He continued a bit farther and was on the point of turning round when again he heard a noise. He paused for a moment—there it was—a gentle splashing. He pushed through the bushes and came out to one of the small streams that fed the river. Bright Eyes was bathing naked in a pool about waist high.

She saw him but made no move to cover herself as she continued to bathe. "Why are you here?" she said.

"I don't know." To see her thus, in all her nakedness, he knew was an abominable sin, totally contrary to his faith. Yet he could not look or walk away; his feet seemed to have taken root. "I said I would stay away from you," he said, "but I cannot."

She said nothing and he watched her hungrily. She was the most beautiful woman in the world, a colorful, exotic New World flower. He fought against her attraction but she was like the call of an alehouse to a drunk. "I cannot!" he cried.

She looked up at him in confusion.

"I cannot," he said again, but he made no move to leave. This was the garden; she was Eve, he Adam. He put his head in his hands and cried. "Why do you tempt me so?"

She said nothing and appeared concerned for him as he approached the pool. He looked down at her, her brown body pulling him closer. Her eyes beckoned. He took off his shirt and boots and breeches and entered the slightly cool water. He took her in his arms. She sighed, rubbing the smooth skin of her face against his ear. He entered her and they moved against each other gently and lovingly. After a while an animal lust came over them and their movements became hurried and rhythmic. Holding tightly to each other, they rode the beast of their passion to its conclusion, finally spinning off into eternity.

Chapter 15

John Newman watched Breuger and Miles prepare the load of skins for transport to the ship. Miles knelt as he tied the bundles tightly with cord. The back of his green linen shirt was stained darkly with sweat. He and Breuger then tied the bundles to willow poles as big around as a man's wrist. These would enable two bearers to carry each heavy bundle. When they had finished, Miles and Breuger stood and looked at John.

"Where did my brother go?" said John.

Miles turned away momentarily to Breuger, who was making a joke, then looked quickly back at John. "He's with the king and the old blind beggar of a priest in their sweat house."

Breuger scowled. "What a vile and disgusting thing that is." A smile appeared on his thin lips. "Samuel certainly does put himself through much in his quest for commerce, does he not?"

John's look was cold and Breuger's smile withered. "Never mind that." John turned away from Breuger to inspect the four bundles of stiff skins. "Is that all of it now?" he asked Miles.

Miles nodded.

Nearby, a group of Coosa men stood waiting. Crying Wolf was among them. Crying Wolf now knew some of the Englishmen's words and listened to their talk. One of the men pointed back toward the village; Swordbrought was coming. "The prince comes!" one of the Englishmen said.

Crying Wolf had never heard this word before. Some of the Englishmen had been disrespectful and so his suspicions were aroused. "What is 'prince'?" he demanded of Brother-of-Samuel.

The man answered too rapidly for Crying Wolf to understand any of his words.

Swordbrought walked up to Crying Wolf. "What is the matter?" he said.

"What is the word 'prince'?" said Crying Wolf.

Swordbrought frowned. "I am not sure. I will ask them." Swordbrought spoke at some length with Brother-of-Samuel, then turned back to Crying Wolf. "He said that a prince is the son of a king, and that he is given the king's power when the king dies."

"*Aieyah!*" said Crying Wolf. "You are no prince! The chief is chosen in council. Tell him!"

Swordbrought looked at the taller brave calmly. "I have already told him."

Crying Wolf looked over angrily at John Newman. "No prince!" he shouted. "Swordbrought is no prince."

John ignored him and spoke to Swordbrought. "Are you in charge of this bunch?" he said.

Swordbrought nodded and looked at the men from the village who would carry for the English. His father had asked him to go with them and the English. Swordbrought was a fast learner and now knew much of the English language. There had been complaints from some of the villagers about the behavior of the Englishmen and Calling Crow wanted to be sure that there would be no trouble. Swordbrought remembered the sight of the Timucua and the stacked boxes of shooting sticks and knew his father was right. If the Coosa people were to stay here, they needed shooting sticks, and if they were to have them, they needed the English. Still, Swordbrought dreaded the thought of his father and Red Feather going off with the skins on the English ship. His father insisted that he was going because he had seen it in his vision, but Swordbrought knew he was going because he was very brave.

Swordbrought called to the men to hoist the bundles. There were seven men; Red Feather had picked them and hadn't thought they would need more than that. But there were four heavy bundles, and for that they would need eight men to carry.

Crying Wolf stood at the pole of the last bundle, which still remained on the ground. One of the men called over to Swordbrought, "Should I get another man to help?"

Swordbrought shook his head and walked over to John Newman. "We don't have enough men," he said. He pointed to the last bundle.

John Newman looked at him dully and then turned to speak rapidly to the frail Englishman who was called Miles. From Miles's words, and from his expression, Swordbrought could tell he thought the task beneath him. Miles looked around at the other man, who was called Breuger, and smiled at some joke between them.

Miles walked to the forward end of the pole attached to the bundle, and together with Crying Wolf, lifted it and set it on his shoulder. Miles spoke with John and Breuger. The Englishmen seemed jovial to Swordbrought, but their words left their mouths too quickly for him to understand what they were saying. They started toward the river trail.

The Englishmen, John and Breuger, walked at the head of the column. Swordbrought followed along behind Crying Wolf and Miles. The walk started off well, the bearers in front maintaining a steady pace. Swordbrought watched the bundle of skins sway slightly from the pole that Crying Wolf and Miles carried as the two very different men settled into the same rhythm. It was very hot, the air full of the smell of flowers and the pungent, muddy aroma of the river. No one spoke. Cicadas ground out a steady chant. The faraway groan of a bull alligator floated through the still air. After a while Swordbrought could see that the Englishman Miles was tiring and having a hard time with the pace. He had lost Crying Wolf's rhythm and the bundle of skins now jerked and swayed awkwardly beneath the pole. Once Miles slipped in the mud while descending a slight slope and cursed angrily at Crying Wolf, accusing the Coosa brave of pushing him.

Nearing the English skiff, they left the trail and forged through the bushes. Miles was very tired, stumbling and cursing angrily. Pushing through some thick ferns, he carelessly let a springy branch swing back and hit Crying Wolf in the face. Crying Wolf angrily tore the branch away as they approached the tied-up skiff. They lowered the heavy bundles to the ground and Miles sighed gratefully and wiped the sweat from his brow.

Swordbrought stood and watched while Crying Wolf went to stand with the other Coosa bearers. John touched Crying Wolf and another bearer on the shoulder and indicated that they should load the first bundle onto the skiff. Crying Wolf and the other man slipped the pole out of the cords and carefully lifted the awkward bundle up onto the skiff's gunnels. Crying Wolf held it in place while the other man climbed aboard. Then Crying Wolf got into the skiff and they carefully carried it forward. Two more were loaded this way.

"Miles," called John loudly. He pointed at the last of the bundles. "You and Breuger get the last one. Put it just aft of theirs and check that the load is well placed so that the skiff does not upset in the surf."

Miles and Breuger picked up the heavy bundle and hoisted it onto the skiff. Miles climbed aboard while Breuger stood in the waist-high water, steadying the load. Then Breuger climbed aboard and they wrestled the bundle forward. As Crying Wolf and the other man were attempting to leave the skiff, Miles clumsily, but not intentionally, bumped into Crying Wolf, knocking him backward. Crying Wolf went over the side and splashed into the water.

Breuger and Miles set their bundle down.

Swordbrought called up to them. "You knocked him into the water."

Miles's face was red but he was smiling. "It was an accident; there was no room."

"Then why do you smile?" said Swordbrought.

Miles shook his head. "Aw, to hell with him, and you too."

Breuger and Miles laughed.

Crying Wolf had regained his footing by this time and was pushing through the water. His face compressed in anger, he reached over the gunnels and grabbed Miles by the shirt.

"No, Crying Wolf," shouted Swordbrought, "you must not."

Oblivious to everything but his rage, Crying Wolf quickly pulled Miles into the water. By the time the Englishman found his feet and rose, sputtering and coughing, Crying Wolf's axe was already in his hand and rising. Swordbrought plunged into the water. He quickly twisted Crying Wolf's arm around behind him, causing him to drop the axe. Miles staggered up the muddy bank as the other Englishmen stood ready upon the skiff, their swords drawn.

Swordbrought relaxed his grip on Crying Wolf's arm and the brave broke free, retrieving his axe from the muddy bottom. Turning, he glared hatefully at Swordbrought.

Swordbrought met his look. "Calling Crow said there was to be no fighting."

Crying Wolf backed away and climbed the muddy bank.

"Let's go," said John Newman as he took his place at the rear of the skiff. Miles and Breuger sat at the oars. Saying nothing, they rowed off, and as the skiff disappeared around the bend in the river, their harsh laughter floated back along the black water.

Chapter 16

Bright Eyes walked into the water of the small stream that was her bathing place. The beaver people had built a dam above and the clear, cool water was waist deep. Bright Eyes had worked most of the morning in the corn, pulling bores from the tender green plants, and this bath was most refreshing. As she wiped the cool water across her belly, she thought about the tiny thing that was now growing in there. She had already told Samuel, thinking that perhaps now he would not go back to England. He had said that he must, but that he would return. She believed him; after all, her father was going with him to bring back the shooting sticks.

She remembered the ugly, frightening face of the Timucua chief and felt a chill. She got out of the water and picked up her things. She had only just finished pulling her skirt around her when she heard someone coming. She was about to run when she saw that it was Red Feather.

Her relief was evident as she smiled shyly at the man her father had chosen for his *tastanagi*. "Oh, it is you."

Red Feather's face brightened hopefully. "Hello, Bright Eyes." He pulled around the skin bag he carried over his shoulder and took a wrapped bundle from it. "It is venison."

Bright Eyes's initial impulse was to reach for it, but she did not. She saw the awkwardness her inaction was causing Red Feather, but still she could not take it. She began to grow angry at his coming here. He could have waited until she had returned to the village and there were others around to offer his gift.

"I was blessed on our hunt," he said, extending the wrapped piece of meat to her.

Bright Eyes still would not take it.

Red Feather looked at her, the slightest quiver about his eyes giving away the intensity of his feelings. "You and your mother will enjoy this."

She didn't like to see this proud man her father had personally trained behave this way, but neither would she allow herself to be pushed. She had chosen the Englishman, Samuel, despite his strange behavior, and Red Feather knew this. Still he pursued her.

"We already have more than we need, Red Feather. Perhaps you should give it to someone who is sick or old." Bright Eyes surprised herself when she said this.

Red Feather's face grew dark. He put the meat back into the bag and went away.

Bright Eyes hurried to the village and her meeting with her mother. She felt sorry for Red Feather but she was angry too. She had decided! Anyone with eyes in their head could see that. No amount of gift giving would change her mind.

Calling Crow sat in the house of Green Bird Woman and stared into the fire. Not far away, his wife and daughter talked quietly as they cooked at another fire. Calling Crow had heard Bright Eyes tell her mother of Red Feather's gift, and his reaction when Bright Eyes refused it. But he was not concerned. Very soon they would leave for England. Over there, Red Feather would not be suddenly saddened by the chance sight of Bright Eyes. And when they came back, there would be fighting, and Red Feather would lose his sadness in the thrill of battle.

Outside, a thick, starless sky engulfed the world. Out on the sea, the English ship was rising and falling on the swells like a gull, waiting to take them and their skins. It had been two moons now since they had agreed on the trade and started collecting the skins. It was good that they were now ready, for, with the exception of Samuel, Fenwick, the old silver-haired iron maker, and a few young men, the English were rude and arrogant to his people. Many people were glad that they were now ready to go away. The exceptions were the four young women who were now ripening with children sired by the Englishmen. Bright Eyes was one of them. These

Englishmen had promised to return with Calling Crow and the shooting sticks, but that could not assuage the young women's sadness. The others who did not want to see the English go were the old people and the young children. The English had given them much to see and hear, and much to talk about.

Just the other day there had been a tumultuous wrestling match that brought out most of the village to the square ground to watch. Calling Crow and Samuel had had great difficulty in calming the passions that the fight had inflamed. But now things would quiet down. Tomorrow there would be a feast in honor of Calling Crow and Red Feather, and the Englishmen, and then they would be gone. That was why Green Bird Woman and her daughter, Bright Eyes, were still cooking at this hour.

Bright Eyes's voice rose as she and her mother argued. Green Bird Woman was not happy that Bright Eyes had given herself to the Englishman, Samuel. Calling Crow was not unhappy with the arrangement. Although Samuel had a wife and child in England, he did seem to care much for Bright Eyes. And Bright Eyes seemed happy with him. That was good to see. They had chosen. Still, Green Bird Woman was not happy about it.

Aieyah! There were bigger things to concern them. Calling Crow's life and dreams had shown him that the white people would keep coming. If the people were to deal with them out of strength, he must form an alliance with Samuel and the English. Bright Eyes's love for him, and the child they would have together, would help in that regard. Now the village had one shooting stick and several braves knew how to shoot it. That was good and would help to scare off any small raiding parties who might think the village an easy target. But when Mantua and his Spanish master returned at the second corn harvest, Calling Crow and his men must be here with twenty of the shooting sticks. Ho! Calling Crow was sure he was going down the proper path. It was good that they were now leaving.

Bright Eyes bade her mother good night. She would be

going to Samuel now. She looked over at Calling Crow and smiled before going out into the night.

Green Bird Woman's face was somber as she banked down the fire. She came over and sat beside Calling Crow. Saying nothing for a while, they looked into the shriveling flames of the fire.

Finally Green Bird Woman spoke. "You know how much all of this has hurt Red Feather. For so long he has been fond of her. I fear for him."

"Red Feather is my *tastanagi*," said Calling Crow, "I need not worry about my *tastanagi*."

Green Bird Woman fell silent. Outside someone walked past the compound, laughing softly. Green Bird Woman put her hand on Calling Crow's. She looked at him worriedly. "What will their baby look like?"

Calling Crow turned to her. "It will look like him."

"*Aieyah!*" said Green Bird Woman, her face screwing up in distaste.

"And," said Calling Crow, "it will look like her."

Green Bird Woman smiled and laughed briefly. Tears came to her eyes.

"I do not want you to go," she said. "I fear you will not return to me."

"Did not Sees Far say that I would?"

"Yes," she said, "that is so."

"I must go," said Calling Crow, "because I alone have had many experiences with the white people. Remember that I was their slave for a long, long time and I know their ways."

"Say no more," said Green Bird Woman. "I cannot bear to think of these things anymore." She caressed his hand for a moment and cried softly.

Calling Crow felt her pain as his own and his heart was heavy. He put his arm around her and they sat close for a long while. Later they lay back on the pallet of skins that was their bed. Soon her cries were of passion, not sorrow, and then they slept.

Chapter 17

The square ground in front of the *chokafa* filled with people well before full day. Women came and went with pots of soup and wooden bowls of roasted meats, fishes and fowls as the people feasted. Calling Crow and Samuel and his men sat at the head of the assemblage as speakers related the experiences of the hunters in bringing in all the skins. Groups of young men and then young women came and danced before the assemblage to the accompaniment of drums and singing. Samuel and Fenwick entertained the group with a tune they played, Samuel on the fiddle and Fenwick on the lute, while two lads danced a jig. The people ate and laughed, filling their hearts with all the joy the occasion brought, knowing that days of uncertainty and sadness lay ahead. Toward the end of the day, when the sun had settled over the trees to the west, a dozen braves approached Calling Crow, Samuel and the others. The one who was their spokesman, a squat, muscled brave with a wide face and deep-set eyes, spoke softly with Calling Crow.

Samuel noted how the other braves in the party looked at him and his men as their spokesman and Calling Crow conversed. Although Calling Crow had taught Samuel many words in the Muskogee tongue, just as Samuel had taught Calling Crow many English words, still Samuel could not tell exactly what the young man was saying to Calling Crow. He did understood enough, however, to feel his anger rising. He listened a while longer, then, unable to control himself, he got to his feet.

John, Fenwick and the others looked at Samuel in surprise as he turned to Swordbrought.

"I think I know, but pray tell me what they have said to Calling Crow," demanded Samuel.

Swordbrought told him straight-faced, "They worry about Calling Crow going away with you. They say they don't trust you. They don't want him to go. They say you will never bring him back. That is what they said. My father has told them that there is no need for them to worry."

Samuel's face was red. "Haven't I agreed to leave two men here?"

"They say you will abandon them here."

"Is that really what they think?"

Swordbrought looked at him solemnly. "Yes."

Samuel turned to Calling Crow as the brave continued to talk softly. "Calling Crow," he said, interrupting the man, "tell him to wait. I have something to say to him and the others."

Calling Crow spoke to his men and they turned and waited for Samuel to speak.

"I have been most happy with the kindness you have shown us these past months," said Samuel to the men. The others around them quieted as they picked up the emotion in Samuel's voice. "We are all grateful." Samuel included his men with a sweep of his hand. "I have seen firsthand how highly you value such things as courage and honor, and I assure you that we English value these things highly too. Because of that I now make this pledge.

"Coosa people . . . I promise you that I will bring your leader home safe to you. When we have concluded our business and return, you will see that the word of an Englishman is as good as the word of a Coosa!"

Samuel looked at the people, most of whom were silently wondering what he had said. He sat and Swordbrought immediately got to his feet and translated Samuel's words for them. The people listened in silence, and when Swordbrought sat, a drumming started up.

Samuel said good night to his brother and the other men as they left for the ship. He had decided to spend his last night here in the village with Bright Eyes. A runner came and spoke quietly to Calling Crow, who then called Samuel over.

"Come with me," Calling Crow said, getting to his feet, "Sees Far has some things to say to us about our voyage."

Samuel saw Sees Far in the back of the *chokafa*. He sat hunched over on a raised platform covered with skins, one of his wives sitting beside him. As Samuel approached with Calling Crow, he wondered what the old wizard wanted with him.

Sees Far smiled when he heard their footsteps. He turned and took something from behind him. It was a small pouch, made of soft doeskin. Its fold-over flap had been painted with a pattern of tiny bird feet, as if a bird had been dipped in different colors of paint and made to walk across it.

Sees Far held it out to Calling Crow. "Calling Crow, I have had a dream about your journey. In it I was told to make this medicine for you. It will bring you and Red Feather back to us. Keep it with you always."

"Yes, Grandfather," said Calling Crow. He held up the pouch to show Samuel. "When we bring home the shooting sticks, the Timucua threat will be no more."

Sees Far nodded. "You can look inside," he said.

Calling Crow opened it. Inside was the corpse of a small black bird, its yellow beak poking out from a mass of shiny, iridescent feathers. Calling Crow closed it and put it into the larger pouch tied to his sash.

"Don't lose it," said Sees Far, "or you can not come back to us."

"Thank you, Grandfather."

"Sa-mu-all," said Sees Far, still having difficulty with the Englishman's name. "I heard you made a fine speech. I know you will bring Calling Crow back in your floating house."

"Thank you," said Samuel.

"You were in my dream also," said the old man.

Samuel's features grew sharp with interest. Sees Far's powers of soothsaying were sworn to by everyone in the village. "What did you see?" he said.

The old man was suddenly somber. "I saw that your circle will close in these lands."

Samuel turned to Calling Crow in confusion. "My circle closes? What is he saying?"

"He means," said Calling Crow, "that you will die in these lands."

Samuel scoffed. "How does he know that?"

Calling Crow's face was grave. "He knows. Don't worry. It is a good thing. He said that my circle will also close here."

Sees Far's leathery face wrinkled even further as he looked toward the two men. "I don't know why this is, Calling Crow, but I saw it, so it must be so." Sees Far looked in Samuel's direction. "You will complete your days on this side of the great water."

Samuel laughed bravely. "Perhaps I should bring my family over and settle here."

"It is a good place to settle," said Calling Crow. "I came here alone and these people made me one of them. They will accept you and yours if you bring them."

Samuel's face darkened with thoughtfulness. "We shall see; we shall see."

The waves rose slowly above the dark sea without a sound as they sought to throw themselves upon the land. Curling forward in their haste, they fell over onto themselves with a loud clap, dissolving into hissing white foam, finally dying with a sigh at the feet of the men who stood on the beach. Calling Crow and Swordbrought stood with Samuel Newman as they watched the dugouts that were already making their way out to the ship. Thirty feet away, the two Irish ship's boys, Patrick and Kevin, stood close together as they stared dolefully at the little ship. A lone dugout canoe remained pulled up on the sand. Two Indian paddlers sat inside, waiting quietly. Red Feather stood alone next to the canoe. The blood-red globe of the sun pushed above the blue of the sea, warming the men with its rays. None of the men spoke. Neither the cry of a passing gull nor the laughter, then hushed words, of the four children who came up behind them disturbed the men, as each of them thought his thoughts, unmoving, as if time had stopped for them.

Red Feather was the first to move, walking over to Swordbrought and embracing him. "Your father will come back to you and the people. Do not worry."

Swordbrought smiled bravely. "Because you go with him, I do not worry."

Old Two Clouds, Green Bird Woman and Bright Eyes came down the beach. At the sight of Bright Eyes, Red Feather climbed into the canoe and sat, turning away. Green Bird Woman embraced Calling Crow tearfully and stepped back. Bright Eyes embraced Samuel and then the Englishman walked into the surf and climbed into the front of the canoe.

Calling Crow approached Two Clouds. "If the Timucua attack before we can return, fight hard. We will soon join you."

The old man nodded sadly.

Finally Calling Crow turned round to his son Swordbrought. He looked deep into his eyes for a few moments, saying everything wordlessly. Finally he spoke. "Good-bye, my son."

A quiver of emotion flashed across Swordbrought's face, but when he spoke his voice was firm. "Good-bye, Father."

Calling Crow walked to the dugout and climbed inside. He sat facing forward and did not turn round.

The paddler in the rear climbed out and dug his powerful feet into the sand as he pushed the dugout off. As a wave lifted the nose of the canoe, he swiftly climbed back in. Paddling powerfully, he and the other man propelled the canoe past the breakers and out onto the calm swells.

Calling Crow stared across the blue sea. The morning sun had singed the air bright orange. Ahead, the many canoes that had taken the people out to see them off now seemed to meld into the ship. As Calling Crow's canoe drew close, the many canoes opened a path for them and they paddled through them, looking into the faces of the people. Calling Crow, Red Feather and Samuel climbed aboard the English ship. Samuel left them to supervise his men in their duties.

Calling Crow and Red Feather stood at the rail and looked back at the land. The long line of returning canoes made a trail on the water from the ship to the beach. Calling Crow spotted the figures of Green Bird Woman, Bright Eyes, Swordbrought and Two Clouds on the beach, watching them. Calling Crow's heart was heavy at the sight of them, and at having to leave his people, but at the same time his heart was full of wonder. He was going to England because that was where his earth path led. It was simply part of the Great Mystery and it filled him with awe.

The *Contempt* moved steadily northward, driven by the trade winds. The days were clear and the sun shone down favorably upon the little ship. At night Samuel steered the ship by the stars and always a lookout stood forward at the bowsprit watching and listening for shoals. Calling Crow and Red Feather spent most of their time by the rail, watching the mysterious coast slip by. One day a large whale surfaced a short distance from the ship. Calling Crow and Red Feather watched in awe as it matched the ship's speed, seemingly aware of their eyes upon it.

"He has come to give us his blessing on our mission," said Calling Crow.

Red Feather watched spellbound, saying nothing. A moment later the huge animal expelled its breath in an upward, explosive gasp of white vapor and disappeared beneath the sea. Calling Crow looked upon the sea with a lighter heart now. Much of the sadness he had felt at having to leave his people had been taken down into the sea by the whale.

Samuel spent some of his time with Calling Crow and Red Feather, explaining the workings of his ship, how it was steered and how the sails were turned to catch the wind. Five days after they had started out Calling Crow saw a familiar promontory, and just past that a little river. His heart raced as he realized that it was the site of his boyhood village. He stayed at the rail, watching the familiar coast as a flood of boyhood memories washed over him. Only when it was too dark to see did he turn away.

Eight days into the journey the air grew noticeably colder. The face of the land changed: sharp granite rocks pushing up through the earth, the thick green covering of broad-leafed trees gradually giving way to a scattering of tall pines. Four days later they encountered floating mountains of ice that dwarfed the ship. Calling Crow asked Fenwick where they were going and he said they were taking the northern route home. The winds blew colder and colder. The men donned heavy capes and hats and, as the cold grew bitter, seemed to shrink inside them.

Calling Crow and Red Feather thought fondly of Green Bird Woman as they wrapped themselves in the heavy buffalo robes she had given them for the journey. She had bought them from a Shawnee trader the year before.

The ship moved slowly northward, turning white with frost and ice, and one day, Samuel turned it back in toward the land. There lay a great, quiet bay, seemingly as big as an ocean. As Samuel gave the helmsman orders to turn the ship and enter, the men speculated anxiously about the dangers of leaving open waters.

John approached Samuel, Breuger and Miles hovering at his side. "Surely you're not going in there, brother?"

"I am," said Samuel, "it could lead to the Northwest Passage."

"We've got a hold full of cargo, brother, this is not the time to go exploring."

"We shan't stay long, John."

"But the danger," said John. "If a storm caught us in there, we might not get out."

Samuel searched the gray horizon. There seemed no end to the bay. Could this be it? he wondered. The passage . . . A way around the bloody Spaniards and to Cathay and Zipangu? "We will sail for two days. If we don't see any evidence of the passage in that time, we shall leave."

John's brow furrowed angrily and he turned and walked off.

Samuel sailed the *Contempt* inside the bay. Massive snow-covered mountains looked down on the tiny wooden ship. The black rock of the mountains was visible in places where the ice and snow had fallen away. Samuel sailed west across the great bay for the better part of the day. As evening approached, there was still no end in sight. Samuel anchored the ship near the shore and the men lined the rails to look out on the empty white land where nothing grew. The temperature dropped rapidly, and except for Calling Crow and Red Feather, who had no facial hair, the beards of the men became encrusted with white frost from their billowing breaths.

The men watched the frozen land, seeing nothing move, fascinated by its emptiness. Then, just before dark, a great white bear appeared as if out of nowhere. It quickly lumbered away out of sight.

The next day Samuel sailed the *Contempt* farther west and discovered a great river. He assuaged the growing fear of the crew with his promise to turn the ship about in the morning and start for home. They turned the ship up the river. They hadn't gone far when snow began to fall, quickly coating the ship. The ropes moved stiffly through the blocks and the sheets became as thick and hard as wood. Their fingers stiff and bleeding, the men cursed the cold and ice as they worked the ship.

Calling Crow turned to Fenwick, who had come over to stand beside him. "Is England up this river?"

Fenwick shook his head as he stared at the misty white land. "No. Samuel thinks perhaps this could lead to the countries of Cathay and Zipangu."

Calling Crow nodded. "I have heard others speak of these places. They say that the people there have worms that weave their cloth for them."

Fenwick tried to laugh but his face was too stiff to move. "That is a new twist." He stared out into the misty whiteness, his usually jolly face growing serious. "Whosoever discovers the Northwest Passage will become the richest man in the world."

As night approached, Samuel anchored the ship as promised. The men stared at the forlorn icy shores as the light began to dim. Fenwick stood silently beside Calling Crow and Red Feather as the light changed to a deep, melancholy blue. Then, wordlessly, he went below, leaving the two Indians standing at the rail. The wind picked up gradually, turning the ship. Calling Crow and Red Feather continued to stare in wonder at the strange barren land. All of the men had gone below by this time except for three who worked above in the ship's rigging. Calling Crow turned to Red Feather. "Let us go inside," he said. They climbed the steps to the halfdeck and went to the door leading down inside the ship. It was locked from the inside and would not budge. "We will try the other door," said Calling Crow, and they retraced their footsteps.

The light was almost gone as they started across the waist. Calling Crow saw the dark figures of the three men working aloft. They were pulling at some ropes. The wind was blowing harder now, bringing with it a terrible coldness as it whistled through the rigging. Calling Crow heard a crack and turned just in time to see a huge thing coming at him and Red Feather. He pulled Red Feather down as the long wooden spar swung by overhead. It came to rest with its farthest end hanging over the icy sea. Men began shouting as they ran to the side.

"*Aieyah*," said Red Feather, "they are trying to knock us into the sea!"

Calling Crow said nothing as they got to their feet. The door up on the halfdeck burst open and more men came running out.

"What happened?" said Samuel.

"The braces snapped," said a man, "and the yard swung away."

"Quickly," shouted Samuel, "run another line through there and secure it."

As the men rushed about in the dark, Calling Crow and Red Feather climbed the steps to the waist and this time found the door unlocked.

Most of the crew were asleep in the great cabin in the stern section of the ship. On the next deck down, the orlop deck, next to the still faintly warm bricks of the cookhouse fireplace, Miles and Breuger, their hands and arms hidden beneath their woolen cloaks, stood with John Newman, who was holding a dim lamp. They looked over at the barely discernible forms of the two Indians, who, with their great hairy robes wrapped tightly around them, appeared to be asleep upon some coils of rope in the dark cable locker. Miles fingered the hilt of his dagger nervously. His face was red from the weather, his pockmarks white and pronounced. "They've as many lives as a bloody cat!" he whispered.

Breuger shook his head. "No," he whispered. "Animal instincts, it is, keen hearing and the like."

Miles pointed over at the Indians with his dagger then looked at John. "Should we do it now?" he whispered. "We could put them over the side when we finish."

John's eyes were as bereft of emotion as two beads of brown glass. "No, not now. Someone might hear. We will wait till we are closer to England. That way we can be sure they will not swim home."

Miles and Breuger laughed softly. They turned and went quietly up the steps to the great cabin.

Despite the icy deck, the men ran to their tasks with a sense of urgency. Calling Crow stood beside Samuel at the whip-staff as the worried-looking Englishman shouted orders to his men. Earlier that morning the lookout high in the crow's nest had shouted down that the entrance to the bay had frozen over in the night. Now, with only the mizzen sail set, they moved slowly past large pieces of floating ice as Samuel attempted to spy a channel back out into open sea.

Samuel turned to scan the jagged mountains off the ship's port side. A long, flat field of ice lay ahead in the distance. Calling Crow, Red Feather and Fenwick stood beside him. "See those peaks there," Samuel said to them. "They form a line which marks the entrance to this bay. That is where we came in."

"Yes," said Fenwick, "but where shall we get out?"

Samuel ignored Fenwick's question as he grimly scanned the misty distance.

Calling Crow looked at the ice field. It extended out into the white mists as far as he could see. Then he noticed a break to the north. "There," he said, pointing, "the sea comes in."

"I see nothing," said Fenwick.

"Where?" said Samuel.

Calling Crow pointed and Samuel and Fenwick squinted and frowned.

"I think you are mistaken," said Samuel.

A few minutes later the men who had crowded together at the bow began shouting.

"I see it," said Fenwick happily, "there!"

Samuel raised his head and smiled. "God in heaven! You're right." He called calmly to the man in the cutaway below them. "Port, ten degrees."

The man wordlessly pushed the heavy lever of the whip-staff to the right and the ship leaned slightly as it turned. A few moments later they passed through an opening not more than five hundred feet across. On either side of the ship, ice fields reached out for them like two great white arms seeking to trap them.

The breeze picked up and the men began cheering as they left the ice behind.

"Set all sails," called Samuel loudly. He looked at Calling Crow sadly. "We will soon pick up the westerlies and sail for England."

"What about the Northwest Passage?" said Calling Crow.

"I'll be back," said Samuel. He turned to look back at the jagged white mountains receding into the distance. "I've never seen a river so broad . . . I'll be back."

Chapter 18

The men of the *Contempt* stepped livelier at their tasks now. After picking up the westerlies, they had sailed for two weeks before strong steady winds before running into the storm that had assailed them for the past two days. Now it was over and each dawn brought greater expectations of a landfall in southern England.

It was three of the clock inside the dimness of the orlop, where Miles and Breuger reclined upon bundles of deer hides. The air was filled with the pungent smell of the hides, and the occasional rustle and squeal of rats. The rats had grown used to the men. Emboldened by their numbers, they made no attempt to hide as they chewed on the skins or attacked what was left of the sacks of Indian corn. A rat as large as a man's boot came out from under a bundle of skins and looked up at Breuger. It then raced across the deck to another bundle. Breuger's hand blurred as he threw his dagger downward, pinning the squealing rodent to the deck. Getting to his feet, he stomped the creature's body under his boot, ending its cries.

Footsteps approached woodenly. Breuger pulled his dagger from the corpse and wiped the blood on the pile of skins before putting it in his belt. Miles sat up expectantly. John Newman ducked his head and entered through the door.

"Samuel sleeps like a babe now," he said. "He won't be waking till tomorrow at dawn or later."

Miles nodded. Neither he nor Breuger was surprised to hear this. Samuel had been awake and at the helm for the thirty-six hours that the squall had banged the ship about.

"Now we will go and feed the fish," said John.

They came up out of the ship onto the foredeck and walked

slowly toward the waist. They saw the two Indians way back on the poop. There were a half dozen men there also, all of them looking down at the two fins cutting the sea in the ship's wake. The sharks had been following the *Contempt* ever since first light, when the cook had dumped the rotting carcass of a deer that had been salted before they left but had not kept.

Miles looked nervously around at some men nearby who were coiling a rope. "What if Samuel finds out?" he said to John.

John looked over at one of the men and the man nodded knowingly. "No one will see a thing," said John, "I assure you."

Breuger laughed nervously as they started down the steps to the poop. The bigger of the two Indians saw them and turned away to speak to the other.

John and the other two men walked across the waist and climbed the starboard stairs up to the poop. Four men leaned over the rail looking down at the wake. The Indians were gone.

"Martin," called John.

One of the men at the rail turned round. "What is it, sir?"

"The savages? Did you see where they went?"

Perplexed, the young man scratched his beard. "I did not, sir." He turned back to look over the rail.

John looked round at Breuger and Miles and then walked to the port steps. "Come on." They walked quickly down the steps and John stopped at the hatch covering the steps leading down to the orlop. He looked wordless at the other two, pulled off the hatch and started down the steep steps. "Leave the hatch off," he called up to Breuger, who was the last one down.

The orlop stretched before them, the cables stacked in coils visible until the light faded up forward.

Breuger came down the steps and pulled his dagger. "They could be hiding anywhere."

Miles nodded.

"I don't think so." John pointed to a nearby hatch that led down to the bilge. "That's where they are. Down with the rats. I'm sure of it. Help me with this."

Miles helped him as he began pulling the hatch off. Above, shouting could be heard. The thud of running booted feet came through the beams. John looked over at Breuger. "See what is happening."

As Breuger climbed up, John shouted to him, "And bring a lamp back! The bloody savages can see in the dark."

John and Miles set the heavy hatch covering aside as the foul vapors of the bilge engulfed them. They paused to get their breath and heard Breuger returning from above. He stopped halfway, calling, "There's a sail off the port bow!"

John looked briefly into the black hole of the bilge, then turned to Miles. "Wait here."

John and Breuger climbed the steps to the waist, John blinking his eyes against the light. "Where?"

Breuger stared across the green sea. "There."

A tiny fleck of white winked in and out of view as the *Contempt* rose and fell in a moderate sea.

"I see it," said John.

"Do you think she's a Spaniard this far west?" said Breuger.

"Could be," said John. "There's always a market for their muskets and wines with the bloody Irish."

Breuger looked back over at the steps leading down. "Perhaps we should wait," he said nervously.

John looked at him angrily. "Let's be done with it."

Breuger nodded and they went back down the stairs. Miles looked up at them. "What is it?"

"Never mind," said John. He looked at Breuger. "Go on up and keep me posted."

Up on the waist, Breuger stared with the others at the growing white shape on the horizon. The lookout's voice boomed out. "She's a Spaniard, a four-master, headed this way!" More men ran to the rails to look out. Breuger saw Fenwick and another man run below, presumably to wake Samuel. He called down to John, "She's headed for us."

John and Miles looked up at Breuger from the blackness of the bilge. "They'll sail closer for a look," shouted John, "and then go on."

Breuger stood and watched with the others. Samuel was

now on deck and the ship loomed larger in the distance, sailing a parallel course to intercept them. It was a huge four-masted galleon of at least a thousand tons. Two rows of ten symmetrically spaced squares along her hull, like buttons on a coat, indicated at least twenty guns per side. With every sail set and a following wind, the ship quickly closed the distance to the *Contempt*.

Forgetting John, Breuger watched the big ship hove to. None of the men spoke as the huge ship drew closer. Twice as long as the *Contempt,* and half again as high, it loomed over them, its guns run out and pointed menacingly downward. Dozens of uniformed men armed with muskets looked down from the rigging as ropes were thrown to the Englishmen. Breuger hurried back down the steps and called down to John on the next deck. John's head appeared above the hatch.

"They're going to board us, John. Come up!"

John's face twisted in anger. "Boarding us? They have no reason . . . They wouldn't dare to board us this close to home."

A loud groan vibrated through the oaken ribs of the *Contempt* as she leaned over from the weight of the Spaniard. Shouting and the thump of running feet came down the hatch.

"For the love of God!" exclaimed John, rushing toward the steps. Miles was right behind him.

The ships were already lashed together when John arrived topside. With the others, he stared up in awe at the huge ship and its many guns. The Spanish captain and his guard peered down over the rails.

Samuel and Fenwick pushed through the men to stand before them. John, Breuger and Miles came forward also. They watched the Spanish captain and four soldiers climb down the chains. The captain walked up to them and bowed. A slight young man, a head shorter than Samuel, he wore a clean mustache and goatee beard. He smiled up condescendingly at John and Samuel. John thought he must have ascended to his captaincy through his father's, or a relative's, influence in court. Two of his soldiers looked like typical Spaniards, with olive-dark eyes and well-trimmed beards. They wore breastplates and comb helmets. The other two were swarthy of complexion and appeared to be of Spanish-Indian blood. Although they too had breastplates and helmets, they wore no shoes.

"Señors," said the captain in Spanish, "who is in charge here?"

Samuel bowed.

The captain shifted his position slightly to face Samuel directly. "I am Captain Valenzuela of His Majesty Philip II's ship, the *San Miguel*."

Samuel nodded. "*Yo soy Samuel Newman.*"

"Ah, English," said Valenzuela, using that language. "Very well, we will speak your language."

"Thank you," said Samuel. "I am commander of this vessel, and this is my brother and partner, John."

The men of the *Contempt* crowded closer to hear what was being said.

"Where are you bound, señor?" said Valenzuela.

"The port of Bristol," said Samuel.

"And where are you coming from?"

"We've come round from Cork, in Munster."

Valenzuela frowned. "Then you were never in the Americas, in the lands claimed by His Majesty?"

"No," lied Samuel.

"What is your cargo, sir?"

"Woolens," said Samuel.

High above, one of the Spaniards chose this moment to disdainfully expel his water. A golden stream of piss fell between the narrow space of both ships. Valenzuela looked embarrassed but said nothing and appeared to be waiting for something. A small, trim man climbed down the chains, his back to them. Reaching the deck, he turned. Unchanged from when they had last seen him in Isabela, it was Señor Gredilla.

Gredilla walked up to stand behind Valenzuela. "That is them," he said softly in Spanish.

"Señor Gredilla," said Samuel, smiling, "I thought you had taken up residence in the Colony of Hispaniola."

Gredilla did not smile. He pointed to John. "That is the one who stabbed the criollo in Isabela."

"You little Judas," said John.

Gredilla's face reddened and he stepped forward, slapping John across the face.

Samuel put his hand on his brother's chest. John's face reddened, but he did not move.

Valenzuela turned and spoke rapidly to his soldiers in Spanish. The men walked quickly to the stairs and descended to the great cabin. Valenzuela smiled and turned away from Samuel and John. He walked over to the rail to speak quietly to someone invisible in the darkened square of one of the Spanish gunports. Gredilla cast an angry look at the Newman brothers, then climbed the chains back up into the galleon. The rest of the men said nothing, the hawsers groaning forlornly as they stretched between the two moving ships.

The Spanish soldiers returned from below, two of them carrying one of the stiff deer hides. They spoke excitedly to Valenzuela and he turned and strode back to Samuel.

"Señor, as you must know, trade with the colonies in the Audiencia of Santo Domingo is limited to subjects of the Spanish Crown."

"By what right?" demanded Samuel.

Valenzuela's tone was polite. "Surely, señor, you know of Pope Alexander's bull giving title of that part of the new world to Castile?"

"Indeed!" said Samuel. "What a lot of rubbish that was. One man in Rome drawing a line around the globe?"

Valenzuela frowned. "Señor, I have no time to discuss it. I am confiscating your cargo."

Samuel's face was red with anger, but he said nothing further.

Valenzuela bowed. He turned to his men and gave them their orders. The Spanish soldiers began transferring the hides to the *San Miguel*.

Samuel, John and the others watched them sullenly. After an hour or so the Spanish lookout called down, "A ship approaches off the starboard!"

The sailors carrying the hides paused expectantly.

"Carry on," said Valenzuela loudly, and the men continued the transfer. In another hour they were finished. Most of the soldiers were back aboard the *San Miguel*, but a gang of six armed soldiers remained with Valenzuela.

Calling Crow and Red Feather came up from below, followed by two Spanish soldiers, one with a large pistol pointed at them, the other a drawn sword. "*Indios*," the man with the pistol called over to Valenzuela.

Valenzuela's eyes widened in surprise. He pointed to John, saying in Spanish, "Take the tall *Inglis* and the two of them aboard."

The sword-carrying soldier stepped toward John, but Samuel's voice stopped him.

"*¡Pare!*" Samuel stepped close to Valenzuela and said softly in English, "I won't let you take them."

The Spanish soldiers grew uneasy, trying to hear what was being said.

The Spanish lookout called down loudly, "The ship draws near . . . two leagues."

Valenzuela looked at Samuel as if he were mad. Valenzuela nodded in the direction of the big guns and the sharpshooters up in the rigging. "Señor, you cannot possibly stop us."

Samuel's face was as red as freshly carved beef. "Yes, señor, your men will surely kill us all, but you will be the first to die."

Valenzuela's soldiers drew nearer, but, not understanding English, did not know what was being said.

Samuel slowly put his hand on the pommel of his sword as he held the Spaniard's eye. "My brother and I will chop you into so many pieces the fish will thank us!"

Valenzuela's face grew taut with fear.

"*¿Comprende ud?*" said Samuel.

Valenzuela said nothing for a moment, then a weak smile appeared on his face. "Señor, my belly is full from a wonderful meal, the sun shines, my hold is full of fine hides . . . I feel very generous today. I tell you what." He indicated John and the two Indians. "I will make a gift of these three to you."

Valenzuela bowed gracefully and called to his soldiers. "Leave them!" The men sheathed their swords and began climbing the chains up into the galleon.

The Englishmen untied the hawsers and the two ships slowly drifted apart. The men of the *Contempt* held their breath as they stared at the bristling guns of the *San Miguel*.

"She will blow us to splinters before she puts up any sail," said Fenwick, voicing everyone's thoughts.

No one said anything as they stared at the run-out guns.

"Why the hell don't they fire?" said John.

"They won't," said Samuel, "not now." He pointed.

The ship the Spaniards had spotted was closing. The red cross painted on a pennant flying high on her mainmast identified her as English. The *San Miguel* unfurled the mainsail and the Englishmen cheered. Valenzuela turned the big ship and she sailed swiftly away.

John Newman was the first to speak. "Thank you, brother."

Samuel looked at him angrily. "If it had been you alone that they wanted, I would have let them take you!"

"Ha!" John laughed loudly, looking at Breuger and Miles. The two men smiled nervously. Samuel glared angrily at them and walked off, Fenwick and the Indians following him.

Breuger looked at the backs of the departing Indians. "Well," he said, "that's the end of the great trading company, eh? All this time and money wasted!"

Miles fingered his dagger as he stared at them. "Yeah. It's been a bloody disaster. Let's get rid of the savages tonight. I'm tired of looking at them!"

John turned to look at them. "No. Don't you dare hurt them."

Miles looked at him as if he had gone crazy.

"They are all we have to show for our great trading venture. We'll have to find some use for them, won't we?"

Breuger nodded appreciatively. Miles screwed up his eyes in confusion.

Chapter 19

To the men of the *Contempt*, the treeless, grass-covered cliffs appeared to push out of the distant mist one morning. Regular in height, they looked to have been carved from the land by a giant with a mighty sword. Now they held back the gray sea like a wall. The sight of the cliffs began to dispel the damp aura of disappointment and impotent rage that had gripped the Englishmen. While intriguing, the sight changed nothing for Calling Crow and Red Feather. Neither man spoke as they stood at the rail, their buffalo robes wrapped around them. The cold salt spray wetted their faces and the rolling deck at their feet. They thought of the past few days' events and pondered their meaning. Calling Crow had wanted to talk to Samuel about the loss of the hides, but he had disappeared below after the big Spanish ship departed.

Fenwick walked by and Calling Crow called him over. "How do we get the shooting sticks now, Fenwick?" Calling Crow asked him.

Fenwick looked at Calling Crow suspiciously. "What do you mean?"

"Now that the Spanish took Samuel's skins, how will he get us shooting sticks?"

Fenwick frowned nervously. "I don't know."

"Where is Samuel?"

Fenwick looked back toward the mainmast distractedly. "Samuel has fallen into a faint from exhaustion and lack of sleep. When he awakes, I will tell him of your concerns." Fenwick walked off.

"It is all a trick, Calling Crow," said Red Feather.

Calling Crow looked at him.

"The men on the other ship will give Samuel the skins later, that is what I think."

Calling Crow said nothing. He knew the Spanish and English were enemies, and that Samuel would not trick them. But Red Feather was willing to believe the worst about Samuel and Calling Crow knew it would be useless to talk to him. Calling Crow saw a small, single-masted ship off the port bow, moving up the coast. He pointed it out to Red Feather.

"It is an English ship," came a voice from behind them.

It was Samuel. He looked stronger to Calling Crow, but he was still evidently deeply disturbed by the loss of the skins. Fenwick stood at his side. Red Feather turned away to look at the sea.

"It is a small fishing boat engaged in the herring trade," Samuel explained. He tried to smile. "I am sorry about your skins."

Calling Crow shook his head. "They were your skins, Samuel."

Samuel frowned. "Yes, I suppose they were. Well, now they are Señor Valenzuela's skins."

"How can we get shooting sticks, Samuel?" said Calling Crow. "We have nothing to trade."

Samuel looked around at some men working. "It will take me longer, but I am sure we can get the muskets. I will have to get them on credit."

"What do you mean," said Calling Crow, mouthing the strange new word, "credit?"

"I will convince the merchants to give me the muskets for no skins now," said Samuel, "and to trust me to bring the hides to them later." Samuel's tone grew somber. "Will you be able to get your people to procure the skins we shall need?"

"Yes," said Calling Crow.

Samuel nodded. "Then I will bring the skins back to England to pay our backers."

"Are you sure they will give us the shooting sticks, Samuel," said Calling Crow, "on credit?"

Samuel nodded and turned away to look at the approaching coast.

"They will gladly do it," said Fenwick emphatically, "because if he does not return with the skins, they will take his house instead."

"One house for twenty muskets?" said Calling Crow, thinking of his own house, a house that could be constructed by a dozen people in a day or two. He looked at Red Feather and then Fenwick, questioningly. "That is good, is it not?"

Fenwick frowned in consternation at not being able to dispel their confusion. He threw up his hands. "One way or another," he said, "they will get their pound of flesh."

Later, with only the mizzen sail set, Samuel stood by the helmsman as he guided the *Contempt* into the crowded harbor. A noisy cloud of gulls circled overhead expectantly, craning their heads as they searched in vain for a meal of fish guts. The harbor was filled with the usual assortment of ships—large English and Dutch galleons, fishing cogs, small lateen-rigged caravels and a dozen or so rowed boats passing between them with passengers or goods. Along the quay, a row of three-floored, peaked-roofed houses and warehouses faced the harbor. Their white mortar facades were X-ed geometrically with massive, dark timbers in the black-and-white style. Some of the buildings had cranes affixed to their upper windows. Hundreds of bales and wooden barrels cluttered the street.

Calling Crow and Red Feather watched from the waist as one of Samuel's men threw a rope to some men on the quay. The *Contempt* groaned as her beams flexed against the quay. A boy spotted the two American natives and exclaimed in wonder. He ran down the quay, telling all he came across about the pair of wild men on the deck of the Newmans' ship. Before the *Contempt* was completely tied up, a crowd had gathered. Seamen, schoolboys, peddlers and fishwives looked up at the two native men with faces of dumb mirth or wondrous awe.

John Newman, Miles and Breuger were the first to leave the ship. John pushed angrily through the crowd, Miles and Breuger close behind him. Their progress slowed by the press of bodies, Miles and Breuger stopped to talk with the crowd. John pushed on, disappearing. Breuger and Miles's faces glowed with self-importance and newfound vigor as they talked about their ordeal. They repeatedly pointed up at the two natives.

Red Feather moved closer to Calling Crow to speak above the noise. "They are going to kill us!" He looked out bravely upon the agitated faces of the crowd.

Calling Crow looked round and spotted Samuel. The Englishman nodded calmly and came up to them. "Let us go," he said.

Samuel and Fenwick preceded Calling Crow and Red Feather down the plank. On the quay, the noisy talk and laughter swelled as the people pressed closer to Calling Crow and Red Feather. An old man, jostled round by the others, found himself face-to-face with the Newlanders and screamed, recoiling in shock and fear.

The crowd continued to grow, pushing in on them. Samuel turned to Calling Crow. "Stay close to me," he shouted.

Samuel pushed roughly through the milling throng, approaching a man with a white beard and reddened cheeks. The man wore a full-length leather jerkin and stood beside a large box full of small, silver-sided fish. The man's hairy, muscled arms were encrusted with a whitish accumulation of fish scales. Samuel shouted into the old man's ear and the man nodded.

Calling Crow and Red Feather followed Samuel and Fenwick into the shop and the old man came in behind them. Wordlessly he closed the heavy door and the wooden shutters, muting the noise of the crowd.

"Why are they so angry?" Calling Crow asked Samuel.

"They are not angry," said Samuel, "just excited. Welcome to England."

The old man then wordlessly led them through the shop and into an apartment in the back. They passed through a sitting room and a great kitchen. Then the old man opened a door and let them out into a quiet, stone-walled alleyway. They hurried down the stone passageway, past puddles of black water reeking with stench and flies. Coming out onto a broad carriageway, they walked quickly toward the fields at the edge of the town.

The crowd continued to linger in front of the fishmonger's shop. With wide eyes and animated faces, they compared the fleeting glimpses they had had of the two savages. Not far away, a boy left a print shop and walked quickly to a posting board affixed to two uprights at the quayside. Using a small hammer and some tacks, he posted a paper upon which was printed:

> In this year, 1575,
> two men were found in new lands
> far beyond Iceland,
> by two merchants of Bristol.
> These men had their bodies painted
> like the Picts of olde,
> and were dressed in animal skinnes.
> They were as rude and wilde as beastes
> and ate their meate raw.

Chapter 20

Calling Crow and Red Feather stood before Samuel's large stone house. Samuel stood up on the steps at the doors, looking down at the other two men.

"What is the matter with him now?" said Samuel in exasperation.

Calling Crow turned to Red Feather and spoke rapidly in Muskogee. "He does not want to enter," Calling Crow said finally to Samuel. "He will wait out here."

"Very well," said Samuel. "But, Calling Crow, you must come now. I want you to meet my wife and child." An old woman appeared at the doors and opened one of them. Samuel entered and Calling Crow followed him. Calling Crow found the house to be much like the boxes the white people used to put their things inside of. It was a grand box for people, with massive thick walls. There were many prettily colored things inside, but Calling Crow did not have the opportunity to look at them closely as he followed Samuel along one of the many square tunnels. Samuel paused and opened the door to another box. "You and Red Feather can stay here."

Calling Crow went inside. The air was hot and stale, and there wasn't enough of it. Calling Crow knew that neither he nor Red Feather would be able to sleep in such a place. "We will sleep outside," he said.

"And when it rains?"

"I like the rain," said Calling Crow.

"You can stay in the spring house," said Samuel. "Yes, that is where you and he shall stay."

"What is that?" said Calling Crow.

"The house is built over a spring and it is cooler there. It is where we keep our food."

A cry came from out in the long square tunnel, then running feet, one pair belonging to an adult, Calling Crow heard, the other to a child. Samuel turned and the whitest woman Calling Crow had ever seen embraced the Englishman tearfully. Her face was oval and pallid, her eyebrows plucked out. A mass of thick brown hair pushed out from both sides of a hat pulled down tightly on her head. Her cheeks were painted with two small red discs. Calling Crow thought that perhaps she had painted her cheeks that way to pay homage to Father Sun. She wore a long black dress down to her feet, but the top was cut open to reveal much of her white breasts. A charming girl clung to her dress. Although dressed like her mother, the girl was evidently in good health, with a full found face and natural color.

"Thank God you have returned to me!" the woman cried. "How did you fare? We worried so for you!" The woman turned to the girl. "Didn't we, Catherine?"

Samuel held the woman's hand and gestured into the room. When the woman saw Calling Crow, her face showed a great fear and she again held tightly to Samuel.

"This is Calling Crow. He is the lord of his town, Coosa Town. Calling Crow, this is my wife, Frances, and my daughter, Catherine."

The woman said nothing and Samuel went on. "He and his lieutenant, Red Feather, will be staying in the spring house for a time."

Frances attempted to smile. "Make curtsey to the gentleman, Catherine," said Frances.

The little girl bowed sweetly.

"I will see that Elizabeth brings some supper for them," said Frances. She walked away, pulling the smiling girl along reluctantly behind her.

"Come," said Samuel, "let us rejoin Red Feather and I will show you the spring house."

As they walked through one of the long square tunnels, Calling Crow asked Samuel, "Why did you build your house so solidly?"

"Well," said Samuel, "it is better that way, I suppose."

"But," said Calling Crow, "what do you do when it is time to move the town?"

Samuel laughed. "We don't move our towns. This town will be here for a long, long time."

Calling Crow and Red Feather spent an uneventful night in the cave-like spring house. When they stepped outside in the morning, a waist-high mist covered the land, and the grasses were wet with dew. Calling Crow looked longingly at the dark, distant patch of forest. Then he and Red Feather walked through the stone gate and across the field to a small stream. They followed it as it snaked across Samuel's land, stopping at the place where the stream dropped down to the height of a man's knee. It splashed onto some rocks and gravel before meandering on and into one of two small woods rising from the mist in the distance. The two men separated to wash and pray silently.

Calling Crow knelt at the stream. As he looked down at the smooth, colored pebbles beneath the water, he thought of his son and wife, his daughter and the tiny one in her belly. He thought of his people, all of them so far away on the other side of the great water. Already he had suffered a major setback in his plan to bring back the shooting sticks. His people desperately needed these guns or they would have to flee from the Timucua. He prayed to his spirit guide for help; he must not fail them.

He heard the flutter of a bird overhead. A dark blur raced toward the distant woods. The smell of strange herbs and flowers intrigued his nose as he rested his eyes on the green grasses growing on the stream bank. He became aware of the voice of the stream. It seemed to be singing to him, offering him reassurance. "All will be well," it sang. "All will be well in time."

Yes, he thought, it is so. Did not Sees Far see that in his vision?

"Yes," the waters sang, "all will be well."

When Calling Crow and Red Feather returned to the spring house, one of the white slaves whom the English called servants was just leaving. She looked back at them worriedly before hurrying into the big house. Calling Crow and Red Feather saw that she had left some meat and bread for them. They sat in the grass as they ate.

After the sun rose to burn away the mist, Samuel came out of the house with Frances and little Catherine. Samuel told Calling Crow he was taking them to his church to pray. A horse-drawn carriage pulled up. Calling Crow was familiar with horses and carts from his days as a slave on the Spanish island of Hispaniola. However, although Red Feather had once seen some Spanish horses from a distance, he had never seen one up close, and he had never seen a carriage. He stood on the road in a state of confusion as Samuel and his family climbed inside.

"Let us go inside," Calling Crow said.

Red Feather remained immobilized by his fear. "No. This is bad medicine. I will not get inside."

Calling Crow climbed up and onto the wooden bench seat with the coachman. Red Feather looked worriedly about and then followed his chief tenuously.

The carriage lurched forward and soon they were speeding along the flat road. Red Feather's fear changed into awe at their flight. Several times he stood to turn around and watch the earth moving rapidly away behind them.

Calling Crow and Red Feather climbed down from the carriage and looked up at the tall dark stone structure. There were other carriages and horses tied up, but the people had all gone inside.

"Why do they come here to pray?" said Red Feather in their native tongue. "It looks like such a sad place."

"This is where their god is," said Calling Crow, "the Spanish god too. They will reside only in great houses such as these."

"Not in the forest or behind the sun?" said Red Feather.

"No," said Calling Crow.

Frances led the way up the stairs of the church and down the stone aisle between the wooden benches. Calling Crow and Red Feather were aware of the people turning to point and talk about them, but they couldn't take their eyes off the strange pictures of red and blue light that shone down from the walls. Calling Crow and Red Feather walked slowly down the aisle. A loud voice, such that they had never heard before, sang out suddenly in a sorrowful wail. They stopped and looked around as the sound grew in volume. Samuel, Frances and Catherine had already seated themselves and turned to them.

Samuel waved to Calling Crow to come forward. "Come," he whispered hoarsely, "it is all right." He pointed to the front of the church, at what looked to Calling Crow and Red Feather like tall straight golden trees growing against the wall. "The organ, only the organ."

"It is war cries!" said Red Feather. He looked around worriedly, sure an attack would come at any moment.

Calling Crow stared at the golden trees. A deep-throated bellow of a voice reverberated in the stone church and he realized that it was the voice of the English god.

The people looked at Calling Crow and Red Feather angrily as the sound grew louder, seeming as if it would shake the very roof off the church. Calling Crow started forward, but Red Feather gripped his shoulder painfully and would not move.

Little Catherine slid off the bench and walked back down the aisle. Smiling shyly, she looked up at the two towering men and took each of them by the hand. Wordlessly, she pulled them along and they sat on Samuel and Frances's bench.

I*n* the large kitchen, Samuel sat on the bench before the fire, eating a bowl of oatmeal with a wooden spoon. He had one of Calling Crow's deerskin shirts on the bench beside him. The garment, of a uniform tan color, had a multitude of tiny pearlescent shells stitched to the sleeves, making a geometric pattern—all of it Calling Crow's wife Green Bird Woman's handiwork. Samuel's brother, John, stood leaning up against the warm bricks of the hearth. Elizabeth swung a blackened, steaming kettle away from the flames, then stirred it quickly with a spoon before swinging it back. She brought a bowl of water and a cloth to Samuel and he washed his hands and lips.

"Do you really think they will loan you the money for the muskets?" said John.

Samuel frowned pensively. He ran his hand over the shirt's beadwork. "After I show them this they will."

John shook his head. "Barrister and Langley are wool merchants, brother. They care not about skins."

Samuel folded up the shirt. "A gentleman by the name of Wilbye will be there. He owns a large tanning and dyeing works in Plymouth. He will sway the others. I am sure of it."

Samuel stood. "Well, John. Frances has awakened by now. I will tell her good-bye and then I'll needs be off. When will I see you again?"

John shook his head. "I will see you in church, brother."

"Very well."

John walked out to the courtyard and Samuel climbed the stairs to his wife's bedroom.

The humidity and heat in the bedroom were oppressive. Despite the opened window on the other side of the room, no air entered as Samuel stood looking over at his wife. Frances sat before the dresser on the only chair in the room. Her servants had already dressed her and she gazed into the mirror, a hairbrush in her hand. She suddenly hung her head disconsolately. He noticed that the milky skin of her neck was reddened by both the heat and her mood.

"You must give this business up, Samuel," she said. "I fear for you."

He said nothing and she looked at him, waiting for him to reply.

"I am sorry," he said finally.

Frances's eyes welled with tears. "Sorry? Do you know what it was like for me while you were gone? Do you know how much I worried?" Her look grew angry. "Do you?"

"Of course," he said softly.

"And you still pursue this?"

He said nothing, turning instead at what he thought was the sound of one of the house servants.

"You have grown odd from your stay in that hot place! Forget Barrister and the others and give up this crazy business."

"Frances," he said in exasperation, "one of these gentlemen has come all the way from Plymouth. If I'm to get money for the muskets, I must go to them."

She turned to him. "No, forget the muskets. Your brother John is in no hurry to go back there. Why don't you show some sense, as he does?"

Catherine's happy, staccato laughter came through the opened window, then Calling Crow's steady voice, then the voice of Anne, little Catherine's nursemaid.

"I cannot forget them, Frances," Samuel said. "I must take Calling Crow and Red Feather back."

"Why?" she pleaded. "They'd be better off here than they would running naked through the forest! Teach them the language. Then they could work in the fields and make their own way."

"No," he said firmly. "They have families! I have promised that I would take them back."

"But that was before the Spaniards stole your cargo," she said. "You are no longer beholden to them."

"But I am," he said emphatically, "because I have given them my word!"

"Samuel," she said, "you are not making sense." She looked at him as if he'd been struck with brain fever, or if he were possessed by the devil.

"I am sorry," he said.

Frances turned away. "And so am I, my dear. So am I." She sobbed into her hands.

Samuel took the reins of his horse from his lackey, Robert, and hoisted himself up into the saddle. Little Catherine waved good-bye from where she sat on the lawn with Anne. Calling Crow and Red Feather sat nearby. Catherine had become quite taken with the two natives, and they with her.

Samuel rode through the gate and turned down the road to town. Frances's melancholia had affected him and he felt as if he were in a state of somnambulism. She would realize how important this all was at a later time when his present efforts would bear fruit. For now, he must try to be understanding of her fears, but carry on just the same. The flower-sweetened air pushed down on him like molasses, slowing all movement. It seemed as if things would soon stop. Samuel was already tired of the tranquil pace of his old, reclaimed life and he felt that if he was not soon off he would never go. He would become immobilized, suspended like a spider fallen into a glass of treacle. To throw off his lethargy, he remembered his thrill at escaping the Timucua. He remembered the deep greens reflected in the black water ponds of that lovely, wild place. He remembered the excitement of hunting deer and turkey with Calling Crow. Another remembrance pushed against his consciousness. Despite his black feelings of guilt, he let it in. It was the memory of the willing, girlish face of Bright Eyes, the memory of her Eve-like, innocent nakedness. He tried to tell himself he was going back because of the promise he had made to Calling Crow, not for her. Yet, memories of her still filled his head; the wanting look in her eyes, her beautiful brown limbs, the feel of her beneath him.

Frances wiped her eyes with her handkerchief. She heard a noise at the door. It was John. "I told you he would not be talked out of it," he said.

She looked at him angrily. "Who put these wild notions in his head, John?"

"Not I, Frances. It is none of my doing."

Laughter floated in the little window. Frances went over and looked out. Catherine and Anne sat on the lawn across from the two savages. Frances felt a twinge of fear. She would talk to Anne about this later. She did not like Catherine getting too close to them.

John joined her at the window. "Catherine is charmed by them."

"Ugh, please! If they would only go away, all this madness would stop!"

"They'll not go anywhere on their own," said John. "They'll need some encouragement."

Frances looked at him suspiciously. "What do you mean?"

"They'll need some inducement to go away. Perhaps I can provide it. I have a business proposition for them."

Frances held up her hand. "Don't say another word, John. I don't want to hear about it. I only want them gone and my husband back. That is all." She started crying softly.

John smiled. "I understand, Frances. Just as I want my brother back. We will speak no more of it."

Red Feather looked down in confusion at the tiny child. "What is she saying?" he asked Calling Crow.

"I am not sure," said Calling Crow. "She wants her and me to do some kind of dance, and she wants you to be our pole, maypole, she said."

Red Feather took the two long strips of red cloth Catherine gave him, the other ends falling to earth. Catherine took one and laughingly handed it to Calling Crow, then picked up the other. "Tell him to hold his hands up to the sky," she told

Calling Crow. He told Red Feather of Catherine's request. "I think it is another of their prayer rituals."

Red Feather's stoic face was unchanged as he raised his long arms up to the gray sky.

"Go around, go around," the child cried with delight as she began dancing about Red Feather's tall unmoving form. Calling Crow followed her.

"Ring around the rosy, pocket full of posies," the girl sang laughingly.

Red Feather turned slowly as he held on to the cloth streamers. It was then that he spotted the sickly white face of Samuel's wife looking down at them. She looked close to death and Red Feather understood why the Englishman was looking for another wife. Still, Red Feather's anger returned; Samuel should have looked elsewhere. Samuel's brother's face appeared at the window beside her.

". . . Ashes, ashes, all fall down!"

Catherine fell backward and burst out laughing, distracting Red Feather. Calling Crow joined her in her mirth, laughing as he sat down upon the grass. Red Feather looked up at the window again but the two faces were gone.

Catherine's slave ran out of the house. "It is almost noon-time, child, time to sup."

Catherine turned away from the woman to Calling Crow and Red Feather. "Almost noon," she cried excitedly. "Come and see! Come!" She took Calling Crow and Red Feather by the hand and pulled them toward the house. Red Feather balked at the steps.

"Quickly," Catherine cried. The woman looked at Catherine worriedly then went inside.

"Let us go inside, Red Feather," said Calling Crow. "She wants badly to show us something."

Red Feather relented and followed Calling Crow into the house. Catherine led them to the biggest room in the house. She pulled them to a thickly padded bench near the wall and indicated that they should sit.

She then pulled herself up between them and pointed to a large wooden thing not far away. The thing had a round face and a wooden tail that wagged back and forth. There were two arrows on the face. The shorter arrow already pointed straight up to the sky, and the other, longer one was moving to join it in little steps. With an almost imperceptible click, the large arrow joined its smaller brother in pointing up at the heavens and the thing erupted in song and music. Red Feather leapt backward over the bench as Catherine clapped her hands together happily.

"Ring around the rosy," she sang again, "pocket full of posies."

Calling Crow joined in. "Ashes, ashes, all fall down!"

Behind an alehouse, three men sat at a table in the dappled shade cast by a trellis full of roses. The alehouse wall behind them was completely covered with curled and age-browned postings and handbills. John Newman leaned back against the wall and propped his booted feet up on a cask beneath the table. He calmly arranged the playing cards in his hand. Across from him, Warren Hopkins, the fat owner of the alehouse, pinched his chin, a mere U-shaped stitch in the fat of his neck, as he studied his cards. To his left, Hugh Collier, a bear of a man with a bald head and a large, bushy gray beard put down the deck of cards and picked up his own hand. Collier owned a fair that traveled the countryside, wintering in Hartford. An old acquaintance of John's, he was here because of an offer the recently returned adventurer had made him. It concerned the purchase of two "wild men" to exhibit at his fair. John had said they might get a chance to see them this day.

As Collier studied his cards, the muted hoofbeats of passing horses filtered through the trellis roses.

"I'll give you fifty pounds each for them," said Collier, "sight unseen."

"No," said John calmly. "I'll not sell them."

"What?" said Collier, laying his cards down. "Then what in hades did you bring me up here for, anyway?"

John continued to study his cards unperturbed. "I'll not sell them. I'll rent them to you, for a percentage of your receipts."

"Ha!" said Collier. "You must be crazy." He picked up his cards.

Drunken singing burst upon them from the opened back door of the alehouse.

"Egads," said John in annoyance, "no more spirits for them, Hopkins."

Hopkins looked over his hand unconcernedly. "Ha! I've heard worse singing in the theater."

John smiled. "I've heard worse in church."

"Aye," said Hopkins, "so have I, especially when it's my wife's turn to solo."

John and Collier laughed softly.

"So, what do you say, Hugh?" John said.

"I already said it," Collier said, "you're crazy!"

Another drunken chorus erupted from inside, degenerating into hoots and guffaws.

"Soon they'll be dancing on your new tables, eh, Hopkins?" said John.

Hopkin's fat face grew pink. "They wouldn't dare." Still, he turned round to look worriedly inside at the dimly visible figures.

A boy ran in from the street and went up to John. "Sir," he said excitedly.

John looked up from his cards.

"Your brother is coming in his carriage. The savages are riding up with the coachman." The boy ran back outside.

Hopkins threw down his cards. "I want to see this." He quickly went out through the arched entryway in the trellis.

"Wait," John called out to him, "let's see your hand first."

"He had a lousy hand," said Collier, "that's what it is."

"How do you know?" said John.

"I looked," said Collier. He put his cards facedown on the table. "Let's go look at these fellows you think I'll want for my show."

John threw his cards down and got to his feet. He and Collier walked under the arch and out into the dying, autumnal light. Samuel's carriage was just turning the corner. A swarm of boys ran in the dust behind it, laughing and shouting at the two Indians seated high up on the bench seat. Despite the laughter of the boys, John felt only anger at the sight. The two savages sat bolt upright and looked straight ahead. The sight of them reminded John of all the money he had lost. Damn their heathen souls! He'd recover some of that if he had to skin them and sell their bloody hides! He went back inside the garden to wait for Collier. One handbill on the wall caught his eye. It was Collier's, and announced the coming of his traveling fair. There were plays and acrobats, jugglers . . .

Outside, the boys chattered loudly, as if they had just witnessed the second coming. Their excitement and wonder was music to John's ears. Surely Collier would see the possibilities. The savages would bring many, many people into the fair, making its owner richer, and providing a nice income for John Newman.

Collier came through the archway and sat down. Folding his hands before him, he said, "When can I take possession of the merchandise?"

For the first time in a long time the shadow of a smile moved John's thin lips. "Tonight."

Chapter 22

As Samuel's carriage wound up the curve of Barrister's drive, Samuel hoped that everything would go well. He had not wanted the two Newlanders to have to submit to this, but Barrister had insisted. The investors all must get a look at the natives and their skin shirts, he said. The carriage lurched to a stop and Samuel got out. As he watched the two natives climb down, he prayed silently that all would go well.

Later, Calling Crow and Red Feather stood on a raised platform that had been built for them in the middle of the great room. They did not use the chairs that had been placed there for them. Most of the people had already inspected Calling Crow and Red Feather closely and now clustered in groups near the food-bearing tables, looking up at them occasionally. The room reeked of the pouches of crushed flowers the women wore about their necks and the burnt odor of the many candles that lit the room like a sky of bright stars. Only one man had questioned Calling Crow about his people and his village. The others had simply passed by, eyeing Calling Crow and Red Feather curiously. The evening passed slowly and finally Calling Crow saw Samuel shake a man's hand vigorously and bow. Samuel started over and Calling Crow could tell by the look of satisfaction on Samuel's face that they could leave.

Calling Crow stepped off the platform to meet Samuel, and Red Feather followed him. Many people turned to watch them leave. Outside, the air was cooler and free of the nauseating smells. "It is done," said Samuel, "they have agreed to lend me the money."

"When will we get the shooting sticks?" said Calling Crow, "and when can we board the ship and start back?"

"All in good time," said Samuel contentedly.

Calling Crow and Red Feather climbed up with the coachman and Samuel got inside. The springless carriage banged and bounced along the blackened road. Almost an hour later it stopped in front of Samuel's house. Calling Crow and Red Feather climbed down as the coachman opened the door for Samuel. A servant with a lamp appeared at the door, waiting for Samuel as the carriage moved away. Samuel turned to the two Newlanders before starting up the stairwell. He smiled briefly. "We will talk more in the morning. Now it's time to sleep."

Calling Crow and Red Feather walked quietly down the carriageway to the spring house. They spoke softly in their native Muskogee. "Why doesn't he get us the shooting sticks tonight?" said Red Feather, "then we could begin the journey back in the morning."

"It will take longer than that," said Calling Crow.

"I don't like it," said Red Feather. "Did you see the way they looked at us in the big house? I don't trust them, especially Samuel."

Calling Crow's voice was full of confidence. "Samuel is an honorable man. He will keep his word. You will see. Soon we will be home with the shooting sticks."

Calling Crow bowed his head slightly to pass through the low doorway of the spring house. He smelled something in the black interior that did not belong there but it was too late to react. A club thudded into his head, stunning him. He lunged at the man who had struck him, knocking him down, but then more men rushed in, piling on him and Red Feather from both sides. Blows rained down upon them and then they were quickly bound up with cords.

All night long, the caravan of carts slowly swayed and creaked along a rutted dirt road. In one of the larger carts, Calling Crow and Red Feather lay, their arms bound tightly behind them. Day dawned and the early winter sun rose and shone dully upon the land. One of the bound men made no sound, but the other moaned in pain. No one went to them. Sour-faced men with switches and whips drove the oxen mercilessly all day without stopping, and on into the night.

*   *   *

The day after the Americans disappeared, Samuel hurried
down the steps of his estate. A boy held his horse for him as
he quickly mounted. As Samuel headed toward the gate, little
Catherine ran over. Anne, her nursemaid, raced protectively
after her. Catherine looked up at Samuel, her eyes wide with
fear.

"Father, they are gone," she said, tears appearing in her
eyes.

Samuel reined in his horse. "I know, child," he called
down to her. "I will find them. Don't worry."

Anne led Catherine back to the house. Samuel rode through
the gates of his estate and down the tree-lined dirt road. His
mind focused on the disappearance of Calling Crow and Red
Feather. He suspected they had come to harm and for that he
felt a great guilt. Perhaps they had gone out walking, straying
onto someone's estate and been killed as robbers. Or perhaps
robbers had accosted them. Something had certainly happened
to them! He simply could not believe his wife and brother's
contention that they had run away. Calling Crow's only desire
was to get the muskets and return to his people.

Samuel looked out across the fields where the row of trees
ended. Divided by low walls of stone, they stretched away
for leagues. At the distant edge of his view, a rainstorm
moved across the sky. He could see the rain coming down
from the dark clouds, waving like a veil in the wind. Up the
road, Samuel saw a man and woman walking a path between
the fields. He reined up his horse on the shoulder of the road
and waited for them. They were country people, and the man
wore a plain, white woolen shirt, black breeches and hose,
and a wide-brimmed hat. He carried a hoe in his gnarled hand,
and a basket full of green and red apples over his shoulder.
The woman wore a wide-brimmed hat and a tan woolen gown
with a pleated bodice; the gown was long and obscured her
feet. She also carried a basket of apples. They walked over
to Samuel.

Samuel nodded. "Have you heard anything of two
strangely dressed men passing through here? They were staying with me but they have disappeared."

The man's thick, white brows rose, etching deep lines in his sun-reddened brow. "How dressed, sir?" the man said.

"They may have been wearing shirts made of skins, smooth skins that look like linen from a distance, and skin garments over their bottoms that they tie around them with a belt."

The woman frowned at the description.

The man's face paled with worry. "Wild Irish, were they?"

Samuel shook his head. "No, they are natives from the new lands of America."

The man and woman exchanged looks of astonished relief. The man shook his head. "We have not seen or heard anything."

Samuel nodded and rode off. The man and woman remained where they were, talking excitedly. Samuel rode on and searched all morning. He had lunch in the town and then continued his search. His frustration made him weary. He had been everywhere and no one had seen or heard anything. It was as if Calling Crow and Red Feather had been swallowed up by the earth. Samuel realized suddenly that with Calling Crow and Red Feather gone, there was no reason to go back to the New Lands, and that meant he would not be going back to Bright Eyes. She would have his child in another four or five months. What would it look like? he wondered. The thought of not seeing it and her saddened him greatly. Then guilt welled up in him. He had a wife and child, here.

He forced himself to think about the present. What about the two natives? Where were they now? He thought of the many things that might have happened to them, none of them good.

Chapter 23

Low marine clouds obscured the winter sky as Swordbrought and the two other hunters moved slowly along the edge of the swamplands. The village had almost collected the last of the skins and would have them ready for Calling Crow and the English when they returned. Ignoring the men, a hidden woodpecker rapped loudly, his tempo rising slightly. The woodpecker ceased, then began again. The cycle was repeated over and over. Upwind of the men, the white-tailed deer they were trailing heard something and turned to look back nervously. They froze. The deer looked straight at the men, its uplifted nostrils dilating as it tasted the cool, damp air. Getting no predator scent, it turned away in confusion and moved toward the forest. Swordbrought and the others followed the trail of the deer into the darkness of the forest. A human cry rang out and many Timucua with clubs emerged from their hiding places. They raced at Swordbrought and his two companions. Swordbrought released the arrow nocked into his bow and it went deep into the chest of a Timucua brave running directly at him. The brave's eyes closed in pain as he went down, the brave behind him tripping over him. Swordbrought turned and saw that his companions were already pinned down under a press of bodies. A club grazed his forehead and powerful hands seized his shoulder. He could taste blood as he spun around dizzily and slipped out of the surprised man's sweaty grip.

A moment later Swordbrought was running back the way they had come, with four Timucua in pursuit. He could hear their breathing behind him. He prayed to his spirit guide, the hawk, and he could feel its power flowing into his legs. Then, like a hawk, he fairly flew over the trail, his feet hardly touching the earth. He soon began to outdistance his pursuers. It was then that the arrow cut his side. If he had not moved to the side to dodge a jutting tree branch, the arrow would have driven itself deep into his back. Another arrow went high over his head and into the trees and then the Timucua gave up the chase. Swordbrought's head, side and leg were covered with blood when he finally ran into the palisade of the village.

All the skin coverings on the many entrances to the *chokafa* were thrown back to admit the light of day, but to no avail. So many people crowded around them that little light got inside and therefore many torches were required to illuminate the interior. In the center of the *chokafa,* the venerable old men sat on their raised, skin-covered pallets, surrounded by the braves, who sat on woven mats in orderly rows according to rank. Other villagers sat in rows around them, filling the entire structure. Bright Eyes was part of the crowd looking into the *chokafa*. With the others, she watched quietly as her brother, Swordbrought, spoke. With a firm voice, he described how he and the others had been attacked and how he had managed to escaped. Swordbrought's face had already been ceremonially blackened by one of the medicine men to indicate that he was in mourning for the man that he had killed. Even from the distance, Bright Eyes could see the large cut and bruise on Swordbrought's head. Along with everyone else, she listened closely to his words, nodding her head in appreciation of his ordeal and his bravery. Despite the support the people felt for Swordbrought, Bright Eyes could feel his great sadness. She knew her brother well. He would be wishing that he had died in the attack, or that it was he that had been taken prisoner by the Timucua.

The old men conferred among themselves for a short while and then Two Clouds rose to his feet. The *chokafa* grew silent as the people waited for Two Clouds to speak. The old man's powerful voice reached the farthest corners of the great building. "The Timucua are becoming bold and we don't have enough braves to repulse them. We cannot wait for Calling Crow to come back with shooting sticks. We have to take action. We should consider moving the village."

A collective gasp went through the people. Things must be bad indeed! Dangerous! Never had they had to run and hide.

Bright Eyes felt another worry tugging at her. She thought of Calling Crow returning and them being gone. If they abandoned this place, could not the Timucua take it over? The thought of her father falling into their hands was horrifying. The child inside could feel her fear and kicked her painfully. With her hand on her belly, she backed out of the crowd. Move the village! Was there no other way? She must find Green Bird Woman and tell her.

In the chokafa, an older brave called Corn Planter was telling the old men about a valley he had found as a young man far to the west. The old men and others listened with interest. A sudden commotion came from one of the entrances. Green Bird Woman pushed into the crowd, followed by Bright Eyes and another young woman, who held a baby on her hip. Everyone turned and looked at them, and the baby stopped its fidgeting and held tightly to its mother, its dark eyes wide and wary. The women sat on the mats.

Corn Planter looked over, angry at the interruption. He turned back to the Council and continued speaking. When he finished, Green Bird Woman rose to speak. Corn Planter stood again. "What is this woman doing, rising to speak?"

Green Bird Woman shrieked like a hawk and all eyes turned to her. "I am not any woman. I am Green Bird Woman! I am the wife of Calling Crow." She pointed her finger at Corn Planter. "And you shall listen to what I have to say."

Corn Planter's face darkened with anger, but he sat silently.

Green Bird Woman addressed her words to all the people in the chokafa. "We should not move the village. Calling Crow and Red Feather will come back to us. Has not Sees Far said they would?"

No one said anything and one of the braves stood. "I say we attack the Timucua now!"

Several braves echoed his words. "Attack!"

"No!" cried Green Bird Woman. "We must wait. All the reports say that they are too many. To attack now would jeopardize the entire village."

The young brave was defiant. "We should attack! I am not afraid to die." He looked round at the braves in the *chokafa*. "War!"

"No!" shouted Green Bird Woman. "I am not afraid to die either." She pointed to the babe on the woman's hip and it clung tighter to its mother. "Would you put that young life at risk? And all the others?" Green Bird Woman pointed to Bright Eyes's bulging belly. "And what about those who have not even come out yet? Do you want their blood on your hands?"

The brave opened his mouth to speak.

"Don't say that vile thing which is on your lips," said Green Bird Woman, "or I shall fight you myself!"

The brave said nothing, and sat back down. Green Bird Woman looked at the people a moment longer and then sat herself.

Two Clouds stood and all eyes turned to him. "There is another course of action that we have not discussed. We could send a brave to the Muskogee confederation at Cussitaw Town. He could ask them to provide us with men to fight off the Timucua."

Two Clouds sat as the *chokafa* buzzed with talk. A man stood and addressed Two Clouds.

"How do we know that they will help us?"

Two Clouds's brow furrowed. "They will help us. We are Muskogee people, are we not?"

Satisfied, the man sat.

Two Clouds turned and spoke with the venerable old men. The buzz of talk swelled while his back was turned, then died when he turned to face the people. "The other old men and I have decided," he said. "Someone will go to Cussitaw Town for help. Now we must decide who this representative will be." Two Clouds sat as the people began speculating on who would be chosen.

An old man, Bent Ears, rose to speak. "Swordbrought should go. His recent escape from the Timucua proves that, like his father, he has strong medicine and the protection of a powerful spirit guide."

He sat as several of the old men nodded in agreement.

A brave stood quickly. "Yes, Swordbrought is brave, and his spirit guide has brought him back to us, but he is too young for this mission. We should send an older, more experienced brave."

With many pairs of eyes upon him, Swordbrought suddenly felt a great sadness. He knew he had done the right thing. After all, he could not have fought off all the Timucua, yet still he wished he had not had to leave the braves behind. He wished that it was he who had been captured, and that it was one of the other braves who had escaped to tell the tale.

Corn Planter raised his hand to speak and was recognized. He glared over at Green Bird Woman and then spoke. "Grandfather, I nominate Crying Wolf to take our request to Cussitaw Town."

Several other braves called out Crying Wolf's name with admiration.

"Why Crying Wolf?" said Two Clouds.

"He has the bravest spirit of all the young men," said Corn Planter, "and despite his young age, he has already killed a man in battle." Corn Planter sat.

Bent Ears rose to his feet. "Swordbrought, too, has killed a man. He has just told us this."

"Yes, it is so," cried out several other braves in agreement.

Swordbrought's heart swelled at the prospect of redeeming himself. They must send him . . .

"But no one else has seen this," said Corn Planter, getting to his feet, "whereas many braves saw Crying Wolf kill the Apalachee brave."

Another brave got to his feet. "It is so," he said. He turned round to the assemblage. "I saw Crying Wolf kill the Apalachee."

Bent Ears waited till the man sat, then addressed Two Clouds and the old men. "Even though Crying Wolf is very brave, he is too headstrong. He follows his own path and does not want to listen to others."

Bent Ears sat and several braves jumped to their feet. "Send Crying Wolf," they cried, "he is the bravest!"

Green Bird Woman walked to the front of the assemblage. She spoke softly to Two Clouds, her words lost in the rumble of voices. She then turned and headed for the entrance, followed by Bright Eyes and the other woman. The buzzing of voices rose in volume when the women had gone.

"Quiet!" Two Clouds looked at the people sternly. He turned and addressed Corn Planter. "Corn Planter, what if Crying Wolf meets two men on the trail? Can he kill both of them and still get to Cussitaw Town."

Corn Planter quickly got to his feet. "Of course," he said confidently. He sat back down.

"What if he meets five men," said Two Clouds.

Corn Planter again got to his feet. This time his response was not as emphatic. "He would kill them, of course." Corn Planter could see that Two Clouds was not finished and remained standing.

Two Clouds probed further. "What if Crying Wolf met ten men on the trail? That is a lot for one man, even for one as brave and strong as Crying Wolf. Could he kill them all and continue on to Cussitaw Town?"

Corn Planter was at a loss for words.

"Sit," said Two Clouds. He looked around at the assemblage. "Strength and fighting prowess are not enough. We have to consider other qualities."

Bent Ears raised his hand and Two Clouds recognized him. Bent Ears rose to his feet and turned to the assemblage. "Two Clouds is wise to show us this. This is why we should send Swordbrought. He has *ottsi,* yes, and he is a good fighter. He is also the fastest brave in the village and has won every race he has run. More importantly, however, like his father, he is possessed of great dignity and is a very convincing speaker for one so young." Bent Ears sat.

In the rear of the assemblage, an old man stood angrily. "What if Swordbrought is killed or taken captive? Would not Calling Crow be very angry with us if we allowed that to happen?"

Bent Ears got to his feet and shook his head. "No! Calling Crow would be very angry with us if we did not give Swordbrought a chance to win honors for himself. Send Swordbrought."

The man sat. The din continued to grow, no one rising to speak, no single argument prevailing. Swordbrought looked around. No one would meet his eyes. A great despair threatened to overwhelm him. Suddenly he felt his father's strong presence, as if he were standing right beside him.

Swordbrought stood. The voices died down and a heavy silence hung over the people. Swordbrought looked at the old men and spoke. "Two good braves are gone today. Coosa Town cannot continue to suffer such losses. Do not send your best braves on this mission. Send me instead and let me prove my bravery. Give me six days to go to Cussitaw Town and bring back some Muskogee braves to help us. If I fail to return, then send another brave." Swordbrought turned and faced the assemblage, his face proud and fierce. "But send me first!"

Two Clouds rose to address the assemblage. "What say you all? Shall we send Swordbrought?"

Most of the hands went up. Swordbrought turned to look out upon the many faces and the majority of the hands went up.

Two Clouds raised his hands. "It is decided. Swordbrought will go."

People began to file out of the *chokafa*. Two Clouds turned round to the old men. "Take Swordbrought to Sees Far. Tell him to prepare him for his journey."

Swordbrought sat on an overturned basket in the dimly lit rear of his mother's large house. Green Bird Woman stood beside the fire. Her shadow moved on the walls as she packed a doeskin pouch for Swordbrought. Although he was glad they had chosen him to take his people's request to Cussitaw Town, he regretted the worry it would cause his mother. Outwardly she would be brave, but he knew her well enough to know she was already worried.

She came over to him with the pouch. Sitting on the mat before him, she opened it up and took out a gray blanket she had woven from the English wool. She held it up to him, squeezing the nap of it between her finger and thumb. "Feel it," she said.

He did. It was a thick, tight weave.

"It will keep you warm wherever you sleep."

He nodded his thanks and she took two wrapped bundles from the pouch and opened them. One contained dried venison, the other parched corn.

"It is good, Mother," he said. He began putting the things back in the pack.

"There is one more thing," she said, smiling sadly. She produced a dried doeskin about the size of a man's shirt. There were stains on it that looked like blood.

"This is what I wrapped you with when you were a tiny little baby." Overcome, she looked over at the fire momentarily, her eyes glossy with held-back tears. She turned back to him and quickly folded the doeskin up. "Take it with you and when you are far away, bury it. Now you are a man and there is no more need of it."

In the morning, the people of Coosa Town went about their business as Swordbrought walked down the path to the palisade entrance. He walked quickly across the field toward the forest. His bow and a quiver of arrows hung from his shoulders and two pouches hung from his belt. One was the pouch his mother had given him, which contained his food and blankets, and the other, larger pouch contained the village's sacred pipe of peace. As a bearer of the pipe, he would be given safe passage by any civilized people he met along the way.

Just before he entered the forest, Swordbrought stopped to take a last look at Coosa Town. He must succeed and he must return quickly. He prayed briefly to his spirit guide, the hawk, and disappeared into the thick, green jumble of plant life.

Toward midmorning he came to the trail that led to the west and began running. He ran swiftly all day without tiring, his footfalls almost silent on the cool packed earth of the trail. At dusk he stopped and found a stream to drink from and a place to sleep.

The night passed uneventfully and in the morning he listened to the waking sounds of the forest as he chewed his corn and meat quietly. When he walked out to the trail, another figure, which had been quietly watching among the trees, melded silently back into the green confusion of vines and leaves. The figure remained motionless until Swordbrought had disappeared, then emerged to follow along at a distance.

Chapter 24

There was not much room inside the hut. The dull morning light entered through a square hole over the bolted door. Calling Crow opened his eyes and looked at the hole. It was much too small for him and Red Feather to crawl through. Calling Crow's fingers reached reflexively for his medicine pouch and found nothing. Of course, he realized with despair, the big bearded man named, Collier had it, along with their bows, arrows and knives. They had been locked up in this place for more than one moon now, ever since their capture and beating. The light increased slightly, form separating from shadow, and Calling Crow looked over sadly at his friend. Because of the beating, Red Feather's right leg had become very stiff and was healing slowly, forcing him to limp slightly. Calling Crow's anger flared as he remembered that night. In the blackness of the spring house, the mens' blows had been so hard-struck that it was only through the intercession of their spirit guides that he and Red Feather had not been severely injured. Calling Crow vowed that before another moon passed he would get them out of here. He would then retrieve his medicine pouch from Collier and find Samuel.

Calling Crow went over to wake Red Feather for Collier's hunt show. It was odd. Red Feather no longer awoke when the sun pushed its rays into the window hole. Calling Crow thought that this was also due to the beating. Red Feather lay so still these days that several times Calling Crow thought he had died in his sleep. These things troubled Calling Crow greatly.

Calling Crow shook Red Feather awake. Red Feather pulled his legs up and sat up on the crude bed. Calling Crow

thought sadly how much damage the beating had done to Red
Feather. Although his bruises would eventually heal, his spirit
had been smashed. His once brave eyes were now vacant
most of the time and he seemed much older than Calling
Crow now, more like an old, old man.

Red Feather stared at the wall blankly, saying nothing.

"The hunt will begin soon," said Calling Crow, "we must
get ready."

In answer, Red Feather merely looked at him dully.

Calling Crow looked out the window hole. Rain was on
the way. He looked again at his *tastanagi*. "Red Feather . . ."

Red Feather turned away and began singing a song of lament.

> "Our Grandfathers are calling me,
> From up where the sun moves across the sky.
> They are calling me to come,
> To the sacred lands . . ."

He stopped and said, "We will die here."

"We will live here," said Calling Crow angrily, "for a
time. Then Samuel will find us and we will go home."

Red Feather came to life upon hearing Samuel's name.
"No!" he said angrily. "You are a fool to continue to believe
in this man! Don't you see that it was he who put us here!"

Calling Crow looked at Red Feather in surprise. Red
Feather had never spoken out against Calling Crow like that.
Calling Crow felt no anger, however. Instead, a twinge of
hope stirred within him. Perhaps Red Feather was rallying.
His eyes blazed with an angry fire. Calling Crow was glad to
see this. Then Red Feather's eyes grew dim again and he
turned away. "I am sorry, Calling Crow."

Red Feather said nothing further, instead staring off at vistas that only he could see.

The day grew gray and the rain had come by the time the
keeper finally unlocked the door of the hut for the hunt. Calling Crow and Red Feather stood bravely as the six men surrounded them. A redheaded giant of a man named Burton
knelt and applied the chains to Calling Crow and Red Feath-

er's ankles. As he was doing this, Calling Crow looked over at the fence. A mob of English people waited there, talking and gesturing as they looked over at them.

Hugh Collier, the old man who ran the faire, shoved his large, hairy face in Calling Crow's direction. He gave Calling Crow his own bow and two arrows. Collier had already removed the sharp shell points from them, then whittled the wooden ends to a duller point. "Let's go," said Collier. "And move more lively, the both of you. They've come a long ways and you must give them a good show."

Calling Crow looked at Collier. How he would have liked to cut this old man's fat belly open and display his prettily colored insides to the crowd. That would be a good show for them.

Collier looked away nervously. He and Burton and the others walked back toward the fence. Calling Crow watched them for a moment, the rain beading and running down his hair and into his face. Red Feather's head hung as he stared at the wet gray earth at his feet.

"Come," Calling Crow to him. "Let us get it over with."

Calling Crow handed one of the arrows to Red Feather and nocked the other into his bow. The ankle chains shortened his stride and clinked loudly as he walked awkwardly toward two solitary trees in the middle of the pasture. Red Feather followed slowly, his eyes downcast as he took small steps. When they reached the trees, Calling Crow turned and looked in the direction of the people along the fence. A boy waved at him and his mother slapped his hand down. The people's expressions grew animated, their eyes big at the sight of him. Calling Crow relaxed the arrow and waited. Red Feather stood still, his head hanging down.

Over at the fence, Burton opened a gate and pushed a small sheep through. The animal ran a short distance then stopped and grazed on a patch of grass. Calling Crow saw a thin column of smoke erupt upward, followed by the report of a musket. The sheep ran in panic toward Calling Crow and Red Feather. Calling Crow pulled the arrow back until the feathered vanes touched his cheek. He said a prayer to his spirit guide. Without a shell point on the arrow, his aim would have to be perfect in order not to cause the animal unnecessary suffering. When the sheep was close enough, he released his arrow. It arced up slightly into the thick, gray sky and down to its target.

The sheep lay motionless on its side on the muddy field. The shouting and laughter of the crowd grew louder as Calling Crow quickly hobbled the short distance to the sheep. He knelt and turned to watch sadly as Red Feather approached in his slow, painful limp. Calling Crow pulled his knife from his belt and began to skin the sheep.

Red Feather knelt awkwardly and stared vacant-eyed at the meat. After a moment he lifted his eyes to Calling Crow. ''Do you know we are dead?'' he said dully. ''We have lost our souls.''

Calling Crow did not take his eyes off his work. He could not bear to look into Red Feather's beaten face. ''Do you want Collier's men to give you another whipping?'' he said angrily. ''Prepare the fire. They are waiting to watch us eat.''

Chapter 25

In the pale light of morning, the spider living over Calling Crow's bed worked steadily and methodically. Calling Crow had been fading in and out of consciousness in the grip of a powerful sickness. Now he was conscious, but almost too weak to move. Seven days earlier, out of overwhelming frustration and despair, Calling Crow had grabbed one of Collier's men through the little window. They had beaten him severely for that and it was then that he had gotten sick. Now they were very careful around him and Red Feather, and Calling Crow saw that what little chance they might have had of escaping was gone now.

Calling Crow looked up again at the spider as it dragged its abdomen past strand after strand, weaving its web. Over on the other sleeping shelf, Red Feather lay without moving. Although he was not sick, his spirit was still broken. Despite Calling Crow's love for his *tastanagi*, he knew sadly that he could now do nothing for him.

Red Feather shuddered suddenly and awoke. Calling Crow wanted to speak to him but no longer knew any words that would encourage him. They had been prisoners of Collier and his show for two moons now. Without Calling Crow's medicine pouch, he could not see how they would ever get away from here. When they weren't penned up, they were chained at the ankles and surrounded by Collier's foul-smelling men. And if they could escape, where would they go? Where was Samuel's house from here? Calling Crow wondered. *Aieyah!* What must Samuel think of their disappearance? Had he stopped searching?

Outside a dog barked. The light of dawn was dimmed by thick dark clouds; another day was upon them. Soon Collier and his men would be coming. This was one of the days Calling Crow and Red Feather danced for the visitors to the fair. The last time Calling Crow had collapsed from the fevers. He didn't know if he could do it today.

Aieyah! What little food that was in Calling Crow's stomach threatened to come up at the thought of the dancing. It was a sham, a show for the people that came to see them, people who looked upon them as half-animal freaks. "Picts," Collier called them.

"You are awake," said Red Feather.

"Yes." Calling Crow again thought of Red Feather's assertion that they had been betrayed by Samuel, that the men that had beaten and enslaved them had been Samuel's men. It was all Red Feather thought about, and it was consuming him. Calling Crow still could not believe it. What now seemed like a long time ago, he had looked into the Englishman's eyes when he had given his word. *Aieyah!* He had meant it. Calling Crow had even given him his daughter. Calling Crow had never been wrong in these things before. Was he now?

Calling Crow heard voices approaching. They would be here in a moment. He sat up; he was soaked in sweat. Fists pounded on the door. Red Feather stood as Calling Crow swung his feet to the floor. The door flew open and the English looked in apprehensively, their beards bejeweled with dewdrops, their skin red from the cold air. "Get out here!" came Collier's bellow.

Red Feather helped Calling Crow to his feet and then took down from the wall the two feathered headdresses Collier's men had made for them to wear during the dance. The headdresses were garishly ugly and comic, brightly dyed pigeon feathers of red, blue and green. Red Feather tied Calling Crow's around his head as Burton knelt and roughly put their ankle chains on. Red Feather put his headdress on his head.

Collier approached Calling Crow and ripped his headdress away. "You'll not be needing it any longer," he said.

One of the men shoved the drum under Red Feather's arm and put the beating stick in his hand. They were led down to the fence where a juggler and a man on stilts amused the crowd.

Burton poked Red Feather with his stick, then turned round to smile at the other Englishmen. "Dance! Beat the bloody drum and dance!"

Red Feather began beating the drum and shuffling his feet, the ankle chains rattling in time. Someone opened the gate and the crowd pushed in around them. Collier and one of his men took each of Calling Crow's arms and led him toward the gate.

Red Feather stopped moving and beating the drum and called over to Calling Crow in Muskogee. "Calling Crow, don't leave me here!"

An Englishman with a stick beat Red Feather on the legs and back and he began again the pathetic semblance of a deer-hunting dance.

Calling Crow tried to hold back but someone struck him on the head, stunning him. "Where are you taking me?" he said in English.

Collier's face was flush with exertion. "You'll find out soon enough."

Calling Crow called to his *tastanagi,* "Red Feather, don't give up! Don't die! I will come back for you." He had one brief look at Red Feather before the crowd swallowed him up. A moment later Collier and Burton roughly pushed Calling Crow up and into the back of a big covered cart. Burton climbed in after him and the cart rolled away.

Cold rain rattled against the canvas roof and sides of the big tented cart which served as Collier's house. Inside, Collier and John Newman faced each other across the two candles burning dimly on Collier's table. The flames moved in the cold drafts, making the figures in Collier's big leather-bound ledger seem to lean every which way.

John removed his red-banded felt hat and put it on the table. He put his feet up on the table. "Bloody wet out there."

Collier grunted as he squinted at the ledger. He scribbled vigorously then put down his quill. "He should be at the brothel by tomorrow morning."

John nodded. "The Turk will tame him, all right."

"If he lives. He's had the ague for a fortnight now."

"They can survive sicknesses that would kill most white men."

"Is that right?" Collier had been loath to send the Indian away. The pair of them were a bigger draw than just one. But it didn't matter anymore. The big one was just too wild and dangerous. The other morning he had reached through his window and grabbed Porter, almost breaking the lad's neck. It had taken all of them to get the Indian off of him after they'd opened the door. Wild man, indeed.

"Well," said Collier, absently, "whether he lives or dies, it's in God's hands." He picked up a cheese sitting on the table and took a big bite. A small avalanche of crumbs tumbled down his great beard, some coming to rest in dark canyons, others catching in the rough wool of his cape. Some of the crumbs fell all the way to the floor, where they would be eaten later by a small colony of mice that lived under the floorboards.

Collier coughed phlegmatically and dipped his quill in the inkwell. He made a quick calculation in one of the few remaining white spaces of a paper beside the ledger on the table. He opened a wooden box and his fat fingers disappeared inside. The click of coin upon coin sounded in the damp carriage and a moment later he produced a small white pouch and set it on the table in front of John. "It's all there, as agreed upon. You can check my figuring if you like."

John picked up the pouch. He was about to pour the contents onto the table when booted footsteps thumped quickly up the wooden steps outside. The door opened on the blackness and young Porter's reddened face glistened wetly in the candlelight.

"There's a gentleman at the gate, m'lord. He's asking about the savages."

"What?" said Collier. "What's his name?"

"Newman."

"Egads," said John, getting to his feet. He dangled the pouch before Collier. "I'll be back." He put the pouch in his pocket and walked out.

Collier turned back to Porter. "What did you tell the gentleman?" he said nervously.

"Nothing, m'lord."

"Good." Collier stood and pulled his cape closer around him. "Take the savage to Burton's quarters and hide him there. Tell Burton and the others that should anyone ask, the savages escaped. Then bring the gentleman here to me."

Ten minutes later, Collier could see some resemblance between the man who now stood before him and his tall, menacing brother, but just some.

Samuel Newman took off his hat. "At the roadhouse in the town they said you had two wild men as part of your show. Do you deny this?"

"Well, m'lord," said Collier, "the truth of the matter is we did have two wild men as part of our show, and a goodly attraction they was too! But they have escaped of late."

Samuel Newman stepped closer, his eyes growing larger. "Then it was true. When did they escape?"

Collier's hand disappeared under his beard as he scratched absentmindedly. "Oh, two or three days shy of a fortnight ago, it was. They attacked my man when he went out to feed them one morning and fled into the woods. I could show you the bloody marks on his neck. No one has seen them since."

Collier saw the lines of concern etch themselves into Newman's brow. "M'lord, why do you care so for a couple of savages?"

Newman waved away the question. He pointed to the hat on the table. "Yours?"

Collier frowned. "Of course. Who else's would it be?"

Samuel continued to stare at the hat.

"I'm sure there must be dozens of them around," Collier said, "all made by the same hatter."

Samuel looked at him. "Could I see where they were being held?"

"Of course, m'lord." Collier lit a lamp hanging by the door and they went down the steps of the cart.

Their footsteps splashed through muddy puddles as they walked in the yellow circle of lamplight. Collier drew back the bolt and bent to walk into the little cottage. The gentleman followed him inside.

Samuel Newman looked around for a few moments at the starkness of the room. Then he knelt and picked something up off the earthen floor. He held it to the light, a woven sash of red and blue, with frayed tassles at either end. It had been stepped on and was wet and caked with mud.

Newman turned angrily to Collier and the older man was taken aback. "How did you come to own these two men?" he asked.

Remembering John's admonition to keep the deal from his brother, Collier fought for composure. "We bought them from some Cornishmen who said they found them wandering about in the forests."

Collier felt a great discomfort as Newman's eyes probed his own. Finally, Newman looked down again at the scrap of cloth he held in his hand.

"I will keep this," he said.

"Of course, m'lord. I have no use for it."

Newman rolled the cloth up and put it in his pocket. They turned to go outside.

"M'lord," said Collier, "if I may be so bold as to inquire, what are these savages to you?"

Newman looked off into the blackness. "None of your bloody business! Just light the way back to my horse and I'll be leaving."

Chapter 26

Crying Wolf had seen the terrain change dramatically the last few days as the trail turned north and west, rising in elevation. There were no more palmetto and the pines were taller, more straight. The earth was drier and Crying Wolf's feet hurt from the many rocks underfoot. Dust rose in the hot air, stinging his nostrils and throat. He bore his fatigue with disdain, however, for soon this business would be over. Swordbrought had put up a strenuous pace and any other brave would have fallen behind, but he, Crying Wolf, had kept up. Now they had traveled far enough away from the village. As soon as he caught up with Swordbrought, he would take the peace pipe away from him.

Crying Wolf ran faster, noticing the distant, smoke-colored mountains visible through a cut in the tree line. A racket came from a nearby hickory as a pair of squirrels argued over something. They disappeared up a branch when they saw him.

Crying Wolf stopped suddenly. There was no longer any trace of Swordbrought's passage. He had slipped off the trail a ways back and Crying Wolf had not noticed.

Crying Wolf turned quickly, his neck hairs rising. Had Swordbrought discovered that he was being followed? Had he circled around to come up behind him? Crying Wolf stared back the way he had come. The forest was quiet, empty. No. Crying Wolf smiled slightly. Swordbrought had not discovered him. He had probably stopped to make camp for the night. Yes. That was more likely.

Crying Wolf started back the way he had come, searching for the place where Swordbrought had left the trail. He would find him, and, if need be, kill him. Then he, Crying Wolf, would go to Cussitaw Town and bring back the Muskogee braves.

Swordbrought sat on a flat rock in a small clearing, eating the last of the dried meat Green Bird Woman had given him. He heard a noise behind and turned, reaching quietly for his bow. Nocking an arrow, he watched the bushes at the edge of the clearing. There it was again, a quiver of movement in the bushes. Swordbrought pulled the vane of the arrow back to his cheek. There was a swish of movement and a large rabbit pushed through into the clearing.

Swordbrought smiled as he relaxed the tension in the bow. Brother rabbit, he thought quietly, thank you for the offering. I would love to have you for my dinner tonight, but I cannot light a fire to cook you. I don't know what people live in this place and I don't want to be discovered.

The rabbit looked at Swordbrought, still not seeing him. Then it raised its nose to sniff the air. Swordbrought suddenly thought of the trickster rabbit stories he had heard as a child and he remembered the village's sacred pipe behind him. Was this rabbit tricking him, distracting him?

Swordbrought turned round and his heart sank. The tall, muscled form of Crying Wolf stood not far away. He cradled the sacred pipe bundle in his arms. He smiled down at Swordbrought.

"You shouldn't leave this unguarded, little man."

"Put it down," said Swordbrought.

Crying Wolf pulled the bundle close to his chest. "Put down that bow first."

Swordbrought put his bow on the ground.

Crying Wolf looked at Swordbrought in annoyance. "I was going to kill you just now, Swordbrought. It would have been so easy! But you are not a bad person, and so I will spare you.

"We are very far from our village," Crying Wolf went on. "You can go away now and no one will ever know what happened here. I will say that I came upon your body and that I took the pipe and went on. Do you understand? If you don't do as I say and go away, I will kill you."

Swordbrought's chest heaved as his rage grew. He got to his feet. "It is you who will be killed, Crying Wolf." Swordbrought pulled his stone axe from his belt. "The people chose me to take the pipe to Cussitaw Town. And I will."

Crying Wolf laughed. He looked down reverentially at the doeskin-covered pipe bundle in his arms, rocking it slowly as if it were a baby. "They should never have entrusted the village's medicine pipe to one as careless and weak as you." He carefully lowered the bundle to the rock and stood up.

Crying Wolf took his club from his belt. "I give you one more chance, Swordbrought. Go away and you can live."

Swordbrought's eyes narrowed in anger. The arrogance of his former friend had grown huge and grotesque. "No, Crying Wolf, I give you a chance to put an end to all of this. Go away now and I will say nothing of this when I return to the village."

Crying Wolf laughed contemptuously. "You will never return." He screamed out a war cry.

Swordbrought threw himself to the side, barely escaping the powerful swing of Crying Wolf's club. Swordbrought swung his axe around and Crying Wolf parried the blow with his longer reach. The two men circled and lunged, their muscles taut as their feet threw up a small cloud of dust into the hot air. Swordbrought's foot turned on a small rock and he lost his balance. Crying Wolf lunged and swung. His club grazed Swordbrought's shoulder. Pain flooded through Swordbrought, but he managed to dance away from the flurry of blows that quickly followed. The two men continued to circle as they eyed each other fiercely.

Swordbrought's breathing was ragged and his shoulder raged in pain as he faced the bigger brave. Crying Wolf feinted a lunge and Swordbrought jumped sideways. Crying Wolf laughed with a triumphant howl. "Look around you, little man," he taunted, "this is where you will die."

Swordbrought felt his strength and speed slipping away, while Crying Wolf seemed to be getting stronger and faster. Swordbrought prayed to the hawk spirit for medicine help. He must prevail for his people, his village! A moment later Swordbrought thought he heard the flight of a swift hawk coming to his aid. It passed a hair's breadth from his head. It was not a bird, however, but an arrow. And it had raced past him and buried itself deep in Crying Wolf's thigh.

Crying Wolf grunted in pain. He dropped his club and fell backward as if dead. Swordbrought whirled about. A tall, wild-looking man with a bow slung over his shoulder was running swiftly toward them. Wearing a breechclout, the man had a thick tuft of hair running from the front to the back of his head.

Swordbrought bent and held up the medicine pipe bundle for the man to see. "You!" he shouted. "I bring the pipe of peace!"

The man screamed unintelligibly and continued to come on.

What kind of man is this that doesn't understand speech? Swordbrought thought. He quickly set the pipe bundle down. The man kept coming and Swordbrought hefted his axe and braced himself.

Screaming out a war cry, the stranger hoisted a crude wooden club and leapt.

The man's club nicked Swordbrought's head, dazing him. Swordbrought felt the man's hands close around his neck. His stink filled Swordbrought's nostrils as they fell backward, the man's body taking the brunt of the fall. They both got quickly to their feet and circled, looking for advantage. Already exhausted from his fight with Crying Wolf, Swordbrought moved slowly. One of the man's swings slashed a bloody scrape across Swordbrought's chest. Reacting with fury, Swordbrought lunged and the bigger man backed up, tripping over Crying Wolf's outstretched leg. Had Crying Wolf moved? Swordbrought thought briefly. The wild man fell backward to a sitting position. Swordbrought rushed forward and brought his axe down on the top of the man's head before he could get up. His closed eyelids quivered spasmodically as blood ran down his face. He pitched forward and was still.

Swordbrought's breath was ragged as he looked down on the dead man. He looked over at Crying Wolf. He was moving, moaning, his face twisted in pain. Swordbrought helped him up and Crying Wolf tried to pull the arrow from his thigh.

The tip had passed all the way through and stuck out the other side.

"Did you stick out your leg?" Swordbrought asked him angrily.

Crying Wolf looked up at Swordbrought and then back down at the arrow. "What? Little man."

Swordbrought pointed angrily to the dead man. "Did you trip him?"

Crying Wolf grimaced in pain as he looked at the dead man. He looked back up at Swordbrought. "You killed him, eh? Now you can kill me, too, little man."

Angry shouting and the sound of barking dogs came from the distance. Swordbrought couldn't see any more of the strange men, but he knew more of them would be here at any moment. He looked back down at Crying Wolf and a great anger filled him. Had Crying Wolf tripped the wild man, cheating Swordbrought of a victory? It would have been better to have died than for that to have happened. Still, Crying Wolf said he had not. Swordbrought would have to believe him.

Swordbrought carefully picked up the pipe bundle and started away. He stopped. Despite the anger and suspicion that were still in his heart, he couldn't leave Crying Wolf behind. He went back and knelt beside him. Swordbrought snapped the front of the arrow off and Crying Wolf grabbed him involuntarily, hissing in pain.

"Help me over to that rock there," said Crying Wolf weakly, "I don't want to be lying on the ground when they come."

Swordbrought helped him to his feet. Crying Wolf exhaled with a hiss as a spasm of pain rippled across his features. Swordbrought walked slowly with him, past the rock.

"There," said Crying Wolf, "help me sit."

Swordbrought shook his head. "No! It'll not be said that I left a Coosa brave behind to be slaughtered. Even one such as you."

Shame darkened Crying Wolf's face. "You must, Swordbrought. You will have to run. Remember, the village must get help from Cussitaw Town."

"Yes," said Swordbrought. He looked over at the almost naked, dirt-encrusted body of the wild man. "Come. We will find a place to hide before his companions get here."

They went as quickly as they could into the dimly lit cover of the forest.

Chapter 27

The covered cart rumbled slowly along the cobblestone road, finally stopping in the early hours of the morning. Calling Crow was sleeping when the men ordered him to climb out. The air was damp and cold and a knee-deep fog clung to the road. Calling Crow shivered uncontrollably as he stood on the stone road. He looked around. Strange lights shone low in the sky, each one seeming to be the same distance from the other. He studied them for a moment in confusion, then realized they were lamps hanging from iron poles. They followed the road that extended out over a black expanse which Calling Crow knew could only be a broad river or lake. There were houses all along the road over the water and one was decorated with round bundles stuck on poles. Calling Crow had never seen such a sight. On the other side of the water he saw a mass of houses and lights. The sight caused him some dizziness and he turned and held onto the cart.

"Bring him up," Calling Crow heard someone say.

A great stone house loomed out of the fog behind the cart, a broad staircase leading up to it. A large, powerful-looking man and a smaller man stood waiting in the doorway. Both were dark in color and were not Englishmen. The big one wore a cloth coiled around his head.

Burton walked over to Calling Crow. "Up you go," he said, and pushed Calling Crow toward the steps. The cloth-headed man watched them silently; the other, who Calling Crow guessed was his servant, stood obediently by his side. The chains on Calling Crow's ankles forced him to move slowly as Burton led him up the steps. Day was dawning and as Calling Crow neared the top he could see more of the many houses here and across the water. Burton stopped and pointed to the road over the water and the houses beyond.

"Pretty isn't it?" said Burton. "That's the great city of London, right across the London Bridge. Up there in the Tower is where Her Majesty, the Queen, and her court rule." Burton looked into Calling Crow's eyes. "You'll not be seeing much of her though, I suspect." His harsh laughter echoed off the cold stone building. "Well, go on up now."

When Calling Crow got to the top of the stairs, Burton called up. "Here he is, Amorgh, delivered as promised."

The big man, who was called Amorgh, turned to Calling Crow. He then nodded to his assistant and they roughly pushed Calling Crow into the house.

To the left and right, stone stairs led up and down. Straight ahead was a large room with a solitary table in the center and chairs arranged around the perimeter. Woven scenes hung from the great room's walls and the place reminded Calling Crow of the room in which he and Red Feather had appeared before Samuel's friends. The memory sent a pang of sadness and pain into Calling Crow's heart. Where was Samuel now? Had he really been responsible for all of this as Red Feather thought? No! Calling Crow still could not believe it.

The iron door slammed shut solidly behind them and Calling Crow turned. Amorgh took an iron ring of keys from his belt and inserted one of them in the lock, turning it with a resounding click. He looked at Calling Crow and scowled. Coughing hockingly, Amorgh spat on the stone floor. He gestured to his helper and he pushed Calling Crow toward the stairs.

How was Red Feather faring? Calling Crow wondered. Calling Crow recalled his last sight of him. Would Red Feather cooperate with Collier until Calling Crow could get them both home? He must! Had not Sees Far said that in his dream he had seen Red Feather returning with Calling Crow? Sees Far was never wrong in such things. Calling Crow went down the stairs slowly and awkwardly in the ankle chains. Amorgh's man, sallow of skin, with a long hook nose, pushed Calling Crow, shouting at him to move faster. Calling Crow turned to glare at him and the man pushed him again, causing him to lose balance. Calling Crow tripped and fell onto the stone landing. He got angrily to his feet and made for the little man, who moved backward with a cry of fear. Amorgh produced a small whip from behind his back and struck Calling Crow stingingly several times on the face and chest while the smaller man regained his courage. He and Amorgh then each grabbed one of Calling Crow's arms and they went on.

Calling Crow started down the next flight of steps. At the bottom they walked down a long corridor and came to an opened, cage-like room. Amorgh and the little man shoved Calling Crow inside.

They shut the iron door with a clang and Amorgh locked it with another key from his iron ring. Calling Crow turned away, hearing the receding click of their sandals on the stone floor. The footsteps went up the stairs and then it was quiet.

The room was empty except for what looked like a bearskin on the floor in the corner. Calling Crow had another spasm of dizziness and sat on the bearskin. He leaned back against the stone wall and sang a lament in his native Muskogee.

> "Oh, land of my ancestors,
> why did I leave you so long ago?
> Your moss-draped trees,
> and black-water pools,
> call to me and I'm filled with pain."

A voice came suddenly from the next room. It spoke in English, yet with an odd accent. "A pretty little ditty indeed. But you had better sleep now while you can. Days are long and hard around here and yours will start soon enough. Sleep now."

Calling Crow found the voice strangely reassuring and slept.

Calling Crow awoke to the clacking of Amorgh's key in the lock. He sat up on the bearskin pallet as Amorgh walked off, the click of his sandals receding down the corridor. Amorgh's hocking cough rattled off the walls and then it was quiet. Calling Crow remained sitting. His fever had lifted but he was very weak. He heard the occupant of the next room stirring. A moment later the man stood in the doorway. He was a thin, broad-shouldered man of medium height, with a thick head of brown hair and a bushy brown mustache and beard. His eyes were bright, with an intense green intelligence. Calling Crow noticed that his right foot was misshapen and his right leg about a hands's breadth shorter than the left. A long, ugly boot he wore made up for the different lengths of his legs. Unlike Calling Crow, he was not chained at the ankles.

"My name is Edward," said the man, "and I am an Irishman. I work here in this place and entertain the people who come here. Come and get something to eat. Then we will work." He turned and walked down the hall with a heavy limp. Calling Crow followed him. They entered a large, dank, dimly lit chamber. Ten small squares, each about shoulder height, divided the room up.

The man called Edward sat at a table in one of the small squares. Calling Crow saw that all of the squares were connected by footpaths. Inside the nearest square, Calling Crow could see a large iron pot half filled with water. It was big enough to cook a large animal whole.

Edward pointed to a round loaf of bread on the table and a wooden plate of foul-smelling English cheese. Calling Crow was so weak with hunger that he took some and ate it. The taste was bitter like the smell, but his teeth felt good tearing through it. He couldn't remember ever being this hungry. Calling Crow ripped a large piece of the bread away, and ate it quickly.

Footsteps echoed briefly off the stone floor. Then the clink of metal keys. The noise faded.

"You've met Amorgh, the keeper of the keys?" said Edward.

Calling Crow nodded.

"He haunts this place like a ghost."

"Yes," said Calling Crow. "He and the other man do not look English."

"They are Turks. The owners of this place, two fine Christian gentlemen, employ them to do the more distasteful things which must be done."

"Are Turks Christians?"

Edward shook his head. "Not this pair. They believe and worship differently. But Amorgh is a great devotee of Saint George." Edward laughed disparagingly. "It is said he has a shrine to him in his room."

"Where is his room?" said Calling Crow.

Edward smiled at him. "No one knows where he sleeps and that's the way he wants it. Once he was poisoned and almost drowned in one of the baths. Another time one of the girls tried to stab him to death. Last year a customer who fell in love with one of the girls wounded him with a dagger."

"Why do Christians have a non-Christian working here?" said Calling Crow.

Edward shrugged. "To do things which good Christians are forbidden to do. People have disappeared, their bodies found later."

"How do you know it is Amorgh doing these things?"

"He's bloody capable of it. However, I will let you form your own opinion of him. And you will, quickly."

"I will not be here long enough to do that."

Edward laughed sadly. "There is no escape from here."

Calling Crow looked at Edward. "I will find a way out. How long have you been in this place?"

"Three years."

"Why?"

"I owe the owners money."

"But you are not chained," said Calling Crow. "Why don't you leave?"

"There are other kinds of chains which can hold one just as tightly as iron."

Calling Crow looked at him in confusion.

"There is something else," said Edward. "Because of what goes on here, very few people know about this place and it is a good place to hide."

"Ah," said Calling Crow, "you are hiding."

"Like you, I don't hold to the same beliefs as them."

"You are not a Christian?"

Edward shook his head. "They found some things in my house and . . ."

Footsteps echoed around the stone wall.

Edward stood up suddenly. "Enough about all that. There is no time." He indicated the man-sized iron pots. "We call those 'the stews.'" He took another bite of the cheese, watching Calling Crow's face intently. "Baths, I suppose I should say. That's where the ladies of this place entertain the paying customers."

Calling Crow looked at Edward in confusion. "Do you mean they dance for them while they bathe?"

The man looked at Calling Crow piercingly, then shrugged. "No, the men and women bathe together, and the women give themselves carnally to the men for gold."

"Ah," said Calling Crow, "gold! That explains it." He looked back at the baths for a moment. He knew that the Spanish, too, had such places. It was a very sad and shameful business. He looked at Edward. "Where are these women?" he said. "Where do they come from?"

"They live at the very top of the house and they come from all over the world. They are slaves like us."

Calling Crow's face grew dark. "I am not a slave."

Edward smiled sadly. He sat and broke off a piece of cheese, then held it out to Calling Crow. "Of course. Have more cheese, for you will need your strength."

Calling Crow's nostrils flared at the sour smell of the cheese, but again his deep hunger overcame his distaste. He ate all the cheese on the plate. "What is it I must do here, Edward? What work?"

Edward pointed to some wood stacked against the wall. "You're to help me carry. We burn a lot of wood to heat the water. You will carry much water too. We make sure the stew pots are hot. That is our job. And then we clean up. The women here make sure the customers get hot. That is their job. And then they clean up, clean out their purses, that is." Edward laughed at his joke and picked up the remaining piece of bread.

Chapter 28

Female laughter and the bull bellow of male voices echoed off the hard stone walls of the bath chamber. The scent of washballs was thick in the steamy air. Imported from Venice, they were made of pressed herbs, oil and rosewater, and the brothel used them liberally. The torch and candlelight blurred in Calling Crow's eyes. He had been three nights in this place now and he moved slowly as he carried two oaken buckets of boiling water, taking care not to be tripped by his ankle chains. When he was not thinking of escape, or wondering where Samuel was, or how Red Feather was, or what was happening in his village, Calling Crow's head seemed to be asleep and the sights and sounds of this place a blur as he went about his drudgery.

There was food—bread and cheese, a soupy gruel—but Calling Crow felt very weak, like an animal that was having its blood slowly drained. Several times Amorgh had beaten Calling Crow and he hardly had the strength to raise his hands to protect his face from the blows. He knew that the reason for this was that his medicine pouch was back in Collier's fair. Without medicine, a brave was weak. No power. The only thing that seemed to rally Calling Crow's spirit was Edward's singing and harp music. When he heard it reverberating off the steamy walls, it was like a candle in the darkness.

Calling Crow ignored the couple in the bath as he poured the hot water to the side. He went on to the next cube. This couple sat naked on the wooden seats as they talked. Calling Crow was embarrassed for them and avoided looking at them. He quickly poured, then moved quietly away. He returned to the boiling caldron to refill his buckets. Amorgh came half-way down the stairs, whip in hand, watching over the chamber quietly. Calling Crow went back to the baths. He poured out the contents of one bucket against the rim of a bath, ignoring the sounds of passion the couple made. He went on to the next cube.

An old man dressed in a white gown sat on the bench. A woman stood naked in the bath, the water up to her waist. Calling Crow did not look at her, but he knew she was very beautiful. He kept his eyes down as he tilted the bucket.

"Stop," said the woman.

Calling Crow still did not look at her.

"Pour over here . . . closer to me." There was amusement in her voice. "I want to feel the warmth."

Calling Crow turned and leaned over the tub.

"Pour closer."

Calling Crow looked at her and his every sense came awake. Her eyes were blue as a summer sky, her lips red and warm, her body voluptuous. She was so beautiful that, for a brief instant, he forgot where he was. She smiled at him and he moved away.

The men were all gone, the women retired upstairs. Calling Crow headed back toward his cell. He passed the stairs that led up to the front door. Edward was off somewhere making things ready for the next day. Calling Crow decided to go up and look around. Halfway up he heard the jingle of metal keys. He froze for a moment, then continued climbing upward. Amorgh's little helper was putting a key into the lock. Calling Crow came up behind him, but the man happened to look around at that moment. He let out a scream and Amorgh rushed in from another room. Amorgh pushed Calling Crow backward, Calling Crow's chains put him off balance and he fell backward. The little man kneed him in the groin painfully. Amorgh and the little man quickly pulled Calling Crow downstairs and locked him in his cell. A moment later he heard Amorgh yelling at Edward. Then it was quiet and Calling Crow passed out.

The next night Calling Crow went about his tasks as usual. Edward said nothing of what had happened the night before and spoke with Calling Crow only as the need arose. When they finished their work, Calling Crow asked Edward if he could go look out onto the garden. Edward nodded, putting a warning into his look.

Calling Crow walked through the kitchen, past the huge, grease-blackened timbers. The cook had long gone to bed, but the bricks of the big walk-in fireplace still radiated much heat. Calling Crow went to the door with the iron grate at the top, which led to the garden. It was locked as it always was. He looked out. The square of the walled garden was black now. Calling Crow thought grimly that even if he could get out there, the smooth stone walls rose straight up to well over the height of two men stacked one atop the other. They looked impossible to scale. And the great house was all locked up and only Amorgh had the keys. There seemed to be no other way out.

Calling Crow prayed to his spirit guide. He must find a way out and return to Collier's fair. Then he could reclaim the medicine pouch that Sees Far had given him. With its power, he would free Red Feather and together they would find their way to Samuel's house and collect the shooting sticks for his people. Calling Crow was suddenly overcome by the immensity of his task, the hopelessness of it. He stood, staring out between the bars, for a long time. A cold winter day dawned on the garden. Slowly the deep green of the grass became visible, its color infusing Calling Crow once again with life, life that had been wrung out of him over the course of his nights in the gray steam. *Aieyah!* It was impossible, but he could only do it with the power of his medicine pouch. He must retrieve it!

Chapter 29

Swordbrought crouched down at the entrance to the cave; Crying Wolf slept farther back. As Swordbrought looked out onto the night's blackness, his thoughts, too, were black. For the past two days they had been able to elude their pursuers, but it had been very difficult. These strange men used dogs in their attempts to hunt Swordbrought and Crying Wolf down. Swordbrought had never heard of this being done before, but it was very effective, and they had been forced to walk through streams to cover their scent track. Who were these men? he wondered. His father had told him of how the Spanish had used their killing dogs to hunt down escaped slaves, but these were not white men. Except for the crudeness of their clothing, they looked like him and his people.

Crying Wolf moaned in his sleep. Swordbrought did not think his wound was life-threatening, but he knew it must be very painful. Crying Wolf found it very difficult to move. Swordbrought thought that once the rest of the arrow was removed, the wound would heal quickly. But who would remove it? Swordbrought realized that he might soon have to abandon Crying Wolf. His mission was more important.

How much farther along the broad trail was the village of Cussitaw? he wondered. For a moment, Swordbrought thought that perhaps he was going in the wrong direction. He recalled his meeting with Sees Far and Two Clouds. No, he was going exactly as they had instructed him. Crying Wolf coughed softly in the back. Swordbrought turned to look at him. When would they find Cussitaw Town?

For a long while now, Swordbrought's ears had picked up no sounds of search in the forest. Their pursuers must be sleeping. Swordbrought thought of Calling Crow so far away in the Englishmen's lands. To Swordbrought, it was the same as going to the netherworld atop the clouds or the one below Mother Earth. He prayed that the spirits would guide his father home safely.

Swordbrought crawled back to Crying Wolf and woke him. Looping the strap of the medicine pipe bundle over his shoulder, Swordbrought helped Crying Wolf to his knees. Swordbrought felt a grudging admiration for the older brave. Despite his earlier treachery, the man could endure much pain and never cried out. Without saying a word, they crawled to the front of the cave and went out into the cool night.

Swordbrought made no sound as they worked their way back to the main trail, but Crying Wolf's movements were clumsy and noisy, and Swordbrought knew that if their pursuers were awake and listening, they would soon be upon them. They reached the main trail and hurried along, Crying Wolf limping badly. Swordbrought picked their way by the occasional glimpses of the starry night sky visible through the thinner canopy of leaves over the trail. Crying Wolf seemed to rally a bit and they made good time along the broad trail. Patches of purple sky appeared between the leaves overhead as dawn approached. Swordbrought and Crying Wolf increased their pace, taking advantage of the greater visibility. Up above, the winged ones welcomed the dawn with whistles, clicks and shrieks. The sky slowly changed to bright blue and it was then that they heard the other sounds, the shouts of their pursuers in their strange language, and the barking of their dogs. Swordbrought and Crying Wolf stopped as Swordbrought turned round to look back. The noise was growing louder; they were gaining. Crying Wolf sat on the dirt of the trail.

"Swordbrought, give me your bow and go on. I can kill two or three of them before they even know I'm here."

Swordbrought shook his head. "Get on your feet. We must get off the trail."

Their progress impeded by the uneven terrain and the bushes and vines, Swordbrought and Crying Wolf moved slower, parallel to the trail. The shouting grew louder; their pursuers were no more than a hundred paces away now. Crying Wolf stopped, his teeth clenched in pain. He leaned against a sapling, bending it over with his weight.

"Little man, go on alone now. I cannot take another step."

Swordbrought looked around nervously. The sound of the others had died; they were listening for Swordbrought and Crying Wolf now. Swordbrought took the medicine bundle from around his neck. He set it down next to Crying Wolf. Nocking an arrow in his bow, he said, "I will return."

Swordbrought worked his way silently back to the broad trail. The forest was unnaturally quiet. He hid himself behind a mass of red maple leaves and waited. A few moments later he saw two men coming stealthily up the trail. Like the others, these two wore only breechclouts, despite the coolness of the weather. They did not have bows, and instead, carried long blowguns. Their large, ugly war clubs hung at their sides, ready for close-in fighting. Swordbrought waited till they were within range and released his first arrow. It pierced the lead man's neck and his hands went to his throat as he gagged and fell to the forest floor. The second man looked around wildly. By the time he spotted Swordbrought, Swordbrought had already released his arrow. The man's reactions were quick and he almost managed to jump out of the way, but the arrow pierced his side. Screaming to alert the others, he fell to his knees.

Swordbrought hurried back to where he had left Crying Wolf. He saw one of the strange wild men leaned over a bush, as if to see what was on the other side. Swordbrought raced forward and saw that the man was already dead, his head bloodied. Crying Wolf looked up at Swordbrought exhaustedly. Not far away one of the men howled like a wolf and another answered. The dogs barked excitedly. They were trying to encircle them.

"Leave me, little man," said Crying Wolf.

"No." Swordbrought took the medicine pipe bundle and knelt to help Crying Wolf to his feet. They made their way back out to the broad trail. The howls increased in number as Swordbrought and Crying Wolf hurried along the trail. Crying Wolf coughed hoarsely, fighting for breath. Swordbrought looked behind and spotted one of the wild men. He stood in full view on the broad trail as he called to his fellows, but he held back. Soon it would be over.

Swordbrought and Crying Wolf followed the trail around a turn, the shouting wild men not far behind. A tall palisade came into view ahead. Swordbrought wondered if it was the home of the strange-sounding men who were chasing them, or if it was Cussitaw Town. He prayed to his spirit guide that it was the Muskogee town, for there was no turning back now.

Crying Wolf gripped Swordbrought's shoulder painfully and grunted in pain. He fell to his knees. Swordbrought looked back down the trail worriedly; the men would be here any moment.

"Come, Crying Wolf," said Swordbrought. "The town is just ahead. We can get help."

Crying Wolf said nothing; his head hung limply. Just then their pursuers came into view. There were eight or nine of them now, armed with blowguns and clubs. Their small dogs yapped and jumped excitedly at their heels. The men stopped momentarily in confusion upon seeing their prey ahead. Swordbrought nocked an arrow into his bow and quickly released it. The arrow went high and then the mob of men and dogs were racing down on them. Swordbrought spun around as he attempted to fend them off. One of the small dogs bit Swordbrought's leg and he whirled about and struck it. It yelped in pain and leapt away. A man struck Crying Wolf on the back of the head and he collapsed on the trail. Swordbrought's axe clipped one man's face and he danced away with a howl of pain, blood streaming from his nose. The dogs jumped and tore at Swordbrought as he whirled to face his attackers. A shrill, warbling war cry erupted from up the trail and five men came running toward them. Swordbrought could tell by the familiar patterns woven into their sashes and breechclouts that they were Muskogee. Soon they were in the fray, swinging their axes in fury. One wild man was knocked backward by the force of a Muskogee blow and the others began running away. After they disappeared around the bend in the trail, an older Muskogee man stepped before Swordbrought. Although the man was shorter than Swordbrought, he was very powerful-looking, with a broad body that looked to have been hacked out of a tree trunk with an axe.

"Who were they?" said Swordbrought, looking momentarily down at the dead man.

"They call themselves the children of the sun," said the man. "They are Yuchi, very bad."

Swordbrought touched the medicine pipe bundle hanging at his side. "I am Swordbrought, from Coosa Town." He looked down at Crying Wolf's inert form. "That is Crying Wolf. We come in peace."

The man nodded. "I am called Fox-Disappears. Let us get your companion inside the village to be cared for. We will talk in there."

Swordbrought nodded in relief.

Crying Wolf had long since lapsed into unconsciousness when they lay him on the skin pallet in the medicine man's hut. Without the flint-hard force of his mind to contain them, Crying Wolf's cries and moans of pain escaped as the medicine man manipulated and removed what was left of the arrow. Swordbrought watched with Fox-Disappears as the medicine man began singing his prayer over Crying Wolf's now-quiet form. An old woman carried a wooden dish in and began applying a poultice to the wound. Fox-Disappears motioned to Swordbrought to go outside with him.

Swordbrought followed the squat, muscled man as he walked swiftly toward the village's *chokafa*. Off in the fields, some of the people of the town irrigated their corn. A woman flung a gourd full of water downward toward the furrows and Swordbrought saw the sun catch and sparkle in the rippling wet curve. Two old men and a naked little girl walked past Swordbrought and Fox-Disappears under the cool shade of the tall oaks that lined the main street of the village. Swordbrought saw no other people. Perhaps, he thought, they were all at a ball game with a neighboring village. If that was the case, they would arrive back before nightfall.

Swordbrought stooped slightly as he followed Fox-Disappears through the entryway of the *chokafa*. Swordbrought seated himself cross-legged on a reed mat across from the village's three venerable old men. Fox-Disappears sat beside him.

The bigger of the three, known as Tall Man, sat in the middle. Despite his fleshy, hanging jowls, Tall Man still had a warrior's face. "Fox-Disappears said that your village is threatened by the Timucua people, and Spanish Slavers, that you need our warriors to help you."

"Yes," said Swordbrought.

One of the smaller old men, with a large round belly, said, "We don't know if these things are true; we only know that you have said them."

"Yes," said the other old man. "You could be drawing our warriors into a trap."

Swordbrought held up his village's medicine pipe bundle. "Why don't we smoke? Then we will talk some more."

Swordbrought took the pipe out of the bundle and performed the pipe ceremony. After they finished and the air was sweet with tobacco smoke, he said, "It seems like a long time since I left my town. My people sent me to you, to bear their story, their plea. This I have done and I spoke true. Now, if you do not want to help us, I shall have to go on until I find some who will."

A runner entered. He went quickly over to Tall Man and spoke softly into his ear. After the runner left, Tall Man spoke. "I have good news for you."

Swordbrought's heart quickened.

"Your companion is awake," said the old man. "The medicine man said that he will be able to walk in four or five days."

"That is good," said Swordbrought. "We will leave then."

"We will send warriors back with you," said Tall Man.

Surprise was evident on Swordbrought's face.

"We believed what you told us," said Tall Man. "We only wanted to hear you speak." He turned to the other old men. "He speaks like the son of a chief."

The two men nodded.

"There is one thing," said Tall Man. "We can only send four warriors back with you at this time."

"Only four?" said Swordbrought, unable to conceal his disappointment.

Tall Man nodded somberly. "We are fighting a war now with the Chellagee people. Our chief and over two hundred of our warriors have been up in the mountains for two moons now. When they return, we will allow them to rest and then send them to Coosa Town to help you in your war with the Timucua."

Swordbrought said nothing and the old man went on.

"Fox-Disappears and three others will go with you when your companion is ready. They will stay with you until the others arrive."

Swordbrought smiled bravely. "It is good, Grandfather! With four men such as these, we will quickly push back the Timucua. I am sure of it!"

Chapter 30

Calling Crow knew the woman who was called Mary was watching him as he walked off with the empty oaken buckets in his hands. He thought sadly of his own woman in his village, so far away now. Despite himself, he turned back to look once more at this exotic beauty, Mary. She returned his look, then turned away, her hearty laughter echoing off the wet stone walls. Even though he knew it was directed at him, it was not mean-spirited and therefore not unpleasant. Besides, she was the only one in the place who acknowledged his presence. She had been teasing him every night now and he had grown used to it. Like the crystalline tones of Edward's harp and the square of green grass in the garden, she was one of the few things of beauty in this sad, gray place.

When the women had all gone upstairs and silence engulfed the place, Calling Crow went looking for Edward. He could find him nowhere, and was starting back to his cell when he heard music. It was a fast, carefree tune. Hopeful and free, it beckoned him. He went to the rear of the house. The music was emanating from the garden behind the kitchen. As he drew near, the music seemed to get under his skin and into his blood. Like fire, it warmed him. Drawing closer, he found it was like laughter; it cheered him. He found himself thinking of the stories he had heard as a child of the little people who lived in the forest. In his head he could see them dancing about as they made their wonderful music. He entered the kitchen and the music became louder. His heart beat faster and faster to the sound. Pressing his face to the barred aperture, he peered out into the blackness of the garden. The music stopped. He waited but it did not resume. Saddened, he walked back toward the baths. He happened to look back

over his shoulder at the heavy door to the garden and saw
that it was now slightly ajar. He went back to it.

Calling Crow opened the door and stepped out into the
garden in the night. Edward sat on the garden bench; his harp
resting on his lap. His faced was badly bruised from an ap-
parent beating and his head hung as if he were asleep. He
opened his eyes at Calling Crow's approach.

"They've beaten you," said Calling Crow.

"Fools," said Edward. "Fools and brutes. They do not
even believe you are a man."

"Who?" said Calling Crow warily. He could see that Edward had been drinking wine or beer.

"Amorgh and his man. They are looked upon by the house
masters as less than men, yet they look on you the same."

"It does not matter how they look upon me."

"You know that you are a man, don't you?" said Edward.

Calling Crow frowned. Wine and beer made men talk
strangely.

"It is high time for you to go home, my friend," said
Edward.

"Why do you torture me so?" said Calling Crow. "You
know I have been trying to get out of here. I have not found
a way yet."

Edward shook his head sadly. "Ah! I have been a bad
influence on you and now you sound like me. You must get
back your fight."

Calling Crow said nothing.

Edward's face grew grimly serious. "A bird appeared to
me in a dream last night and spoke to me. It said that you
must soon be on your way, that it was very important."

Calling Crow stared intently at Edward. "Yes, but I have
lost my medicine pouch. Collier took it from me, along with
my weapons."

"What is this medicine you speak of?" said Edward.

"It is what your people call magic," said Calling Crow.
"Tell me, what kind of bird was in your dream?"

Edward seemed puzzled at the question. "A crow, of
course. The old ones knew it as a sacred bird. It told them

where to build their towns, it guided them in their travels, helped them settle disputes.''

Calling Crow looked at Edward questioningly. ''And you believe in the crow?''

Edward looked up at the night sky. ''Crows never lie.''

Calling Crow followed Edward's gaze. The walls of the garden rose straight up, as if the two men were at the bottom of a deep box. High above, thin, stringy clouds raced beneath a silver moon set in a cold, ebony sky.

''What else did the crow say?'' said Calling Crow.

Edward looked at him piercingly. ''It said that when the moon is full you should come out here to the garden. You will find three rocks arranged upon the ground. Dig in the middle of them and eat what you find there. Then you will be ready to go home.''

''I am ready now,'' said Calling Crow. He turned away from Edward and walked to the corner of the garden. He ran his hands over the smooth stones of the walls. There were thin, shallow spaces in between the blocks that made up the wall. He jammed his fingers into these cracks and pulled himself up a few feet off the ground. Edward watched him with amusement. Calling Crow's ankle chains rattled as he dug his toes into the cracks and slowly, painfully, climbed to about half his height from the ground. His fingers began to bleed, the blood running down the gray wall as he rested. The muscles in Calling Crow's back and legs rippled from his exertions and his breath came in gasps. He looked up at the sky and continued slowly upward. He was out of reach by the time Amorgh and his man ran out into the garden. Calling Crow heard them, but did not turn his head as he clung to the wall.

Amorgh looked at Edward incredulously.

Edward laughed. ''He is quite a climber, eh? Like a fly.''

''You let him climb up?'' shouted Amorgh.

Edward laughed. ''Aye, and he may climb out of here yet.''

Amorgh motioned to his man and he jumped at Calling Crow, but he was too high to reach. Amorgh grabbed the smaller man. ''Go around in case he gets over.'' The man ran off. Calling Crow resumed his slow climb, Amorgh flailing upward at him with the whip.

"Look at him go," said Edward laughingly. "He's going to make it!"

"He'll never make it. No one can climb to the top." Amorgh angrily swung the whip upward and it wrapped itself around one of Calling Crow's feet. Calling Crow stopped climbing. He shook his foot slightly and the whip fell away just as Amorgh hung his weight on it. Amorgh fell backward onto the grass.

Edward laughed drunkenly and Amorgh struck him in the face with his whip.

Calling Crow continued his slow climb. Half the wall still stretched above him. Below, Edward and Amorgh looked up as they watched him.

One of Calling Crow's bloody feet lost its purchase and he swung outward from the wall, hanging now only by his left hand and foot. He dropped heavily onto the grass. Amorgh ran over and kicked his inert form. Putting one foot on Calling Crow's back, Amorgh looked over triumphantly at Edward.

"I told you no one could climb this wall! No one."

"It does not matter," said Edward. "He is too wild. You cannot hold him."

Amorgh scowled. "Perhaps you are right, not with iron chains. But, as you know, there are other chains, invisible, but stronger than mere iron." Amorgh smiled triumphantly. "I shall bind him even more tightly to this place. You shall see."

Amorgh tucked his whip behind him as his man ran back into the garden. "Get the savage into his cell!" he shouted before walking back into the house.

Strangely, when Calling Crow awoke the next morning, the chains around his ankles were gone and his cell was unlocked. This change intrigued him. Surely Amorgh and his man would be watching him even more vigilantly now. What was Amorgh planning?

At night, Edward disappeared somewhere as Calling Crow carried the water buckets and fed the great fire that heated the water. He kept his eyes on the ground as he worked and gradually the noise of the place died down and the people went away. The great house grew very quiet. Calling Crow had started back to his cell when a blur of yellow streaked across the sad gray of the walls. Turning, he saw nothing. Then a tiny yellow bird fluttered around the wall and raced toward the front of the house. He followed it to the bottom of the stairs, but it had disappeared up.

Calling Crow noticed a strange thing—a cold breeze pouring swiftly down the stairs, as if the door at the top were open. He had never noticed this before. He crept closer, thinking that Amorgh and his men must be hiding, that it was some kind of trick, but there was no one there. Intrigued, he placed his foot on the first stair. The river of air stopped! Despite that he decided to go up. There might be a way out.

Calling Crow climbed the stairs quietly and found the door to the house locked firmly from within. He was about to go back downstairs when again the little yellow bird darted by. It fluttered up the stairway that led to the women's quarters at the top of the house. Calling Crow started up, but saw no one. They were all asleep. Was there a way out up above, a window he could climb out of? He lay his feet down silently, slowly mounting the stairs. He came up into a long corridor with many doors. One of them was open halfway, the dimly lit interior beckoning. Again, he wondered if this was a trap set for him by Amorgh and his man. It didn't matter though, he decided. If there was even the slightest chance of escape, he must explore it. He went to the door and looked in.

Soft golden light illuminated the room. Mary smiled at him from where she sat upon her bed, an oil lamp burning on a small table beside her. She was wearing a gown the likes of which he had never known existed. It was magical, like a light veil of mist in the morning. It allowed the eyes to see through it to her body. The tiny yellow bird sang happily inside a wicker cage. Calling Crow stepped inside the room and closed the door. The caged bird suddenly grew quiet.

Calling Crow looked over at the bird and it jumped from branch to branch of the little dead tree that was affixed to the inside of its cage.

"His name is George," said Mary, as she watched the little bird jump about. "Your wildness scares him."

Calling Crow said nothing for a moment, staring instead at the aperture that was cut into the stone wall. Flanked by two wooden shutters, the window was too small for anyone but a child to squeeze through. Cool night air moved through it teasingly and he could smell the river in it. A small room had been cut into the other wall. The curtains which covered it were not completely closed and he could see that it led nowhere and was simply a place for Mary to hang her clothes. He looked back at her.

"I thought maybe you wouldn't come," she said.

"I thought this was a way out of here," he said sadly. "That is why I came."

"There is no way out," she said.

Calling Crow again looked around the room. A wooden chest of drawers sat on one side of the room; a single chair under the window on the other. The bird began to sing again tentatively in its tiny voice. Mary ran her hand over the bedclothes. "Bolt the door and come here. Amorgh and his men are away, but I don't know how much time we have till they return."

Calling Crow threw the bolt and went over to her. He sat

on the edge of the bed, mesmerized by the sight of her. She was even more beautiful here than she was downstairs. He looked through the magic gown at her soft white breasts, her wide hips and the tawny hair of her womanhood. She took his hand and placed it upon her leg. He felt as if she'd placed a spell upon him and stared at his hand, marveling at the smoothness and color of her skin against his own.

He took his hand away. What was she doing to him? "Do you know when Amorgh and his men come and go?" he asked her.

She ignored his question. "I dreamt of you last night," she said.

Calling Crow looked into her eyes. They were as deep as the sea and he was sinking into them. "I have dreamed of you too," he said, "even when I am awake. Many times."

Aieyah! He got to his feet and turned away from her. "That is not why I came up here."

"Are you sure?" she said softly.

He turned his back to her. "Yes. Tell me, where does Edward go at night?"

"He changes into a bird and flies away."

Calling Crow turned to her. "You have seen this?"

Mary shook her head solemnly. "No, but everybody knows it is so. He is a sorcerer. He talks to the angels."

"The angels?"

"The spirits in the trees, the water . . . That is why Amorgh has not killed him. He is afraid of him. Haven't you noticed?"

"Yes," said Calling Crow slowly, "He will strike him, but he seems afraid to go further. How did Edward come to be in this place?"

"He made an enemy of a priest in the countryside. They said he was conducting ceremonies in the old ways in the forest at night. They could never catch him, of course, but then someone found secret books hidden in his house and he had to go into hiding."

Somewhere in the house a heavy iron door closed. The sound reverberated through the stone walls.

Mary got out of the bed. "It is Amorgh," she said. "You

must go now or you will get a whipping for being up here."

Out in the quiet of the stone stairway, Calling Crow could still see her beauty before his eyes. Despite that, his longing to be away from this place flared anew. Amorgh and his man went away from time to time. Mary knew when. Perhaps she could help him get the key . . . Calling Crow's mind raced ahead. He must get back to Samuel's, and soon, and then he and Red Feather could make the crossing for home. In one moon's time the villagers would be harvesting the first corn. Then they would plant the second corn. Inside Calling Crow's head a tiny voice cried out in panic. Was it already too late? No! he thought emphatically, pushing the thought from his head. Had not Sees Far told them they would return in time? *Aieyah!* It must be so! But he must hurry!

Chapter 32

Reginald Burton wiped his whiskered lips with the back of his hand and lowered the tankard to the thick oaken table with a loud thump. He looked around the Talbard at the other customers—shopkeepers in aprons, iron mongers with blackened hands, tailors, their doublets riddled with pins, gaunt-faced hod carriers—all of them clustered in groups at different tables, laughing or arguing loudly as they slowly drank themselves into a pleasant numbness. In the other, smaller rooms, the gentlemen talked quietly and calmly, leaning forward on occasion to get a word in to a confidant over the noisy racket. Burton sighed contentedly and took another swallow of his beer. Back at Collier's fair, the smaller wild man was still bringing in many customers and the show was making much money. Collier had sent him in to the city to purchase their bread and provisions as he usually did. But this time there would be a special side trip to the brothel. He had a message to deliver to the savage. It was part of the plan Collier and Amorgh had decided upon to take the fire out of him. Burton frowned. If he were running things, he would do it with a whip. In a week the savage would be licking his boots.

Burton fingered the money in his purse. While at the brothel he would combine a little of his own pleasure with Collier's business.

A serving girl suddenly appeared before Burton, startling him. She leaned forward to pour for him and his pulse quickened at the sight of the ripe young breasts beneath her bodice. She seemed repulsed by his interest, pulling away to disappear quickly into another one of the dingy rooms. Burton cursed and drained his tankard. He put a copper on the table and got slowly to his feet, pushing through the crowd to the door.

Outside, the light of late afternoon hurt his bloodshot eyes. He looked around, getting his bearings, then began walking in the direction of the brothel. More noises assaulted him on the busy street, but they were of a more musical kind. School-boys sang and shouted shrilly to one another as they made their way home; shoppers haggled as fishwives called out their wares; somewhere a blacksmith's hammer clanged rhythmically on an anvil. Burton hadn't lain with a woman in months and his lust began to build as he drew closer to his destination. A clubfooted beggar brushed by him and he reflexively put his hand over the purse in his breeches' pocket. Soon he could see the bell tower of St. Saviour's Church rising on the left above the tall houses and shops, then, straight ahead, the pincushionlike display of pike-mounted severed heads which crowned the southern gateway of the London Bridge. The sight cheered him, for he was almost there. Quickening his pace, he whistled a tune.

Burton sat on the wooden bench, his wide shoulders sag-ging, as the woman left to go get food. He was exhausted, having just passionately spent his seed. Someone approached and he looked up vaguely. It was the savage, carrying two buckets in his hands. The savage recognized Burton, but Burton ignored him. He was going to enjoy this as much as possible. He looked wordlessly at his feet.

The savage did not go away. "Where is my friend?" he said in a plaintive tone.

"Go away," said Burton.

The savage put the buckets down and came closer. "Where is my companion? Is he well?"

Burton felt himself growing angry. He wondered who had first taught this savage to speak. Having the English language issue from his savage lips was an abomination. Burton stood and spotted Amorgh across the room. He nodded subtly. It was almost time to put the knife into this fellow.

The savage stepped closer to Burton—and touched him! "Where is he?"

Burton's face's reddened in anger. "He is dead!" he lied. "Dead! Now, go away!"

"No," cried the savage, "not dead!"

Burton looked at the twisted features of the savage and laughed. The savage stepped closer, putting his hands around Burton's neck, pushing him backward. Burton struck at him, astounded at the man's strength. The savage shouted hysterically now in his native tongue as he continued to push Burton backward. Where the hell was Amorgh? Burton wondered as he began to lose consciousness. A crash of sound brought Burton to. He sat up on the stone floor. Amorgh and the other Turk were wrestling the savage away.

Burton got to his feet, cursing bitterly. He spat as the savage's screams echoed off the walls. Silence hovered in the room for a moment, then the talk and laughter slowly returned. The girl rushed up. "Beer," Burton demanded. He rubbed his throat. "Bring me a bloody beer."

Calling Crow awoke in his cell in a stupor. He got up slowly, his body aching and stiff from the many kicks and blows Amorgh and his man had inflicted upon him. The stones of the house reverberated only silence now and he went quietly next door to Edward's cell. He was gone, his door open. Calling Crow saw a wooden barrel of beer sitting on the table and took it back to his own cell. He drank thirstily, delighting in the cool rasp of the beer against his parched throat. So, Red Feather was dead. The thought seemed to have melded into his flesh and bones now, so that they, too, screamed out in pain, along with his heart. Calling Crow held the barrel up and drank more of the sweet liquid. So, Sees Far had been wrong after all! Calling Crow drank more. If Sees Far was wrong about Red Feather, then could he not have been wrong about Calling Crow returning to his people with the shooting sticks? *Aieyah!* He hated to think these things, but they were possible. Calling Crow drank more and more, and slowly, mercifully, discovered that he didn't care.

He staggered out into the corridor and headed for the stairs. Mary's door was open this time, too, and he quickly entered and bolted it. "Where does this Amorgh sleep?" he demanded. "Tell me!"

"I heard your friend is dead," she said softly. "I am sorry."

Hearing this, he felt all the anger go out of him. He went over and sat on her bed. He cried drunkenly. "Where does this Amorgh sleep? Tell me and I will kill him!"

She put her soft hand upon his head, pulling him to her breasts. Her flesh was warm and inviting. Unable to stop himself, Calling Crow ripped away her gown. She threw her head back and smiled as he mounted her, giving herself to him joyfully, and with a passion that amazed and inflamed him.

Later as he lay spent, she ran her fingers across his lips, looking down at him. George, the caged bird, sang prettily and unafraid, filling the room with his songs.

Mary leaned down and kissed his head. "I dreamt of you again last night."

Calling Crow said nothing.

Mary frowned. "It was most strange. In my dream there was a man with an arrow in his hair. Even though you had already killed him, he came from the beyond to threaten you."

Calling Crow turned away from her.

Mary took a metal thing shaped like a small pot with two tubes coming off of it from beneath her bed. She then took a red silk pouch from beneath her pillow and removed a black sticky substance from it. She broke a piece off as big as a finger tip and kneaded it into a round ball. Calling Crow's sorrow and anger were building again, but he was intrigued by her actions and watched her closely. Mary took a candle from the table and lit it on the lamp. She held the candle to one of the tubes of the metal thing. She then placed the other tube into her mouth and drew upon it. As the candle flame bent at the waist, kissing the black ball, Calling Crow realized the thing was a strange medicine pipe. There was liquid somewhere inside it and it made a gurgling sound as sweet flowery smoke emanated from its top. Mary exhaled and handed the pipe to Calling Crow. He drew on the pipe, pulling some of the strange smoke deep into his lungs. After a moment he relaxed some, his anger and worry beginning to dissipate.

Mary turned to him, her eyes as red as blood. She smiled sadly. "Better now, eh?"

Strangely, as if it were someone else doing it, Calling Crow nodded his head. They continued to smoke and seemed to grow smaller and smaller until the bed became a vast, treeless landscape. Finally Calling Crow fell into a deep, deathlike sleep.

Chapter 33

Despite the coming of autumn, the sun burned down from a clear blue sky as Swordbrought, Crying Wolf and the file of four Cussitaw braves emerged from the forest and started across a field of cane grass toward the Coosa Town. Crying Wolf stopped and the four men behind him waited.

"Swordbrought," he said.

Swordbrought turned.

"I am not going back," said Crying Wolf.

"Crying Wolf, you must." Swordbrought's face was big with disbelief. "You will get a hearing before the Council and I will tell them of all that has happened. They will give you a chance to prove yourself again."

"For what I have done there can be no second chance, Swordbrought. I have no people anymore. I can never again show my face in Coosa Town."

"You are wrong, Crying Wolf," said Swordbrought sadly.

Crying Wolf shook his head. "No. I am not wrong. All the things they said in Council are true. You are the best representative of the Coosa people. The Council chose well."

Crying Wolf turned away. Limping slightly, he ran back into the forest and disappeared.

Swordbrought started toward the distant palisade, the Cussitaw braves following him. A group of boys playing outside the timbered walls spotted the men. They watched warily, ready to run into the safety of the palisade. As the men drew closer, some of the boys recognized Swordbrought and they all ran out to meet him. The boys were smiling and talking as they approached but quickly lapsed into a wary silence when they realized that Fox-Disappears and his three men were not of their village. The boys followed the men inside, but hung back a dozen paces, talking quietly and speculatively.

The file of men moved along the village streets, followed by a growing crowd of curious children. Some idle people noticed the men's appearance and stopped their talking to watch them pass. In the cornfields, men broke up the ground with fish-bone hoes, the muscles in their backs rippling under their sweat-glistening skin, while women jammed finger-deep holes into the earth as they deposited seeds there in a swift motion. These took no notice of the arrivals.

It was dark by the time the Council was ready to formally receive Swordbrought, and Fox-Disappears and his men. They entered the torch-lit *chokafa* and seated themselves across from the Council of Old Men. Two Clouds was the first to speak. He got to his feet and looked at Swordbrought and the others. He then turned and addressed himself to Sees Far.

"Sees Far, Swordbrought has brought back warriors to help us in our fight against the Timucua, but not as many as we wanted."

Sees Far nodded gravely and the other old men smiled at this.

Two Clouds turned back to Swordbrought. "Swordbrought, why have you brought back only four men?"

Swordbrought rose to his feet. "Grandfather, that is all they could spare. The Cussitaw people are off fighting a war against the Chellagee people. When they finish, many more will come here and help us."

Two Clouds nodded. "If we are still here. Mantua and his men are a day's march south of us."

Swordbrought nodded toward the squat Muskogee brave, Fox-Disappears. "These people saved my life. With their help we will repel the Timucua."

Two Clouds turned to the other old men. "Well, I think we chose well to send Swordbrought. He did what was asked of him."

The old men nodded in agreement and Two Clouds turned back to fix his hawkish eyes on Swordbrought. "Sees Far tells me that he never sees your father anymore in his dreams, but that he is sure he isn't dead.''

''I am sure that he will return to us,'' said Swordbrought. Sees Far nodded solemnly and Two Clouds went on.

''Swordbrought, we cannot wait any longer for Calling Crow. We must take action soon. Take Fox-Disappears and Little Bear with you and find out what Mantua and his men are planning. They already have over two hundred braves in their camp. That is more than enough to overrun our town and take our women and children prisoner. But they appear to be waiting for something before they attack. You men must go and find out what that is. We must know how much time we have!''

Swordbrought's smooth, young face grew grim. ''Of course, Grandfather. We will do what you wish.''

Always, the effects of Mary's smoke stayed with Calling Crow long after he left her bed. These days he moved in a stupor through the steamy cubicles, carrying wood and pouring water. The shouts and bawdy laughter of the people no longer bothered him as they rattled off the wet stone walls, clattering in and out of his ears. Even more strange, Edward's kind voice was only a reverberant noise to Calling Crow now as he moved about his tasks. Only the occasional echoing strains of Edward's music penetrated the thick fog that had enveloped Calling Crow's heart. When he heard the music, it was like the sight of a colorful spray of yellow flowers in a sunny clearing after one emerged from a dark cave. Then it was gone and the dark and quiet again engulfed him.

Calling Crow did not know why they had taken his chains off, or why they left his cell unlocked. He tried to understand it, but his mind no longer seemed capable of clear thought. This night, like all the others, he looked up to see that the door that led to the women's rooms was open. He quietly mounted the stairs to Mary's room. They made love as if outside of time, their passion a meal they lingered long over, both giving and tasting all the flavors they'd enjoyed over a lifetime. Then they smoked and the pipe sucked Calling Crow dry of all sorrow and pain. This night he noticed that along with his sorrow, his body was drying up. He was lighter, weaker, like a gourd left to dry in the sun. They slept.

Sometime before morning Calling Crow and Mary awoke to the heavy thud of the front door. Voices argued loudly. Calling Crow went out and Mary followed him. They heard Amorgh's familiar cough and Edward's voice, and another voice that Calling Crow had not heard in a while—Collier!

Calling Crow and Mary crept closer around the stairwell. Amorgh and his man and Collier stood on the landing facing Edward. Collier wore a great black cape, having just come in from the cold. His breath billowed as he accosted Edward. "What did you take?" he demanded.

"What are you talking about?" said Edward.

Amorgh and his man grabbed Edward from behind, bending his arms around. They were hurting him and Calling Crow could not go to him; the black smoke had taken all his courage. All he could do was hide and watch with Mary.

"Don't play innocent with me," yelled Collier. "Someone broke into my carriage . . . and Porter says he saw you in the town last night."

"I'm free to come and go as I please," said Edward.

"Yes," bellowed Collier, "and I'm free to tell a certain sheriff where you are hiding yourself these days. Now, what did you take, you bloody thief!"

"You have nothing that I would want," said Edward with scorn.

"Filthy Irish liar!" Collier grabbed Edward, turning him about. They fell to the ground and Collier rolled on top, straddling the smaller man's chest. Edward cursed and laughed drunkenly. Collier grabbed him by the hair, lifting his head. Calling Crow opened his mouth and Mary held her hand there, quieting him.

Collier slammed Edward's head into the stones. "What did you take?" he demanded. He slammed his head again with an awful thud. "What did you take?"

Edward did not move as thick blood pooled beneath his head.

"You've killed him," said Amorgh worriedly.

Mary cried out and made the sign of the cross. The men looked up in surprise as Calling Crow staggered down the stairs.

"Get him," shouted Amorgh, as he and Collier rushed up. No longer strong, Calling Crow was easily pushed back and overcome by the men. They beat him and took him back to his cell.

*   *   *

After Edward's death, Calling Crow went about his tasks mindlessly, barely feeling the occasional sting of the whip. He continued to go to Mary's room, but they no longer made love. They were both too saddened and empty. Instead, they smoked the pungent black tar that Mary kept beneath her pillow. It sent their souls on journeys to distant, featureless lands full of warm drifting fogs and devoid of people and animals. Once Swordbrought, Green Bird Woman and Bright Eyes appeared to Calling Crow. Bright Eyes held a child, his grandchild, out to him. He sat up on the bed and threw the bubbling pipe away as if it were a live thing. It clattered metallically across the floor as he turned to Mary, his eyes full of tears and blood, "I must leave this place! I must go home. Tell me where Amorgh sleeps."

Mary, her own eyes bloodied and vacant, calmly shook her head. "Then he will kill you too."

Calling Crow stared at her, knowing he should feel anger and rage, but he could feel nothing. There was nothing inside him anymore. He left the bed and crawled across the stone floor to retrieve the pipe.

"You need more, is all," said Mary, placing another black piece of death in the pipe's bowl. Calling Crow quickly held the candle to it and drew on it. The little flame curled over the edge of the bowl like water running over a fall as smoke gurgled through the thing. Calling Crow passed it wordlessly to Mary as the faces in his head dissolved. He fell back upon the bed. Soon his soul embarked on another journey to the strange dead lands.

Chapter 35

T*he* topknotted Timucua braves made no attempt to hide themselves as they stood up in the dugout canoe and paddled out into the river. Many more braves lined the banks, sitting relaxedly or standing to talk and watch the men in the canoe. From their hiding place across the river, Swordbrought, Little Bear and Fox-Disappears watched one of the Timucua lean out and jab downward with a five-pronged spear. He triumphantly hoisted a wriggling fish, its silver sides flashing bright sunlight. "He is the biggest one!" The voice drifted across the water clearly, as if the speaker were right next to the hidden Coosa braves.

"Look," whispered Little Bear, pointing at some Timucua working farther up the riverbank. The men waded in waist-deep water as they pounded wooden stakes into the river bottom. "They are building a fish weir . . . on our land!"

Swordbrought watched, noting how the very big brave, Little Bear, quivered with rage after his pronouncement. They could do nothing now however, for there were simply too many. Indeed, there were too many Timucua for the village.

Swordbrought ignored the noise the Timucua fishermen and workers made as he listened to the forest behind him. They had been here three days now and, even though they had left no traces of themselves, they must never relax their vigilance.

Fox-Disappears tapped Swordbrought on the shoulder. Swordbrought turned to watch the tall Timucua chief, Mantua, carefully make his way down the mud-slippery bank to the river. Mantua bent at the waist to splash himself with water, then looked at his top braves.

"Avila brings in his ship in two moon's time. We will get

our camp ready and stock up on fish and meat. Then we will attack and take our slaves. When Avila arrives he will pay us in thundersticks and long knives.''

The braves raised their axes skyward, shouting in anticipation. Then their voices dropped as they discussed further with their chief.

Swordbrought's face was grim as he turned to the other two men. ''We have seen and heard enough,'' he said softly. ''Let us start back before it gets too dark.''

As they quietly made their way out of the thicket, a movement caught Swordbrought's eye and he pulled his fighting axe from his belt. Little Bear and Fox-Disappears pulled theirs also. A loud cacophonous chorus of Timucua war cries erupted from all around as twenty or thirty men rushed at them. Swordbrought aimed a blow at a powerful-looking brave but he deftly parried it. There was no time for a second blow; several large braves slammed Swordbrought painfully to the ground. Before he went down, Swordbrought had the satisfaction of seeing Fox-Disappears land a bloody blow to the head of a Timucua brave. Then they were being dragged swiftly across the shallow river, a man on each arm. Swordbrought felt badly that he hadn't taken them home the night before. Now it was too late. He prayed to his spirit guide that their deaths would be swift and that he'd be brave.

Chapter 36

As Calling Crow carried the boiling water to the baths, Edward's death was before his eyes. The picture would not go away. In Edward's death he saw the death of others far away. They would soon die because he was here and powerless to help them, and there was not enough black smoke in the world to alleviate the pain of that realization. Slowly he went about his final task of damping down the fire beneath the great caldron. As he stared into the flames, the heat burning his face and arms, he found himself thinking of his peoples' story about the coming of medicine. The story told how once there was no pain and sickness in the world to afflict people. Life was good for a long, long time. Then, people offended the animals by killing too many of them and not showing gratitude for those they had killed. The animals held a great council and decided to send sickness to the people. People suffered so much that eventually the animals took pity on them. They appeared to the holiest of the people while they dreamt, and told them what plants they should use to cure their sicknesses. They also told them how to use the sweat lodge to heal themselves.

A pile of half-burned logs suddenly collapsed, startling Calling Crow. A knot of wood popped, blue gasses hissing in escape. Calling Crow thought of the time before they left to come to England, of the many deer they had killed to get the skins for the shooting sticks. Sees Far had offered a prayer to the deer people, but perhaps Calling Crow's own prayer was not sincere. Perhaps he still did not have the forgiveness of the deer people. Was that why his life had turned into such an unbearable sickness? Inside his head a small voice said, "Take a sweat bath and heal yourself." He looked around.

One of the copper tubs in the corner had a man-sized hole in its base where the metal had rotted out. Calling Crow had an idea.

He went into the other room and got one of the thick canvases that were sometimes placed upon the stone floor for the lovers. He draped it over the top of the broken tub and then ran a rope around it, making the canvas as snug upon the tub top as the skin on a drum. Then he scooped up a bucket full of the glowing embers and dumped them on the metal floor inside the tub. Immediately he could feel the heat rising inside. He crawled out and got another bucket of embers. He crawled inside, emptying the bucket making a tall, radiant mound. He spotted a wicker basket of wet cloths outside and pulled it in after him to plug up the hole. The heat built quickly and he fought for breath. Pungent sweat poured from him, forming a steaming pool about him. Soon his skin sweat no more and turned as dry as a leaf. His consciousness waned as he sang the medicine songs. He thought he could smell his own hair burning but he stayed where he was. He must cure himself. Finally he could stand no more. He was burning up. It was then that he felt the presence of an old friend, the medicine man, Sees Far, sitting beside him. Sees Far smiled at him in encouragement and he passed out.

Calling Crow awoke sprawled upon the metal floor of the tub. The embers had cooled and he pushed the charred, crumbling remains of the basket away and crawled out. He felt that something was coming. He looked around in the dark. The great house was deathly quiet. He thought he heard music, a ripple of notes from a harp! He headed toward the kitchen and paused to listen. Hearing nothing, he was about to turn and go back toward the stairs that led to Mary's room. Then it came again—a cascade of tinkling notes, like a hand drawn quickly across the strings of the harp. He ran to the kitchen door and found it unlocked. He went out.

The garden was empty. Of course it would be empty, he told himself sadly. He became aware of a growing pressure in his head and looked up. Above the box formed by the garden walls, clouds were racing past a huge full moon of polished bone. He remembered Edward's words and looked down at the grass at his feet. In the silvery light, he easily located the three rocks.

He knelt on the soft earth. The bright moonlight seemed to tickle the inside of his head as the wind moved his hair. Leaves skittered about the garden path like noisy bugs. He dug into the damp earth with his hands, down as far as his elbows. His fingers touched a soft object. He pulled it up and brushed the dirt from it. A small pouch, it was decorated with tiny bird feet prints. *Aieyah!* This pouch was from his other life, that other world! Calling Crow suddenly thought of Mary up in the top of the house. His flesh remembered her warmth. He remembered the magic black smoke that took away all pain and memory. For a moment he considered putting the pouch back in the earth and covering it up. Then the moon seemed to immobilize him and the wind and leaves spoke to him, whispering encouragement. He saw old Sees Far handing him the pouch so long ago. Again he thought he heard Edward's harp, then a loud squawk came from above. Calling Crow looked up to see a large crow perched on the top of the wall. The crow looked at Calling Crow curiously and then spread its large wings and flew away.

Calling Crow understood what it was telling him. It was time to leave this place. He got to his feet. Remembering Edward's instructions, he opened the pouch. He brought the tiny carcass to his mouth and chewed on the harsh, desiccated flesh. He coughed, fighting back the urge to retch. As he ate it he felt himself straightening, standing taller. He took a deep breath and stretched, and his bones cracked and popped loudly. He felt strength flowing through them. He looked at the pouch in his hands and remembered how the faded painted bird feet pattern had once held a rainbow of colors. He saw vividly his attractive, loving wife and his strong son, his village and his people, his mission. Tears filled his eyes and he screamed out his war cry, his voice echoing off the boxlike walls and up to the moon. Tonight he would leave this place, one way or another.

He headed for Mary's room as realization flooded through him. It was after Amorgh took off his chains that she had sent her little bird to bring him to her room. It was her pipe and black smoke that had made him weak and small, that took away his memories and his pain, thereby robbing him of his rage and the strength it would impart to him. She did these things for Amorgh. The realization hurt him, but he knew it must be so. And she must know where Amorgh, the keeper of the keys, slept. She must!

Mary waited for him eagerly. The weather was colder than usual and she had closed the window. Now she longed for his warmth beside her. George sang his tiny songs from his cage but they did not cheer her much. Nothing cheered her, or Crow, since Collier and Amorgh killed Edward the music maker.

The door opened and she looked up. It was Crow. He was different, though. She could see that a great anger possessed him and he seemed to have grown larger. He closed the door and latched it.

"Tell me what you have known all along," he said. "Tell me where Amorgh sleeps."

She could not tell him. No matter how much she wanted to. She said nothing and he came closer. The room was very still and quiet.

"Tell me!" he demanded.

"I don't know."

"*Aieyah,*" said Calling Crow. "I will wait. Tonight you will tell me, Mary."

She said nothing and he said, "Why is George locked up?"

Mary remained silent as Calling Crow opened the cage and put his hand inside. George hopped on his finger and he went over and sat on her bed. Calling Crow stroked the little bird's head with his finger. He brought him close to his lips and said to him, "You must know where the keeper of the keys sleeps. If only you could talk, you would tell me, wouldn't you?"

George flew off, fluttering around the room twice, finally disappearing somewhere behind Calling Crow. He turned around and did not see him. "Where is he?" Calling Crow said.

Mary said nothing, looking over quickly at the closet.

Calling Crow followed her look, suspicion darkening his face. He went over to the closet and pulled the curtain aside. There was a dark crack where the walls met. He had never noticed it before. Had the bird disappeared in there?

Calling Crow pushed and the wall gave way to the blackness of a corridor. Stairs led up.

He looked at Mary. "What is this?"

Too frightened to speak, she said nothing.

Calling Crow disappeared into the blackness of the corridor.

Mary took the pipe from the floor. She kneaded a soft plug of opium into a ball and put it in the bowl. She was about to light it when George fluttered back into the room, settling in her hair. She carried him to his cage and put him inside. Returning to the bed, she lit the pipe. As the smoke began to make her smaller, she thought worriedly that when Amorgh came down he would kill her. She could see his small black eyes and feel his large sweaty hands around her neck. She took another gurgling draw on the pipe and the thought became less terrible. It became intriguing. Would he kill her? Would he not fear the owners? How would he rationalize it? Suddenly another thought struck her. It might be Calling Crow that would come down the stairs. Would he kill her? He had cause: she had helped to keep him here. He knew that now. She sucked at the pipe hungrily as this new, sad, terrible thought filled her head. The smoke ran through her veins now, warming her against the cold speculation. Fixing her eyes blankly on the closet, she continued breathing through the pipe. Finally her fears shrank to mere motes of pollen and drifted away on a slight draft.

Calling Crow took the stairs two at a time, quickly arriving before the door at the top. He opened it smoothly, the leather hinges making no noise. Along one wall was a large shuttered window, some moonlight coming through the cracks. At the far end of the room a large canopied bed sat. Calling Crow crept silently over to it and looked down. Amorgh's sallow-faced helper slept peacefully there, but the big man was missing.

Calling Crow heard something behind and turned. Amorgh's arm went around Calling Crow's neck. "Khoudi!" cried the big man.

Amorgh's friend jumped from the bed and pulled a dagger from his belt as Amorgh wrestled Calling Crow backward to the floor. The little man ran with the dagger outstretched and Calling Crow caught him with his feet as he sprang, pushing him backward with all his might. The man crashed splinteringly through the shutters, a cry escaping his lips as he fell to his death.

The little man's death distracted Amorgh for only an instant, but it was all Calling Crow needed to twist out of his grip. He bounded to his feet as Amorgh took a sword from the wall. Amorgh swung and Calling Crow dived out of the way. Calling Crow grabbed the heavy covering off the bed and threw it, netlike, over Amorgh's outstretched arm and sword. It slowed the big man down enough for Calling Crow to reach him and pounce on him. A tiny cry escaped Amorgh's lips as Calling Crow's hands closed around his neck. Amorgh dropped the sword and struck at Calling Crow, scratching him. Amorgh squealed hoarsely as all of Calling Crow's pain and anger passed into his hands. Amorgh's hands fought for a purchase on Calling Crow's body, then lay still at his side. Calling Crow's hands had minds of their own and they squeezed and squeezed until Amorgh's neck was the thickness of a young boy's wrist. Amorgh's head flopped onto his chest and then onto the stone floor with a thud. Calling Crow took the keys from his side. He spotted a cloth sack by the bed and tucked it into his sash. He would use it for Red Feather's bones. He had already decided to go back to Collier's, find the bones and take them home. Otherwise, Red Feather's spirit would roam these foreign lands in sadness forever. He hurried back down the stairs.

Mary's eyes were as red as two setting suns and she seemed frail and childlike. He realized that he had never really seen her this way before and it was very sad.

He held up the keys. "He is dead. You are free."

She smiled sadly. "Come here."

Calling Crow sat on the bed. She laughed sweetly, sitting

up to run her hand over his face. "Stay with me."

He shook his head. "It is time for me to go now; you can go too."

"Open the window, please," she said.

Calling Crow did as she wanted and the cold, river-scented night air poured into the room.

"Now open the door to George's cage."

The little bird had been singing merrily in its tiny voice, but when Calling Crow opened the cage door, it stopped. It looked at the opened door nervously, but did not move.

"He knows that to go out there is to die," said Mary. "Poor thing, the starlings would make a quick meal of him."

She turned to Calling Crow. "I am no longer young. I, too, would not fare well outside. Besides, I am happy here."

Calling Crow looked at her sadly. He did not want to leave her here, but he could do nothing for her. He left the room and went quickly down the stairs to the big door. The second key he tried opened it and he went out into the night. He looked once toward the river, and the bridge tower with the long things jutting from it, and then hurried away from the city. Caressing the medicine pouch hanging from his belt, he said a quick prayer to his spirit guide. His prayer was good, because with every step he could feel his power growing, and himself becoming invisible. He saw two men coming toward him on the road and deliberately passed very close to them; they never knew he was there. Soon he left the city behind.

As the light of day began to gather, Calling Crow hid himself under one of the large structures the English penned their animals up in. As the sun moved across the sky, he slept fitfully, the shouts and talk of the English field workers drifting under the structure. Several times men and women snuck inside the structure to couple quickly and furtively, going out again soon afterward. When darkness fell, Calling Crow again took to the road, heading in the same direction, away from the city. In the middle of the night he saw a familiar compound, Collier's fair.

Calling Crow's heart was heavy as he crept through the tall hedgerows that surrounded the place. He came across the pen where Collier kept the pigeons he and his men so loved to eat, and broke into it. He quickly killed eight of the cooing birds, then tucked their wrung necks under his belt. He located the place were he and Red Feather had been held captive. He crept over to the small structure and peered into the barred aperture, at the dingy interior. He did not think they would have left Red Feather's bones in there; the English buried their dead, but perhaps there was a clue as to where they buried him. He saw the bottom of one of the sleeping shelves. All his sadness came back to him now as he mourned his friend. Then something came into view—a foot!

From inside the hut a voice moaned and a figure moved into the patch of moonlight. It was Red Feather. He looked out in confusion. "Who is there?"

"You live!" said Calling Crow, not being able to contain his joy. "I thought you were dead."

Red Feather came to the door, his hands curling around the bars as he looked out. "No," he said, "I did not die. I waited for you but I was beginning to think that you had died."

Calling Crow shook the heavy door but it wouldn't budge. "I must get you out of here quickly."

"Yes," said Red Feather. "The keys are in Collier's wagon, along with the keys for my leg chains, and our weapons too."

Calling Crow was already hurrying across the dark field. He crept silently around the side of the wagon, noting the pale light that issued from some cracks. He heard the scratch of a chair; Collier was in there. Calling Crow remembered Collier's hands slamming Edward's head into the stones and he decided to kill the Englishman. Footsteps hurriedly approached and Calling Crow froze in the darkness. Several pairs of feet clumped up the steps and he heard muted voices. A moment later the feet thumped down the steps and hurried off. Calling Crow waited in the darkness for a moment and then crept inside. His heart sang when he spotted the black iron key ring hanging from a wooden peg on the wall. From some wooden pegs on the other wall he took his and Red Feather's bows, their axes and their quivers of arrows.

Later, Calling Crow and Red Feather stood against the

hedgerows. Calling Crow tucked his iron axe under his belt and looked around. He pointed out the woods in the distance to Red Feather. As they hurried along, Calling Crow hoped the woods would be deep and thick enough to conceal a fire. He wanted to cook the pigeons, for they were both very hungry and had a long, long way to go.

Chapter 37

The moon had not yet risen when Calling Crow and Red Feather left the woods. They walked parallel to the road, but an arrow's flight away, through the plowed fields and through small woods. They walked in silence, keeping their distance from the scattered dwellings, some of which showed the golden glow of fires from their windows. Occasionally they would be forced to climb over one of the small stone walls that snaked through the land. Once they stopped in a garden long enough to pull up and eat some roots growing there.

The moon rose finally, a gibbous moon, giving off soft silvery light. Uncomfortable with the wide open expanses of fields, the two men hunched over closer to the earth as they walked. They methodically watched the road before and behind them for any signs of movement. There were none.

They walked in silence as the moon moved across the sky. Calling Crow frowned at something ahead and stopped.

"What is it?" said Red Feather softly in their native Muskogee.

"The road splits in two ahead."

"So?"

"One goes on, going higher into the hills; the other goes that way."

Red Feather searched the dark distance where Calling Crow's arm was pointing.

"Which goes to Bristol?" said Red Feather.

"I don't know," said Calling Crow. "We shall have to ask."

Red Feather said nothing, instead turning to look at Calling Crow in puzzlement.

Calling Crow started walking again. "Come. We must find someone to ask."

Richard Burke, a fifteen-year-old shepherd boy, stared off at the distant hills. Keeping one eye on the rocks that jutted out of the soil like ancient bones, he followed the slowly grazing sheep as they moved in the direction of a field higher up. He felt an inexplicable chill upon his back and turned around suddenly. For a moment he thought he saw two figures on the distant horizon. He screwed up his eyes and there was nothing. He walked on.

A large round rock, nearly as tall as he, cast a black shadow like a well and he thought of the story of the knight Tannhauser. It was said that it was on a night such as this when he came upon a cave that led down to the underworld. A beautiful woman could be seen down there in a sheer, billowing dress of silks. She was Venus the nymph and he descended to her, disappearing for seven years. As Richard passed by the shadow he felt a chill. Did he hear something? He hurried away from the shadow, remembering the story of St. Patrick and the entrance to purgatory. Richard thought he heard a gentle footfall behind and turned suddenly.

"You, wait."

The voice was faint and strange-sounding. A ghost? Richard turned and ran over the rocky ground, frightening the sheep that now hurried along with him. Richard's frantic uphill flight caused him to pant loudly. He ran onward, finally coming up against a large upthrust temple of rocks known to the local people as the Rockpile. Over the top, Richard saw some high wispy clouds racing beneath the moon.

"You," came the odd voice again, "stop!"

Richard turned. At first he saw nothing, then two shadows separated from the others and moved a bit closer.

Richard's panting increased. "What do you want?" he cried.

"Where is the town called Bristol?" said the ghost.

Richard's voice trembled. "The low road," he blurted out. He pointed. "Take the low road."

It was a few moments before Richard realized the ghosts

had gone. He moved a few steps forward and stopped. Seeing and hearing nothing, he called to his sheep and hurried home.

The next day, a small notice was affixed to a signboard outside the village church. It read:

"Richard Burke, the shepherd boy,
was pursued and harassed by ghosts last night.
Running for his life, Richard managed to escape
his pursuers until they trapped him against the Rockpile.
There the ghosts demanded of him to know
the way to the town of Bristol.
It is thought by some that Richard hath
stayed too long in the bright moonlight
and that it hath driven him mad."

Chapter 38

Calling Crow and Red Feather looked out from the woods at Samuel's estate. The windows were golden squares; torchlight flickered on the lawns just in front of the house. The rest of the lawn was hidden by the stone walls.

Armed only with his iron club, Calling Crow started across the fields. Red Feather carried the bows over his shoulder as he followed behind. When they came to the wall, they could hear distant voices.

"There are many people in there," said Red Feather. "Perhaps we should wait in the woods and go in tomorrow."

Calling Crow listened to the voices a moment before talking. "Perhaps, but I want to see who is there. Help me over the wall."

Calling Crow paused at the top and looked down at Red Feather. "Wait for me here. I will come back."

Red Feather nodded and Calling Crow dropped down inside the walls.

Calling Crow headed for the house. As he drew close, he saw that the people had evidently gone inside. Animated voices and the occasional strain of a musical instrument reached his ears. Outside, two torches still burned brightly, just down from the main entrance. Calling Crow decided to go around the back. He came to an open window and moved closer. The smell of tallow wafted out, but the dimly lit room appeared empty. He was about to climb inside when he heard a sound and turned. Two men were walking by. One carried a torch. The other was Samuel's brother, John. They saw him. "You!" said John. "How in the devil did you get back here?"

"It *was* you!" said Calling Crow.

John pulled his sword and turned to his companion. "Get the others."

The man ran off and John stepped boldly toward Calling Crow.

Calling Crow pulled the iron axe from the rope belt around his breeches. "It was you who put us in that place," he said.

John ran forward and swung his sword. Calling Crow dived out of the way as a shower of leaves and debris fell around him. John cursed and ran at him, raising his sword for another blow. His face suddenly screwed up in pain and he pitched forward onto his knees. A feathered arrow protruded from his back.

Red Feather approached and stood in the dim light. "I will not let you out of my sight again," he said. "Always, I am afraid I will lose you and I see that I am right."

Calling Crow was about to reply when Samuel ran up. He knelt and stroked his brother's head. He felt his neck for the pulse of his life's blood. "He is dead!" he said in an anguished voice. Bowing his head, he mumbled some prayers, crying sadly. Then he stood and looked at Calling Crow and Red Feather in shock. "You! You are back!"

"Of course we are back." Red Feather had another arrow nocked in his bow, this one aimed at Samuel's chest. "You put us in the fair. Now you shall die like your brother."

"What is he talking about, Calling Crow?"

"Your brother and some men took us that night, Samuel. They took us to Collier's fair and locked us up there all this time."

"How do you know it was he?" said Samuel in anguish.

"It was he, Samuel. Look inside yourself and you will see. It was he."

Calling Crow turned to his *tastanagi*. "Put down your bow, Red Feather. It was John that did this thing to us, not Samuel."

"Calling Crow, you don't know how much it hurts me not to listen to you. But you have always been blind in this thing. Long ago Samuel must have put some spell upon you, don't you see? All our suffering is his doing and I shall end that now." Red Feather pulled the vane of the arrow back to his cheek as four Englishmen ran up with torches, bathing the area in heat and light.

"Red Feather," said Calling Crow, "tell me something, for I am confused. How can it be that my very own right arm no longer does my bidding?"

Red Feather trembled, then released the tension in the bow.

"Get them," shouted the men, seizing Calling Crow and Red Feather, pinning their arms behind them.

"Kill them," shouted one of the men, pulling his sword.

"No," said Samuel, turning to the man. He looked angrily at Calling Crow as he spoke to the man. "Go to the garrison and get the soldiers. The law shall have them. We will keep them here until the soldiers arrive."

One of the men struck Red Feather, knocking him to his knees. "Bloody savages! Soon you will both hang."

Samuel stared coldly at Calling Crow. "Put them in the spring house."

Chapter 39

A *large* fire burned beside a dead willow tree in the middle of the clearing the Timucua were using for their camp. Back a hundred feet, Swordbrought, Little Bear and Fox-Disappears strained uselessly against the hide cords that bound their hands painfully to the tall poles behind them. The Timucua had held them prisoner for three days now, and tonight Mantua would decide what should be done with them.

Swordbrought heard a tiny noise. He turned to see Crying Wolf creep from the shadows near the river. He crouched beside him, cutting his cords. Swordbrought's arms fell to his side, temporarily, uselessly numb. Crying Wolf had turned to go to Fox-Disappears when four Timucua braves cried out and ran over. Crying Wolf spun round with the knife, slashing one brave across the throat. The man went down but several others were soon upon them and they were quickly overcome and tied up again.

"Bring them now," came a loud voice from the fire. The Timucua cut Little Bear and Fox-Disappears down. Crying Wolf struggled and a Timucua brave clubbed him over the head. He and another brave dragged Crying Wolf by his hair through the mud as the other braves pushed and shoved Swordbrought, Little Bear and Fox-Disappears.

They stood close to the big fire, its heat burning them. The tall Timucua chief, Mantua, emerged from the crude hut that had been built for him. He stood before each of them in turn, inspecting carefully. Grabbing Little Bear by the hair, Mantua yanked his head closer to look into his eyes, then pushed him away. He pointed to Crying Wolf, who was lying supine on the ground, his head to the side; one of the braves had his foot planted upon his neck.

"Let him up."

The brave stepped away and Crying Wolf got slowly to his feet.

"Bring me a torch," Mantua called.

A brave ran up with a torch and Mantua took it, holding it so close to Crying Wolf that all could hear his hair singeing. Crying Wolf did not move.

"Yes, I remember you. The one who fought so hard. You would deny us our due?"

Crying Wolf said nothing, instead looking through the Timucua chief.

Mantua sneered and came back to stand before Fox-Disappears. The squat Muskogee brave's face was flint hard; no emotion escaped his eyes. Mantua studied him a moment longer, then walked on to Swordbrought. He shook his head in puzzlement, then held the torch close as he studied Swordbrought's features. Sudden realization lit up his eyes and his face twisted into a gruesome smile.

"Now I know where I've seen your features before," said Mantua. "The one who is guided by the crow, the one who left a feather with me to show me that he could have killed me. He must be your father."

"Yes," said Swordbrought. "He is. And he will drive you and your men off and kill you."

Mantua backed off and laughed. He addressed the four captives collectively. "My men have endured much over the past several moons." He looked over briefly at Crying Wolf. "One of their favorite warriors is now dead and they demand blood revenge. One of you will give them the satisfaction they crave."

Mantua stood before Fox-Disappears and glared at him angrily. Fox-Disappears did not flinch. Mantua then stood before Crying Wolf. Crying Wolf scowled at him angrily. Mantua stood before Little Bear and the big brave smiled disdainfully. Mantua moved on to Swordbrought. Mantua then nodded to one of his men and he cut the cords around Swordbrought's wrists.

Mantua smiled. "You must deliver my message to your father, the Crow warrior." He reached into his medicine pouch and took out a black feather. He handed it to Sword-brought. "Give this back to your father. Tell him I will be coming for your people soon. Tell him that I will personally deliver both of you to the Spanish!"

Mantua turned and pointed to Crying Wolf. Several Timucua braves rushed forward and grabbed Crying Wolf, dragging his struggling form toward the small dead willow near the fire.

Mantua pulled his knife and approached Little Bear and Fox-Disappears. He cut their wrists free. "All of you, come. You will sit with me."

Crying Wolf had already been tied to the tree. After Mantua, Fox-Disappears, Little Bear and Swordbrought sat, a large Timucua brave stepped out of the crowd and approached Crying Wolf.

"Swordbrought," Crying Wolf called out, "save my name! Tell the village what I tried to do! Tell your father I died brave!"

The large Timucua brave took a knife from his belt. He cut into the flesh on Crying Wolf's broad back just above the shoulder blades. Crying Wolf flinched, but did not cry out. The Timucua brave then sawed and tugged, pulling the brown strip of skin down to reveal the wet flesh beneath.

Mantua looked over at Swordbrought and the others. Swordbrought looked away angrily. He looked instead at Little Bear's and Fox-Disappears's faces. They were expressionless. Swordbrought hoped his own face would show nothing.

The Timucua brave started another cut, pulling and tugging. Crying Wolf shuddered. His breath whistled rapidly as the outer skin of his left side hung down from his waist like some half-removed garment.

Swordbrought watched, struggling to keep his face expressionless. Inside he forced his mind to recall all the lessons his father and Red Feather had taught him of the way of things and of the Great Mystery. He recalled climbing a tree with some other boys to witness a snake raiding the nest of a woodpecker, the snake eating the hatchlings one by one as the mother flew about, shrieking out her horror and despair; he remembered his father waking him with a touch and the

two of them watching a panther bring down a buck deer twice
its own size; he remembered the deer's brave, doomed struggle with the panther's jaws clamped around its throat; he remembered his own, clumsy first kill, when his arrow hadn't
penetrated the deer's side deeply enough; he remembered
looking briefly into the glazed, shocked eyes as he quickly
cut the deer's throat. Now this bloody thing tied to a tree,
that panted and writhed, that no longer looked like a man,
this was part of the Great Mystery, too, as much a part of the
Great Mystery as a hawk in flight or a hailstorm . . .

But, despite all of these things that he knew to be true, way
down inside Swordbrought, in a tiny little place where no one
but he ever went, there was intense revulsion, pain and breath-
taking horror, and sadness, too—all of which he would not
allow up and out now, not yet, knowing that at some later
time he could exorcise it, perhaps at one of the festivals, or
in the sweat house. Then he could endure the pain and mourn
for this man whom he had grudgingly grown to respect and
love as a brother. But now all he would do was watch emo-
tionlessly with the others, not showing the enjoyment of some
of them, but not showing any weakness either.

Chapter 40

Calling Crow and Red Feather sat in the blackness of the spring house, their hands bound tightly behind them. Neither of them spoke and they heard no noise outside, save for the occasional whinny of one of the horses in the barn. Half the night had passed before Red Feather finally said, "So we will die here after all."

Calling Crow said nothing.

"At least we will die together," said Red Feather.

"No," said Calling Crow, "we will not die. We will go home."

"How?"

"Samuel will take us, just as he promised that day."

Red Feather laughed crazily. "Calling Crow, still you cannot see that which is right before your very eyes. Samuel hates us for his brother's death. He does not want anything but our deaths."

Calling Crow's voice was calm as he answered. "Red Feather, where is your faith? It doesn't matter what Samuel wants . . . He will take us back, just as Sees Far has said. You will see."

In the lamp-lit hall, Frances clutched little Catherine tightly. Crying uncontrollably, the girl knew not what had happened out in the garden; she knew only that her mother and father were arguing angrily.

"I cannot do it," Samuel said agonizingly. "Yes, they have killed my own brother, but it was because John stole them out of here that night. He took them and—"

Samuel's lackey, Robert, entered, his reddened bald head etched with a mass of worry wrinkles.

"Get over to Fenwick's house quickly," said Samuel. "Take my horse."

Robert bowed as he waited, knowing there was more. He tried not to look over at the lady of the house and little Catherine, who continued to cry woefully.

"Tell Fenwick to get William, and enough men to crew the *Contempt,* and get them here within two hours. Tell him to promise them privateering shares, if he has to, but get them here."

Robert hobbled quickly out of the room.

"You can't go, Samuel," Frances said, "not after this. They have demonstrated their savagery. I fear for you."

He looked at her. "I must. I cannot leave them here to hang!"

"What about her?" Frances looked down at the crying child. "You'd go off and leave her again?"

Samuel came over and knelt before Catherine. "I'll be coming back, child. Father will come back."

Catherine reached out to her father, but Frances would not let her go. "John was right to take them to Collier," she said.

Samuel drew back. "You knew!"

"Yes," Frances cried, "I knew. And he was right."

Samuel got to his feet. "See that John is buried properly, Frances. Now leave me, for I am too saddened by all of this to argue further."

Frances picked up Catherine and rushed from the room.

Calling Crow and Red Feather heard the crunch of boots on the paving stones. The door was unbolted from outside and the black silhouettes of several men stood before them.

"Get in the wagon." It was Samuel's voice.

Calling Crow and Red Feather walked out onto the path and climbed up into the wagon. The other men climbed up and sat behind them, saying nothing. The wagon lurched and swayed along the bumpy roads until it finally came into the town. The wheels rattled on stone for a while and the wagon finally stopped before a large building. The men jumped down. Someone unlocked the door and a man went inside, returning a few moments later holding a torch aloft. Calling

Crow could see Samuel clearly now. Fenwick was at his side in the front seat of the wagon.

"Samuel," said Calling Crow, "why do you not listen to me? I want to tell you all that has happened to us since we were taken that night. Then you will understand."

Samuel did not turn and said nothing. Fenwick turned to look at Calling Crow curiously.

Calling Crow went on. "Samuel, I knew you would come."

Samuel turned to him, his face hard and angry. "You did not have to kill him."

"Samuel," said Calling Crow patiently, "he would have killed me if Red Feather had not shot him with his arrow."

"I will speak no more of it," said Samuel. "I am here for reasons of commerce. I have the muskets and for these you have agreed to pay us in skins. I am here because that vast place that you come from does not belong only to the bloody Spaniard. And, yes, I am here because of a promise I made a long time ago." Samuel looked away. "From this day on, I will speak to you only concerning matters of trade."

Two of the men came out of the building carrying a long wooden box. Calling Crow knew it held the shooting sticks. The men went in and out repeatedly, and soon the wagon was stacked high with the boxes.

Calling Crow could no longer see Samuel and Fenwick in the front. "Let us go," came Samuel's voice.

The wagon moved off slowly, passing the darkened houses and shops. Soon the tall masts of ships came into view.

Calling Crow and Red Feather stood on the poop of the *Contempt* as Samuel and his men made ready to cast off. The ship drifted out from the quay. The wind was gentle as it came off the land and over the buildings, shifting direction and making gentle slapping sounds in the canvas. When they rounded the harborage, the wind picked up, heeling the ship over slightly. When the buildings were very tiny, Calling Crow and Red Feather saw the orange glow of torches arriving on the quay and then they were out of sight of the town.

Chapter 41

The crossing was uneventful, the *Contempt* moving up the Florida coast after six weeks at sea. Then, when they were still two or three days away from Coosa Town, a storm came out of the south and the little ship was driven north with a fury. They anchored in the lee of some small, tree-lined islands, hidden from any ships that might sail past. Samuel reckoned that they were no more than a day's march from the village. They brought the muskets ashore in three trips. The next day they set off for Coosa Town, leaving six men on the ship. With twelve of Samuel's men carrying the heavy boxes and barrels, they moved along the forest trail slowly, arriving at the palisaded village toward sunset. A growing crowd followed them as they walked along the main street. Reaching the *chokafa,* they left the noise outside and entered the large, airy structure.

Calling Crow approached the seated old men, as Samuel had his men lay the boxes down in two neat piles. Calling Crow felt nothing but coldness from the English leader and wondered if he could still trust him. Samuel's desire for trade, what he called "commerce," burned fiercely in his heart, but would this desire make him a reliable ally? Calling Crow did not know. These English were almost as puzzling to him as the Spanish had been. He decided to watch them closely and put the question aside for now. He spoke rapidly to the old men in his native Muskogee, then came back to Samuel and his men.

"Sit," said Calling Crow, indicating the mats spread out in front of the old men.

Samuel and his men seated themselves before the old men and Calling Crow sat facing them. When the people had quieted, Calling Crow stood and addressed the council and the attendees, telling them of the wonders of England. He told them of their capture and imprisonment, but left much out, instead praising Samuel for his role in getting the shooting sticks and taking them back across the great water. Halfway through Calling Crow's talk, four women ran into the airy structure, hovering near the entrance. Green Bird Woman cried out at the sight of her husband. Calling Crow paused briefly and turned to her. He was very happy to see her. His daughter, Bright Eyes, stood beside her mother, cradling his grandchild in her arms. He longed to go see the child, but that would have to wait. He went on with his report to the Council. Green Bird Woman wiped away a few tears with her hand as she listened with the others. Bright Eyes watched her father closely, surreptitiously looking over from time to time at the group of sitting Englishmen. Samuel noticed her and craned his head to get a better look at the child. Failing, he again turned his attention to Calling Crow and the old men. When Calling Crow finished his talk, the old men concluded the meeting and the people began leaving.

Outside the *chokafa,* the light of day had faded. Samuel left the side of his men and went over to where Bright Eyes stood with some other women.

"You look well," he said to her, not touching her.

She nodded shyly.

Samuel looked closely at the child and was taken aback. He had known all along that it was probably his, but still, part of him thought it might have been fathered by another man, perhaps Red Feather, who, even now, watched Bright Eyes from a distance, his eyes haunted and sad.

But the child *was* mixed; there was no doubt about it. Its skin was the color of its mother's, but its hair was auburn and its features angular. Samuel stepped closer to it, staring down in amazement. It was a boy. He saw himself in the tiny face, and guilt and discomfort threatened to overwhelm him. He felt faint and looked around.

He called his men over, then turned back to Bright Eyes. "We must pray over the child," he told her.

She nodded worriedly as the Englishmen got to their knees. Bright Eyes then knelt and held the child upon her knees so the men could see him. Samuel intoned the Lord's Prayer as a crowd of people gathered to watch. Some of them knelt and moved their lips in sincere imitation of the Englishmen.

Calling Crow and four of his men approached when Samuel had finished.

Samuel got to his feet and turned to Calling Crow. "I have named him John. I shall bring a parson with me on my next trip and have him baptized properly."

"Bright Eyes has already named the child," said Calling Crow.

Samuel looked at her in surprise.

"I call him Little One Who Listens." She looked at her father and smiled. "Now I will call him John Who Listens."

Calling Crow nodded and indicated a dozen men who had gathered behind him. "Samuel, these men are going to begin gathering the skins to repay your debt. They will start tomorrow. My son is calling all the braves together for a war council. We will pick the braves who will use the shooting sticks. I want to begin teaching them how to use them tomorrow. Our enemies, the Timucua, are very close now and could launch their attack at any time."

Samuel nodded. "Very well. Where are the two lads we left here? Patrick and Kevin?

"They ran away," said Calling Crow. "Two Clouds thinks they may have been captured by the Timucua."

Samuel frowned. "I will have some of my men make a search in the morning."

"As you like."

"Where can my men and I stay?"

Calling Crow pointed to the *chokafa*. "They can stay in there tonight. Tomorrow I will have my people construct some houses for you."

That night Swordbrought, Red Feather and the Muskogee brave who was called Fox-Disappears, sat in the *chokafa* across from Calling Crow. A few feet away a single fire cast its wobbly glow, and over at the far wall, Samuel and the twelve Englishmen sat together. Calling Crow welcomed Fox-Disappears and then they smoked the pipe of peace together.

Afterward, as Calling Crow carefully wrapped up the pipe, they mourned the passing of Crying Wolf by recounting stories of his courage and fighting prowess. Then Calling Crow asked Swordbrought to report on everything they had seen at the Timucua camp. When he finished, Calling Crow's eyes were fierce. "Now we will give the Timucua a good fight. We must begin training the braves in the use of the muskets."

Swordbrought took the black crow feather from his medicine pouch. "Mantua of the Timucua people told me to give you this, and to say that he would personally turn us both over to the Spanish slavers."

Calling Crow's eyes showed amusement. If not for the dangers Mantua posed to his family and people, he could have enjoyed this contest with the Timucua leader. He reached out his hand to Swordbrought. "Give me the feather. I will return it to Mantua at the first opportunity."

For the next three days, an air of tense expectancy hung over Coosa Town. Scouts were sent to watch the movements of the Timucua and the people of the village worked busily from sunrise till after sunset, making arrows and gathering rocks to be thrown from the palisade by the children and old men and women. Samuel and Calling Crow drilled the Coosa braves and Fox-Disappears and his three braves in the use of the muskets. Fox-Disappears, who impressed Calling Crow greatly, was promised one of the muskets for his own when the battle concluded. Periodically the rattle of musket volleys echoed from the forest and caromed through the village. When this happened, the people would stop what they were doing and listen for more. On the fourth day the scouts returned with grim news. A force of roughly two hundred Timucua, many of them armed with muskets, was approaching the village. As evening drew near, Calling Crow brought the musket-armed braves into the palisade, positioning them on the catwalk that Samuel had advised be built on the inside of the timber walls. Calling Crow then met with his top braves, and Samuel and his top men, in the *chokafa*.

"The Timucua will probably arrive tomorrow afternoon," said Calling Crow, "or perhaps by evening."

Samuel shook his head. "Your musket men are not ready.

They reload much too slowly, some of them improperly. They need at least another week of drilling.''

Calling Crow nodded. ''That is true. But now they are not afraid of shooting sticks.'' Calling Crow looked around at his men proudly. ''They will not freeze upon hearing the thunder of the muskets. And after they fire their own muskets, they can pick up their bows. After they exhaust their arrows, they can pick up their axes and knives.'' Calling Crow looked around briefly at the Englishmen, then back at Samuel. ''When do you and your men leave for your ship?''

''We will leave first thing in the morning,'' said Samuel.

A runner entered the *chokafa* and hurried over to speak with Calling Crow. Finishing, the man ran out again.

Calling Crow turned to Samuel and pointed to the west. ''A large group of warriors has been spotted in that direction. It will take them only as long as two or three of your English hours to reach here.''

''Are there any Spaniards among them?'' asked Samuel.

''My scouts saw two.''

Samuel nodded slowly. ''My men and I will stay in the village until it is safe to travel. Then we will wait for delivery of the skins at the ship.''

Calling Crow nodded. He reached behind him and brought out the pipe. ''Will you join us in a smoke, Samuel?''

Samuel got to his feet, his men doing the same. ''No. We will go out to the palisade and wait there.''

All night long Samuel stayed on the catwalk with his men, periodically peering out at the darkened forest. Calling Crow and his men were now painted for battle. They squatted in small groups and talked quietly and excitedly among themselves. Calling Crow came and went, talking to his leading braves and scouts. Before first light, a thin mist exuded from the forest and drifted across the fields, obscuring them from sight. Everyone was tired and tense and there was still no sign of the invaders. Samuel and Fenwick lay down to rest and were almost on the point of sleep when a shout rang out. Samuel awoke to see Calling Crow and Red Feather looking out onto the fields. Calling Crow saw him and exclaimed, "They come!"

Everywhere people were moving. Men pointed their heavy muskets at the tree line, resting the barrels between the logs of the palisade. Women and boys grabbed fist-sized rocks from baskets and waited expectantly.

Men emerged from the forest and walked boldly through the chest-high mist. It was hard to see them clearly, but there appeared to be very many of them. Samuel watched them gather for a while and then he went over to speak with Calling Crow.

Calling Crow turned to his men. "Do not fire until I give the word," he said.

Their legs obscured, the invaders moved quietly through the mist like ghosts, coming ever closer.

Samuel called to Calling Crow as every eye watched the advancing men. "They are now within range, Calling Crow. You should give the order to shoot."

Calling Crow said nothing. The invaders moved ever closer. Suddenly a voice sang out happily. "Not enemy!" it said. "Not enemy!" It was Fox-Disappears. He ran over to Calling Crow. "They are from my village. They are Muskogee men from Cussitaw Town. Don't shoot. Tell your men not to shoot!"

"Don't shoot," called Calling Crow, and the word went quickly up and down the line of men.

"Put down those muskets," shouted Samuel. He ran along the catwalk, grabbing the muskets from the men and laying them carefully at their feet.

Fox-Disappears called out a greeting to the men and one of them called back, recognition in his voice. Soon everyone was shouting and the fort erupted in a loud, excited buzz.

Samuel's ears hurt from all the singing. The newly arrived Muskogee Indians filled the field against the palisade wall, jumping in time as they sang a compelling battle song. Calling Crow stood in their midst, Red Feather, Swordbrought and Fox-Disappears about him as he talked with the leader of the newcomers.

Fenwick waved Samuel over to the palisade and they both

looked out. Three of Calling Crow's men were hurrying toward the palisade opening. Samuel watched them thread through the shouting, dancing mob of warriors to shout into Calling Crow's ear. It was time.

Calling Crow raised his musket to the sky and the others did the same. The warriors ran toward the palisade entrance. Calling Crow caught Samuel's eye, inviting him and his men to join them in their battle. Samuel looked away. It was then that he saw Bright Eyes farther down the palisade, her tiny baby strapped to her back. Together with an older woman, she was carefully stacking rocks between the palisade logs. Even though he was too far away to see the baby, in his mind he clearly saw that tiny face. The thought of him and her up here with musket balls filling the air horrified him. Along with that thought was the certain knowledge that she would not retreat to the relative safety of the village interior. There was no point in asking her.

Samuel turned to Fenwick and his men. "Do you want to join them in their fight?" he said.

Fenwick frowned. "Our business is commerce, m'lord, not Indian fighting."

"That is true," said Samuel, "but if Calling Crow and his people do not prevail here, there will be no commerce."

An older man named Nicholas grew agitated. "Commerce or no," he said angrily, "we should go to the ship."

Samuel shook his head. "We won't be going anywhere until this is concluded. It's too dangerous."

"I say we fight." It was William, their smith and pilot. He looked angrily in the direction of the forest. "There are supposed to be two bloody Spaniards with them and I'd like to get my hands on one of them, I tell you. I'll wring 'is neck like a pigeon's."

Samuel looked at the others.

The large, flaxen-haired, ruddy-faced farm lad named Philip, brother of Tom, who was killed on their first trip out, came forward. His hands shook at his side as he spoke. "I understand these Timucua Indians are the same lot that killed my brother. I want to fight."

Samuel looked at the others.

"Aye," said Taylor, a middle-aged, barrel-shaped stevedore from the docks, "we'll fight." The others nodded their heads.

"Let's go then," said Samuel.

They climbed down the ladder and fell in behind the river of braves pouring out of the palisade.

The Coosa and Cussitaw braves spread out, moving in a wide mass through the trees of the forest. Calling Crow was at the forward edge of the movement, watching closely for signals from his scouts ahead. The forest was silent, the four-leggeds and winged-ones having already either hidden themselves or fled. Calling Crow was convinced an attack would turn things to his advantage. After all, Mantua and the Timucua had a good idea of the relative strength of Coosa Town and probably figured that they would fight a defensive strategy within the walls of the palisade. But everything had changed with the arrival of all the Muskogee braves from Cussitaw Town.

Calling Crow saw one of his scouts motioning them to a halt. He called to his men and watched as the scout crept stealthily forward. A solitary musket erupted and the scout staggered backward, clutching his stomach painfully. He fell and another musket erupted. Then, a moment later, another, but there was no coordinated volley of musket fire. Calling Crow waved his men forward, indicating that they should flank the approaching column of Timucua. The braves began moving into the thicker foliage ahead and the fighting grew in intensity. Still, however, the firing was sporadic. The Timucua had been surprised and shaken by the attack; Calling Crow was sure of this. This was why they did not deploy their men skillfully. The battle would be over quickly and so Calling Crow raced forward with the others to enjoy it while it lasted.

A Timucua darted from behind a saw-palmetto where he had been hiding. The man was surprised by the absence of his comrades and Calling Crow easily sidestepped his attack, swinging his iron axe to drop him in a heap. War cries split the morning air as small groups of men closed and fought. Calling Crow ran ahead, coming to a small clearing. It appeared that the Timucua had abandoned the battlefield. Over by the edge of the clearing, Calling Crow noticed two of the Englishmen. One was stretched out on the grass and appeared to be badly wounded. It was Fenwick. Samuel knelt by his side, ministering to him. Calling Crow heard someone coming up behind him. He whirled about, his club at the ready. It was Swordbrought. He fought to catch his breath, then he spoke. "It is a complete rout, father. The Timucua were totally surprised by our numbers and the muskets. Now they are running for their lives!"

Calling Crow smiled. "Tell Fox-Disappears to pursue them only as far as the swamplands and then to return. I don't think we will have to concern ourselves with them again."

Swordbrought nodded obediently, turned and ran off.

Something moved smoothly across the periphery of Calling Crow's field of vision, then froze, Calling Crow turned and saw a man run out of the cover toward Samuel. The figure wore red breeches and a breastplate of Spanish armor, and carried a Spanish sword. A familiar, tiny arrow was woven into his topknot. Before Calling Crow could move, Mantua had struck the Englishman a glancing blow to the head with the flat of his sword, knocking him flat.

Calling Crow began running as Mantua knelt to take Samuel's scalp. Mantua was tugging Samuel's head backward when he turned and saw Calling Crow. He leapt to his feet and swung the steel sword at Calling Crow. Calling Crow's axe deflected the blow and Mantua twisted quickly out of the way. Calling Crow swung again, the blow glancing loudly and harmlessly off Mantua's breastplate. Mantua whirled and Calling Crow leapt backward. The long sword gave Mantua the advantage. Mantua swung again and again, the tip of his sword slicing open Calling Crow's medicine pouch. A black crow's feather fluttered to the ground between the two men. "I wanted to return my gift to you," said Calling Crow. "Why don't you pick it up?"

Mantua snarled and ran at Calling Crow, swinging his sword powerfully. Calling Crow parried a swing and managed to land another, normally stunning, blow to the Timucua warrior's armor-protected chest.

Mantua pressed his attack, backing Calling Crow up with

a series of whistling blows. Mantua slowed suddenly, distracted by something Calling Crow could not see. A musket ball whizzed dangerously close by, followed almost instantaneously by a thundering boom. Mantua eyed Calling Crow hatefully. "Next time we will settle this," he said, then turned and disappeared into the thicket.

Calling Crow heard people running up behind him. It was Swordbrought, Red Feather and Fox-Disappears. Fox-Disappears's musket was still spewing smoke. He and Red Feather paused to speak to Calling Crow, but Swordbrought ran on, pursuing Mantua.

Calling Crow called his son. Swordbrought emerged from the thicket a moment later, his face set with angry determination. "He is alone, Father. I can catch him."

Calling Crow shook his head. "No. I am the one who must confront him. Our paths run together. When the time is right, he and I will meet again. Then one of us will prevail and the other will die."

A moan came from the direction of the Englishmen. Samuel sat up weakly; blood ran down his face. They went to him and Fox-Disappears knelt to inspect his wounds. "He was hit quite hard on the head, but his skull is intact." Fox-Disappears moved over to look at Fenwick. "This one appears to have been stabbed with a lance. We'll have to get them back and let the healers tend to them."

Samuel awoke. Something covered his head and eyes and he could not see where he was. There was a steady roar in his head and the sound of someone crying . . . or was it singing? He wasn't sure. Then he seemed to be flying dizzily through the air. He sank back into unconsciousness.

Light seeped through Samuel's eyelids. Someone had removed the covering from his eyes and head. He looked up into the bent sapling rafters of a small hut. He tried to move his head, but his neck shrieked in pain. He realized that the steady sound was a heavy rain; he could feel its dampness on his cheeks, the rest of him being covered with skins. A withered face looked down at him briefly and he realized the other sound was singing. It was the old conjurer, Sees Far. "What happened?" asked Samuel.

Sees Far disappeared and another face came into view, a pretty face, Bright Eyes. "The one called Mantua hit you on the head," she said. "He was about to take your scalp when my father stopped him."

Samuel blinked his eyes in confusion. "I don't understand."

"At the battle. You were tending to your friend."

Recollection flooded through Samuel. "Yes. I remember now."

Bright Eyes had disappeared from view and he called her back. Again she hovered over him.

"Bring your father here. I want to thank him."

The smile went from Bright Eyes's face. "You must sleep now, Samuel. Sleep."

Samuel grew angry. "No. I must thank him and I must do it now."

Worry gripping her features, Bright Eyes moved out of view. Another head appeared above Samuel. White-haired, red-faced, it was William.

Samuel reached up and grabbed William's doublet. He tried to pull himself up, but dizziness overcame him. He fell back. "How are the men, William?" he said weakly. "How is Fen?"

William smiled. "The men are well. Fenwick is walking, has been for two days now."

"Two days?" said Samuel incredulously. "How long have I been lying in here?"

"Eight days, m'lord."

Samuel closed his eyes. "Eight days . . . It is very strange. It seems like only a moment ago I was looking down at Fen and then . . ."

"Yes, Sir," said William, "by the grace of God, eight days. And in that time we accumulated well over half the skins we'll be taking back with us. The Indian king says we'll collect the rest in a month's time. Then we can set sail for home."

"Go home?" said Samuel groggily.

"Yes, sir, to England."
"Oh, yes, go home, to England."

Over two hundred miles south of Coosa Town, at the Spanish island garrison on Parris Island, a longboat slid onto the beach. Señor Pedro Avila, the slaver, and a half dozen Indians stepped out into the knee-deep surf and walked up the beach. Avila pointed to the shade cast by the palisade, and the Indians waited there as he headed inside the palisade to the largest of the newly constructed adobe buildings. As Avila walked wearily into the commandant's quarters, he was not happy over the report he had to make.

Over by the window, General Ruiz, a pudgy, middle-aged man with muttonchop whiskers, sat at a desk, reading a ledger. His face ran with sweat and his white linen shirt was soaked, his soft, hairy chest showing through the thin material.

Avila walked up to the desk and bowed.

The general put down his ledger tiredly. His face clouded over with anger and disappointment. He had been counting on this expedition to succeed. His percentage would have enabled him to buy his way out of this hot hellhole. "I have heard," he said, "that you and Mantua did not have much success this time."

Avila nodded sadly. "The other *Indios* attacked. They had many, many more men than Mantua's scouts had reported, and muskets too. It was totally unexpected and put Mantua and his men on the defensive."

"Mantua was routed, eh?"

"Si," said Avila begrudgingly.

"Very well," said Ruiz tiredly. "You can go now."

Avila did not move. "Mantua would like to attack again."

Ruiz frowned. "What? If Mantua was fool enough to let some of his muskets get away from him, then he deserved the defeat he received."

"But, sir," sputtered Avila defensively.

Ruiz waved away Avila's words. "No! Let him choose another target. What was his haul? Three slaves?" Ruiz laughed disdainfully and picked up his pen. "Tell Mantua to reconnoiter the area south of here. Reports are that there are many displaced *Indios* there that could be easily captured."

"There is more, sir," said Avila persistently.

"What?"

"Sir, they weren't Mantua's guns."

"Then whose were they?" Ruiz asked in angry exasperation.

"I'm not sure, sir, but there were white men in the village. Mantua said they were Englishmen."

"English!" Like everyone else, Ruiz had heard the rumors of an English settlement somewhere between the Castillo de San Marcos at St. Augustine and the Bahia de Santa Maria de Jacan. His hatred flared at the thought of the English pushing into their territory. He got to his feet and leaned forward. "Are you certain?"

Avila nodded vigorously. "Mantua says he almost got the scalp of one of them."

"Bring Mantua and the others in here. I want to hear it from them myself."

After Avila left the headquarters, Ruiz looked out the window at the wildly forested mainland. An English settlement! It was like a gangrenous sore on the Floridas and would have to be cauterized. Nearby, not two hundred yards away, the tall-sided, stout-hulled galleon *Madre de Dios* lay at anchor. A five-decker, there were over eighty cannons on her. They could get some of them upriver on the long boats, or, if need be, there were two carriages on board; they could haul two of the biggest overland . . . This beautiful ship could carry over five hundred soldiers and *Indios* if need be.

A mosquito hovered around Ruiz's neck. He swatted at it and it refused to go away. Ruiz smiled. This operation would be news all the way back to Court. It would be his passage out of this miserable swamp!

Yes, if there really was an English settlement, it would have to be burned immediately. He would wipe it off the map of Florida and leave not a trace.

Many torches lit the *chokafa*, their quivering light moving over the people crowded inside. The Muskogee braves from Cussitaw Town formed the largest group and Fox-Disappears sat at their head. Not far from them, Fenwick and a dozen Englishmen sat in a tight cluster. Samuel still rested in Bright Eyes's house, although he was almost fully recuperated.

Calling Crow stood and picked up the sacred pipe. He beckoned and Fenwick and Fox-Disappears got to their feet, joining him. They sat and the people silently witnessed the bond being cemented between them. Afterward, Fox-Disappears and Fenwick returned to their places.

Two young women entered the *chokafa* carrying a bundle between them. They lay it before the leader of the Cussitaw braves. Fox-Disappears's broad face was dark and serious, but Calling Crow noticed him look up briefly and fondly at one of the women, White Flower. Fox-Disappears had already gotten her mother's permission to marry her and would not go back to Cussitaw Town with his men. After he and White Flower married, they would move into her house and he would be adopted by her clan.

Two braves entered next. One of them carried a large, English leather pouch full of musket balls, wadding and other things for the muskets; the other carried a barrel of black powder. After they left, Fox-Disappears stood and held up the two muskets Calling Crow had given him earlier. One of them was Fox-Disappears's, the other was Calling Crow's gift for Fox-Disappears's chief.

Fox-Disappears raised the two muskets high over his head and turned slowly to show his men. After he sat, women dancers filed in and drumming started.

As the women began their stomp dance, Calling Crow's heart should have been singing. After all, they had just routed the Timucua force, and Fox-Disappears's new Coosa wife, and his dependance on Calling Crow for powder and musket balls, would bind tiny Coosa Town tightly to the Muskogee confederacy for a long time. Calling Crow's heart should have been soaring like a hawk, but instead he felt a twinge of premonitory worry. Something was not right. Vague, like an ache in his bones on a cold morning, the feeling would not go away.

Chapter 42

The two Coosa boys, Flat Head and his friend Fish Boy, had done well on their hunt. A fat raccoon hung over Flat Head's shoulder and two long rabbits hung from Fish Boy's belt. They had been gone two days now, skirting the forest along the sea to the south of Coosa Town. Now the sun had set and the air was hot, humid and still. They looked for a good place to spend their second night.

They came upon a small copse full of leafy deadfall. As Fish Boy cleared a sleeping place for himself, Flat Head climbed a nearby birch tree to tie their game up out of reach of four-leggeds.

"Is the light out there?" Fish Boy called up to Flat Head.

The night before they had seen a strange apparition near the sea. A bright, white diamond of light, it had appeared in the distance like a low-lying star.

"There is nothing tonight," said Flat Head as he tied up the game. He climbed down and lay out his sleeping skin across from Fish Boy.

"Maybe it was a spirit," said Fish Boy as he looked up into the blackness, "or the sun come down from his home in the sky."

Flat Head said nothing for a moment. He didn't think it was the sun; it wasn't bright enough. It might have been a fire, but he had never seen a fire that big! "It is gone now," he said finally. "We can tell Sees Far about it when we get home."

The boys fell silent and soon slept.

Half the night had passed when Flat Head suddenly awoke. He was puzzled, for he had heard nothing, and smelled nothing, yet all his senses were alive and warning him of danger.

He sat and listened. Strange, there were only the sounds of crickets and frogs, the drone of the mosquitos. So what had awoken him?

He got to his feet and climbed up into the game tree. The strange light was back! This time it was much brighter and appeared to wobble and move.

A nearby noise startled Flat Head and he almost fell out of the tree. It was Fish Boy, climbing up beside him.

"*Aieyah!*" said Fish Boy. "So bright! It is the sun come down, just as I said."

Flat Head said nothing.

"Should we go see?" said Fish Boy, a slight quiver of fear in his voice.

Flat Head was frightened, too, but could not let his younger friend know this. "Of course," he said.

They climbed down and started warily down the trail. After walking for a long time, they left the trail and began moving through the trees. They finally came to the edge of the forest and peered out across the expanse of sea grass. A light, brighter than the sun, had lit on the beach ahead. Warped, indistinct figures moved before it, dancing perhaps.

Fish Boy touched Flat Head on the arm. "It is spirits," he said. "We should go."

Flat Head thought it might be men. He hoped that it was men, and not spirits.

Both boys stared for a few moments longer, mesmerized by the beauty and intensity of the light. Flat Head's curiosity grew greater than his fear and he turned to Fish Boy. "Stay here. I want to go up a little further so I can see better. Then we will go back to the village."

Flat Head waited until Fish Boy squatted down safely out of sight among the bushes. Then Flat Head moved off. He felt brave, but, strangely, despite the growing cool of night, he was bathed in sweat.

Flat Head moved stealthily between the dark trees and palmetto, pausing periodically to peer out at the light. Unfortunately, staying within the cover of the forest prevented him from getting closer to the light. He stopped, straining his eyes as he watched the tiny figures that seemed to dance in front of the light. He knew it was not cold this night, yet he was shivering. It must be spirits, he decided. They had cast a spell over him. He started back to Fish Boy.

On the way back, Flat Head slowed several times to peer back over his shoulder at the eerie light. Fortunately, it was not following him and he reached the black patch of bushes where he had left Fish Boy.

Flat Head crept over to the spot, but Fish Boy wasn't there. Flat Head felt he was far enough away from the light to safely call Fish Boy's name, and he did, but received no response. Flat Head checked the area they had come from, back for about the distance of a bow shot, but still could find no trace of his friend. Feeling his courage slipping away, Flat Head forced himself to go back to the place where Fish Boy had disappeared. By now, Flat Head was shivering uncontrollably with fear and loss. A tear pushed its way out of his eye and he rubbed it away. He must be brave! He managed to calm himself briefly, then thoughts of Fish Boy pushed into his head. Where was his good friend now? Had the spirits taken him away to the netherworld? *Aieyah!* He should never have left him here alone. He was too young. It was Flat Head's fault! What would Fish Boy's mother think of him? The others? Flat Head took one more look at the light and its attendant spirits and then hurried away.

A light rain fell from a gray sky as Calling Crow crawled slowly along the sodden ground through the maiden cane grass. The surf rumbled mightily not far away and an occasional seabird cried out hungrily. Flat Head's light had, as Calling Crow suspected, turned out to be a large fire. Its attendants had inexplicably abandoned it in the middle of the night and drifted southward. Day would soon break and Calling Crow wanted to get closer to the site of the fire before he went back to hide in the forest. He crept closer. Despite the steady rain, the fire continued to smolder, issuing a sulfurous plume of smoke that shifted direction with the wind.

Calling Crow had seen no evidence of Flat Head's friend, but he had seen many prints on the ground, evidence of men, not spirits. He wondered sadly what the boy had told them.

Calling Crow continued crawling toward the fire until he could hear the rain hissing into the red-hot embers. He lay still. The wind moved from time to time, wafting the heat and sulfurous smoke back over him, and it took all his strength not to cough. He turned his head to take a breath and, in the growing light, glimpsed the flat impression of a booted Spanish foot in the mud. It told him what he had suspected: the fire-tenders were guiding a ship in to harbor. Perhaps they would be back this evening to throw more wood upon the fire. He turned round to make his way back to the tree line and froze. Two Timucua, their lances held at the ready, tracked something through the grass. If their game took them in the right direction, they would cross his track.

Calling Crow raised his head slightly to take another look around. Seven or eight other Timucua gathered on the beach on the other side of him. He was surrounded.

Where was Mantua? Calling Crow wondered, as he lay, unmoving. Either Calling Crow or he would soon give the other a warrior's death. Of that Calling Crow was certain.

The rain falling on Calling Crow's back tapered off to a wind-whipped drizzle as the light grew. The sea rumbled and sighed, rumbled and sighed, as he lay motionless, occasionally glancing back to locate the two Timucua trackers. Whatever they were stalking had taken them away from him. *Aieyah!* His prayer had been heartfelt and his spirit guide had responded. He looked back at the others on the beach. They were looking out at the place where the sea met the sky. Calling Crow's face darkened as he saw what they were looking at. There would be no more guiding fires; the ship had already anchored.

It was the largest ship Calling Crow had ever seen, looking to be two or three times the size of Samuel's ship. Calling Crow's initial reaction was anger. Why did the Spanish people keep coming? He wanted to fight them, to wait with his men for them and drive them back into the sea. But he knew that his people were too few, and he knew that there would be many soldiers on the ship, maybe even horses. He noted the many rows of cannons and he remembered seeing first-hand what that many big iron guns could do to people on a beach, despite the distance of the ship. It was good that they had long ago moved the village well inland.

Calling Crow took another quick look behind him and gripped his iron axe firmly. The two hunters had taken a turn back in his direction. He would have to fight his way out or die here. It was only a matter of a few moments before they would cross the path he had made in the grass.

A shout came from the Timucua on the beach. As a wave lifted it up, Calling Crow saw several heads in a Spanish longboat, all but one topped with hats. The hatless head had a small arrow hanging downward from a topknot of thick black hair. The boat and the heads disappeared in a trough between the waves. A moment later Calling Crow saw the Spanish rowers ship the oars as a wave caught the boat and drove it swiftly toward the beach. The Timucua who waited on the beach shouted again and the two men behind Calling Crow gave up their search and began running toward the others.

Calling Crow managed to make it back to the tree line without being seen. He would have liked to stay and see the extent of the Spanish force, for he was sure it would be a much larger, more powerful force than had last been sent against his village. But for that reason he decided to go back to the village right away. They would have to flee, and many of the people would be opposed to this, given their ignorance of Spanish power and weaponry. He must convince them or they were doomed to slavery. He thought briefly of his own captivity on the Spanish island, of his never-ending toil in the gold pits, the constant whippings and the snarling, killing dogs, and a deep anger and disgust welled up in him. He must make his people realize the danger, and quickly. He turned and ran back toward the town.

Those who could not fit into the *chokafa* crowded around the entrances to hear Calling Crow's address to the people. Calling Crow, Red Feather, Fox-Disappears and a half dozen other top braves sat at the front, across from the old men. Samuel and his men sat in a position of honor to Calling Crow's left as he faced the people. The combined voices of the people raised a cacophonous din in the large, airy structure until Calling Crow stood. The noise died down and the people leaned forward as they listened to Calling Crow talk of the Spanish threat. During the pauses in his talk, the pop and hiss of the small sacred fire could be heard.

"I have seen all these things before," Calling Crow went on, "as have some of you. But, this time it is much worse. The Spanish ship is the biggest I have ever seen and will surely unload many men with shooting sticks. The village must be moved."

This last statement elicited cries and shouts throughout the *chokafa*. An old woman wailed sadly. "Leave these lands? I would rather die here."

Many other old people echoed her words.

"We can fight." The top brave called Swift Arrow got to his feet.

"Yes," said Calling Crow, his powerful voice charged with anger, "there will be fighting, and I will put myself in the midst of it, along with you and the other braves. But . . ." Calling Crow slowly moved his powerful, outstretched hands across the crowd and the people watched mesmerized. ". . . Still we must move the village, otherwise the young and old will be killed or, worse, enslaved."

"What does the Council say?" said another brave.

Calling Crow remained standing as he turned to look at the Old Men sitting on their skin-covered, raised pallets behind him.

Two Clouds raised his hand. "Calling Crow is right in this. We must move the village." He turned to look at the other Old Men. One by one, they slowly raised their hands, all but Sees Far.

"Sees Far," said Calling Crow, "what do you say?"

Sees Far's voice was very faint and the noise died as people strained to hear his words. "Calling Crow is very wise in the strengths and ways of the white people. That is why we should do as he says."

Moans and cries rippled backward through the people as they passed Sees Far's words along.

Swift Arrow again got to his feet. "No!" he shouted. "We

must not do this. We should stay and fight. If we flee with young and old in tow, eventually our enemies will run us down. It is better to keep them here behind the palisade walls while we braves go out and fight the Spanish.''

Murmurs of agreement swept the crowd.

"Yes," shouted Calling Crow, "some braves *will* stay behind and fight; that way the enemy will think that the village has not moved. Then these braves will break away and join the rest of us. You, Swift Arrow, will be one of them, but I must lead the village away from here!' "

Evidently satisfied by Calling Crow's choice of him to stay behind and fight, Swift Arrow sat down.

Calling Crow went on. "The people will leave, but they will not be run down and captured by the Spanish because they are going away on the English ship. It is hidden up the coast and we can reach it in two days.''

The crowd gasped as every set of eyes turned to the cluster of Englishmen. Samuel nodded his head slowly and a buzz of worried speculation filled the air.

"Can the ship carry them all?" said Two Clouds.

"Samuel says that it can," said Calling Crow.

The people talked fearfully among themselves until Calling Crow raised his arms for silence.

"It is decided," he said. "Gather your things up without making any noise. We will leave this night in the darkness after everyone is ready."

Children cried and harsh voices erupted in argument and worried speculation as the people filed quickly out of the *chokafa*.

In was the middle of the night, and the little sacred fire in the *chokafa* had no effect on the cold air. However, the comforts of a roaring fire were farthest from the minds of the people assembled inside. Against the far wall, the Council of Old Men looked fierce in their war regalia, despite their great age. Mantles of whitened deer skin, ceremonially decorated with red paint, covered their now-sloping, boney shoulders, and conical caps of whitened deer skin crowned their wrinkled faces and hard-set eyes. Mounted on the wall behind each man were his war club, medicine pouch and sacred pipe.

Calling Crow had just been consecrated as the war chief and sat just forward of the Old Men on another raised, skin-covered pallet before the sacred fire. His red-painted big shirt of deerskin, cinched around the waist with a ceremonial sash, exuded red anger. Around his neck, the severe black of the crow feather necklace seemed to have magically broken his head apart from his body, giving him a forbidding, spectral appearance. To Calling Crow's left, the village's ark, a long, intricately decorated rectangular basket, sat upon a woven reed mat. Inside the basket were the village's medicine—consecrated bundles and vases. The thickest and sturdiest of the vases was still empty. This one would receive the embers from the sacred fire when it was time to go. A carved pole passed through two hide thongs woven into the basket would enable the two young men selected by the Council to carry the ark safely.

Closest to Calling Crow, on his right, sat Red Feather, Fox-Disappears, Swordbrought and Samuel, and farther off were the leading warriors of the village, six in all. All the men had dressed brightly so that if they died during the fighting, they would look good when they stood before the Great Spirit.

A messenger came and bowed before Calling Crow. "Most of the people from the river side of the village are ready to go."

"How many are you waiting for?" said Calling Crow.

"Only four, old ones. They should be ready soon."

"Good," said Calling Crow. "Have them assemble now in the square ground with the others."

The man ran out. Two Clouds, his jowly cheeks now firm with determination and concern, called over to Calling Crow. "How long will it take us to get to the English ship?"

Calling Crow looked at him calmly. "About a day's march, perhaps a little more, depending on how fast the old and children can travel."

A whisper of a voice called out. It was old Sees Far, who had again taken ill. "Calling Crow," he said, "I cannot tell what the hour is. Will we be able to leave before daybreak?"

"Yes. There is only one man who has not reported. After

we hear that his people are ready, we will go. That will be soon.''

Another man quickly entered the *chokafa* and walked over to bow before Calling Crow.

''All is ready.''

''How many all together?'' said Samuel.

''One hundred and sixty,'' said Calling Crow.

No torches burned in the wide, dark expanse of the square ground as the people clustered together protectively. Calling Crow and Red Feather walked through the people, answering questions and offering encouragement.

Calling Crow was pleased. The people were orderly and most seemed bravely resolved to do what they must. Few of them knew of the terror Spanish weapons and horses could unleash, yet, despite this, they obeyed. This touched him deeply. As he and Red Feather were returning to the head of the square ground, a torch-bearing warrior ran up to them.

''People are already outside the palisade,'' the man reported excitedly.

Calling Crow turned to Red Feather in puzzlement. ''How could that be? No one gave the order to begin the march.''

The man shook his head worriedly. ''Not our people, the invaders!''

''How many?'' said Calling Crow.

''We're not sure. But seventeen lights have been counted, equally spaced around the palisade.''

Calling Crow's voice was steady. ''Red Feather, go back to the *chokafa* and tell the Council and top braves. I will return after I have a look.''

Calling Crow turned to the messenger. ''Tell the people to go back to their houses and remain ready to go. We will soon decide what must be done.''

The man turned and waded into the throng of people.

Calling Crow ran toward the front of the palisade. Fox-Disappears, Swordbrought and Samuel spotted him, and caught up with him as he climbed the stairs to the fighting platform.

They looked out. Six torches were visible, spaced evenly

in the blackness in front of the forest. It was impossible to determine how many men there were, however. Someone climbed up the ladder behind the four men.

The others turned to look at him. It was Red Feather. They looked back out at the lights.

"Why haven't they attacked?" said Fox-Disappears.

"They are here to hold us up until the others arrive," said Calling Crow. "They want us as slaves."

None of the men said anything further as they looked out at the distant pinpoints of light. Finally, Calling Crow said, "Red Feather, send out two scouts to determine their numbers and positions. I will go to the Council now." He turned and headed for the ladder, the others quickly following him.

The mood in the *chokafa* was grim. The Old Men looked at Calling Crow and the braves expectantly.

Two Clouds was first to speak. "Perhaps we should go as planned. The braves are all eager to fight. They could draw off the invaders until the others are away."

Calling Crow answered thoughtfully, "I have sent scouts out to find the strength of the enemy. Let us wait till they report before deciding what to do."

"It appears," said Samuel in English to Calling Crow, "that they will lay siege to your village."

Calling Crow nodded as the other Coosa watched him and Samuel intently. "We can resist them from behind the walls," said Calling Crow, "but not forever."

Calling Crow turned to Fox-Disappears and said in Muskogee, "We will once again have to ask the braves at Cussitaw Town for help."

Fox-Disappears nodded. "I could go."

"I want a younger man to go," said Calling Crow. He looked at the Council. The Old Men raised their hands in agreement.

Swordbrought stood. "I will go," he said. "I know the way now."

"No!" Swift Arrow got to his feet. "I have been near there before and I can find it easily. I will go!"

A tall, slim brave called Fire Heart stood. His dark eyes

were fierce with determination. "I will go with you," he said. "That way one of us will get through."

Little Bear got to his feet, his massive bulk looming over the other three braves. He looked at the council. "Send me. I have a better chance of getting there than either of them."

Calling Crow looked over at the Old Men.

"Swordbrought," said Two Clouds, "you will stay here this time." Swordbrought sat and Two Clouds looked solemnly at the three remaining braves. "We will send Fire Heart this time, then, in three or four days, we will send Swift Arrow. Little Bear, there will be much fighting here. It is better that you stay."

Little Bear sat and Two Clouds looked at the other Old Men. They raised their hands in agreement.

Calling Crow turned to the braves. "It is decided. Fire Heart, you will go immediately. Tell the Cussitaw Council that this time there will be many more men arrayed against us, and that they will probably begin their attack with the dawn. Go now." Calling Crow looked at Swift Arrow. "You will go in three days' time, to insure that one of you makes it. I will tell you when."

Later that night, Calling Crow and Red Feather watched Fire Heart lower himself from the palisade and drop to the ground. The bright pinpoints of torchlight could be seen on either side in the distance as Fire Heart's slim form glided toward the blackness of the forest. When Fire Heart melded into the relative safety of the trees, they relaxed some. Whether or not he made it to Cussitaw Town would depend on his personal medicine power, his speed and his fighting prowess.

Calling Crow and Red Feather climbed down from the fighting platform and started back toward the *chokafa*. Fenwick ran up to them. "Your Lordship," he said to Calling Crow, "there's a messenger at the gates!"

Calling Crow and the others followed the short, rotund Englishman as he ran awkwardly toward the fighting platform near the palisade entrance. Winded, Fenwick paused at the steps, breathing heavily as Calling Crow and Red Feather and the braves climbed the ladder.

Samuel met Calling Crow at the top. "There he is." Samuel pointed to the closest torch.

The bearer of the torch was unrecognizable in the distance. His voice boomed out loudly in Muskogee. "Coosa people! You cannot escape. Give up now before the Spanish soldiers arrive!"

A fierce anger welled up in Calling Crow at the sound of the voice. It was Mantua.

Chapter 43

Pedro Avila sat in the middle of the long dugout canoe as the Timucua paddlers stood. There were six of them and they sped the canoe along very swiftly, despite the strong current running in the opposite direction. Although the sun was warming the day, a rainstorm had recently moved through the area and the creek was higher than usual, with much debris moving downstream. One of the paddlers pointed to a long, dark shape on the bank. At first Avila thought the unmoving shape was a log, and then he realized it was a large alligator that had crawled up to feel the weak sunlight on its back. Avila thought grimly that these creatures would get more to eat than was normally their due if the fighting for the village proved heavy.

At a great bend in the creek, the Timucua turned the dugout toward the bank. Avila disembarked at the barely recognizable camp and walked along the muddy bank. He saw one of Mantua's headmen squatting down to talk with some other braves. The man got to his feet and led Avila quickly along a path that came off the muddy riverbank. At one point they passed though a clearing and Avila could see the tops of the palisade's timbers rising above the trees. They came to a grove of pines in which several dozen braves sat around talking.

Avila's guide paused and pointed to where Mantua slept under a crude shelter. He lay on a pallet of skin spread upon a bed of sphagnum moss. Avila walked over, intrigued, for it sometimes seemed as if the Timucua chief needed no sleep.

Mantua opened his eyes at Avila's approach. He started to get up and then noticed something upon his chest. Unconcerned at first, he then quickly swiped it off as if it were a venomous spider. Avila watched it flutter to the ground and noted that it was only a black feather of some kind. He could not understand the normally fierce Timucua's fearful repulsion and thought that perhaps he was still not completely awake.

"General Ruiz sends his regards," said Avila.

Mantua grunted as he got to his feet. He yawned loudly and scratched his buttock. "When will he send the big thunder stick?"

"Soon, tomorrow perhaps. They are already unloading it from the ship."

Mantua grunted his approval and looked over at his men.

"The general wants you to position all your men around the palisade."

Mantua looked back at Avila in annoyance. "There is no need. I already have a dozen sentries around the town."

"I know," said Avila tactfully, "but the general is concerned. He thinks that they may attempt to flee."

Mantua scowled. "They will not flee! With their women and children, their old people in tow, where could they go that my men could not run them down?"

Avila frowned. Mantua could be as stubborn as a mule. "Double your guard then, and I will send you a cask of wine tonight."

Mantua looked at him hungrily. "Send the wine. Good. Then we will talk some more. Now we will eat."

Calling Crow, Samuel and Red Feather stood on the ramparts looking at the distant tree line. The men hidden in the forest could not be seen, but every now and then a puff of musket smoke blossomed like a white flower from the deep green, followed by a booming report, giving them away. No one had been hit by the wildly inaccurate long shots, and the Coosa and Englishmen on the ramparts returned fire. Calling Crow glanced up at the blood-red clouds over the trees. The sun had already set and soon it would be dark enough for him and the others to leave the palisade. The last report Calling Crow had received was ominous in its implications. The

Spanish had mounted a large gun in one of their longboats and were preparing to bring it up the river.

Calling Crow frowned as he thought of the impact such a thing would have on Coosa Town. Not only would the noise and the sight of the thing's belching fire and smoke frighten the people, but with it the invaders would quickly breach the palisade walls. The Cussitaw Town braves would not get here for at least another five days. There was only one thing to do; tonight they would attack and steal the cannon. Calling Crow had already worked out a plan with Red Feather and Samuel. Red Feather would lead a group of braves who would launch a diversionary attack against the main camp of Timucua, while Calling Crow and his braves, along with Samuel and three of his men, attacked the guards and stole the cannon. Calling Crow's scouts had reported that the cannon was tied up at the mouth of the river and guarded by at least eight Timucua. Calling Crow's plan was risky, but if successful, it would leave the palisade walls intact. Then, hopefully, they could repel the attack that would soon come.

In the *chokafa,* the drum-driven wailing of the singers abused Samuel's ears. He tried to ignore it, to appreciate the primitive passion and sincerity in the voices, but the feverish ague that had assailed him after the blow to his head had lately returned, and it would allow him no pleasure. Not five feet away, two men sat on the reed mats beating their drums. The blind priest's two young helpers moved about, using a hawk's feather to waft smoke from a clump of herbs over Calling Crow and his braves. Samuel coughed, the smoke catching in his throat. He thought that Calling Crow did indeed look fierce in his war paint. His red ochre-painted war axe looked as if it were already smeared with the blood of his enemies.

Samuel turned round to look at his own men, the motion sending aches up and down his neck and a shuddering chill deep into his bowels. He had had the fever for two days now, and with the ministrations of Bright Eyes and her many teas, it seemed to be receding, but not quickly enough. Fenwick smiled in amusement, but Philip and Taylor looked bewildered and uncomfortable. Samuel knew they did not like the noisome ceremony, but because he had chosen them to go along to take the cannon boat, Calling Crow had insisted they be present for his priest's blessing too.

"Although it looks nothing like one of us praying to the Lord, God, on bended knee," Samuel had explained to them earlier, "still, it is their way of asking God to protect them during battle."

When the ceremony concluded, they moved out to the darkness and headed for the palisade wall. Samuel and his men carried muskets, although they had agreed to use them only as a last resort. The swords they wore would, hopefully, enable them to dispatch without much commotion the Timucua savages guarding the cannon.

Up on the fighting platform, Calling Crow talked quietly with Red Feather and his squad of men as they looked out at the distant torches. Samuel turned to his own men. In the dim moonlight, Fenwick's small, violin-shaped figure was dwarfed between the hulking height of Philip the farm boy and Taylor's bearish bulk. Samuel hoped that Fen would fare well. Initially, Fenwick had argued for trying to reach the ship, but Samuel had countered that it would be impossible, pointing out that the savages could move much faster in the forests and more than likely they'd all end up as Spanish galley slaves, with only a lifetime of whippings and toil to look forward to. That sad forecast had given Fenwick enough resolve to volunteer for the cannon attack and Samuel hoped his horror-driven valor would sustain him during the entire maneuver.

Samuel looked back at Calling Crow. Strange as it was, he realized that his fate, and the fate of his men as well, was now bound up with Calling Crow and his people. If they could triumph here, this could be the point for England's long overdue entry into the Americas. Trade and colonies would follow eventually. There would be trips to Court, an audience with Her Majesty. Perhaps a governorship. If they were defeated, well, they would all suffer the same fate.

As Samuel studied the distant forest, he heard Calling Crow utter some command in Muskogee. Red Feather and his men immediately dropped down over the palisade wall, disappearing into the darkness. Then, Samuel and the others waited while Calling Crow searched the black night. For what? Samuel wondered. What could he possibly see from up here? Samuel turned to watch one of the distant pinpoints of torchlight. It seemed to divide into two and them fuse together again. He blinked his eyes and his head ached. Someone touched him on the back. A Coosa brave's hideously decorated face hovered close by and Samuel involuntarily stepped backward. "Go," the man said softly in his language. Samuel touched Fenwick's sleeve, indicating he should get the other two. Samuel watched the brave walk off. To see one of them suddenly come at you from the darkness, he thought, would be enough to stop many a heart cold. He hoped it would have a similar effect on the Timucua savages.

Down on the ground, Samuel and his men followed in file as Calling Crow and the squat, broad-shouldered brave called Fox-Disappears led the way across the darkened fields. They entered the forest and worked their way north. Samuel stumbled along, his head dizzy, making more noise than he should. After what seemed like half the night they came to the riverbank and a long dugout canoe which Calling Crow and his men had evidently hidden there. Samuel gratefully sat in the middle and soon they were gliding down the black river. Calling Crow's men were so expert at paddling the long boat that the only sounds that reached Samuel's ears were the occasional splashes as fish jumped to take the many flies and mosquitos Samuel could not see, but which continued to bite voraciously at his exposed flesh. Samuel grabbed the gunnels as a dizzy spasm ran through him. In his fevered state, there seemed to be no up or down, only black, and the movement of his head to the strokes of the rowers.

The canoe slid onto land with a gravelly rustle and stopped. Again they walked quietly through the darkness beneath the trees. A hand forcefully grabbed Samuel's shoulder, urging him to his knees. Samuel turned and motioned Fen and the others to kneel quietly. Turning back, he tried to see in the dark what Calling Crow and the others must have seen, but there was nothing. They knelt quietly for a while. Samuel was on the verge of asking Calling Crow why they had stopped when he heard it—the distinct tramp of feet upon leaves, the cracking of a branch underfoot, a softly muttered reproach in that strange tongue. Not ten feet away, a number of men were marching by, yet they were invisible to Samuel. After the tramping sounds had receded, they moved on. They walked for half an hour or so until Samuel stumbled into the brave in front of him. The file had stopped.

The brave pushed Samuel forward and he knelt beside Calling Crow and Fox-Disappears as they peered across a small field at something. At first Samuel could see nothing, then the dark outline of the boat became visible against the starlight reflected in the water. It was tied up upon the bank. Two savages stood beside it, looking at the water. Samuel knew there should be more, but he could find none.

Calling Crow raised his hand and pointed. Samuel's eyes strained. Yes, there. Back twenty feet or so, he saw five more savages sitting in a circle.

Fox-Disappears gestured to two of his braves and they all crept to the left, silently wading into the water. Samuel and his men quietly pulled their swords and followed Calling Crow and the other two braves as they crept forward. When they were a hundred feet away they stopped and knelt to wait for Red Feather's attack on the main camp. It was not long in coming.

A distant musket cracked and the Timucua got nervously to their feet. Bent low, Calling Crow immediately crept forward and the others followed. Several more muskets boomed in the distance. Calling Crow raised his axe and raced forward silently. The Timucua never had time to raise his own club as Calling Crow's blow knocked him backward. Calling Crow turned to engage another Timucua.

Samuel saw a Timucua rushing at Calling Crow from behind. Samuel intercepted the man and he quickly redirected the direction of his axe, grazing Samuel's right arm. Samuel dropped his sword painfully and the savage howled with delight. Philip came out of the blackness and swung his sword, almost severing the Timucua's head from his shoulders. Samuel's right arm hung limp and useless at his side.

He picked up his sword with his left as he heard splashing and grunting behind. Fox-Disappears and the others were engaged in a fierce struggle on the long boat. Philip and another savage thrashed about violently in the river.

A large mass seemed to float past Samuel as Taylor and one of the savages fought, grunting and cursing, their movements a macabre dance. The savage was big and powerful, but Taylor had evidently grabbed him from behind, pinning the man's arms to his sides. The savage still gripped his axe tightly in his right hand and twisted and kicked furiously as he attempted to put Taylor off balance. Taylor, for his part, looked reluctant to let the man go. Samuel saw why. Taylor had somehow lost his sword.

Samuel's arm was still useless from the blow the Timucua had given him. He saw Fenwick sitting on the ground. He had evidently been knocked there and was in some kind of stupor.

"Fen," called Samuel softly, "get up and help him."

Fenwick looked blankly at Samuel for a moment.

"Over there," Samuel hissed.

Fenwick got to his feet and saw the two men struggling. Grabbing his musket by the barrel, he rushed over. Fenwick struck the native on the forehead. The man's legs buckled and Taylor let him fall to the ground.

Samuel walked over as Taylor glared at the collapsed native menacingly.

"Is he dead?" said Samuel.

In answer, Taylor pulled Fenwick's sword from his side and stabbed the man. He handed the sword back to Fenwick.

Calling Crow suddenly appeared out of the darkness. "The cannon is ours," he said. "We must take it away at once."

They went over to the Spanish longboat. Fox-Disappears and two of his braves were already aboard, Fox-Disappears examining the cannon closely in the dim light.

Samuel rubbed his arm and gratefully felt strength coming back into it. He knelt beside Fox-Disappears to inspect the cannon. It was firmly lashed with stout cords in the center of the longboat.

"Quickly," said Samuel, "Philip, Taylor, take the oars. Let's go!"

As the others got aboard, Samuel went forward. He found several kegs of powder, a dozen cannon balls, and four bar shot. One of the latter, if it struck the palisade squarely, would open it wide enough to drive a carriage through.

He worriedly called to the others in the darkness. "Hurry!"

As the heavy boat moved slowly away from the bank, Fenwick turned and pointed. "Samuel, they've spotted us!"

Five or six torches raced toward them.

Samuel shouted, "Pull, men. Pull hard!"

Taylor and Philip put their backs into the oars. They were quickly joined by Fenwick and Fox-Disappears. The boat had moved about thirty yards from the shore when the men with the torches reached the bank. Three Spanish soldiers carried long muskets and five or six Timucua braves waved their war clubs wildly. Two of the braves immediately jumped into the water and began swimming toward the boat. The Spanish knelt and fired a volley from their muskets. The shots struck the water, sending up geysers of spray. As Samuel was reaching for his own musket, the boat leaned over suddenly, almost knocking him overboard. Two Timucua braves were attempting to climb aboard. Fox-Disappears made a move toward one of them and the man grabbed him by the hair and pulled him overboard. A moment later the other Timucua was in the boat and struggling with one of the Coosa braves.

"Look!" shouted Fenwick.

Another four or five Timucua swam through the black water toward the boat.

A wave of dizziness came over Samuel. He shouted over to Calling Crow. "We'll never get the cannon out of here. Cut the ropes! We'll have to dump it in the river."

They began hacking at the thick ropes that secured the heavy cannon in the middle of the boat. A Timucua brave surfaced aft and attempted to climb up onto the gunnels.

Samuel turned to him, sword drawn, and the man sank back into the water. Samuel leaned his weight against the cannon, trying to move it. Calling Crow joined him in the effort, then one of Calling Crow's braves, but the cannon would not move.

Samuel shouted over at Philip and Taylor. "Leave the oars! Help us!"

The two Englishmen joined the others alongside the black bulk of the cannon. "Heave!" called Samuel. For a moment nothing happened, then the cannon slid with a groan, crashing up against the port gunnels. Before anyone could react, the boat flipped up and over as if a giant had surfaced beneath it. Samuel felt a knock on the head as he went into the cold water. He spun around and down. He was a tiny thing, sinking into an ink pot, blacker than night. A dark shape drew close, a grisly-looking hag. She embraced him, pulling his face close. She forced her tongue into his mouth. Cold and wet, like a raw clam, the tongue pushed its way past his gullet, starting down his throat. He gagged reflexively, and pushed her away. Clawing his way upward, he broke the surface, vomiting and coughing hoarsely. He looked around in a panic as his feet fought for a purchase and churned the depths uselessly. He was drowning, as the others must be. He went under, then fought for the surface. He gasped for air, spotting what he thought to be the riverbank opposite from the Spanish and their savages. He thrashed, doglike, clawing for land—for the love of God, let his feet feel land beneath them. The current spun him round and he thought he saw someone or something, one of the horrid alligator beasts—behind him. He cried out, continuing to claw for the land. Sputtering, swallowing water, his lungs and throat burned like fire as he fought for breath. Then, mercifully, he felt soft mud beneath his feet and crawled up onto the bank. Coughing, vomiting, he collapsed.

Samuel lay quietly. The distant shouts of men echoed across the water, but they were becoming less frequent and more faint. His breathing slowed, becoming regular again, and he felt his strength returning. He heard a rustling in the bushes. He felt for his sword. Thank God! It was still in its sheath. He pulled it quietly and looked up at the black jumble of the forest.

His breath left him as he saw two large black shapes leave

the trees and move down the bank toward him. They would be savages; his men must have drowned. Lord God above, had he been saved from a watery grave only to be cut into pieces by the savages? He forced himself to his knees as they drew closer. He was about to leap upon the first of them when the man spoke. "Who's there?" It was Philip! Mother of God! And Taylor was behind him.

"It is me," he hissed at them.

The two shapes stopped.

"Samuel?" said Taylor tentatively.

Samuel got slowly and unsteadily to his feet. "Yes. I think someone hit me on the head, or perhaps it was the boat."

Philip put his arm around Samuel, steadying him. "Where is Fen?" said Samuel.

"We don't know, sir," said Philip. "We were working our way back in the hopes of finding both him and you. I'm afraid he must have drowned."

"How did you manage to get ashore?" said Samuel.

"A barrel, sir," said Philip. "It was very buoyant and we both held on and made our way. It was God's grace, it was."

Taylor grunted his agreement.

Neither Samuel nor Taylor said anything for a few moments. Then Samuel spoke. "We had better find the dugout. That's where Calling Crow and the others will be. They swim like fish and it's likely some of them survived."

Taylor pulled his sword and led as they moved clumsily through the brush along the banks. After walking for almost an hour, Taylor stopped and peered through some bushes. Philip and Samuel knelt behind him.

"What is it?" whispered Samuel.

"I'm not sure," Taylor whispered, "I think there are people on the other bank. See! Something's moving there."

They crept closer, carefully climbing down the slippery mud of the bank.

Samuel stared across the smooth blackness of the river to where he thought Taylor was pointing, but still could not see anything. He turned round to Philip. "Do you see anybody?"

"I think so, but I cannot tell who they are."

"Go over," said Taylor, "and get a better look."

Philip looked round at Samuel plaintively.

Samuel nodded. "See if you can find a piece of wood to take you across, lad. Take a look and tell us what you see."

Philip disappeared into the blackness of the bank. After he had been gone awhile, Samuel whispered to Taylor. "Do you see anything?"

Taylor shook his head. "Nothing now," he whispered, and the two men stared in silence at the river, the noise of the frogs and crickets assailing their ears.

After a while Samuel got to his feet. "Come, we must attempt to get back to Calling Crow's town."

"What about Philip?" said Taylor.

"We cannot wait. The savages will be searching the river up and down."

As Samuel began climbing up the bank, they heard the sound of an owl nearby. Taylor stopped.

"Come along," said Samuel, turning round.

"Look," said Taylor, pointing to the river.

Something was gliding downriver, drawing closer. As it drew near, they saw it was a canoe. Fox-Disappears worked a paddle up front as it slid up onto the bank, the current turning it sideways. Philip sat in the middle, along with Fenwick and Calling Crow.

Samuel and Taylor quickly climbed aboard and the paddlers pushed the canoe off and headed it upriver. Samuel turned round to Fenwick. "Thank God you're alive!" he said quietly, "I though you had drowned."

Fenwick pointed to Calling Crow. "I would have been feeding the alligators by now if his lordship, Calling Crow, had not pulled me out of the river."

Samuel turned to Calling Crow. "We don't have the cannon, but neither do they."

Calling Crow watched the dark riverbank as Fox-Disappears and the other braves smoothly propelled the canoe upriver with quiet, even strokes. "Samuel," said Calling Crow, "can they pull it up from the river and use it?"

Samuel stared into the utter blackness as he answered. "Yes, but it would take them weeks, perhaps months." Calling Crow's voice was tinged with pleasure. "That is good."

"With all the men and muskets they have down there," said Samuel, "this will only buy us one, perhaps, two days."

"We will fight them off until Fire Heart brings back the Cussitaw braves."

Samuel said nothing, his thoughts as black as the river they moved upon. He pictured Bright Eyes and her baby back in the town. How long would it take the Spaniards to breach the palisade? He took the thought no further, the reality of their situation being too grim.

Chapter 44

Samuel's ague returned and he shivered uncontrollably as Calling Crow's braves pulled the dugout up onto the riverbank. Well north of Coosa Town, they formed a file and crept through the quiet of the forest. When they neared the town, Calling Crow's braves skillfully avoided Mantua's sentries, and before dawn's light they huddled against the palisade wall. Calling Crow warbled a birdlike signal and a crude ladder was lowered. A moment later they were within the safety of the town. Samuel's men went to sleep in the *chokafa*. Samuel made his way through the now-familiar dirt streets. Drumming, singing, and the occasional trill of an Indian flute filled the cool air.

Bright Eyes was kneeling before the cook fire when he entered. She smiled up at him and he went over to look at the child. He stared down at it in wordless fascination. She came over to him and felt his clothes.

"Wet," she said, and went to one of her many baskets to fetch him a skin robe. He stepped out of his clothes as she dipped a conch shell into one of her pots. After he wrapped himself in her warm robe, he sat down on the sleeping pallet. She brought him the shell full of hot tea. He sipped it noisily, but despite its medicinal powers, exhaustion overcame him and he lay down and fell instantly to sleep.

He awoke, feeling her naked warmth beside him. Outside, the rain was coming down hard. Despite the night's blackness, he knew she was awake. He pulled her close and rolled atop her. "Kiss, kiss," she said softly, and he kissed her lips tenderly. He mounted her and they made love slowly with the sound of the rain all around them. Bright Eyes pushed him off and slipped on top of him, putting him inside of her.

She rode him with cries of joy till they spent themselves and fell back to sleep.

The wind-driven rain lashed the thatch of Green Bird Woman's house with a gentle rhythm. Dawn would not break for another three hours and Calling Crow lay in a deep sleep. Despite this, he was aware of the rain and other sounds—water being poured into a pot, the fire noisily consuming a large stick just thrust into it, and, very far away, a baby crying. Then a voice came, a voice he was vaguely familiar with, and Calling Crow began his steep climb up out of the netherworld of dreams.

The voice spoke rapidly, agitatedly; it said, "They told me I must tell him!"

"You go!" This was Green Bird Woman. "I will tell him when he wakes; he must sleep more."

Calling Crow climbed higher, coming out of the warm netherworld, feeling the wet coolness of the house now, smelling the sweet smoke and the turtle soup.

"He must be told now!"

"Go," said Green Bird Woman softly, but harshly. "I will tell him soon."

Calling Crow was awake now. "Send him in," he called over to Green Bird Woman.

"*Aieyah*," she said. "You should rest some more. The others will deal with this."

Calling Crow got to his feet. He was stretching when the young man stood before him. His name was Thunder-From-The-Sea, and his face was pinched with concern.

"A scout just arrived," the young man said. "He reported that the Spanish appear to be making something on the beach, but what it is, he cannot say."

Calling Crow glanced at the entryway. "Come," he said. "We must get over the wall before it gets too light."

Green Bird Woman watched worriedly as they ran out of the house and toward the palisade wall.

The rain had stopped and the sun was well up when Calling Crow and Thunder-From-The-Sea climbed up into a tall, gnarled mulberry tree. Hidden in its thick greenness, they watched the many Spanish and Timucua braves moving about on the beach in the distance. Calling Crow saw the boat drawn up in the sand and the structure erected beside it. Mostly Spanish soldiers crowded around the thing and Calling Crow could not tell what it was. Out on the sea, the huge Spanish ship rocked gracefully with the swells, its many sails furled. Calling Crow and Thunder-From-The-Sea watched for a long time. They were ready to leave their perch and go closer when something changed. The Spanish formed into a long, thin line which stretched from the thing up to the tree line. They began moving slowly and then the thing separated into two. A long black shape followed the line of men moving into the forest, leaving a scar in the sand of the beach.

Calling Crow began climbing down.

"What is it?" said Thunder-From-The-Sea.

"It is the end of Coosa Town," said Calling Crow. "Come, we must run. There is not much time left."

Bright Eyes was looking down at Samuel when he opened his eyes. Her tea had worked its miracle and Samuel's fever had gone. He felt his strength returning, and along with it, a feeling of hope. With the cannon boat out of the way, perhaps they *could* hold out in the palisade. Calling Crow had just sent another brave to Cussitaw Town for help and he was sure it would be forthcoming.

Bright Eyes frowned and touched him on the chest. "You stay," she said in halting English. "Ship go. Ship come back. You stay."

He smiled sadly. He would, of course, return to England when the skins were ready. She must know that, he thought, despite her question. It was the best possible solution. The trading post he would establish here would give him reason to come and go. He would see Frances and little Catherine, and he would see Bright Eyes and the boy too. Destiny had dictated that he belong to both worlds. No one could force him to choose one over the other.

"I will go with the ship, but I will come back."

"No go," she said angrily.

He said nothing further.

She turned away from him and got to her feet. She quickly pulled her gown over her. Taking the boy from his pallet, she went out into the early morning mist.

The figure up on the fighting platform noticed Bright Eyes moving toward the place where the stream passed under the palisade and came into the town. He had been hoping she would come out of the hut. She carried the baby with her and swung it from side to side as she sang in a whisper—"Heya, heya, I have loved and now my heart is heavy."

Silently, unseen, he dropped down from the parapet and followed at a distance. Somewhere in the billowing clouds above, a hawk cried out as it searched the ground in vain for food. Quietly, stealthily, the figure caught up with her and stopped.

She turned, suddenly aware of him. Red Feather said nothing to her, and she did not run away from him. Instead she continued her singing. He stepped closer and still she did not run away. They stayed that way for a while, her singing and rocking her child, him standing his silent, watchful vigil, until the village began to wake.

She looked at him once more, kindly, he thought, and then she walked back in the direction of her house.

Samuel stood up on the fighting platform with his men as a fine rain fell, turning the surrounding land a dull, greenish gray. They watched a mass of smoke billowing up from the trees about a mile or so to the south, where the main group of Timucua Indians made their camp. A boy climbed the ladder behind them and tugged Samuel's sleeve.

"Keep a sharp eye on the tree line," Samuel said to his men. "I'll return within the hour." He climbed down the ladder and followed the boy back to the *chokafa*.

Under the flicker of torchlight, Calling Crow sat before the Old Men. His right-hand man, Red Feather, his son, Sword-brought, and the Cussitaw brave, Fox-Disappears, sat beside him. A few feet away, the town's top braves sat in a cluster.

Calling Crow gestured for Samuel to sit.

"Samuel," he said, "I have seen something which is very bad."

Samuel nodded and Calling Crow went on. "The Spanish and their Timucua allies have taken another cannon off their ship. All night they worked, putting it onto a wheeled cart. Now they are pulling and pushing it here. We will have to leave the palisade."

Samuel frowned. It was ominous. Because Calling Crow and he had successfully attacked the cannon boat, the Spanish and the Timucua would have too many soldiers and braves guarding this gun to attack it directly. "How long do you think it will take them to get it here?" he said.

"Two days at the most," said Calling Crow. "The trail from the sea is wide."

"Yes," said Samuel, "but it is boggy in places and the cannon is very heavy. That might add another day. But you are right. We must leave."

"Yes," said Calling Crow. "Are you sure your ship can carry us all?"

Samuel nodded. "What about the Cussitaw Town braves?" he said. The thought of Bright Eyes and the baby having to flee frightened him. It would be very dangerous.

"If Fire Heart reached Cussitaw Town," said Calling Crow, "they will arrive in another three or four days. Too late for us."

Samuel nodded, lapsing into grim silence.

Calling Crow turned to the Old Men and told them of his recommendation. They talked softly among themselves for a few minutes and then Calling Crow said, "We will leave tonight."

"Calling Crow?" It was Sees Far.

"Yes?"

"Last night I had a dream that a great white fog will descend on the land. It will be so thick that no one will be able to see anything."

"It is good," said Calling Crow. "We must get everything ready."

"No," said Sees Far, "it will not come tonight."

"When, Grandfather?" said Calling Crow, concern in his voice.

"It will come tomorrow night," said Sees Far.

"Calling Crow," said Samuel. "We must not wait! If they get that cannon through the bog faster than we anticipated, well . . ." Samuel left the thought unspoken.

Calling Crow said nothing as he looked at Red Feather and the top braves. Finally he turned to the Old Men. "Sees Far has never been wrong in these things. I say we wait until tomorrow night."

Two Clouds said, "You speak wisely, Calling Crow. We will go tomorrow night."

Calling Crow looked at his top braves. "Some of you will attack the main camp of Timucua. This will help divert them while we evacuate the people."

Red Feather, Little Bear, each of you pick five men and bring them back here. Swordbrought, go tell the headmen to get all the people ready. We will go tomorrow night."

Samuel, Taylor, Philip and the other Englishmen stood upon the fighting platform, clutching their muskets tightly.

"To have conjured this," Fenwick whispered in awe, "the ancient, blind one is a powerful sorcerer."

"He did not conjure it," said Samuel, "he dreamed about its coming."

The Englishmen said nothing further as they looked out upon the thick, cold fog lapping against the palisade walls like a milky white sea. It had come out of the woods in the middle of the night and now looked thick enough to walk upon.

Someone climbed up onto the fighting platform behind them. It was Swordbrought. "It is time," he said softly.

They climbed down. A mist was gathering within the palisade walls, but it was nowhere as thick as what lay outside. Samuel and Fenwick followed Swordbrought past the thick column of people and possessions. Men with bows over their shoulders carried large baskets and bundles. Interspersed between them were their women, also carrying baskets and bundles, with babes and small children asleep in their arms. Samuel saw Wilfredo the black and Gregorio Rojas the Spaniard and their families among them. In the middle of the column, they passed a phalanx of muscled, fiercely painted and armed young braves. The old men councilors, the village's ark and its bearers, Calling Crow's wife and several other revered people of the town were all in their center. Sees Far the conjurer was tied to a large brave's back for the journey. Bright Eyes stood behind him, John-Who-Listens asleep on her back. Each person carried a length of cord which would enable them to follow along behind one another in the fog. The sight soothed Samuel's nerves. No one would be able to see them this night. They could only be discovered by accident. And if that happened, well, he and his men would be at the front of the column. He could get back here quickly, and with the phalanx of braves around her, she and the boy were as well-protected as was humanly possible.

They came to the head of the column. Calling Crow wore his red battle paint and carried a red lance in one hand, his large iron club in the other. The tiny carcass of a small black bird was affixed in his hair above his ear and he wore his big shirt painted with a scene depicting the *Contempt* riding very low in the water with many people crowded upon its decks.

Red Feather, Little Bear, and about a dozen other braves, formed a tight knot as they faced their chief. Samuel understood that these were the men who would divert the enemies' attention by attacking the main force of Timucua.

Calling Crow stood before them, speaking softly, but at the same time fiercely and powerfully. The braves raised their clubs and lances skyward and then it was time to go.

Calling Crow watched Red Feather and Little Bear lead the braves at a trot back along the column toward the palisade entrance. As they passed, Samuel heard the people calling softly to them to be brave. The fog swallowed them up and all was quiet.

Calling Crow motioned to Swordbrought, and Samuel and his men. They walked to the front of the column, where they joined two older braves, Calling Crow's best trackers. They would read the ground and guide the villagers through the fog. Calling Crow led the column to the palisade wall. Several stout men rushed forward and removed two of the tall timber uprights which had been loosened during the night. Thick fog poured through the breach, running along the ground like milky water. They waited in silence until the muted sounds of the distant diversionary battle erupted. The people took up the cords that linked them together and walked through the breach and into the thick fog. Samuel had to check his match continually, bringing the cord up to his face to blow on it till it again glowed cherry-red; the dampness threatened to put it out.

General Ruiz paced nervously in the clearing. Beside him the big cannon waited on its carriage, five gunners standing by to man it when given the order. Dozens of heavily armed men, all of them wearing breastplates and helmets faced out into the trees around them. The fog was blowing into their camp, patches of it moving across the ground like ghosts. General Ruiz's men watched them warily, holding their crossbows and harquebuses at the ready.

General Ruiz stopped his pacing. He thought he heard muted, sporadic musket fire. He listened closer, but heard nothing further. He turned to a tall sergeant carrying a cross bow. "Sergeant Valencia, we cannot wait any longer. Take a half dozen men and go and find Avila and his Indians. We must begin the attack."

As the big soldier gathered his men, a shout came from the distance. Avila the Slaver and Mantua ran out of the fog and into the camp, followed by at least forty of the fiercely painted Timucua Indians.

General Ruiz called over to the tall sergeant. "Wait, they are here."

Avila ran breathlessly up to Ruiz, Mantua standing back a few paces.

"Well," said General Ruiz impatiently, "are the bravos in position for the attack?"

Avila shook his head. "It is too late," he said, "the villagers have escaped."

"Impossible," said General Ruiz. "With all the braves surrounding the village, how could they get through?"

"They sent some of their men against us while the others slipped away in the fog."

General Ruiz slapped Avila across the face. "You let them escape?"

Avila's face quivered slightly. "Mantua had the bulk of his men on the major trails. If not for this fog we would have detected them leaving."

General Ruiz's eyes bulged. "All of them gone!" he shouted. "This is your fault!"

"We captured three," said Avila.

"The English?" said General Ruiz hopefully.

Avila shook his head. "No, three bravos."

General Ruiz scoffed and turned away. He called to his sergeant. "Valencia, form the men up. We are going back to the ship."

Sergeant Valencia began shouting; men ran to form ranks.

Mantua walked up behind Avila and spoke in his ear.

Avila called to General Ruiz over the noise. "Sir, I told them they would be paid tonight. I would like to give them a partial payment. They will track the town people down in the morning when the fog lifts."

General Ruiz glared at Avila as if he were mad. "Fool, there will be no payment! They are gone and it is your fault."

Avila turned to Mantua to explain but the Timucua chief had already heard enough. With a scream of fury he swung his axe, clubbing Avila over the head. Avila dropped down dead from the blow.

General Ruiz ran, shouting, into the center of his men. "Close ranks," he yelled, "close ranks."

Mantua shouted an order to his braves and they unleashed a rain of arrows. Several soldiers cried out in pain but most of the arrows clattered harmlessly off the Spaniards' armor.

General Ruiz's men formed a tight iron ring around him and the gun as they began moving backward. The Indians followed, aiming for the gaps in their armor as they fired their arrows.

"First rank, fire!" General Ruiz called out, and the harquebuses boomed. Several of Mantua's men fell dead.

"Second rank, fire!" Again the harquebuses boomed and Timucua braves fell with gaping, bloody wounds.

"Ready the gun," came General Ruiz's call, as more arrows clattered against them.

From his long association with Avila the Slaver, Mantua

knew what a big cannon could do to a mass of men. He shouted a warning to his men and they melded into the surrounding trees, continuing to fire their arrows at the retreating Spaniards.

The long column of Coosa people walked slowly, but steadily. At one point Calling Crow recognized the distant sound of cannon fire, but he did not stop the column to listen further. The night passed without incident, and in the morning, the sun penetrated the fog, tingeing it with a pale white glow. Calling Crow held up the column briefly and the people said nothing as they ate quickly of the parched corn they all carried in their pouches. No longer needing the cords that linked them together, they tucked them away and began walking again. They moved faster now in the strange glowing light.

Under the thick canopy of the trees, the fog survived unharmed by the sun for most of the day. Despite the length of the column, and the numbers of aged and children among them, they traveled at a surprisingly fast clip. Samuel felt that God must have been with them. They would make the ship now; he was sure of it. At full day, when they were only a half day's march from the *Contempt,* two of the Coosa braves that had been part of the attack force rejoined the column. Calling Crow ordered the column to halt, and he, Sword-brought, the top braves and the Old Men moved off the trail to counsel. Samuel and Fenwick joined them.

One of the returned braves had a bad eye, partially closed by some infirmity or other, probably at birth, and it was he who did the talking. Samuel knew enough of the Muskogee language to understand what he was reporting. He and his fellow brave were all that was left of the attack force, the others having either been killed or captured. The other brave said suddenly that he thought that Red Feather and Little Bear had been captured and were alive, but he could not be sure. He lapsed back into silence and let the lame-eyed one finish the report.

Afterward, Calling Crow spoke quietly with the Old Men. Finishing, he called Samuel over.

"Fox-Disappears and I are going back with one of these braves to try and free the others," said Calling Crow. "Wait for us on your ship for one day only. If we do not return in that time, take the people far enough north so that they will be safe."

Samuel nodded. "I think we could wait longer once everyone was aboard," he said, "but, of course, I will do as you wish."

A commotion came from behind them. A knot of people talked loudly and excitedly. Green Bird Woman called out to Calling Crow and he went back to her.

Samuel looked over at Swordbrought. "What is it?"

The young man frowned. "My mother is very frightened. The medicine man, Sees Far, has asked to see Calling Crow before he goes back. Sees Far said that it will be the last time he sees him and he wants to say good-bye."

Samuel looked back to see Calling Crow facing his tearful wife as some other women tried to console her.

"Why do you go back?" said Green Bird Woman. "Send some of the younger braves."

Calling Crow knew he would never know peace if he did not go back. "I will be back," he said to her.

"Calling Crow," Green Bird Woman said sadly. "Once the Spanish took you away and made you their slave. Don't go!"

"Green Bird Woman." Calling Crow's frown revealed his concern. "Take heart. We will be warmed by many more fires before we part."

Green Bird Woman smiled bravely. "Yes. You are right." She wiped away her tears with her hand. Calling Crow waited a moment and then they embraced and stepped apart.

"Be brave, my love," Green Bird Woman said. She turned away.

Calling Crow walked over to where old Sees Far sat on the side of the trail.

"Is that you, Calling Crow?" said the ancient medicine man softly.

"Yes, Grandfather. It is I."

Sees Far smiled. "Come close."

Calling Crow knelt and Sees Far waved a smoldering bundle of tobacco leaves at him, wafting the smoke over him. "Just as the black crow cannot be seen at night," chanted the old medicine man, "so you shall be invisible to the Timucua people."

Calling Crow chanted a song to summon his spirit guide and then he got to his feet. He motioned to Fox-Disappears and the returned brave called Sleepy Eye. The three men raised their lances to the pale disc of the sun as they cried out their war cries. They ran back down the trail.

From where they hid themselves, Calling Crow, Fox-Disappears and Sleepy Eye could not see Coosa Town, but the thick cloud of black smoke rising from it drifted over them. Ashes fell down through the tree leaves like a strange, warm snow. They listened to the distant screams of the Timucua braves, wild and drunk with the euphoria of violence. Calling Crow saw no Spanish and he decided that they must have already taken to their ship, leaving the Timucua to spend their rage on the abandoned town.

Calling Crow motioned the others to follow him and they moved closer to the river. They saw several groups of braves across the water, all of them with bundles and pots taken from the town, some of them wearing extra layers of skin garments they had taken. Calling Crow saw no evidence of Red Feather and the other missing braves, however. They followed the river in the direction of the sea. At the place where the river bent, where it was shallow enough to cross, they spotted a group of five Timucua braves standing on the opposite riverbank talking.

"Look," said Fox-Disappears, "back in among the trees there is something."

Calling Crow peered at the distant tree line. Just inside the darkness of the forest there appeared to be at least three more men. "Let's go closer."

Staying under the cover of some stunted dogwood trees, they crept closer. Calling Crow motioned the other two to stop. There, about one hundred paces away in the trees, Red Feather, Little Bear and another young brave were tied up to

some trees. Dark bruises covered Red Feather's face and he
sagged against the cords. Little Bear stood erect, staring ahead
angrily through badly swollen eyelids. The other brave's head
hung and much dried blood covered his chest. Calling Crow
thought he was already dead.

Calling Crow motioned to Fox-Disappears and Sleepy Eye.
They backtracked, then crossed the river. Nocking arrows into
their bows, they hugged the stunted trees and vines along the
muddy bank as they crept closer. At Calling Crow's signal,
they released their arrows and two of the Timucua fell dead.
Calling Crow and the others screamed out their war cries and
ran at the three startled braves who were left. Fox-Disappears
struck one Timucua in the head, killing him instantly. Calling
Crow killed another brave before he could retrieve his axe.
Sleepy Eye ran to engage the third Timucua as Calling Crow
and Fox-Disappears ran over to cut the men down from the
trees.

Calling Crow quickly cut Red Feather free as Sleepy Eye
continued fighting wildly with the other Timucua. Red
Feather stumbled weakly and Calling Crow put his arm
around him to support him. Fox-Disappears cut Little Bear
free. Fox-Disappears then cut the third brave's cords and he
fell down dead.

Little Bear shook his shoulders, slapping his arms and
wrists to bring the blood back into them. He took a war axe
from one of the dead Timucua and ran back to where Sleepy
Eye was fighting. He hit the Timucua on the back of the head
and he fell dead. "I am sorry," he said to the surprised Sleepy
Eye, "but he abused me so much I could not help myself."

Sleepy Eye, his sweaty chest heaving after his long fight,
eyed the big brave angrily, but was too spent to say anything.

"Are there any more alive?" Calling Crow asked Red
Feather.

"No," Red Feather said weakly, "all dead."

Calling Crow was about to ask Little Bear the same question when four more Timucua burst out of the cover of the
trees, screaming out their war cries. Calling Crow let go of
Red Feather and turned to meet one of them. The brave used
his momentum to knock Calling Crow down. The man pulled

his knife and lept. Small, desperate battles raged around Calling Crow as he fought to keep the Timucua's knife away. The brave was very powerful and Calling Crow was still stunned. They fought furiously over the knife, neither one giving ground. Calling Crow said a heartfelt prayer to his spirit guide. *Aieyah!* He had come all this way! He must take his men back with him. Finally he found the strength he needed to turn the Timucua's knife around and into the warrior's chest. The man's blood spurted out and he lay still.

Calling Crow sat up and looked around. Red Feather was unscathed by this latest attack, but still unable to get to his feet. Sleepy Eye and the man he had been fighting both lay dead or dying. Fox-Disappears and a Timucua were still fighting with drawn knives and Little Bear sat on the ground in a stupor. Calling Crow was getting to his feet when a Timucua brave appeared under a tree not twenty paces away. He released his arrow.

"*Aieyah!*" Little Bear's large form lumbered out of Calling Crow's peripheral vision and into the arrow's path. Calling Crow heard it go into Little Bear with a thud. Little Bear groaned, but continued charging forward, his axe held high in a massive hand. The surprised Timucua pulled another arrow from his quiver, but was too slow. Little Bear's first blow knocked him to his knees, his second, killing him.

Little Bear turned. The arrow protruded from his thorax and a froth of blood bubbled out with every breath he took.

Calling Crow helped the big man sit down against a tree. Fox-Disappears came up to them, breathing heavily, his arm supporting Red Feather.

Calling Crow knelt beside Little Bear. "Can you walk, brother?"

Little Bear shook his head. He pointed to the opposite bank of the river. Ten or so Timucua braves ran along the muddy bank.

"They haven't seen us," said Little Bear in a hoarse whisper. "You must go."

Calling Crow lay his hand on the big man's shoulder. "The Great Spirit has witnessed your bravery, Little Bear. You have earned an eagle's feather. I will bring it to you myself when I enter the netherworld.''

Little Bear nodded weakly then looked worriedly in the direction of the approaching Timucua braves.

Carrying Red Feather between them, Calling Crow and Fox-Disappears moved back into the cover of the trees. Despite Red Feather's weakness, they moved quickly along the wide trail, away from the scene of the fighting. The sun had reached its zenith, and Calling Crow calculated that they could reach the ship before sunrise if there was no more fighting.

Several hours later the trail turned, running parallel with a long stretch of sandy beach. Calling Crow and Fox-Disappears left Red Feather in a copse of bushes and went out onto the beach. Breathing heavily, they looked up and down.

''Perhaps we should take the beach,'' said Fox-Disappears.

Calling Crow nodded. ''Yes. We can go faster. Then when it gets dark we will go back into the forest. Come on.''

Fox-Disappears did not move.

''What is it?'' said Calling Crow.

''We're being followed.''

Bright Eyes sat in the sand on the windy beach with the others, giving herself up to her exhaustion after their long walk. An occasional gull cried overhead and the sea rumbled and sighed serenely. John-Who-Listens slept soundly in a basket next to her. Around them, some of the people were very sad and cried openly at having had to flee their town. Most seemed resolved to what had happened. But, Bright Eyes guessed, like her, they probably had doubts deep down in their hearts about what lay ahead. Placing their trust in the English had been hard enough for them when their leader Calling Crow was among them. But now that he was gone, they must be very worried.

Bright Eyes was very worried. She thought about the story that had quickly circulated just before Calling Crow and Fox-Disappears went back for the others with Sleepy Eye, the story about what Sees Far had said about not seeing Calling Crow again. *Aieyah!* Did he really say that? How could they set off on such a risky trek without Calling Crow to guide them? It was unthinkable.

One of the braves sitting near Bright Eyes got to his feet and pointed at the water. She got up and turned to look. Samuel was returning in his boat to take the next group out to the ship. The sight of him cheered her, but not enough to dispel her worry totally. She turned and saw Green Bird Woman watching the place where the trail had brought them out to the beach. She was waiting for Calling Crow to step out of the forest. Bright Eyes thought of her father far away somewhere, trying to bring back the tall, sad-faced Red Feather and the others. The image of her former suitor's face made her sad. She looked over at the approaching boat. Samuel waved.

Aieyah! she prayed. Great Spirit, help me. I am so confused. As if in answer she heard her baby cry. She went over and knelt down to him. His brave, insistent cries blotted out all her confusion and sorrow. She leaned closer to speak to him and he settled back into sleep.

Samuel called to her. He wanted her to get in the boat. She picked up her baby and walked over. Green Bird Woman continued to stare at the trail.

"Mother," Bright Eyes said.

Green Bird Woman did not hear her.

Bright Eyes placed her hand on her mother's shoulder. "It is time to go to the ship."

Green Bird Woman turned to her sadly. "I won't leave here without him."

Bright Eyes knew her mother meant this. She had to get her on the ship. Then maybe Samuel could help her. "Mother," said Bright Eyes, "you must spend the night on the ship. It is safer. Then you can come back again tomorrow."

Green Bird Woman nodded reluctantly. Bright Eyes took her hand and they stepped into the boat. The Englishmen pushed it out into the surf.

Chapter 45

Calling Crow and Fox-Disappears hurried along the beach, Red Feather supported between them. They paused, and Fox-Disappears looked back. With Red Feather blocking his view, Calling Crow could not see. "How many are following us?" he said.

"Strange," said Fox-Disappears, "only one man. He is very far away, however. We could easily lose him in the forest when it starts to get dark."

"No," said Calling Crow. "You take Red Feather and go on. I will stay. It is me he wants."

"Calling Crow," Red Feather said weakly. He tried to say something, but pain and exhaustion overcame him and his head hung limply.

Fox-Disappears hesitated, looking at Calling Crow expectantly.

"Go quickly," said Calling Crow. "Tell them not to wait for me."

Fox-Disappears hoisted Red Feather over his broad shoulder. He looked once more at Calling Crow and then hobbled away under the weight of Red Feather, melding into the shade of the forest.

Calling Crow walked down toward the sea. He spotted the tiny figure away in the distance. Waves crashed and sighed as Calling Crow sang a medicine song. "I am the anger of my people," he sang. "I shall strike down my enemies and lead my people to freedom."

The sun began to dip behind the trees. By the time it was gone, the figure was only a bow shot away.

Calling Crow pulled his iron axe from his sash and waited. Mantua slowed to a trot and then stopped. He pulled his war club from his belt and faced Calling Crow. "I prayed you would wait and give me a fight."

Calling Crow faced him. "Despite the cowardly things you have done, I will give you a warrior's death."

Mantua laughed. "I don't think so, Grandfather. It is I who shall bring *your* long journey to an end." Mantua lunged forward.

The two men fought hatefully, but skillfully, jabbing their lances, parrying each other's blows, their swinging axes blurring as they whistled through the afternoon air. Grunting and cursing, they closed quickly to deliver their blows, and sprang quickly apart. The younger Mantua pressed Calling Crow, moving him back toward the forest. Mantua's club whipped over Calling Crow's head and he ducked and rolled out of the way as a shower of leaves and debris rained down. Calling Crow lunged, swinging hard at Mantua's head, but his foot caught on a root and he lost his balance. In that instant, Mantua jabbed with his lance. The flint point went into Calling Crow's side.

Calling Crow's eyes narrowed in fiery pain as Mantua cried out happily. "There will be many more of them," he said boastfully. "I want this to last a long time."

Calling Crow could feel his strength beginning to run out of him. Mantua feinted with his lance and swung his axe in a crushing roundhouse. Calling Crow's lance cracked in half as he deflected the blow. He threw the useless lance away as Mantua smiled and pressed his attack. Calling Crow prayed to his spirit guide for help as Mantua continued to back him up. Calling Crow knew that if he didn't do something now he would soon be dead. Long ago, he had created this iron axe that was in his hand to lead his people to freedom. While still a slave, he had watched the Spanish priests as they made iron. Then, after winning his freedom, he had summoned all he had seen, praying as the priests had prayed, and made this thing. Now all must come to fruition. He put all his prayers into this thing, and threw it with all his strength. As if it had wings, it flew the distance between them so quickly that Mantua did not react. It struck him on the nose with a thud. Stunned, the Timucua chief dropped his own axe, but managed to keep his feet. Before he could recover, Calling Crow pulled his knife and ran at him. They fell to the ground. Mantua's face ran with blood, but he held Calling Crow tightly, trying to buy a few seconds until his senses returned. Calling Crow felt his strength going quickly. Dizziness threatened to overwhelm him. He heard a tearing sound and a sickening realization washed over him; Mantua had ripped away his medicine pouch!

Calling Crow's strength flared with his rage and he broke out of the younger man's grip. He plunged his knife deep into Mantua's chest and the big man shuddered and died.

Calling Crow pushed him away weakly and sat up. He grabbed for his medicine pouch, but the dead man held it firmly in his grip. Calling Crow took his knife from Mantua's chest. He would have to cut the man's hand off.

Before he could do it, he heard shouting. Getting slowly to his feet, he went farther out onto the beach. The sun had set and the sky was blood-red. A long ways down the beach ten or more Timucua braves ran in his direction. They had not seen him yet. They would be the advance party for a much larger group. He must get to the ship and warn them. He must go.

He went back to Mantua and again tried to remove the pouch. The hand would not release it. The shouting grew louder, closer. Calling Crow staggered into the forest.

In a large patch of shade, Bright Eyes sat on the wooden deck of the ship. She looked over at her mother. Like many others, Green Bird Woman stood at the rail and stared at the trail head. Shaking her head sadly, Bright Eyes left John-Who-Listens with her friend Owl-Woman and walked over to Green Bird Woman. She stood silently beside her.

"John-Who-Listens has slept through all of this," she said to her mother. "I think he must have been very tired before we left the town. Perhaps it was the drumming and singing."

Bright Eyes realized her mother wasn't listening. Instead, Green Bird Woman raptly watched the shore. Bright Eyes followed her look. Two tiny figures had come out of the forest and now stood on the beach. People began shouting and a moment later the Englishmen departed in their boat to pick them up.

Later, Bright Eyes crowded around the rail with the others as the boat pulled alongside the ship. Fox-Disappears climbed up as some others helped Red Feather over the rail. People cried and shouted.

Green Bird Woman called out to them anxiously, "Where is Calling Crow?"

Bright Eyes pushed forward to listen to what was said.

Fox-Disappears went to Green Bird Woman. "He stayed. There was someone following us and he stayed to fight him. He said not to wait for him."

"*Aieyah!*" Green Bird Woman turned away tearfully. Bright Eyes went to her to console her, but it was no use. Her mother was deep in her sorrow and Bright Eyes couldn't get through to her.

Just before dark, Bright Eyes spotted Sees Far on the back of the brave who was called Porcupine. She thought again of the story. What had Sees Far really said? Maybe someone had misinterpreted his words. She decided to offer Sees Far some food. He must be hungry after all of this, and afterward he might tell her what he had said earlier. She called over to the brave.

The brave called Porcupine turned to her.

"I have some food for him," Bright Eyes said. "Bring him here."

When Porcupine approached, Bright Eyes asked him to kneel. She lifted a bowl of wetted, parched corn up to Sees Far, calling his name. He was asleep and she was about to leave him alone when his head fell back. His mouth gaped open and a large fly exited it, buzzing lazily away. Bright Eyes screamed.

Several women rushed over as Green Bird Woman knelt down beside Bright Eyes. "*Aieyah!* Bright Eyes, he is dead."

The brave called Porcupine nervously attempted to get to his feet.

"Hold still," Green Bird Woman said to him harshly, "let us get him off first." They lifted Sees Far off Porcupine's back and laid him down on a bark blanket someone had spread out. Sees Far's body was curled up like a leaf. His hands had closed into fists and his skin looked like old, polished wood.

The little, round Englishman named Fenwick and the big Englishman named Philip came over. "The ship is overcrowded," Fenwick said to Bright Eyes. "We will have to bury him ashore."

Bright Eyes told her mother what Fenwick had said.

"*Aieyah,*" said Green Bird Woman, looking up at the fat little Englishman, "he's as light as a small child. What difference will he make?"

Bright Eyes translated and Fenwick answered, "I am sorry. There is not enough room on the ship. All the dead will be buried or thrown overboard." Fenwick and Philip picked up the blanket to carry Sees Far to the boat.

"They are taking Sees Far," Green Bird Woman shouted to the others. "The Englishmen are taking our eyes!"

People crowded around the Englishmen blocking their way. They set the body down in frustration.

Two Clouds and another of the Old Men walked over and the people parted to let them through. They knelt beside the body and spoke with Bright Eyes.

Samuel came over to Fenwick. "What happened?"

The little Englishman glared over at the crowd of natives. "The old wizard died, but they won't let us bury the body."

Two Clouds stood and turned to Bright Eyes. "Tell your Englishman we will not have Sees Fars' ghost wandering this place alone. If he stays, so do we."

Samuel understood most of what the old man said. His face was pained and drawn as he turned to Bright Eyes. "The old man stays. But tell them all that we must go in the morning when the tide has risen. This is Calling Crow's wish."

Bright Eyes relayed Samuel's words to the others. Then she went and got a large basket. She and Green Bird Woman picked up the old medicine man's blanket-wrapped body and placed him in the basket. Then Green Bird Woman went back to the rail to take up her vigil.

Bright Eyes looked down at the basket and fear threatened to overwhelm her. There were so many dangers, and so many

little ones and frail old people. Now they had lost their keen-
est pair of eyes. *Aieyah!* Would they also lose their chief,
Great Spirit? She, too, turned round to look at where the trail
brought them out to the beach. She prayed that her father
would come back to them soon. With Sees Far gone, they
needed him now more than ever!

Samuel stood beside the helmsman's cowl and looked out
on the throng of Indians lining the decks. Many of them still
kept their vigil at the rails, hoping to see Calling Crow. Sadly,
Samuel realized he probably would not return. Like the old
sorcerer who had just passed away, Calling Crow also seemed
able to see into the future. Perhaps that was why he had insisted they not wait for him.

A mild breeze washed over the ship and Samuel shivered.
Despite the relative warmness of the early winter weather, he
wore a thick woolen cape, for his ague had returned. Unable
to sleep, he had gotten up with the dawn. Their predicament
was not good. Although the sound was ten feet deep on av-
erage, and could accommodate the *Contempt*, there was a
sandbar in the channel that sounded at only seven or eight
feet at high tide. With the added weight of all the Indian
people, the *Contempt* was drawing too much water. They
would go when the tide was at its highest and hope and pray
for the best.

The day wore on, the tide rising, but there was no sign of
Calling Crow. Many of the Indian people began singing their
songs of lament. The wailing assailed Samuel's ears, seeming
to make his fever worse. He leaned back against the rail dizzily.

Someone shook him. It was Fenwick. "Are you all right,
m'lord?"

Samuel nodded.

"We have to go now," said Fenwick. "William tells me
the tide has peaked."

Samuel shielded his eyes from the painful, glaring light.
He looked over to where Bright Eyes sat with her mother.
Both women would hate him for this, but they must go. The
Timucua could be tracking them at this very moment.

"Get them ready to hoist sail," said Samuel. "I will bring up the anchor."

Fenwick moved off, stepping carefully between the Indians.

Samuel waited till the men were in the rigging, ready to unfurl the sails, before giving the order to weigh the anchor. Four men began pushing the capstan round and the *Contempt* turned slightly as the slack came out of the cable. One of the native women began screaming. Samuel looked over. It was Bright Eyes, pushing her way through the people to him.

Tears filled her eyes as she came up to him.

"We must go," he shouted, "I am sorry."

"No, no," she yelled over the noise of all the activity, "look!"

Samuel looked to where she was pointing. A solitary figure stood on the beach.

"It is Calling Crow!" shouted Bright Eyes. "You must get him."

Samuel ordered a boat be put out and not long afterward the English oarsmen helped Calling Crow aboard. His side was bloody from a wound and he could hardly keep his feet. Green Bird Woman rushed to his side and supported him. "It is time to go, Samuel," said Calling Crow. "They're coming."

Samuel nodded weakly and walked over to the helmsman's shelter where Fenwick, William and Philip stood waiting. Calling Crow and Green Bird Woman followed. The anchor came up and the *Contempt* drifted a little to starboard as Samuel headed her for the narrow channel.

"Look," cried Fenwick, pointing to port.

Timucua braves crowded out of the trail head onto the beach. Some of them ran into the surf up to their waists, but went no farther. Their numbers grew till there appeared to be several hundred of them. Brandishing their lances and clubs menacingly, they watched the little ship move listlessly up the slough. Spotting the channel that cut between the two seagrass-covered spits of land, the Timucua began running along the beach toward it.

"We must get through the first time," said Fenwick, voicing everyone's fear. "They'll not allow us a second chance."

"Philip," said Samuel, "get forward with the sounding line." As Philip ran off, Samuel turned to Fenwick. "Fen, get a dozen men and braves up here with muskets ready. If they get too close, give the order to fire."

Samuel called down to the helmsman as Fenwick ran off. "Turn her hard to starboard."

The *Contempt* turned sluggishly in the mild wind as she headed for the channel opening. Calling Crow almost lost his footing and Green Bird Woman struggled to support him. As the little ship approached the bar, the wind died and she slowed, drifting to port and the sandy bank. People screamed as the ship began to lean over. Timbers groaned and a sigh came from the sandy bottom as the hull drove up against the bank.

"Did we stove anything in?" Samuel asked William.

"No, I don't think so." William turned and looked back, his thin white hair fluttering in an errant breeze. "But even if we did, it may not matter."

Samuel turned to look. The Timucua were racing down the sandy spit. They would be within arrow range in another minute.

Samuel looked up at the flaccid mainsail. A spasm of dizziness hit him and he grabbed William's shoulder to steady himself. "Where's our bloody wind?" he cried.

Calling Crow put his hand on Samuel's shoulder. "Take heart," he said, "Emissee will provide."

"What did he say?" said Fenwick.

Samuel held up his hand. A moment later a strong, hot wind sprang off the land. The sails filled and the hull slid scratchily away from the bank as the *Contempt* again began moving.

The dull brown of the sand bar was now visible beneath the water ahead. Philip called back, "Six feet, sir. Hardly enough."

Samuel cursed. "Six bloody feet it will have to be!"

Picking up speed, the *Contempt* drove toward the channel. The ugly brown mass of the bar slipped beneath them. With a sickening, scratchy sigh, the ship ground to a stop.

An arrow shattered loudly against the mainmast, falling

about their feet. Another arrow ripped into the sail, hanging up.

"Here they come," said Fenwick.

The Timucua charged down the beach. A mild wind continued to blow, filling the sails uselessly as the ship sat, leaning over slightly.

Red Feather, Fox-Disappears and a half dozen other braves took positions at the rail beside Samuel's men.

At a nod from Calling Crow, they let loose their arrows into the leading group of Timucua. Several fell, sprawling, onto the sand.

"Fire," Samuel called. The muskets thundered. Acrid smoke washed by in the warm wind and several Timucua lay bloody on the sand. The others quickly ran over them.

Arrows flit angrily through the air. Several Timucua waded into the slough toward the *Contempt*.

Samuel pulled his sword, looking back sadly at the old people and children crouched down upon the decks. "All their bloody dancing and praying—for naught!"

Calling Crow hoisted his axe and Green Bird Woman helped him to the rail. No one spoke as the natives closed the distance.

A single wave rushed down the narrow channel toward the *Contempt*.

"For the love of God!" said Fenwick. "Do you see it?"

Samuel nodded. "It's the hand of God."

The water rose ever so slightly and the *Contempt* began to right herself. With a rasping groan, she slid off the last patch of sand and sailed free.

Calling Crow raised his axe triumphantly and his men joined him in shrieking out their war cries. A few errant arrows landed in the sea as Samuel turned the ship. Moments later they were well away under full sail.

Chapter 46

Down inside the ship, Green Bird Woman and Bright Eyes worked tirelessly over Calling Crow. He had fallen unconscious after their escape from the Timucua. For two days they poulticed his wound and attempted to keep him comfortable. Calling Crow drifted in and out of dreams. In one of them, Mary came to him, her little yellow bird sitting on her shoulder. "Beware of the man who wears an arrow in his hair," she said. "Even though you have killed him, still he threatens you from the grave!" In another dream, Mantua held Calling Crow's medicine pouch out to him. When Calling Crow reached for it, the ground gave way and he fell down a deep hole to the center of the earth. After a long climb back up, he opened his eyes.

Green Bird Woman and Bright Eyes looked down at him. "Where am I?" he said.

"On the English ship," said Green Bird Woman. "We are going away." She took his hand and held it to her face. "To where, I cannot say, but at least we are together once again."

Calling Crow sat up quickly. His eyes closed involuntarily in pain as he clutched his side. "How are Red Feather and the other braves, and Samuel and the Englishmen?"

Green Bird Woman gently pushed him back down. "Lie back. They are alive. We have poulticed your wound and it has only now stopped running. Soon it will heal if you allow it."

Calling Crow felt where his medicine pouch used to be. "My medicine is gone. Bring Sees Far to me. I must tell him."

Bright Eyes came close. "He is dead, Father. He died just before you came back."

"Did they leave him back there?"

Bright Eyes shook her head. "We have brought him along."

Calling Crow sank back to the pallet. "Good . . . Sees Far dead. *Aieyah!*"

Bright Eyes ran a cool, moist chamois of doeskin along her father's brow. She got to her feet. "I will go tell Samuel you are awake."

Two days later Calling Crow was on the deck of the ship, watching the coast slip by. He saw a familiar promontory, then a grove of tall pines. He called to Samuel and the Englishman joined him at the rail. Soon they spotted a little river emptying into the sea. They were approaching the site of Calling Crow's boyhood village of Tumaqua.

Samuel hove the ship to and dropped the anchor. Calling Crow stayed at the rail, his eyes drinking in the sight of the familiar coast as a flood of memories washed over him.

Despite his weakness, Calling Crow was on the first boat that put off from the ship. Soon he was walking the overgrown paths, kneeling to inspect the faint impressions of the long gone houses, running his hand along the hole that used to be his village's fire well. His heart was heavy, but at the same time he felt a great hope growing inside him. Things had come full around; his circle was closing and it was good.

Calling Crow directed his people to build their town in a wooded area just south of where his boyhood village used to be. A fire well was dug and the sacred embers taken from the villages' ark and placed inside. People began to build the *chokafa* over the fire well, and that night the flickering flame of the new town's sacred fire burned within. The *Contempt* was unloaded in a day, and after two days, several huts were up, fashioned from bent-over saplings and roofed with thatch. Calling Crow and Red Feather had regained much of their strength. Swordbrought, along with several other top braves, led several exploratory patrols in the area and found no evidence of recent habitation. Sees Far's body was put up in the trees to dry. Later, his bones would be cleaned and properly disposed of, some of them going to chosen braves for their medicine pouches. The *Contempt* lay at anchor a cable length from the sandy shore and every day the little English boat went out to load more skins, and roots and herbs that Samuel had collected.

Samuel again fell sick with the ague just before the *Contempt* was fully loaded and ready to sail. He lay in Bright Eyes's little house near the fire. This time, Bright Eyes's teas and medicines had no effect and the fever gripped Samuel completely, slowly squeezing his life out.

Fenwick and William sat near Samuel's unconscious form as Bright Eyes sang a song of lamentation. Samuel cried out suddenly and Fenwick and William went close, looking down on him.

Bright Eyes daubed Samuel's brown hair with a chamois of wet doeskin. Samuel's eyes opened wide and he stared upward, but appeared not to see them. "Fen," he cried.

Bright Eyes hung her head and cried.

"M'lord," said Fenwick, "what is it?"

"Fen, it is cold. Cold! The ice will soon form and we will be stuck."

Fenwick looked at William sadly. "Yes, m'lord. We should be away."

Bright Eyes got to her feet and ran, crying, from the house.

"Fen," said Samuel, "I see it!"

"What m'lord?"

"A circle round the sun!"

"M'lord?"

"The circle has closed."

After they buried Samuel, the *Contempt* sailed. When the trades filled the little ship's sails and she rushed homeward, the Englishmen threw the strange musty-smelling roots and tree bark into the white wake, keeping only the deer hides for sale to the tanning houses. Calling Crow watched the *Contempt* until it disappeared in the sea. Weeks passed and the little town grew to thirty small houses and a granary. Acorns were gathered and several fish weirs constructed. Red Feather had completely recovered from his beating at the hands of the Timucua, and Calling Crow noticed how the tall, sad-faced brave hovered near Bright Eyes and her little baby, his eyes watchful and protective.

Calling Crow should have felt good about all these things, and he did, but there was still an emptiness in him. He knew this was because of the loss of his medicine. Despite this, he grew steadily stronger, and so did the little town. Then an owl took up residence in a tree near Green Bird Woman's house, calling out every night. Calling Crow's wound opened and a odorous pus issued from it. No poultice or tea that Green Bird Woman concocted could stem its flow. A feeling began to grow inside Calling Crow. Something was coming. Try as he could, though, he could not get the feeling to come quickly, or show itself in the open, and it remained hidden. He decided to seek a vision.

Red Feather and Swordbrought built Calling Crow a platform in the forest, in the highest tree they could find. They helped him climb up to the platform and left him there. Only the winged ones perched nearby remained to keep an inquisitive eye on him. Calling Crow fasted for three days as his platform bobbed and swayed like a canoe upon the sea. Without sleep, he cried out and and chanted to his spirit guide to grant him a vision. On the fourth day he collapsed.

Swordbrought had gotten up with the sun. He planned on going to his father, to stand a vigil at the base of the tree. It had been five days now and he was worried. As he headed across the fields, toward the forest, a man walked toward him, an old man, clutching an eagle's feather. Swordbrought didn't recognize him at first. Although his hair was long and he was dressed like one of the people, his skin was light like the whites, and sickly, and he was very thin. When the man drew closer, Swordbrought saw the wound in his side and realized the man was his own father. Weeping, he ran to him and put his arm around him, helping him back into the village.

Many people crowded into the still-uncompleted *chokafa* to see Calling Crow after his vision quest. Calling Crow sat at the head of the people, the Old Men behind him. It was very quiet, only the voice of the sacred fire could be heard as Calling Crow looked slowly round at the assemblage.

"Soon I will die," he said. A collective cry went up and he raised his hands for quiet. "My life with all of you has been good. But I am glad I am dying now. It is a good time to die."

"What did you see in your vision?" said a young boy.

The boy's father scolded him for speaking out. Others in the gathering speculated quietly on what Calling Crow might have seen.

"It is all right," Calling Crow said to the boy's father. "I wanted to tell you all what I saw. I saw a time many lives in the future when people will fly through the sky like birds."

"*Aieyah*," said Green Bird Woman in awe, "they will fly?"

Calling Crow nodded weakly. "Our people will be gone by then."

A deep moan of sorrow rumbled through the *chokafa*.

"Who are these flying people?" said the boy after a few moments.

Calling Crow's face darkened as again he thought of his vision. "People of all different colors—white people, yellow people, black people, even red people. Their square houses will cover Mother Earth like a fungus on a fruit, and their many fires will burn holes in the sky. Birds will die in flight, falling down to earth. Father sun will grow hotter in his anger, killing the fish, the four-leggeds and many, many people. Then, when things are restored to balance, life will be good once again."

Chapter 47

The day that Calling Crow collapsed, the wind stopped blowing. Despite the winter season, the heat grew oppressive, and there was no end to it. Calling Crow gripped his eagle's feather tightly as he lingered for days near death, growing thinner and thinner. In daylight his body was bathed in sweat and his expression was as one who is dreaming. At night Green Bird Woman lay at his side, periodically waking to daub his brow and spill a few drops of water between his lips.

One night a familiar sound woke Calling Crow. A great wind had come up and raced happily through the trees. It was Emissee, giver and taker of breath. The leaves sang out their joy with a loud clattering. Calling Crow realized that Emissee had come to bear his spirit away to the netherworld. As a chief, he had been charged with protecting his people. And that he had done. He was ready. The town was ready, fields laid out, the hunters bringing in game. Swordbrought had grown into a man. Red Feather watched over Bright Eyes and her little son. All the bad things Calling Crow had seen in his vision would not come for a long, long time, until all his people were gone. Yes, it was time.

Soon Calling Crow would see all who had gone before him. He would look into his father's eyes once again and feel the embrace of his mother; he would see Swordbrought's mother, Juana, and Caldo, the great chief; he would see the good Spanish priests, Fathers Luis and Tomas, the wise old men, Mennewah, Rain Cloud and Sees Far, the big brave Little Bear—everyone who had ever meant anything to him. He would fight again with the Timucua chief, Mantua, winning back his medicine pouch. Ho! It would be very good.

The leaves fell in a torrent from the trees, some of them rattling on the thatched roof, others skittering and chasing one another along the hard-packed dirt of the compound. Now Calling Crow was one of the leaves way up in the highest tree. He looked down on the sleeping village and wished he could say good-bye to his people, one by one. But there was no time. Emissee was waiting.

A withered old leaf not far from Calling Crow broke away with hardly a sound. Now the wind twisted Calling Crow to one side and then another, tugging at him harder, insistent. Shouting out his war cry, Calling Crow let go and took his last breath. The wind bore him away over the darkened village. The white sand beach flashed by and he sailed out over the sea. Then he was gone.